Sin Eaters:

Devotion Book One

Sin Eaters:

Devotion Book One

Kai Leakes

www.urbanbooks.net

Urban Books, LLC
97 N18th Street
Wyandanch, NY 11798

ISBN 13: 978-1-60162-415-4
ISBN 10: 1-60162-415-8

First Mass Market Printing June 2014
First Trade Paperback Printing August 2012
Printed in the United States of America

10 9 8 7 6 5 4 3 2 1

Distributed by Kensington Publishing Corp.
Submit Wholesale Orders to:
Kensington Publishing Corp.
C/O Penguin Group (USA) Inc.
Attention: Order Processing
405 Murray Hill Parkway
East Rutherford, NJ 07073-2316
Phone: 1-800-526-0275
Fax: 1-800-227-9604

Prologue

It is said that our kind was born on the cusp of life and death. Over the ages, many would become blinded by oblivion, but others will carry within them the truth as we do.

Their creation spawned in love by which was forbidden for our kind. A child of unique heritage was born by a disciple, the true first disciple, later to be named an immortal. This disciple protected her child and was forever watched by her love, her mate, the first guardian.

This union was specially chosen by the One God to produce a protector who would grow with his seed, the messiah, in order to walk the destined path of righteousness. Others would be born during the childhood of the messiah, called to protect, watch over, and defend innocents of the time.

The protector, this first child, would grow to watch over the blessed seeds of the One God, his son, and his son's cousin the Baptist. They would train and become cultured in all that is holy and all that is worldly to better understand their roles in society.

This education would take place by the three disciples, chosen because of their wisdom to be at the birth of the One God's son. These men would also be anointed with the gift of immortality to also advise the children born to protect the messiah, becoming the first council of true crusaders. Undeniably this would be considered to have occurred in the lost years of the One God's child's life. But who are we to interrupt the human world's history?

Much information about this tale of our heritage is lost to the normal human world and is protected by current disciples, prophets who were born into this chaotic world today. But in our world, a world where our history has been eradicated due to the First Fall, and later the Second War in protecting the young messiah, this tale of the First, the Light, and the creation of the Dark has been lost as our kind are hunted by our dark cousins.

As is our right as heavenly beings and our right to save our kind from being hunted and eliminated, they now innately fight our eternal enemies without the true knowledge of what we are. The history of our generational battle encoded in all of our blood has left our kind blind from the truth that they need to win and protect the innocent.

With the altered tale of the young messiah which is now taught to the younglings of our kind. The tale of the first protector, who would change with the death and rising of the messiah, forever shifting into what we are now, is also lost, and our greatest weapons know not who they are and their purpose, and are shunned from their own kind, as it should not be.

Chapter 1

Today . . .

Metallic, sweet, and mind-intense flavor filled the air. The quiet that floated around made the hair on passersbys in the night stand up, as if the already chilly wind wasn't enough to have them shivering from its touch. Rich, ebony-black swallowed the alleyway, keeping the individuals occupying it secure and sequestered away from all who dared peek down the tight tunnel. Water idly slid down the asphalt street, mixing with oil, the shiny slurry causing trash to skate against the cracked asphalt surface, where cushioned, midnight-colored Timberlands stalked back and forth. The quick glint of light cascaded like a pulse near the booted body.

The individual inhaled in even, shallow breaths while listening. All sound seemed to be absorbed away as if in a tornado. This marked silence instantly triggered the timed attack, an attack that had the individual's body expand with power, velocity, and well-checked strength in anticipation.

If you were one of the many idle flies hovering in the nearby dumpster, you would've been amazed at the sight of the superhuman individual running in an almost flying position and landing on the second hulking form in the alley. The rise of a scent that had cats meowing and arched in defense on the railings of a window and under a parked car filled the air again.

The crisp, white glint of light slashed through the night air, landing against the second bulked individual as the attacker hissed. In a fraction of a blink, claws the size of an oversized lion's hacked the air as tentacles dipped out near the blind spot of the attacker, making the being jump in the air. Bringing down a well-honed piece of metal onto the second bulked individual, a wash of headlights momentarily revealed a male human, his contorted body stretched into a crude form. The precise slash against the horrendous entity's flesh resulted in the familiar smell filling the air once more.

The Attacker crouched low in a resting battle position. Taking in shallow, calm breaths, the Attacker watched as the thing turned to attack again, running full speed.

A tapping rhythm on the alleyway due to the entity's Italian leather wingtip shoes caused the Attacker to hum, throwing the entity off mark. A light sheen of perspiration kissed the Attacker's forehead with each calm intake of breath and hummed note. The Attacker lived for this. Loved it and desired the hunt of creatures such as this.

Strategizing the next move, the Attacker thought back to how this prey was hunted. A quiet smile flashed across the Attacker's lips. It wasn't hard to get to the sick bastard. The Attacker posed as the entity's preferred choice of target, an angry teenager, who wanted nothing but to get away from his parent. It made the Attacker clutch the blade that nestled comfortably against his palm in anger at the obscene and pornographic discussions that occurred with the demon.

It made it even easier to identify that this monster wasn't the shrewd Italian entrepreneur he portrayed himself to be, but was in fact a succubus-level, soul-polluter demon. These were the most degenerate of demons, feasting off the pain of the victims through lewd sexual means, debilitating torture, and flesh eating.

Knowing this, it silently pleased the Attacker to stalk and mentally threaten the demon's territory by baiting it, since these demons were known for their territorial nature.

Allowing the demon to believe they were to meet up outside of a popular artist's concert, the Attacker led the demon to the alleyway through simple mind manipulation, and the rest is history. Shuddering with a lethal dose of pleasure and battle tactics, the Attacker's body tightened with the wait as the breeze in the alley lightly brushed against skin.

Sidestepping within the low crouch, the Attacker pivoted and flipped forward with the agility of a panther and produced a silver gun. Suddenly, bullets exploded in the air. Glimmering and glowing metallic objects penetrated the thrown-back body of the beast, causing it to howl in pain.

The Attacker ran full speed, his gaze locked on the bullets as they hit each expertly calculated point on the demon's body. Landing a blow to the entity's ribcage, the muscles in the Attacker's bicep tightened with the impact of breaking bones and tearing flesh.

Seething with anger, contempt, disbelief, and hate, the demon attempted to slash at the Attacker with its claws. Its teeth dripped with a mixture of its own blood and a liquid miasma. The beast slammed the Attacker into the side of a building, breaking bricks and creating a crater in the wall. Elated, the demon rushed like a bull, ready to launch another attack of teeth and claws.

The Attacker was not amused as he braced himself, pivoting out of the way with a deep guttural grunt. He released another round of bullets into the slashing, bleeding beast and watched him fall.

High-pitched human screams erupted from the beast as it lay on the cold, glistening, wet pavement, its twisted, contorted body writhing as the Attacker casually walked over it, kneeled down, and grabbed it by its neck.

Watching slowly, the entity howled and hissed. Its eyes begged to be left alone while fleetingly fighting back. Its tentacles and claws melted away into a very human hand as the once demonic thing revealed its true form during its wails. A disheveled-looking, handsome, muscular man dressed in an Italian-designed, straight-from-the-runway suit coughed up blood and wheezed in agony. The clawing man murmured in unintelligible sentences, his sun-kissed olive skin slowly fading into a murky grey. Wrinkles of decay and diseases emitting from his once-handsome frame seemed to slosh away with every scream of pain and anger, and flowing oak-colored hair drifted away like dust in the wind.

The man reached out and attempted to tear at the Attacker's throat. Flashes of the demon's past life of darkness flowed into his vision; they showed through the eyes, and a briefly-flashed smile of the Attacker's photogenic face.

Hunching over in a swift movement that would rival and shame a snake—if a snake could be shamed—the Attacker hissed. He clutched at the man's engorged heart to pull it to its surface, and the man screamed in garbled terror.

"Ashes to ashes . . . " was whispered in the air as the Attacker pulled the heart from the man's cavity. He ferociously bit into the side of the screaming man's neck, tearing and biting, until his mouth seemed to fuse with the writhing man's jugular as rivers of blood sloshed everywhere.

The scent that filled the air seemed to get darker and richer, almost chocolate-scented as the Attacker drank and twisted the pulsating warm heart from the man's chest, forcing him to release a shrill in the air so loud, the nearby cats in the alley ran off in fear. The man in the suit lifted from the ground as the Attacker embraced the body into a tight hug.

Light filled the once-dark alleyway as blade-like feathers exploded from the Attacker's body. The man in the suit evaporated into a thick, ruby red-visceral mist that slowly expanded in the air, and as if it had a mind of its own, the mist hit the Attacker's body in a strange embrace.

The Attacker's wings spastically arched into a blinding, glowing width, spreading in the air, as he arched up and cried out in an almost passionate euphoria. The emotions, the pains, the suffering, the lust, the passions, everything that made up the structural sins and lives of the entity's past victims, filled the Attacker. The satisfying fear the attacker had embedded inside of the demon's own DNA during the battle added an erotic tranquility to the sinful richness of the souls being reclaimed within.

As the Attacker drank, the miasmic evil of the demon, the forced taint of innocent victims and those humans who were just as dark as the demon who fed on them connected with his pure essence. The Attacker's body shook with the intake of the mist, making him genuflect and reach up in the air. A new pulsating and glinting silver light exited the Attacker's body and propelled into the stars, out of the atmosphere.

The release made the Attacker land into a quiet crouch, with him standing and taking slow intakes of breath. Glowing perspiration rested on the Attacker's brow, while swirling tribal tattoos kissed his biceps and hard abs, blending into the muck of the entity's remains.

Brushing off the particles of demonic flesh, claws, and blood from the fight, the Attacker ran an idle hand over his face. His eyes briefly closed while taking a moment to step back into reality and his battle wounds healed on their own. Licking the remaining blood from his lips, his fangs slowly retracted, as did his silver dark wings, disappearing altogether, to reveal his well-toned, chiseled, milk-chocolate skin.

The Attacker's well-kept ebon locks brushed down his back, reminding him to knot it into a ponytail. He sheathed and hid his once bloody blade into his spinal shield and restored the much-needed moonlight to what had been a death-silent alley, letting the voices of oblivious innocents fill the void around him.

He smoothed his black slacks and made his tailored black jacket appear. Then he slid it over his now freshly cleaned linen white shirt and walked out of the alley, whispering a cleansing protection prayer. The prayer would take care of any residue of evil from the entity, and block the memory of anyone who might have been in the alley during the fight.

The Attacker, as if nothing had happened, coolly strolled to his black-and-silver Escalade while texting on his cell. He flashed a fangless smile to a pair of gawking women as he closed the door then pulled into the exiting traffic of departing clubgoers. The soft, thumping music in his truck blended into the busy sounds of the night, while the purring of the cats returned to the alleyway, resuming the frigid tranquility of the city nightlife.

Chapter 2

Her body ached from standing for twelve hours. It was overheating from the constant steam and Dutch oven-feel of the sweltering confines she was in. Her muscles kept clinching with the onset of a cramp, and she was just downright tired. Yet none of this could stop the constant thoughts of what needed to get done. She had a flux of customers flowing into her establishment, demanding her signature work—no, her art, as she preferred to think of it. And people yelled all around her as they busied themselves with the many orders going out.

Sanna's lips slightly tilted up into a soft smile as she let her gift flow through her. She painted her vision on the plate in front of her and sprinkled the seasonings of her love over the roasted beef loin braised in a Creole wine and onion reduction sauce. The roasted loin nestled on a pillow of grits, asparagus spears, and sautéed collard greens.

Yes, Sanna was a culinary artist, and her restaurant, Aset, was a five-star hit in St. Louis. She was proud of her baby. She paired the culinary art with her passion for soul food, while showcasing other artists in the St. Louis and East St. Louis area. She loved it. Her restaurant was creating such a buzz, people from Chicago, Atlanta, and Washington, D.C. had been blowing up her phone with catering requests and offers to open up another restaurant. She was blessed, and she knew it. And she was always grateful for her blessings.

But if she didn't close her kitchen down soon, she was going to pass out. She had forgotten that she had promised her godsister that she would stop working overtime in the restaurant. She had hired a trusted crew of people, her friends from culinary school. They would shut the restaurant down by one in the morning and get everything done before having to get up again and arrive at the restaurant again at eight in the morning to start all over again. It was grueling, and she was always tired. But she had learned to balance running the restaurant and having a life.

She was twenty-seven, a curvaceous and healthy size fourteen, with thick curly black hair, and long, caramelized crème brulé legs on a five eight frame. It took a long time for her to come to a place where she was happy with her ample bosom, slightly plump rear, and overall plus-size glory. She had overcome the teases and harassment of her youth and didn't give a bit about how men or women judged her looks.

She knew she was pretty. Had many tell her they loved her milk chocolate-colored eyes that exquisitely formed into an almond shape that framed her delicately curved face and pouty lips. She also had many tell her how they loved the feel of her skin, and marveled at how soft yet firm she was. Her godnieces loved to lay on her and just sleep while feeling secure against her.

She smiled as she put the final touches on her chocolate truffle soufflé cake with caramel mousse and lavender powdered sugar.

Yet, even though she had learned to love herself, she was insecure. She couldn't help it, not with the ghosts of her teen years still peering from locked and closed doors in her mind. She had dealt with those demons, but it didn't mean that they didn't try to scratch at her from time to time. She often felt those demons were the reason why she had become so afraid of relationships, and why she hadn't had a serious one in years, but she was fine with it as best as she could be. This is who she was now. The young girl in her past wasn't the mature successful woman she had become. She had plenty who had tried to date her now because of her elevating status, but she was blessed with a mother who'd taught her all about the games men play and what the loss of true love could do.

Closing her eyes as the final plate went out, her chocolate-covered hands rested splayed out against her workstation as a sharp pain suddenly tore through her temples. Her brows furrowed as she tried to deal with the sensation.

"Damn!" escaped her lips. She rode the pain as flashes slashed across her vision. This was the tenth migraine she'd had this month, each one getting worse, with more flashes of light.

She couldn't understand it, and she prayed every night that they would stop. Sometimes she would wake up in the middle of the night drenched in sweat, as the headaches and flashes interrupted her sleep. She thought one day she was going to pass out from it at work, but it never happened.

Sanna had decided then to go get a complete physical, which turned out to be of no use. Her doctor couldn't figure it out, nor could the other five doctors she had gone to. Her mother was worried for her but kept saying that she'd get used to it. All she could do was look at her mom, mouth slightly dropped, staring at her as if she had been drinking.

Get used to it? The hell, she would get used to these attacks on her brain, she was very close to saying, but before she could, another stab to her mind caused her to blank out, experiencing flashes of many different people, some she didn't know, places and situations she never could understand juggling around in her mind.

These flashes were like her own mini-movies. Sometimes she liked what she saw, but many times they scared her to her core. She could never remember the full tales or details, but she'd learned to begin to write down whatever she could remember, especially the constant erotic dreams she kept having about her and a mystery man. She could never see his face or anything. The only thing she could do was sense him, his body, his scent, his heat, and feel the slickness of his skin as he lay near her side, tracing her body with his large hands. She could also feel his weight as he sat at the foot of her bed. Yeah, he kept her comfortable at night, safe, so she couldn't complain.

Tears fell down her cheeks as she stumbled out of the kitchen to head to her private office. With the hallway wall as her anchor, she fell into a black abyss and sobbed as another memory raked her brain.

A year ago, Kyo had taken Sanna to BJC Hospital downtown. They had been looking at an empty historic building with a representative from Protection Corps, an architecture and restoration firm, wondering if this was the spot for a nice upgrade to their restaurant. The art deco feel of the granite and marble walls called to her. She couldn't believe she had found this treasure, especially with a lot of old buildings in St. Louis being torn down. She felt this was what they needed, this old building that filled her with a sense of hope.

Walking away from Kyo and the flirting representative, Sanna took in the huge, comfortable space with a beautiful street view and great access, especially for parking. She was happy she went with a new firm that had a taste for rehabing old buildings throughout St. Louis, East St. Louis, and Alton, IL. She loved the respect they gave to the buildings and land. The firm made sure that the buildings they worked on were eco-friendly, which was especially important to Kyo. The building's statues of standing guards from Japan and Egypt as well as Native American guards had drawn Kyo as soon as Sanna showed them to her. They couldn't believe they had both driven by this prime piece of property and never noticed it. Six months later, they were its sole owners.

Sanna smiled, looking at her marble stairway with beautiful Egyptian etchings. The work was exquisite, and one could tell it was all carved in love. Reaching out, she let her manicured fingernails softly brush its smooth surface. The heating marble melted and slid against her fingers, making her touch the etchings more as she stared in amazement, not noticing each intricate marking softly glowing with her strokes.

She inhaled sharply as she heard a sudden, soft humming song fill her mind and being, while her body fell with a hard thud, pain searing through her.

The migraine made her think of the time when she'd had it so bad that she had to be hospitalized. She was twenty-one then and in culinary school. One moment she was vying for a chance at working in France as a sous-chef for an exchange program, the next she was waking up in the hospital looking at a set of her old childhood drawings her tear-streaked mother had given her.

Her migraines had always brought forth strange images, but she had no idea that even as a child she'd drawn those very scenes. Each bright well-drawn squiggle had depicted her life in the present. She was an adult, surrounded by her family, owning Aset restaurant, and a tall man stood behind her, with his hand on her waist as darkness tried to reach for them. Her drawings took her mind off the reality that she was laying in the hospital because of her blackouts, even though the images scared her.

This time it felt worse than when she was twenty-one. She clutched the side of a nearby wall, a slight pain continuing to sucker-punch her temples. Her body felt as if it was overheating when she stumbled into her private office.

Tears of pain slid down Sanna's soft cheeks as the blackout took her over, making her twist and turn. The images were coming faster and harder every day now, as if she had to help someone or something. Each image flashed past her like she was in the middle of a live slide show, the gust of force of each picture stinging her cheeks as she reached out in pain. She felt her mind split as she fell to her knees on the floor of her office, her psyche begging for the pain to stop. She was sure she was dying.

Fighting for the pain to stop, she swung at invisible hands as she heard the distant shouting of a scared voice demanding that she wake up and get up. She felt the hands rock her and pull her as the images suddenly sharpened around her mind then broke into a piercing scream in her mind, "*Get Out!*"

Breaking out of her vision, she jerked up, sweat blanketing her brow. Instinct had her push herself up into a low crouch with an urgency she had never felt in her life. Fright-flight had her suddenly running as she noticed Kyo leaping over falling debris and flaming pieces of their restaurant falling from the ceiling. She didn't understand how her baby was on fire. Yet, as she looked around, she swore she saw a lone body with glowing eyes watch her then begin to chase both her and Kyo.

She heard Kyo hiss as her body suddenly compressed and slid through a narrow opening, pulling Sanna with her.

Blinking at that smooth move, Sanna didn't even want to ask how the hell her homegirl had just pulled that off. Their baby, Aset, was on fire, and something was chasing them hard.

"I got you, sis!" Kyo yelled as she clutched Sanna's hand. Carefully pulling her up as she ground her feet and tried to keep her cool.

Sanna sputtered, her head spinning while her body tensed with adrenaline, "Aww, hell to tha naw. Kyo, you see what the hell is happening?"

Looking around, Kyo shook her head, tears filling her eyes at their restaurant in disarray. She herself couldn't believe what was going on around them.

Kyo had been waiting for the last patron to leave. She had just happily put up the wedding cake she'd made for a customer who'd begged for her custom sugar art to be used on it while they were both in the kitchen working their asses off.

She knew Sanna was finishing the last sample dessert for the patron, and so instead of keeping staff on hand for one man, she'd decided to let the last remaining waiter clock out. As co-owner she would handle whatever else needed to be done.

They both hated working overtime and making staff stay late just for one customer, but they had decided to always treat the last customer with no less hospitality than any other customer, an approach that brought great reviews to the restaurant. So today wasn't any different with this patron.

The handsome man kept eyeing Sanna and watching both of them. Kyo wasn't offended. She had seen many quietly observe her and her "sister," thinking of ways to flirt with them. It amused her, but this time it felt a little off.

Kyo wanted to smile and flirt back, but something kept making her skin crawl. The man commented on how beautiful she was and how her skin seemed to shimmer with starlight.

"Oh, thank you. That's just lotion," she lightly commented. She had to chuckle and try to please the customer as she waited for him to leave.

People often commented on the soft glow of her skin and how it seemed to shine in certain light. She was used to it. Her skin had always had that glow. Her own mother had the same glow and didn't think anything of it. Kyo always put it down to her dark-complected mother, who was of Okinawa descent.

Kyo stood at a statuesque five eight with a curvy, athletic build. She loved playing with her thick black hair, getting it in spiked asymmetrical bob haircuts with a single stripe of color in her eye-covering bang.

Her mother and father had always said her personality came out in her art, and it was her art that introduced her to Sanna. They grew up together in North County and went through everything together, including defending their friendship, because in St. Louis it wasn't often that a young black girl was seen with a young Asian girl, or a young Asian girl with one jade-green eye and one ever-changing hazel eye for that matter.

From the day they'd met in kindergarten during finger painting, to them both going to college, to Kyo dropping out of med school and, later, both of them enrolling in culinary school at the same time, they'd stayed with each other like white on rice. She always felt she had to protect her best friend through everything, and it didn't bother her in the least bit. Sanna's battles were teaching her to protect herself, and it made Kyo proud to call her "sister."

Her mind still recalling what had happened prior to the attack on Aset, Kyo was ready to ride out as she stood in the kitchen. She was tired, and when she saw her sis stumble to her back office with another migraine, she knew it was time to close shop for the day. Her best friend's blackouts scared the religion into her. That's how bad Sanna's fits were, and that always made Kyo act as her guard of sorts.

Kyo had walked into the front room to collect the patron's dishes, but the way he watched Sanna as she left the back kitchen made the hair on the back of her neck stand at attention. Smiling at the patron, she reached for the empty cup and dessert plate. She flinched as the man grabbed her wrist. Her eyes narrowed as he gently stroked the soft underside of her wrist.

It took every ounce of patience to not slap the taste out of him as he murmured, "Hmmm. You and the chef are such artists and exceedingly good with the tastes and flavors presented."

She watched as he held firm to her wrist and leaned in to inhale her perfume. This man had the audacity to lean in and brush his lips against her flesh, making Kyo jerk back, as if millions of stinging ants were eating at her skin. She quickly clutched her wrist as she unconsciously scrubbed it while quirking an eyebrow and staring at the man.

"Excuse me, but I think it's beyond time that you leave, sir."

The man slowly smiled and looked up at Kyo with dark eyes. "Your friend is in pain. I think she needs your help."

Kyo was about to curse the man the hell out when she heard a thud come from somewhere in the back of the restaurant. Absentmindedly rubbing her ear, it tripped her out sometimes

at how good her hearing and sight were. She
thought she saw the man bow with his hat and
exit the restaurant when she turned to gather
his bill. But something about the eeriness of the
moment made her quickly move to the front of
Aset and lock the door.

Concerned about her sister, Kyo headed from
the front of the restaurant to the back, rushing
down the hallway to check on Sanna in their
shared office. As she rounded the corner to the
office, she heard an explosion come from the
main dining room. Stopping in her tracks, she
quickly re-routed toward the dining suite. She
saw the table where the man had been sitting on
fire.

Confusion, anger, and a sudden fear hit her
hard as she tried to stop the fire with a nearby ex-
tinguisher. White foam sprayed around her, but
nothing stilled the flames that moved as if it had
a life of its own. All around her, items exploded,
and the straw that broke the camel's back was
when the kitchen exploded. Nothing made sense.
Nothing seemed to be occurring naturally was all
she could think as she ran to Sanna's office.

Her pulse quickened as she sprinted though
the restaurant and burst into the office. Her body
felt as if it was on fire, and her limbs suddenly
felt like sturdy liquid as she shook Sanna awake,
who lay in a crumbling heap on the office floor.

Fear chewed at her heart as she watched her best friend twisting in pain, a soft sheen of sweat kissing her brow.

Sanna was speaking in a strange language again, as Kyo always noted during her blackouts, but it freaked her out even more that as she yelled and shook Sanna, trying to pick her up and wake her, she understood what Sanna was saying.

A piercing screech hit the air as Kyo heard, "Get Out!"

The words seemed to explode from Sanna in a jumbled ramble, making both of them jerk back as Sanna woke, hoisted herself up, and ran.

As they ran down the hall, all Kyo could think about was protecting her best friend and getting out. Looking around she swore—no, she knew she saw that strange man standing in the middle of the dining room around the flames watching them, a dark, sinister smile on his face.

She innately knew he wasn't human when his eyes flashed an unnatural, glowing yellow. *They burned like flames*, she thought as she caught up with Sanna, who she swore was moving like a jaguar.

The man flicked his nail, and a flame burst over the women.

Kyo instinctively ducked and slid into a backflip, dodging the attack. "The hell is going on?"

ran in her mind and fueled her attempt to get herself and Sanna out safely.

She yelled in fear as she saw that same man leap and rush after them like the fire that was engulfing their restaurant. She believed she had to be dreaming, until Sanna confirmed in so many words that she too saw that "thing of a man."

Kyo suddenly swung a hand out, pushing them both out of harm's way. At the same time, Sanna rolled and gave a floor sweep of her leg.

Both women looked in twin shock as the body of the man chasing them abruptly stopped in the middle of the flames and combusted by a flashing light. The impact of that hit was so strong, it knocked both women out of the restaurant and into a safe spot across the street. Later they would swear that, after they'd watched their beloved restaurant almost burn down with all of their hard work, they'd felt comforting hands guide them out. Those very hands, Sanna knew she had felt before, although she couldn't remember where.

Chapter 3

"Damn, cuz! You smell like death." Sarcasm laced the deep drawl of Marco's curled lips.

The Attacker strolled into the shared complex he lived in with his House family. Though he was of the House of Vengeance, or V'ance, as is the ancient name by birth, he also lived in a mixture of Houses, mainly his own established household and his cousin's House of Templar, or T'em.

By right, because of his ranking birth, he was able to form his own sub-house within their unique culture, due to his Society caste, and out of necessity to survive he did so, just by happenstance. He and his cousin jokingly called their home House of the Unknown, or as he'd heard from the underground, they were being called the House of Dusk.

Throwing his coat down on the floor, the Attacker rolled his shoulders. With one stroll, he plopped on his couch with his leg resting on the swirling glass table in front of him.

Marco slowly shook his head as he watched his cousin from beneath his thick, dark lashes. A wisp of smoke escaped from his well-formed lips as he relaxed with his cigarillo.

Private memories of the past strengthened the unity between the two men as they joked with each other. He was his cousin's Shield. He would ride or die for his blood, and nothing was going to change that, because he knew his cousin was his Shield as well.

"Feels good to just sit, ya know. Was out there on the grind, man, and got hit with double duty," his cousin replied.

Marco sharply inhaled through his teeth and let out a deep rumble as he eyed his exhausted brother-in-arms. Fatigue made his typically erect stance slump as he noticed the powerful undertone of strength emitting from him as he rested on the couch.

He had fed. This was good. When his cousin ignored his base nature, it usually resulted in an almost diabetic shock. Fever would take him over. Convulsions commanded his body, as an inability to breathe and complete weakness of the form would have his cousin locked in his room for days until he fed properly. It wasn't a good look. He was damn sure glad none of that was going to happen as of now.

"That's why I stay to my role, and I just watch, man. I don't get involved. Don't hafta, on the real," Marco replied, letting out another stream of smoke as his cousin let out a low laugh.

Marco raked a hand over his intricately braided dark hair, scratching his scalp as he sat up and rested his forearms on his thighs, looking his cousin in the eyes.

"*Escucha*. When you gonna tell the parentals, man? You been trying to live in both worlds, and ya can't. Don't know why you won't let me just watch her. She fine as hell, and I don't got a problem watching. Hell, baby gotta body like . . . " Marco licked his lips as he let the image blend into his high. He leaned back in a laugh.

The Attacker, smooth like a panther, shifted up from the couch steadily observing him with a lethal gaze, the sound of metal hitting glass as he dropped his gun on the table in a noncommittal warning.

"Ha! I'm clownin' on ya, cuz. I know what's up. So what happened? What made you work double time today? A girly like that shouldn't have had you workin' like this. *¿Comprendé?*"

The Attacker crossed his arms over his chest. His arms creating a barrel of muscled, tattooed flesh as he calmly sat back and thought over everything that had happened.

"First off, Marco, shit was mad good today. The hunt was as it is. Saved some humans from being polluted, was on my way to do my duty and watch but got delayed, my man. Found a hit that just couldn't be allowed to live." The Attacker rubbed his chin before continuing on, speaking with his hands. "You know, Pops and Ma are not going to understand what's happening with me. Hell, I don't even know. I'm supposed to be a Guardian like you, but naw. I been like this since I found ya, man."

Marco flinched at the memory, his thoughts abruptly turning dark. "Mmm-hmm, I remember. You fed off them, and I thought you were coming after me. Man, you not supposed to be able to do what you do, Khamun. You are like me. You watch, but you remind me of the Stalkers."

The Attacker calmly slid back into the conversation and finished Marco's statement. "Yeah, and I saved ya ass that day and learned how they are my prey."

He slowly stood to walk into the kitchen and grab a cold drink as he heard music thumping in the library, which connected to sitting area.

Studying his cousin Marco from the edge of his bottle of beer, Khamun casually replied, "Calvin mixing again?"

As the music flowed seamlessly in their mutual home, Marco nodded his head.

Plopping back down on the couch, the Attacker took a swig of his beer and exhaled. "So I needed to feed. You know how it is. So it wasn't easy to find that Italian cat that I been stalking for some time. You remember the *pedo*?"

Marco agreed and took another puff as he listened, his mind ticking with the intel. Finding that bastard took the team on an emotional roller coaster. The children he took, the girls and boys he hurt, would forever add to the lists of haunting dreams which he knew his cousin would relive at night. Taking in the sins of demons and purifying them always came with a cost, and that cost was sleepless nights for several weeks.

"It was good. I needed that kill, and it balanced me out to watch my Guide. Been watching her for so long, trying to stay in the rules of the Guardians, but something is up with her. I noticed some shit today. After I got my dinner, I rolled out and went to watch her and her godsister. Everything was on point like normal. But, cuz, she doesn't feel like a normal human, man, nor does her girl." Sitting forward, Khamun tapped the edge of his bottle against the table, lost in thought.

"I read the records on her, been watching her when I got this role at nineteen, but her difference hit me hard today, Marco, and it's not jiving that the Cursed are watching her too."

"Why now?" Marco quizzically asked.

Khamun shook his head. "They've been watching her. They started coming around both of them for nine months now, heavy. Been providing me with good targets too, but today was different."

Hesitating, he tapped his ankh ring against his bottle. "Naw, let me go back. You know we can't interfere as Guardians, but you know me, I have to. She's been having blackouts again and almost ended up in the hospital yet again, man. I'm not down for that, so I been helping her, ya know."

Marco gave a grunt and nodded. "Yeah, yeah. Been giving her succubus dreams. I know, cuz."

"Marco, man, that's not what the light does, bro, not succubus dreams. It's been . . . I don't know. Passion always heals, right? No harm in that."

Marco howled in laughter and choked before taking another puff. "Naw, you know where I come from, *acere*. But, my man, you got moves like a succubus and like a Stalker, but I know that ain't what we do over here. So no harm. You was healing, not hurting. Not being The Attacker. I got ya back, family. But outside from all that standard intel crap, on the real, what got you smellin' like burnt ass, man?"

Khamun flashed a smile and snorted, "Fuck off, man! You know what it is. Pure unadulterated demon, and now they are no longer watching them. They are now hunting them. My guide had her usual blackout today, and her homegirl had to deal with a customer that wasn't who she thought he was. You know law dictates that we can't get involved unless they attack our guides, and guess what"—With a slam of his fist, Khamun dissolved into the Attacker persona, his eyes darkening in anger. "Muthafucka was feeling himself and breached that line, man."

Marco's voice lowered, and his eyes flashed. "What kind of demon?"

Marco's voice passed him by as his mind played a mental rewind of the events. Everything that happened made the Attacker shake his head, checking his own anger.

"¿Khamun, qué clase de demonio?"

Khamun regarded his cousin as he hunched his shoulders and replied, "It's cool. It wasn't her, but it was a Warlock."

Marco threw his smoke in the air, and it disappeared with a clap as he grunted, "Damn! What the hell do they want with your guide?"

Fury made Khamun push his empty beer bottle. He watched it roll on the table as he raked a hand through his locks. "Listen, it gets sick. Punk hunted them and played with them. My girl was having spasms, hard ones. The Warlock went in hard on my girl's godsister and set they spot on fire, man. I tried to wake her up, but her mind was locked to me. And when I say lock, I mean spiritual barriers were on her. What I just say? My guide, my human, she is not what I thought she was, and they know it. Neither is her girl."

Khamun glanced around the room with a pause as he replayed the whole incident in his mind. "I had to set that shit straight, had to get to them, but my girl's godsis was on it, and so was my guide. When they escaped that Warlock, they looked like *us*, Marco. They are not what I thought, man! Humans wouldn't escape what that Warlock threw at them. My guide's bestie, Kyo, threw a gargoyle spell at that punk, and it knocked him back. Bastard was shocked, man, and I had to act fast. I pushed him back in the building, while moving them across the street, and cut that asshole's head off and fed."

Before Marco could say, "What the," Calvin appeared behind the couch, standing with his arms over his chest.

He bellowed, a scowl flashing across his handsome face, "What the fuck! How a human female do something like that?"

Khamun just shook his head and let out a sarcastic laugh. He pounded a fist with Calvin's while reclining.

"I'm not even done. Let me tell you what I saw my girl do in the building. Baby was moving faster than a nut, damn it!"

Everyone in the room laughed hard.

Khamun continued, "When Kyo held her hand to help my guide, Sanna ran, dropped into a floor split spin to dodge the Warlock, while making him fly back against a wall. And, my brothas, Kyo fell back into a backbend and slid under a blocking beam over the door, holding Sanna's hand as they ran outside. Damn, man! Y'all know the rest. That shit was raw."

Calvin leaped over the couch, making it shake with his weight. Expertly landing in a sitting position next to Khamun, he exclaimed, "Baby girl acted like a Gargoyle. Khamun, what cha think?"

Running a hand over his face, Khàmun sat back as he eyed his crew. "What do I think? I think that her skin was letting off the defense markings of a gargoyle, and her eyes sparkled like stone, man. Somehow, some way, that woman is a gargoyle, and all this damn time, no one in Society, none of the seers have documented this shit right here. Come on, man. One is a gargoyle, and the other, I can't tell yet, but the Cursed want them both and can sense them better than us! Who are these women? Calvin? Marco?"

His boys sat quiet, each one in a different pose as they either rested near the couch or sat on it.

Khamun closed his eyes and rubbed his temples. "All I can think is, muthafucka, please. This shit right here is not on that okeydoke tip."

Marco suddenly stood and walked out of the room. Snatching some keys, a cold chill followed him as he headed to the garage.

Khamun clicked into action before his cousin and was already sitting out in his Escalade before his last statement sank into everyone's mind.

Holstering his weapons and lowering his cap over his head, Calvin followed suit and sat on his cycle. With a glance to the moonlight, Calvin revved his cycle. His third eye sprung open at the sound of a comforting motherly voice, syncing with his psyche as images flashed before him.

Visions fed his mind as he understood what was going on. He put a gloved hand in the air for the fellas to see within, and both Macro and Khamun listened as he entered their mind.

"None of the seers could feel this, but we can't go after them like this. We hafta hit them women at a different angle, so you can still do what you do, Khamun. I'm being told that they're at their fam's home and being questioned by the Blue."

Brows furrowed, Calvin's jade eyes illuminated as he licked his lips and tilted his hooded head to the side. *"Yo, your moms, Lady Eldress is channeling some heavy info, Khamun. She said she's been trying to position us where we can help the ladies, but since the other seers ain't having her dreams, she thought she was having memories of past guides we've helped. She's upset—naw, scrap that—she's pissed."*

With a quick glance at Marco, who was ready to do damage, Khamun clutched the wheel of his ride, mentally listening to their brother-in-arms relay what they needed to know.

"*She said, 'Go protect, go interfere.' Know what I'm sayin? But do not make yourselves known to the ladies, not yet. Ya heard me? She said to use the business to help them out, tell them that we heard what happened, and we want to move them to the building they had been looking at ASAP and that the fee will be taken care of because of what happened. I have to put a protection barrier around their homes, you know, do my thang, fo' sho.*"

Marco chimed in with restrained anger, "*Comprendo. So we don't let 'em know what we are, but they get to meet the men behind the business. Let's do this. I feel their asses surrounding the guides, bro. We need to move out.*"

Khamun clenched his fists, sitting back and thinking, while a nerve in his jaw began twitching. He zoned out as he thought over the whole game plan. "*Okay, this is what we do. We wait some days to let them know who Protection Corps is. I need to hunt those bastards. We need to hunt them bastards. They stepped over into my territory . . . our territory.*"

Marco flashed a brief dimpled smile, and his fangs lengthened. His grey eyes darkened, and he heard Calvin load his gun and strap it to his back, while adjusting himself on his bike.

"A'ight! Slayer to Stalker, blood to blood, time to make it do what it do, *familia*!" he shouted out loud.

Driving off from their complex, Calvin glanced over his shoulder as he watched the massive building cloak itself in a mirage-like shimmer, appearing as a destroyed shipping dock. He had to remember to thank his adopted sister, Kalika, for choosing a great spot when she came back from India. Kali was their local tech Mystic and Slayer. She wasn't a traditional Mystic, which always made her feel like an outcast, but that made her perfect for this house full of outcasts.

Calvin couldn't wait to see his sis again. He still recalled how they had fallen into each other's life back in Harlem at the park eleven years ago. That meeting was the catalyst in learning that he was an Immortal. More than that, in this new life of his, he was now a partial Mystic, something he didn't realize he'd come back as. All of his lives, he could remember being trained as a Slayer. He even remembered being gifted with immortality in the bayous of Louisiana.

It made him smile and tighten his large hands on the handlebars of his cycle in fury. That life didn't give him the happy memories he wanted, except for being gifted, but it was what it was— life. Now, he could only trip over how his lives had evolved. Outside of being a protective big brother to Kalika, he was a young thirty-year-old music producer. That was his thing. In all his lives he could channel the emotions, the history of people gone, which helped him define his sound and produce the type of music that always left a positive message in your heart, while making you kick it in the club, if need be.

His bro's called him the Poet, the Renaissance man, or Mr. Black Panther, and he was cool with it. He was about his music and his family. Do or die was his motto. Mess with either, and you messing with death. He was an old-school Slayer. Hell, he had come up with many of the tactics of hunting from back in his old lives in the bayous, in Harlem's roaring twenties streets, and as a 'Nam vet who'd joined the Black Panthers. He was about survival and the hunt, and he knew he was the go-to man about it all.

Calvin was a lean six eight, hazelnut-hued, football player-built brother with soul-searching emerald-colored eyes. He had to laugh when he thought about his eyes. Them eyes right here messed up many a woman's sexual walls of protection, had him breaking them down like a train. His eyes marked him as a Mystic, and he was a damn good one at that.

Despite the fact that he was born and raised in Harlem, it was commonplace for many Immortals, or Disciples as they were called in Society, to still make a second home in the birthplace of their first life, and the same was true for Calvin. He spent many summers in "Nawlins" visiting his grandmother, who in the Nephilim Society would be called a Prophet, a human male or female, gifted with the abilities of a Mystic or just a Seer. Some kept the history of the Nephilim Society; others were just Guides and helpmates to innocents or Vessels.

These lessons were taught well to him and Kali. The family motto of them all ran deep in their minds. So they learned the rich history of their family and relatives. Kali and he both trained and spoke with their cousin Bishop, or Unc as Calvin always called him, who was like a second father to them both. They met and played with their close-in-age cousins, Sanna, Darren, and Amara, while keeping the Nephilim part of the family tree quiet from his young human cousins for their safety, as was typical in the Nephilim Society. It wasn't uncommon to have human family out there in this massive world.

Spending so much time in New Orleans left him with a mixed accent that blended into a sensual drawl that helped liquefy many females when he sang or spat his rhymes. He had to thank the Lord for that gift; it also helped lure many Cursed females to him, as an expert Slayer should be able to do.

Calvin pulled off his skull cap and narrowed his eyes, scanning the darkness before him. Observing the quiet downtown city streets of the Lou, he ran an idle hand over his low-cut fade, which had swirling African spiritual protection symbols artfully and carefully cut on one side of his hair in a part. He inhaled sharply and silently sent a prayer chant of protection over his brothers and the guides they intended to keep away from the Cursed. He put his cap back on and rolled out as the light turned green.

Khamun closed his eyes as he sat outside his Guide's mother's house, the cool night air idly flipping his locks. He rolled his shoulders as he heard Calvin pull up, hop off his bike, and quietly get in the backseat of the Escalade as if he hadn't a care in the world.

One of the first rules younglings were taught in Society was, silence is golden, and the Attacker, or the Reaper as he preferred to be called by his bro's, took that rule to heart. It was what fed them, kept them on their toes, and helped him find his prey, oh so well, and tonight wasn't going to be any different.

Picking up his cell, he punched three digits and waited. "Lenox, relocate the contractors to the Nile building. Yeah, they overstepped the boundary. You know what to do." Disconnecting his cell phone, Khamun motioned for his brothers to move out, informing their minds that they would take out the Cursed watching the Guide's house. He closed his eyes as Calvin inhaled sharply and whispered a teleportation prayer.

Landing in the back of an empty house, he heard his bro's land at the same time in different sections of the quiet neighborhood surrounding Cursed entities. He smiled. It never stopped to amaze him how his senses responded to the hunt. It was mind-blowing, almost addictive.

Quietly stalking, he scaled the side of the house, propelling himself upward, and stood on the roof in a low crouch. The adrenalin in his system made the muscles in his body twitch with anticipation and a slight calmness as he inhaled the cool night air. Cutting into the night, his amber eyes sliced through the darkness and slightly glowed with the touch of the moonlight.

At twenty-nine, Khamun was a Reaper. He had no other term to call it, because he still didn't know what he was. No one in Society, not even his own parents, could understand his extra abilities. So the first time he went on a hunt, which wasn't purposeful, and he fed from his first victim, he had decided to never tell his parents that their dear son was something unheard of.

His wings expanded into the night as he flew in the air, gliding into a leap, and landed on the top of a nearby car. He descended so lightly, not a sound was made as he jumped off and sprinted to the back of his Guide's house without the Cursed knowing. Skidding to a halt, his fangs crested as he crouched low behind his Guide's mother's garage.

The air near the garage was filled with a putrid smell, and he knew a Cursed Gargoyle was near. Extremely near. His gloved hands fisted. He was tempted to retrieve a blade but opted to use his hands for the kill. He loved the feel of a Gargoyle's flesh tearing in his hands as he sent the beast back to hell.

Resting a solitary hand on the soft grass, he was furious as the energy of the land let him glean what had occurred. They brought Gargoyles, which meant the S.O.B.s were on a mission to reap havoc. It wasn't making sense. What was it that had a team of Cursed ready to kill his Guide? Usually, it was a simple Light-ver-sus-Dark scuffle, an I-want-what-you-got war when it came to Guides, but this was different. This was more than one Cursed warrior here; it was a small team.

Coming back to reality, he clutched the grass and clucked his tongue as a nerve ticked in his jaw. Well, this was just interesting. He knew many parts of the Lou had areas where old slave and forgotten graves used to rest, or old church plots, but this was more. This was both. He grinned.

His Guide's house happened to be resting on old holy land blessed by Native Americans, then later the Church through the generations. He could read the history and feel the pain of the past in the souls being cut off too soon due to bigotry, fear, pure animosity, and more.

His Guide's mother chose a proper house location, and now it was time to handle what they came to do. He felt his brothers in the midst of the fight already as he waited for the Gargoyle to come his way. Rolling his sleeves up, intricate prayer symbols swirled on his forearms as he kept a palm flat on the land and another resting against the garage.

Marco was on a mission. He felt his cousin searching the neighborhood like a mad man. He reached for the barrel that was securely strapped on his back and moved quietly yet quickly, shielding himself in the shadows. He wondered if she was here. He couldn't deal with the actions he would have to take if she was.

He eyed a Hunter who had backed up into his way. He stopped in the middle of the street then slowed his stride to a deliberate stroll, lighting a "trinity," as they called it in Society.

Trinities were rumored to be named after the three wise Disciples who'd first introduced the rejuvenating three-spiced herb anointing, and healing, non-addictive cigarillo to Society.

Putting the trinity out, he kept it in his mouth as he slightly nodded to the Hunter, who kept looking at him. His eyes scrolled over his staring target, and he kept his cool, silent and assessing. This was a female Hunter, dressed in dark colors that accented her deep-swept curves. He almost hissed when he saw a white collar adorning her neck, because this let him know the House she represented, another thing that marked her for death.

Marco chuckled softly and crossed his arms over his hard chest as he walked around the Hunter. His voice lowered into a drawl as he let his accent roll off his tongue, "Ey, so how long do we have to be out here watching like this?"

Marco had to laugh because the Hunter was still confused. He loved newbie Hunters who still couldn't tell if he was Light or Cursed. He watched as the newbie shrugged and returned her attention back to the house. His eyes stayed focused on the Hunter and the house as he stepped closer.

The intensity of the closeness made her finally speak. "She a potential, waiting for the word to get her."

Marco rocked back and forth on his heels, chewing on his cigarillo, his hands calmly sliding in his pockets. "Aw, like you were *chica*, huh?"

Within a span of a heartbeat, before she could reply, Marco reached and grabbed the Hunter by her delicate neck and whispered, "Shhhhhhh! *Escucha*. Play with me." He felt her struggle while he dragged her from view.

She tried a swift kick to his head, which he promptly blocked, still gripping her neck. Her sharp grunt and growl revealed her fangs as they glinted in the night with each jerk of her body.

As she twisted, he held her tighter then turned her to face him. His voice dripped with an icy, malicious drawl. "Let me tell you who I am. I am the grey, and you are no more."

Recognition lit her eyes as they flashed red, and she pushed to attack, rasping, "Traitor!"

Kissing her angry lips, he blew the smoke from his relit trinity into her mouth and watched her choke on it. Her eyes widened at the assault of blessed smoke. She screamed, and he let her go. He stared in deep contention as she clasped at her throat, while still trying to attack him.

Re-crossing his arms over his wide, solid chest, he sighed and continued to watch with a bored expression on his face as she fell to her knees and looked up at him. Her wide eyes flashed with frozen fear.

Marco kneeled down before his target and blew more smoke in her face and pushed her head to the side, exposing her neck.

The frightened Hunter reacted in innate fright-flight reaction, reaching out to claw his face.

Unfazed, Marco's bite was quick like a cobra's and purposely painful. The Hunter paled, letting out a final scream as white light exploded from the street and side of the building where they were, dissolving her into ash and ambers.

Standing, Marco licked his lips. He savored the taste of her sudden fear of the Light he had poured into her system. With that bite, he was able to connect to that fear of the Most High unto her soulless body, spreading it through her tainted body.

Turning to walk away, he placed his trinity in his mouth and hummed, "As they say, give up the ghost. Let her know that when you see her again in Hell, bella."

Calvin landed with a thud, cracking cement, as an Anarchy Snatcher blasted him with a punch to his chest.

"Dayum!" escaped his lips as he flipped forward and rolled into a low crouch, holding twin scythe blades in each hand. His massive shoulders shifted as he rolled his neck, cracking it. Working a prayer spell into each blade, his emerald eyes softly glowed, as did his tats on the back of his cocoa-rich neck and shoulders. He slowly rose to meet the Anarchy Snatcher coming his way.

The attack was fast. Objects lifted in the air, hauling toward Calvin as the Snatcher ran head on into him, swinging, his long nails protruding like thorns.

Ducking each advance, he leaned back as the Snatcher's long claws tried to stab into his heart. Using quick footwork, he had to dodge parked cars as he landed skin-searing blows to the Snatcher's body.

"Hey, homie, getcha hits right. Then I may be scared. Ya heard me?" Calvin slid over the hood of a nearby car. Producing a holy water-infused, electric nuke ball of light, he threw the spear at the venom-spitting vamp and watched the Snatcher leap away. A mantra of curses swarmed into his mind as he maneuvered himself around the car.

Lookie here. This bussa is fast. Calvin landed into a running back stance, his massive frame hunkering low as he sprinted down the street to draw the Snatcher out into open space. He knew it was life or death when dealing with a Snatcher. His body was cut up good by the hard-hitting vamp, but he knew what he had to do to kill it.

As he ran, he saw a flying Dark Gargoyle hunting his movements. Glancing back, he noticed the Snatcher was still following. Tracking both targets that came his way, Calvin sprinted around a corner and found a brick. He pulled his hoodie on and lifted the brick. After tossing it between his large hands like a football, he hitched it as hard as he could and threw it at the Dark Gargoyle, sending an exploding prayer with it.

The wind was suddenly knocked from Calvin, making him feel as if an asthma attack was forming. The spells were weighing heavy on him, draining him, and affecting his breathing. He needed better recovery time. Being a partial Mystic was limiting and, frankly, sucked ass. With a sigh, he chewed on some Qua gum, aka spirit gum, to quickly give him some energy. Embers of dead Dark Gargoyle rained around him as he strolled, relaxing and brushing the ash off his body.

Quietly waiting, he closed his eyes and listened to the screeching approaching Snatcher, who was drawn by the exploding Dark Gargoyle, as he kept his back to the entity. His hands fisted at his sides as he heard the signature clicking vibration a Snatcher makes when producing its Cursed venom.

Generations of spells filled his mind, some he wasn't able to work but knew, others he used on a daily basis, and others he had created himself.

He let the rhythms of each spell fill his spirit as he began to bob his head to the internal rhythm he was creating with each swirling spell. He could literally smell the Snatcher in his personal space, ready to attack. His eyes suddenly cascaded into white light, and Psalms and spells spilled from his lips in song. Each note carried in the air, making the Anarchy Snatcher back away in pain, the song swirling around the vampire.

Crooning to the melodies in his mind, body, and soul, Calvin rock-stepped back into a capoeira martial arts kick. The quick motion allowed him to divert his moves and stealthily bring down his scythe blades to slice the Snatcher in half. The vampire shred into miasmic pieces, due to the combination of Calvin's blades and spell.

Calvin smiled as he landed against the ground in a resting stance. His blades, the ground, and the block lit up like a lamp, a signal from his brother-in-arms. Calvin's soul calmed in satisfaction as his spell doubled back and worked the second part of its purpose.

Everything that was covered or touched by the Cursed enemy was suddenly washed in healing and cleansing white light that purified everything it touched.

Exhaling slowly, Calvin pounded a fist to his heart and pointed to the heavens with thanks.

***

Scoping his area, Khamun scanned the house and stopped. A sensational ting flowed over him. His body tightened in heightened desire as he mentally caressed her. She was tense, confused, angry, and hurt. He could taste her tears as she sat on her bed. She was exhausted at having to answer multiple questions. He wanted nothing more than to walk into her room, pick her up, and soothe her pain, but he couldn't. She wasn't his world. Well, she wasn't, until he saw her best friend turn into a Light Gargoyle, and he was currently occupied.

Quick like a cobra, he reached out in front of him. His prey hissed in his arms as the Reaper's wings exploded in the night air, encompassing the demon. The energy within the neighborhood sizzled and snapped, connecting with him as he channeled it. Khamun woke up the Light powers, and a white wall of energy lit every street, house, and car as holy land was reclaimed.

Grunting, the Reaper's arms bulged with the strain, twisting and turning. The little S.O.B. didn't know what hit it. Khamun was the Reaper, and the thing was his prey.

Khamun absorbed his victim's screams as it tried to leak acid from its teeth and tried to ineffectively gash at him.

Suppressing a laugh, the Reaper heard a crack. The Dark Gargoyle went limp in his arms as he absorbed the entity's essence, and the Light barrier fried the rest of the monster's dead husk, saturating the air with the metallic scent of Cursed demon flesh. Flames then ash decorated the skies as the Light finished off the Dark Gargoyle's approaching Master.

The sound of a still screaming Cursed Hunter stuck in the light barrier triggered the Reaper to pull out his blade and approach the hissing and suffering entity. With a quick flick of his wrist, he made the warrior think he was about to slice him in half as he whistled in amusement, holstering his blade.

"Your kind fucked up by coming into my territory." The Reaper smiled even more while circling the writhing Hunter, toying with his prey. "Tell me what you were looking for, and I'll send you to your master right now. Or I'll watch you burn from the inside out some more. Your pick of the cards, cousin."

The trapped and screaming Hunter twisted as he tried to get loose. Sudden fear for the first time in his long-lived life filled him as he gazed up. He couldn't understand any of this. He wasn't supposed to fear this Angel. He was ready to die for his Cursed family. But as he stared into the glowing amber eyes of the Guardian in front of him, fear ran down his stuck legs as he felt the Light eat him from the inside out. Last-minute thoughts flickered in his mind as if he was on death roll, and all he could think was, torture and pain was his kind's birthright. But who knew the Light could throw it back in righteous balance? Maybe he'd chosen wrong.

With a tilt of his head to the side, the Reaper looked deeply into the Hunter's terrified gaze, and he lowered his voice. "Maybe, you did." Then, quick as a blade, he ripped through the Hunter's chest. He tore out his prey's still beating heart, wrapping his fingers around his spine and pulling both free at the same time.

Fear was frozen on the Hunter's face, and he sputtered, the life in him fading. "What are you?" faded in the air as the Hunter's body dissolved in the Light.

Dropping the dissolving remains, the Reaper walked away, brushing his shoulders off. With a shrug, he casually said, "I don't know," and looked into the house, searching for his guide.

Listening and connecting instantly with her stressed mind, he saw her standing in the shower. Swirls of hot water glowing from the prayer protection spell that was released slid down her soft breasts, curved hips, and ample rear. He had to stop himself from phasing into the shower to kiss and slide her hardened nipples into his ready mouth.

Inwardly pissed at the rules that kept Guardians like himself from interacting with Guides one on one unless they were in danger, he couldn't do what he really wanted to, which was to sink deep into her hot, sweet, wet tightness.

Stepping back at the sound of Calvin's tan boots on pavement, Khamun turned and gave his bro a pound with his fist. Assessing his boy with an inward chuckle, he noticed the blood on his leather hoodie jacket, jeans, and hands. Calvin was a beast with his Mystic and fighting skills. Khamun knew whatever got in Calvin's way wasn't coming back alive.

"What it do, bro? She all right?" Calvin wearily asked, his eyes scanning in the dark.

Kicking a lone basketball out of his way, Khamun rolled his shoulder and pulled his spilling locks back up into a knot. He then ran his ash-covered hands over his pants. "Yeah, she's cool. Your spell kept everything invisible to the innocents."

Calvin suddenly dropped to the ground squatting, his hand touching glowing grass as he quirked an eyebrow and scrunched up his face in amazement.

"Yo, what the fuck, man! Where this holy land come from?"

Turning, both men eyed Marco as he strolled in smoking and resting his gun against his shoulder. His eyes were flashing, silver disks circling his irises as he frowned. "*Mira*, the whole block is lit up. That's what's up."

Lost in thought, Khamun remained silent as he stared at the house then walked away. Heading to his ride, he slid his hands behind his neck.

Both Calvin and Marco glanced at each other.

Marco lit another trinity, and Calvin adjusted his hood, sliding his earbuds in and cranking up his iPod as they trailed behind in silence, scanning the house on their way out. Both men were satisfied at the fight they'd had today. Everyone had gathered a little bit of info that they would need to present to the Lady Elderess, Khamun's mother Neffer. Until then, it was time to roll out.

Chapter 4

"Sanna!"

Knocked out, yet slowly waking up, Sanna sighed and sank deeper into her soft warm bed. It was comforting to be at her mom's, even though a part of her wanted to be at her own home.

Last night was fit for a soap opera. Her mother was angry when she saw her daughter and god-daughter surrounded by police and firefighters, and covered in soot. The moment they entered her home, she instantly put her foot down and demanded that her daughter stay.

"Sanna, get up!"

Chipped manicured nails peeked out from under the sheets. Snatching at the half falling pillow, her small hands quickly placed the pillow over the bump of a head under the sheets. Sanna didn't feel like dealing with the aftermath of losing her restaurant. Her body was tense and sore in every crevice. All she could think about was taking another hot shower and lying in bed all day. She was slowly thinking about both, until her whole peripheral vision began to shake behind her closed eyes.

She abruptly sat up with a jerk and looked through her blurred vision, and her mother hazily came into view. With a sulking huff, she pushed down her curly, frizzy hair. Her hair had earlier been styled into thick, fluffy natural curls that fell past her shoulders. She had been channeling Jill Scott, when she had it done, but now it was a fuzzy mess after having washed it. But she didn't care.

Right now she was wondering why her mom was shaking the hell out of her, and if it would be personal suicide to push her mother out of the bed and kick her one good time, before going back to sleep.

Grouchy, Sanna sighed. "Yes, ma'am?"

Tamar Steele was considered a small, calm woman with a temper when she was ready to release it, and last night, her spirit broke into a thousand pieces as she felt the same things that hunted her husband long ago had returned to hunt her baby girl. Eyeing her disheveled daughter, she could clearly see the bruises and strain on her child's body, and it put the anger of God in her, especially when she saw the same markings on, and fear in, her godchild. Both of her daughters looked as if they had stepped out of a war, and burning house.

The paralyzing fear from last night flashed in her mind again as she rubbed her temples and exhaled. She pushed the thoughts away in order to stay strong for her daughter and not panic over almost losing her. She was sure her children were more than she hoped they were.

"A representative from that architect, restoration realtor business is here. He needs to talk to you right now, baby."

Sanna looked at her mother with hidden tears in her eyes, flinching from the soreness that filled her frame. "Ma, I'm not ready for that right now. Can we do this later?"

Tamar inwardly heaved a sigh, shaking her head. "Baby girl, get your ass out that bed now and come talk to this man. He said this can't be moved to another time. Kyo is out there with him right now. Both of you are strong, so go talk to him."

Sanna grabbed her fluffy cotton robe and slid it on. As she slowly shuffled down the hall of her mom's house, sadness filled her. Her restaurant was in ruins. All her money and time had gone to hell, and now she had to relive it and listen to how much money it would take to try to rebuild what she and Kyo had just invested in. Tears threatened to fall as she walked down the hallway.

Rounding the corner, Sanna saw Kyo chuckling as she sat eating some French toast in her mother's kitchen. Ready to pop off a smart remark, she froze as a pair of startling icy blue eyes—no, grey—No, they were blue, but they stood out so strong, she wanted to blink but couldn't. Those eyes filled her with calm, healing relief. All she could do was stare at the owner.

"Hello, Ms. Steele. I'm Lenox . . . Lenox Ma-cLeod. I'm here at the request of our firm to discuss the loss of your property. And it looks as if I'm also here to enjoy a wonderful breakfast."

A reassuring smile came across Lenox's strong, five o'clock-shadowed, sexy jaw, and she felt the soreness and pain in her body disappear with a shake of his big hand. The man stood a towering six foot eight, she guessed, with jet-black curling hair that was pulled into a ponytail at the nape of his neck.

Sanna had to count her breaths as she watched the man pull out a chair for her. He moved smoothly, like a man who knew he was suave, but not in a conceited manner. Suddenly images of single friends she could hook this guy up with flashed in her head as she sat. The man was astounding. He had a soft light-bronze tone to him that suited his rugged, sophisticated Scottish and African American heritage. His light goatee that rested on his cut jawline accented his full, shaped lips, his defined muscles moving under his relaxed Armani suit. She couldn't lie, she was impressed, and really relaxed, which she couldn't understand, but since the pain in her body was now gone, she couldn't complain.

Taking a seat, she looked at the array of French toast and scrambled eggs on her plate. "We are willing to seek ways to work with getting Aset back up and running, but I hope this doesn't skyrocket our payments with you all. It was—things are not making sense. I'm sorry," she said with a smile.

Sanna was taking small bites and talking. She abruptly put her fork down and rubbed her temple, as memories flooded her mind. She felt her body tense. Her hands began to shake, and her mind swirled. Welcoming the impending blackout, Lenox's voice sliced through it all, producing a sense of calmness within her, erasing the pain.

"Ms. Steele—Sanna, if I may, that is not why I am here. Well, it is, but please, listen. Protection Corps understands the unusual circumstances to the loss of Aset, and we have decided to turn this situation into a positive by currently relocating all of Aset into the building you had been looking at last week, the Nile building."

Kyo, cupping her café mug to her lips, almost choked on her coffee as she and Sanna both mirrored the same shocked look.

"What?" escaped both women's lips in unison as they leaned toward each other.

Lenox smirked and took a bite of his French toast. It had been a long time since he'd had such a delicious batch of French toast. With all the work he and his fam did to guide and help in the city, breakfast wasn't something eaten all the time.

Studying both beautiful women, Lenox inhaled and snipped at each pain circuit running through Sanna's body. The woman had been lit up like a Christmas tree, pain flowing through her whole body. The same was going on with Kyo as well, but as he glanced at the pair, he noticed these ladies' energy lines were not like those of the typical human.

Softly laughing, Lenox took a sip of his café-worthy coffee. "Let me explain again. Your loan in Aset has been moved over to the new property without any increase or rate change due to the fire. Our investigation crew clearly saw that the fire was no fault of yours or anyone employed by you. Because of this, and the fact that we recognize that Aset is extremely important to the welfare of the Three Points of St. Louis, we've decided that this change is good."

Sliding the new unsigned contract across the beautiful oak table, Lenox smiled. He was damn good at what he did. Law was his thing. Though he mainly worked with overseeing contractors and their negotiation within the company, this smoothly written document was his cardinal contract. It would bring nothing but double security and blessings upon the women in this household, even if they didn't know it. But glancing up at the matriarch of the house who had just walked in, he felt that maybe his perceptions might be off.

He watched the women huddle around each other and begin talking in hushed voices as he leaned back. As he slowly drank his refilled cup of coffee, he studied them and inwardly chuckled. The women were beautiful; he could clearly understand why Khamun always came back from his sentries tired, stressed, and angry. These women had auras around them that demanded any man with a right mind protect them, lay down law on anyone who came into their lives and tried to harm it.

Calmly soaking in Sanna's image, he absentmindedly nodded as the women asked him questions pertaining to the contract. Sanna was beautiful. The way the light soaked into her soft, thick wavy curls of hair, frizzy and pulled up into a free-form puff, brought a comforting feel to his heart. He could see her running around with many children while handling business with her restaurant. He could see her with her many hobbies, and he could clearly see the happy man standing by her side protecting her 'til the day she died, her husband Khamun.

Lenox abruptly sat up, raising an eyebrow at the vision. He wasn't a seer. The only time something like this happened was if something extremely important and dangerous was about to happen, and he was being called to go lose himself in the Society libraries, searching for needed information, all due to a Denotation vision.

Replaying the image in his mind, he shook his head. No, Khamun wasn't her husband.

He stood protective over Sanna watching, happy yet sad, pain in his expression. Dark feathers lay around the pair as he reached to take Sanna's hand and froze, unable to touch her. Sanna sat watching her children. Tears of blood he hadn't noticed before slid down her cheeks, as the children who had his amber eyes disappeared in the darkness that overshadowed the pair. He could hear Kyo's screams in the background. Sanna's skin suddenly glowed.

With a quick look over the women of the house, he quickly stood and reached for his phone. "Excuse me, ladies. I must make a call."

Hastily moving out of the kitchen, he walked outside and hit two numbers. "Eldress V'ance y A'lor, Society is in danger. I just was given a Denotation vision, which I must research."

He knotted his brows in concern, listening to the comforting warm voice on the other side as he nodded. "Yes, Eldress, it is steaming from this. Okay, they are being protected as was requested . . . blessings upon thee."

Closing his cell, reflex almost had him grabbing his wrist blade and slice across the delicate neck near his shoulder. Only grace and his training stopped him when he recognized the aura behind him before she could sense the attack.

A soft smile played at the corner of his lips as he looked down at the striking beauty in front of him and quirked an eyebrow. He appreciated that cutie moved like a stealth ninja.

"Hello, Kyo."

Beaming, she glanced up. She didn't know why, but when he was near, she noticed that her pains went away. He was really comforting, and she felt like she could tell him everything. And the fact that he was oh so yummy didn't hurt at all.

Kyo walked up to him a little closer and decided to get to know him. "Are you okay, Mr. MacLeod?" She leaned against a porch beam and studied him out the corner of her eye. Playing it cool, she idly carved into the wood with her nails as she waited for his response.

Crossing his arms over his wide chest, he rocked back and forth, looking out into the sunlight as he listened to her soft voice. "I'm good. Just had to handle some business on your and Sanna's behalf, of course."

Kyo began to rock back and forth, mimicking his movements. "Well, look, we talked it over. Sanna would have been standing here as well, but we went through it that night. She is still dealing with it, as am I, so . . . " she said, observing the man out the corner of her eye.

She inhaled and looked up into the calming, understanding, and trusting eyes of the man before her. She had to stop herself from choking on her rising tears.

"We thank you, and we've combed through the papers and see we have no choice but to accept. Hell, we'd be fools not to, so thank you. We'd like to feed you and the execs when everything is finished."

With a curt nod, Lenox replied, "Of course. I'm sure the execs won't object to that." He inwardly cussed.

This joint watching of these women was not going to work in his personal opinion. These ladies were too loveable, too sensual, too open, too honest, too everything he and his bro's wanted in women that they couldn't find in Society. Yeah, he was really going to be kicking Khamun's ass shortly.

Heading back into the house, Lenox slid his hands over the back of his neck, cupping it and rubbing as he exhaled. Yeah, this was going to be interesting to handle.

Water dripped on Sanna's already frizzy curls as she pulled it back into a high ponytail. She sighed, walking around the building. It was raining outside, and for some reason, it seemed the dampness had followed her into the building. Placing her wet coat over an idle chair, she stopped, her mouth dropping. *This ain't right.*

Over three months of working on the new restaurant, and the designs were coming out perfect. But this was something new that she was looking at. The walls to the soon-to-be Aset Reborn were covered with intricately drawn pictures and phrases written in kanji and hieroglyphs. It was so beautiful, all she could do was stare as she heard humming then singing swirling around her.

With a quirk of her eyebrow, she turned to look around as the singing grew stronger, making the hair on her body stand. Her libido began to go crazy with the caress of the deep sensual voice flooding her senses. Walking farther into what would be the dining area, she slid by the covered piano and stopped.

The image was beyond words. Squatting with paint splashed over thick, muscled, jean-covered thighs, A white A-cut tee that seemed to be battling with a barreled chest flashed across her vision and made Sanna lick her lips, her eyes continuing their traveling. A towel hung from a well-rounded, rock-hard rear, as muscle-strained arms, with paint splotches that seemed to be kissing mahogany chocolate skin made her breath hitch. Ebon dreads pulled up into a braided ponytail had all sense of knowledge being taken from her mouth, as she watched the fine man sing and paint a magnificent mural.

All she could do was watch him, as strong hands with long sensual fingers blended color after color and applied it to the wall. Glowing swirls of script seemed to briefly flash before disappearing, making her shake her head in confusion. She quietly licked her lips, as her eyes traveled over his stone jawline. Something about this stranger made her want to run her tongue over the clean-cut goatee and taste the soft plump lips that were belting out her favorite song.

Shaking herself she inwardly chastised herself for being stupid. She needed to find out who this fine brotha was and who told him to put such wonderful work on her walls.

Kyo had told her that the new crew was coming in and out of the building, but this man right here, she had to count her breaths. She felt like she knew this man but didn't, so this wasn't going to work. What would she look like jumping some man, just because he was artistic, could sing, and was fine? No, she needed a moment to think. To ask the appropriate questions. Such as, how long had he been working on the mural, and other questions, to steer away from ogling the man.

Sanna shook away the butterflies plaguing her stomach and put a smile on her face. Intent on speaking with the man and finding out exactly what he was painting, she turned on her feet and ran into rock-solid chest. The scent of rich, aphrodisiac-filled cologne hit her senses hard as she looked up with a shocked expression. Her eyes roaming up that solid chest, that man smoothly tilted his head down to hover his lips over her own and kissed the taste, the sense, and the panties off her body. Her stomach clenched in building desire and heat, and her toes curled.

She could see in her third eye, his paint splattered fingers all over her silky skin as he gripped her and pressed her to his rigid bulge. Her body let out a shake of ecstasy as she let her hands reach up onto his locks and held on to dear life. She had never felt so right at home in her life. She felt everything in that one kiss. That kiss scared her and pushed her deeper into his touch. His taste seared itself into her very swollen core and overheating blood.

The slam of piano keys, jilted her, making her turn, then return back to the waiting lips of the bold painter. Blinking, she looked around and saw that he was gone, and no evidence of anyone ever being there with her.

Walking up to the mural, she saw it was fresh paint, but it was in a wet dry state. Her arms crossed around her as she sighed. Damn! She was tripping. This was too much. Did she need someone so bad that she was imagining sensual encounters?

Biting her lower lip, she huffed and went back to looking around the almost finished restaurant. Something made her pass as she inhaled. She could swear she still smelled the cologne and feel the taste of the kiss.

Frustrated, she grabbed her coat, locked up and headed back out into the melancholy rain. *This is some utter bull*, she thought as she headed to her car. Maybe the blackouts had finally gotten to her.

Sitting in her car as the rain doused the window shield, she whispered a prayer. She and Kyo had been blessed that everything was going right again. The restaurant was being rebuilt. Their clientele hadn't been lost, and in fact had grown. She had also been able to send up some money to her brother Dare, also known as Darren, for school. He was in his junior year at the University of Chicago with Kyo's brother, Takeshi, or Take as their family always called him.

Smiling at the incoming text from her brother, she had to shake her head at the message and its protective tone: Send more food now, need sweets for the ladies ASAP. Love you sis and don't let any brothas touch you or it's on.

Both men were twenty-four with GQ-meets-everyday-guy-on-the-street facial features, which had her getting bats to fight the women off them. Dare and Take were men who loved to excel. They were damn good at their schooling, so much so that they stayed on the dean's list, even when pledging Kappa in school. Yeah, those two young men were a good catch, and it didn't help that their swag was so honest that, without being rude, they always sidestepped women who weren't up to par. This, of course, helped them gain equally honest women as significant others.

She had just sent another gift package to her baby sister Amara a week ago. Amara was Darren's twin, born two minutes behind Darren, which was why they called her the baby of the family. She was the sassy one, always saying something smart to anyone who disrespected her intelligence or her family. That is why she gained the nickname Truth. Yet, she was always respectful about her sassiness, never hurting anyone unless in defense.

The only way people knew that Dare and Truth were twins was because they had similar hand movements, and they shared the same eyes, skin tone, and dimples. That was it. Everything else, resemblance-wise, reminded people of Sanna. Both Amara and she shared the same curly hair, but Mara's was a dark sandy brown, which she got from her mother. She also shared Sanna's height, curvy body, and smile.

D.T.T., as the family called them, were like the Three Musketeers. You could not break them apart, until Amara got accepted into Spellman and the guys went to Chi-town. Sanna's phone never stopped ringing with calls from Truth seeking sisterly advice about the men of Morehouse and the surrounding Atlanta area who tried to holler at her, or just to talk. Sanna loved her like she loved herself. Truth reminded her of their mom at times, with her wit, sass, and intelligence. That was what made her the head of her pre-med program and a great youth leader in Atlanta.

Suddenly dizzy, she looked up. Everything around Sanna seemed to slow in suspended animation. The rain. The people. Even the sound of her favorite song seemed to drone away as her mind and emotions dipped behind that secret wall of loneliness. She counted her breaths as they came out shaky and slow. She hated these bouts of sadness, as she thought of everyone around her having someone.

It didn't also help that she relied on the bouts of fantasy she had like today that often reminded her of being single in a lonely city. It was rough to try to condition herself that she was strong, independent, and was fine with just dating and flirting.

She wanted what everyone else wanted, but she felt that no one was going to come her way. Kyo had always been telling her to stop searching for her keys, whatever that meant, but Sanna couldn't help her heart. If someone was coming to be her everything, then they were taking too damn long. This was why she cooked and sent care packages to the twins and her godbrother. Why she loved to hear their happy responses and Facebook status brags. This was also why she loved what she did with her restaurant and working with Kyo. It calmed that threat of her inner anguish bothering her and tearing at her self-esteem.

She frowned at the continuing slow suspended motion of the rain as she turned her car on to drive off. Something wasn't right, but she couldn't put her hand on it. The back of her mind itched, and something made her play with her cell, using her thumbnail to shift it up and close it.

The sudden buzzing sound of her vibrating cell made her jump. She looked at the incoming text:

DARE & TAKE. R HURT & IN HOSPITAL. COME FAST.

As she quickly sped home, she just couldn't understand it. They had just sent her a message to send another care package, then now this?

This wasn't right at all. The blood was slowly rushing through her veins as she drove down Natural Bridge and Kings Highway. The pouring rain blurred in slow motion before her eyes, forming into tunnel vision. Her brothers were lying in the hospital and she didn't know what their condition was. This couldn't be happening. She wanted the drama to stop. She felt like her life had been going into this course of the unknown ever since her restaurant had burned down, and she was now utterly out of balance with it all.

Kyo was in a moving dream. She sighed as she tossed in her bed. Her psyche made her feel as if she was comfortable in her bed while her dream played out. She could taste the air as she flew in the damp night sky. Raindrops splashed against her skin and face as her hair hugged the side of her cheeks and jaw. Silently running through the night sky, the pumping of her blood made her take dips, twists, and turns. Illuminations flickered and danced, greeting her like Christmas lights, while the city skyline opened before her. The city was hers, and she loved it.

Light as a feather, she jumped and landed against a nearby building. Scaling the wall and using her nails as anchors, with a grunt and a sharp heave, she landed on top of the roof. It felt as if she was hovering as she looked down the art Greco-Roman building. Her silk sheets felt as if they hugged her body like soft, ultra impenetrable, spandex-like wrappings. She sighed and let the sheets drop calmly against her back, feeling it shift into her spine and disappear. She loved her dreams of flying. Everything felt extremely real as she crouched low over the edge to peer at the silent streets down below.

An ambulance pulled into the building, and she focused her hearing as she found what she was looking for. Her baby brother lay dead to the world, scratches over his tattooed arms, bandages keeping his wounds sealed and clean. Tears threatened to fall as she hissed at the blood she suddenly smelled. She focused on her godbrother Dare, who lay just as beaten up as her brother. By both men's wounds, she could tell they had caused the same amount of damage to whoever attacked them.

Abruptly standing, she tensed, and the hair on her nape stood to attention. She turned in a battle swing, her nails hardening like they always did into diamond-hard spike tips.

She had sensed her pursuer the whole time, so when she swung, she smiled as she almost hit him. His familiar hiss rent the air, and she kicked back into a low stoop, pausing briefly to run at him. He smelled so good and blended into the wind with his movements as his deep chuckle caressed her between her legs, making her tighten with sudden need.

Annoyance and hot-blooded lust hit her like a double-edged sword, making her quickly shift her thoughts. She didn't need to go there right now, like he always made her. She wasn't here for that, not in this dream, no. It was time to hunt the one who hurt her family, not battle-dance with this mysterious man of her dreams.

As she watched him, she backed away while he stood back in the shadows. She kept her hunkering stance and sidestepped to fall backwards off the edge of the hospital roof. Opening her arms, she felt her sheets wrap around her. Only, it wasn't her sheets, but wings. While they opened in the wind, making her hover, simultaneously her familiar dream opponent grabbed her and pulled her back up on the rooftop.

A flash of shock ran across her face as she glared. Ticked off was an understatement. She felt him hold her in place as she struggled against his hard, warm body, his hands finding the right places to grip her tight.

"I'm not here for this! Let me go!" she yelled, feeling him slide his hand behind her neck.

He whispered against her earlobe, "I know." His head tilted as firm yet soft lips brushed against her, tracing over her sensitive spot at her nape.

The quick jump of her pulse seem to excite him as he followed its beating rhythm and trailed his mouth over her smooth skin, teasing until he found her soft, plush mouth. That touch alone made her stop her fight as he deepened his kiss and his mind melted into hers. His familiar taste invaded her senses as his similar wings wrapped around her body, making her shiver with desire as his mating scent filled her senses.

Kyo knew this man so well, like she had already met him in her waking reality, but he could never see his face, only feel it. She understood that he was like her in every way, and that he was tall. She felt like a child in his arms, but only slightly.

"It saddens me that you are not here for me to teach you more about your lineage flower. I know you're here about your fam. We're on the same page, so stop struggling, and let me get this kiss before we go hunt. A'ight?"

His words penetrated her mind as his body molded with her. She bowed her head forward, and he rocked with her, their kiss deepening as his tongue entwined with her own. She moaned as his kiss turned into a battle dance they were both very used to.

She felt her leg slide up his hip as his kiss seemed to somehow give the impression that he was kneeling between her legs and sealing a passionate kiss against her opening flower. *Yeah, he knows what he is doing*, flashed in her thoughts as his dragon flew with hers.

Her lover's tongue flowed and ebbed into her yin and his yang, making her pant against his rock-solid body. She was ready to crest, and he was ready to make her release, but she had to fight. They couldn't mate like this tonight, yet she tasted his need and he tasted hers. They both had been without each other for some months.

Yeah, they needed this reunion, her mind said, as her diamond-hard fingernails slid over his low haircut. Her nails traced over his eyebrow, as if reading braille, and his sideburns that formed into a thin goatee, the light scraping of her nails not cutting him one bit. Her fingers continued their search, memorizing the ink-black, magnificent ruby-and-gold dragon irezumi fluidly flowing against the side of his neck and disappearing over his shoulder.

He was effectively distracting her, and she knew it. But where she wanted to run and protect her brother, her body clearly had no intention of going.

Her body shook with the rhythm he was creating per his kiss. His tongue sensually pushed and fought with hers, expertly vibrating and dipping, making sure she felt it in the core of her heat.

She bucked and tore her mouth away from the dragon kiss as she came against him. His need made him seal their kiss again with her fiery, quick release.

As he held her tight against him, cradling the back of her neck, her body opened like a flower as her climax ebbed. His soft kisses at the side of her neck soothed her rising embarrassment. She felt him leave a mating bite on the back of her shoulder and neck. Using dragon heat to heal it, he sat them both on solid ground as he held her, studying her face.

His power allowed him to see her in her dreams, and the stronger she became, the more of him, she would be able to see. He smiled at the ancient power. It upset him that he wouldn't remember any of this, nor would she, until both of their dragons, or Gargoyles as they were labeled, were ready to "awaken" or in close proximity. Hopefully, this marking would help her find him in his reality, and vice versa. He could only pray.

Looking around as they settled in the quiet, secluded park he had guided them to, the pair slid apart. Need sucker-punched her in the gut, making Kyo push her opponent against a nearby oak and slide her hand down over his swelling bulge. Wisps of rain kissed Kyo's face and eyelashes as the skies opened and rain spilled hard and beat down on the pair. Their pulses synced and heated up their body with need, while vapors of steam sizzled from their bodies.

Unknowingly to Kyo, her dream lover studied her. *She looks so beautiful when in the mating heat.* Her eyes carried the lighting of the moon against its jade glowing surface as her lithe body sliced through the falling rain, making him ache with more need. Her golden dragon wings expanded with her arousal, their majestic span filtering the flickering lights of nearby buildings and cars into a soft, seductive glow around them as they brushed against his silver dragon wings.

He couldn't help whispering against her delicate earlobe, nibbling her slightly, "Baby, come put it on me." Reaching out to hold her hips, he groaned then hit her with a transforming spell that changed her tight black jeans into a tight short skirt.

He watched her grip the oak as he bit his lower lip. His shaft wept as he glanced at her moving up the side of the tree to straddle him, using her wings and his hands as an anchor.

Kyo leaned back, keeping her balance as she got the itch to use her free hand, and slowly searched behind her to release her dream lover's straining thickness into the wet midnight air. His thick head sprung out quick like a blade, and she felt it slap against her rear, making her gasp with desire.

She didn't know why she knew how to pleasure this man like this, but she innately knew him. This was her only man. He'd been in her dreams forever. He was her first when she was twenty-one, and it all happened in her dreams. It frustrated her sometimes, but not on nights like this when the lovemaking seemed so real, felt so real.

She knew what she wanted, how she wanted it, and how he liked it. She took his aching shaft in her hand, squeezing, watching his lips part with need as she slid her hips down and up, gliding him inside her yearning, waiting haven. Yes, she knew this man. The only parts of him she could see were his sexy smile and thick member. He was so delicious, made for her only, fitting her so well.

She gasped, "Yes," as his hips met her swirling thrust, making their skin glow in the night.

Pleasure had her cradling the side of the tree. Her free hand fisted into his low-cut hair, grabbing enough to slightly pull as his hands squeezed the soft mounds of her rear and pulled them into the familiar fight of their sensual rhythm.

The rain covered them in a cooling but intoxicating waterfall spray of droplets as they both quietly battled to get the other off first. It was a necessity for each other, because who ever came first usually woke up first, and tonight Kyo wanted to make him come first.

Their descent into decadence always left her with a smile on her face and utterly satisfied in the morning, which was why she always looked forward to these dreams.

She moaned and stretched against his thrusting body as he opened her shirt and took a cinnamon nipple into his warm mouth. His dragon fangs caused an erotic friction that had her riding him harder against the oak tree. He bucked up against her softness, seeking to hit the pleasure principle of her core and heat. The pulsating tightness in his sac pushed him forward and up, until he heard the sweet, honey-coated vibration of her dragon song pouring from her lips. Her song had him seeing the rain around them slow and sparkle like diamonds in the night sky.

He held her close, inwardly begging for her to not stop, to keep going as he squeezed and pulled out of her. He saw the tears of frustration in her eyes as he captured her mouth, stood her on the ground, flipping her as she pressed her flushed face against the oak tree.

Letting the tip of his tongue trace the outside of her earlobe as she tried to turn and look over her shoulder, her wings spreadeagled in need. Anticipation made her claw at the tree when the tip of his head caressed the swell of her rear, enticing him to lightly trace her swollen lotus lips from behind.

She heard his sigh as his hand reached to stroke her belly in a lazy swirl that painstakingly found the moist, throbbing curve of her bud. She knew he loved it when she arched her back for him in this position, so she did just that, her eyes shutting at his eager strokes.

She wanted to keep her cool, but she couldn't stop the plea from escaping her mouth as he slowly circled her bud, making her arch against his hand. Her growing need seemed to fuel his touch as his fingers dipped in and out, making her pant and bounce against his teasing head and commanding hand.

Yeah, her dream seemed to be lasting longer than ever, but she couldn't complain at all. He was so good, she knew she was turning into a fiend. The rain slid in a slow caress down her back as she waited to see what he would do next.

Pulling her back against him as he opened her legs, he let his fingers tease her warmth as he circled his finger around her saturated bud. She was so wet, she coated his fingers. He wanted to taste, but they were outside in seclusion and soon had to return to reality, so he did what was needed for both of their sakes and entered her waiting, slick warmth. He watched her head fall back as she held on to the tree for dear life.

His sudden entry had her thanking the Most High for his gift of dreams as she felt his thrust guide her back to her climax. She didn't want him to stop for anything. She felt his shaft swell even harder inside of her, making her legs spread wider as her ass jolted backwards to feel his sac kiss the mounds of her rear. She could feel his desperate need to go deeper, and she obliged, wrapping her legs tight around his waist as she pushed him deeper into her core.

He was at his breaking point, but he wanted to watch her beautiful, jaded eyes flash like a rainbow as she came. He heard her curse again as he flipped her and lifted her, thrusting back inside to press her against the oak. He took her mouth and gave a final dragon kiss as they both rode their familiar rhythm and came.

Dragons were known for their girth and length, so he praised the Most High that this was nothing but a dream because he knew for damn sure she'd be knocked up tonight if he had his way. Tasting the rising sun, he whispered against her calming body, feeling her thighs holding him closer as he kissed her.

He whispered, "I took care of the hunt earlier, looked after both of ya brothers. Baby, I got you when you don't even know it."

Her moan at being upset because she didn't get to be the one to hunt, and of equal thanks, blended with her eager dragon kiss as she melted against his soft lips. That moment of calm made

them both relax as the rising sun ended their
mating dream.

The last thing she heard was her lover's sensual drone brush against her ear, "Protect your
Vessel," before she finally surrendered to sleep.

Kyo felt her floating, hovering body fall back
into her waiting bed as the sun slapped her
against the face. Grumbling, she heard a crash
and a loud curse in the guest room, which had
her jerking out of bed with a start. She looked
around confused, her bob disheveled, and the
sheets around her a crumpled mess.

In that moment, before feeling as if she needed
to attack, Kyo heard Sanna yell, "I'm okay. I fell
outta the bed again. Go back to sleep!" She shook
her head with a tired laugh.

With a groan, Kyo collapsed back against the
bed, pulling her pillow over her head. Some
nights Sanna would fall out of her bed, and Kyo
would find her tangled up and flushed, just like
she herself was right now. *Damn!* She knew her
godsis was having a heated dream too. But, right
now, she was wishing she could go back to that
oak tree. Hell, she could smell the grass, the rain,
and the night air. She could even still feel the
man between her legs.

Frustration made her whine as she dug deeper
under the covers, pushing a pillow between her
legs, her mind churning.

Sanna had ended up driving to her house late last night after checking the new restaurant. Momma Tamar had demanded that Sanna check the new restaurant, so she could relax and check on her new baby. Sanna instead had bypassed her own home and crashed at Kyo's spot, a nice little message abruptly left on her voice mail beforehand, just to let her know that she would be using her key.

Something was up with her bestie, and somehow she knew it wasn't good. She had heard her crying all night until a calmness hit her and kept Kyo from waking her up to ask her what was going on. But she had every intention of finding out why Sanna insisted on coming over and why was she upset, once her body stopped throbbing due to horniness.

Annoyed Kyo slid out of the bed and stalked to the shower, kicking imaginary items out of the way. Yeah, they both had come hard in her dream together, but she still was frustrated, yet extremely satisfied. Passing by her bathroom mirror as she turned on the shower water, she saw her nails had dirt. She looked at her shagged reflection and frowned. A twig and leaf lay comfortably in her disheveled hair, making her feel as if she was a contented wood nymph. All she could do was slowly raise an eyebrow and stare slack-jawed. *How the hell did that get there?*

Chapter 5

The welcoming heat of velvety smooth, sticky and slick wetness flowed on his hands as he studied the quietly smiling lips in front of him. His eyes flashed in the night air, and he coolly looked over the twitching, panicking Stalker as he held his prey calmly against a brick wall. It amazed him how easily they fell to fear when their own deaths, past and now present, flashed in their soulless minds and empty hearts. Their kind lived off terror, yet somehow they always succumbed to begging, pleading, and demanding that he not snap their neck. Unfortunately for the Stalker, right now he wasn't in a pardoning mood.

This time, he was enjoying keeping the entity alive. The Stalker's husk of a beating heart pulsed in his bloodied hands. Jaded, he took the Stalker's claw and chewed on like it was a toothpick while he watched his prey squirm.

He was pissed, as usual.

Sexual frustration was a bitch, and he'd just been slapped multiple times. Add that to the new stress of having a Guide whom he couldn't figure out why she and her friend were both beacons for the Cursed and its brood. The math was playing out in his head, but it wasn't adding up. His brief discussion with his mother had him understanding the possibility that the one named Kyo, being a Gargoyle, was also a part of his mission. That frustrated him royally. He was officially feeling as if he was in a constant car accident and wasn't dying anytime soon.

He was at his wits' end. That was all he could say he was feeling about it. Otherwise he would've had a massive headache, and he wasn't about to stress himself like that. He needed to focus and figure this out before the Cursed took another intended for the Light. He squeezed the pulsating decrepit heart as he leaned in and tugged, causing the smirk on the Stalker's face to disappear.

The Reaper's voice dripped like molasses, ready to smoother and seal the very breath from the entity as he probed, "Explain to me, why are you here?"

The Stalker hissed, his fangs snapping like a dog's as he squirmed and pushed at the wall, trying his best to get away.

Amused, the Reaper just calmly held on and watched the pitiful struggle.

Khamun had found him near his Guide's home attempting to break the prayer line surrounding the house, but of course, he couldn't have that, so he snatched the Stalker and pinned it up against a neighbor's nearby garage wall.

"I can do this all night and day," he coolly stated. "And we know how your kind doesn't like the light, so I ask again. Why-are-you-here?" The last sentence was drawled and stressed with a tight squeeze and tug.

The Stalker tried to swipe at him again. His eyes bulged out with a hiss. Fear swallowing the entity until it finally broke his gurgled silence, "Uggg! You know why, bastard!"

"Hmmm. If I did, you would be dead already. This is not the normal snatch-and-take your kind is known for. This has turned into a battle, so again"—He squeezed and began to tear a vein away as the entity screamed.

"Just kill me!" the Stalker screamed as he tried to swing again.

The Reaper sighed. He tore an arm off, flipped it, and used the hand to point at the Stalker. The blood was so dark red, it almost looked black, painting the side of the garage.

"Ahhhhhhh! Because we need them. We need them before you take them!"

Khamun cocked his head to the side as he quirked his eyebrow. "You say that like I don't know, so let's try this again."

With a drop of his hand, he tilted the Stalker's neck to the side and bared his diamond white fangs as they lit up in the moonlight. Drinking from a Stalker was like millions of needles shredding through its body, which made it pure torture for the victim and sure pleasure for the Reaper.

"No, no! Wait! Wait!"

Khamun squeezed then bit down hard. Ravenous, he tore and ripped at the Stalker's aorta as he drank ever so slowly, knowledge filling his mind. Then he saw it. He saw their plan to take his Guide and kill her friend. He saw their intention to give her the Cursed bite and make her into one of them. He saw them planning something worse for his Guide, something more than the bite. Something he couldn't understand as the knowledge flickered. Shit wasn't kosher. Which had him pissed. He lessened his siphoning before the Stalker could die without telling him all he needed to know.

"Tell me!" he growled.

The Stalker made the mistake of laughing out of spite.

Very wrong move, Khamun thought as he pulled the Stalker to him. His nails dug into his prey's skull and ripped, exposing brain matter, and the Stalker screamed in the night, its eyes rolling into its head.

With a shove, the Stalker went flying as Khamun held its pumping heart and let it go. The exposed heart seemed to pulsate as it steadily beat from his prey's open cavity.

The Attacker got ready to ask again, but the entity spoke up fast, "She is a Vessel! An Oracle!

We need her, so we can use her knowledge of your kind."

Khamun's mind froze for a millisecond before he could process how they could figure out something like that. An Oracle . . . his guide was a Vessel and an Oracle. This was paramount.

The Stalker panted on as he crawled, looking around for an escape. Fear sparked in his eyes as every sin he committed compounded on him, breaking his will like a twig as the Attacker wrecked his body with each sin. Each dark act the bastard had ever committed flashed before him.

"I don't know how they knew. I believe the Dark Lady found her. We were to find the Vessel and bring her to the Dark Lady."

Khamun quietly processed the information as he studied the Stalker and snatched him up again. His hand immediately wrapping around his prey's protruding heart. He had to hurry. This one was a newly made Cursed, and so the torture was too much for a new breed. This was why Khamun kept him alive for so long. He was enjoying this hunt.

The Stalker tried to shake his head but stopped when he saw that he couldn't, because of the Reaper's hold on him.

"Then you are not alone, huh? Where is her pet?" Khamun restrainedly asked.

"I—I do not know. She should have been here to stop you, bastard! She should have—"

Khamun heaved a sigh and bore down on the now jerking Stalker. His fangs sank in deep as his Reaper wings abruptly expanded into the night sky, blanketing them both. He let go of the heart and let the Stalker try to push him off, but of course, he couldn't, as Khamun gained his fill, pulling back with a snap of his jaws. His blade shifted from his wrists as he stepped back while slicing the Stalker in pieces.

He watched in satisfaction as each piece lit up and disappeared. The miasmic sins of the Stalker reached out to him to nourish his craving as he bowed forward and sent the discharge up to the heavens. The sins of this monster were sinister. The bastard was a serial rapist and killer, loved to kidnap pregnant women and slice them open as he molested them before displaying their bodies like art. A human like this made for a satisfactory candidate for the Cursed, and giving him the bite only made the sick monster worse.

Yes, this kill, this bit of vengeance was definitely a righteous one. Panting from the intense cravings and catching the scent of more prey, Khamun swerved, climbed to the top of a garage, and jumped off the side of it as he turned and made contact with fresh, supple flesh. A resonance in the air made him duck as razor sharp blades whipped at him and sliced his bicep. The sound of metal on metal filled in the air. He swung his blade up, cutting a thick, lush thigh as he grinned and stood up to head butt a beautiful face.

The inertia made him bounce back. His vision focused before him. He watched as what he and his boys called the Medusa fell back onto her haunches and licked her bloody, plush lips. Sharp glinting fangs dipped low as she made a clicking noise that irritated him. She was thick and sensual. If she was on team Light, then any man would've tried to get at her, regardless of her coldblooded visage. But right now, that wasn't the case, and what was sensual was also lethal.

Sidestepping, he felt winded. Laws of the battle had him watching closely as her braids gracefully fell over her shoulders. Those bitches had blades skillfully woven between each thin braid. Her steel-hard nails systematically hid sacks of Cursed poison. Her coco syrupy skin was glossy with her sweat as he studied the pin-like protrusions of her spinal cord that lined her back like jewelry and added a creepy feel to her human appearance. To say she was lethal would be an understatement. This chick was a weapon herself.

She wore skintight black pants and a low-cut, belly-showing tank that displayed her high, full breasts. The black diamond-inlaid choker around her delicate throat told him what house she came from—A'archy.

She was a high-level Stalker and Cursed Gargoyle, nothing like any demon ever recorded in the Libraries. He could see a glimpse of a tattoo on the side of her breast cage, but he couldn't make it out. All he could see was a rush of kohl-lined brown eyes making their way toward him.

He smirked, welcoming the fight. His blade fluidly sliced through the air to swing out and make contact with her supple flesh yet again. This was the bitch's Pet, and he knew a battle with her for damn sure would be one he would enjoy. Sidestepping and following through with his fist, he let his knuckles hit her beautiful jaw, and the Medusa screeched and flew backwards.

He grimaced. Then he smiled. His boy Calvin had noticed the fight and was running full speed to assist, sliding over the hood of a 4x4, his guns blazing. He must have followed him there or had a vision of him fighting tonight.

"Go heal, chump! You have poison in your system!" Calvin shouted with a beaming smile as he held his hand in the air, levitating the screeching woman.

Khamun shook his head, ignoring his brother-in-arms' request as he leaped in the air, making contact with the entity. The force caused Calvin to slam them both to the ground with a grunt.

Khamun rolled to his side, holding his ribs and watched from across the street as his brother went into action.

The Medusa's heels tapped against the concrete roadway. Both men smelled the sudden saturation of poison coming from her. They knew from previous intel that they had to keep away from her nails, her bite, and those bladed boots of hers, each of which she used to inject poison into her prey.

Calvin's Khemetian protection tattoos and symbols on the side of his low fade glowed with his power, and his emerald eyes burned bright, ready for battle.

The Medusa grinned with excitement as she bounced up and ran after him.

Calvin smirked, ducking from flying objects being hurled at him, and skidded to a halt. Arms crossed, he stood in a b-boy stance as he waited. Adrenaline made him fist his hands as he dropped to the ground. Swift and precise, he hoisted himself up on one hand to spin-kick the screeching banshee down the street. Expertly landing in a backflip, he followed as she swung her nails at him in a frenzied attack.

"Ey, you don't know who you fuckin' wit, little momma. Ya heard me?" Calvin said in his thick New Orleans accent.

"And you don't know who you are playing with, baby." The Medusa seductively walked toward him, crouching low to sharpen her nails against the street pavement. "Your accent is horrendous. Must you debase the queen's language so?" Flipping her braids over her shoulder, she suddenly pivoted then jumped toward him in a spiral turn in the air, hitting his back with the skill of a martial arts master.

"Yeah, shawty, enjoy it. Shit!" Calvin hissed as he pushed back and swung his blade at her, its metal edge making contact with her razor braids. Sweat covered his face as he watched the Medusa clutch her arm, blood sliding over her fingers while he ran in a zigzag.

Calvin heard Khamun let off a round of Light bullets from his gun as he crouched low, holding his side, his leather trench coat moving as he aimed. He knew he had to help get his bro out of here. Poison was affecting him, and he could see it in his glowing eyes.

The Medusa laughed, her lithe, curvaceous body quickly jumping and pivoting from each bullet before she landed right in front of Calvin, stopping him in his tracks. Quick as a flash, she grabbed him by his shirt and pressed him against a car. Her plush blood red lips parted near his neck, to expose her slowly extending fangs.

Calvin held his blade against her belly as she sharply inhaled his scent.

"Mmmm," she moaned as her nails dug into his shirt, cutting the fabric but not flesh. Her brown-sugar eyes flickered with glee while she studied his features. "You both are so fun to play with," she muttered. Her tongue slipped out, thick yet thin like a snake, and its ribbed satin surface slid over Calvin's jaw and neck as she found his mouth. Her free hand gripped his jaw as the pad of her thumb ran over his lower lip, and she forced her tongue in, kissing him deep. Her plump lips drew his lower lip into her mouth as she sucked and tugged, before letting go with a satisfied smirk.

"Get off me!" Calvin spat.

The Medusa chuckled, jumping back.

Calvin's anger caused him to move quickly to ram his blade into her, but he missed her by mere second.

At the same time a high-pitched sound pierced the air. Its tone made both men clutch their ears and fall to their knees as the Medusa looked down the street, smoothed her braids, and sashayed away.

Calvin tried pushing up to follow her but ended up watching her flip over a car and disappear in the night.

Her voice echoed back, "I am being called back, but we will all play again later."

Khamun shook his head as Calvin glanced around, wiping the sweat from his face with a grunt. His tattoos and symbols faded with the drop of his energy. Calvin glared, pissed. His body clearly had drained the large amount of magic used in battle.

Languidly walking toward a now standing Khamun, he inhaled sharply then laughed. "Damn!"

"What?" Khamun looked down at his wound, smelling the rank poison while he limped toward his car.

Calvin was close behind him, mirroring his movement with a slight limp. "Let me get that shit outta ya system, homie," he muttered. He turned his face, scrunching it up in a scowl as he reached out toward his boy.

Puss seeped from the cuts inflicted on Khamun, making him grunt in pain. Khamun's body could usually reject poisons, but since this was known to be lethal, Calvin had to act fast.

Going into his hoodie, he pulled out an anti-venom shot that he was able to make earlier. This was going to be brutal. When administered, the shot always hurt in the worst way, so he had to help and do his job. With one hand on Khamun's chest, he held his bro down as he grunted and clutched his teeth from Khamun's swing then lunged.

"Damn, man! Why I have to get cold blocked? Shit, I wasn't the one going after that chick."

As Calvin probed his wounds, Khamun shook his head, cringing. "I know, damn. That shot hurts every damn time. My fault, fam."

Calvin just chuckled low in this throat as he watched the wound expel the poison while he collected what he could for more anti-venom. "Don't even say it, man."

Running a hand over his locks, Khamun stood and looked over his body. "Say what, chump?"

Flashing a lopsided smile as he nodded, Calvin looked over his own battle scars. "That you're hardheaded? Ha!"

"Agreed. But you gained another chance at the Medusa because of me," Khamun replied.

When Calvin didn't respond, Khamun quirked his eyebrow while he held back a deep laugh. "Yeah, I thought so."

Khamun couldn't help but glance at his best friend's bouncing shoulders as Calvin laughed with him. Calvin had been studying the Medusa for a while now, and this little encounter had further piqued his interest.

Satisfied, both men clapped each other on the back and whispered a spell to fix smashed cars, broken lights, and damaged buildings.

"Ey, Khamun, on the real, girlie flicked that tongue like a freak, brah. Oh my damn! That shit was boss!"

With a glance around the neighborhood, making sure the sound barrier was still up, Khamun turned and shook his head at Calvin. A smile played at his lips as he lightly laughed. "Seriously?"

Calvin headed to his bike and nodded, flashing his pearly whites. "Yeah, shawty is crazy as hell, but that tongue was da business. Ya dig!"

A half-smile played on Khamun's lips. "Damn! And I thought I was crazy."

Khamun hopped in his car and followed Calvin away from his Guide's neighborhood. Sanna crossed his mind. He was satisfied that the Cursed couldn't get near the section of the neighborhood anymore, now that it was barricaded with prayer and Light guards.

Lenox sat quietly, his head cocked to the side. Lost in thought, he swallowed a huge chunk of the Granny Smith apple he held in his hand. "Okay, tell us that again," he said as he leaned forward, one foot propped up, the other stretched out.

Khamun sighed as he looked toward the ceiling. He had collapsed on the floor as soon as he'd strolled in, and Calvin had taken his normal seat, the couch, one leg propped over the armrest.

"My Guide is a Vessel . . . an Oracle."

"Shit! You got to be kidding me. Another Oracle?" Lenox sat incredulous as he continued on, "Your mother is one of a few Oracles we have left globally. She is also the only Eldress Oracle in this region. Do you know how huge this is?" Lenox almost shouted but remembered who he was addressing. He sat back and calmed down, his mind reeling with this new knowledge. "She is the last Oracle, bro. We lost the last surviving one in Houston."

Khamun rubbed his temples as he tried to stay calm himself, keeping himself from getting up to pace or blow some shit up.

"He could be lying, saying anything to throw us off their scent," Marco replied, a flicker of amazement filling his voice as he also tried to process this knowledge.

"Naw, man." Khamun paused then slowly stood one arm over his chest, the other resting on his forearm like the thinker. He glanced at the Societal crest that marked their house. It lay spray-painted over the fireplace mantle in an edgy design that made it unique to them. "That was truth. I read it in his blood as he died. He couldn't hide that from me. Shit. You know this changes everything now."

Everyone in the room bowed their heads. It now meant that they could no longer watch. They now had to step into play and protect the only recently surviving Oracle born into existence. His Guide. Sanna. Everything now clicked for him.

Slowly pacing, Khamun cupped his forehead. "It all makes sense now."

Lenox's voice gained everyone's attention as he spoke. "All right, gentlemen, let us work this shit out for my man. The lawyer as well as the Warrior in me, without uncertainty, is prepared to go to war."

Khaman continued to pace the room. He motioned and counted on his fingers while he spoke, "One, when I was first assigned to them, I kept getting vibes that they both weren't what they seemed. The longer I worked with them, the more I noticed. Two, that shit at the restaurant kicked it off for me. Why? Because before all of this I kept getting Gargoyle vibes from her, and now we find out she is one. Shit! Third, both women fucking don't know what they are and will be going into their ripening now that the Cursed is surrounding them. We have to get them out of there now, because they won't stop until they have her and kill Kyo. Game over. They win again and weaken us yet again."

A cold anger filled the room as every male's eyes flickered and changed colors as they nodded.

Lenox fisted his hands as he leaned, his elbows resting against his thighs. "It is going to be the Reckoning and a fucking shame what we are going to do to those bastards let alone what we will do to them if they ever lay a hand on that young woman. This is our vow."

They couldn't let another innocent person, let alone another new blood, get snatched, tortured, and turned into pure evil against their will. If this happened, yet again another innocent would become a liability to the Light. They couldn't let that go down.

The scales were already tipping in favor of the Cursed, and now Society was in a fragile state of being. The team knew without a doubt this war was about to go deeper than ever. Nothing was going to stop them from protecting what was theirs.

A sudden click at the entrance of their compound had guns and blades being drawn, as a still silence took over and the door creaked open.

Orange and red silks caressed the opening door, and small painted nails appeared palms up, "Hold on!"

Every male sighed in unison and put their weapons away as Calvin hopped off the couch. He took a couple of long strides to the massive industrial steel factory door and reached out to pull in a small, dark-haired body to him, embracing the figure in a bear hug.

"Kali," Calvin's molasses-deep voice softened as he looked down.

Kalika stood shaking her wavy jet-black, shoulder-length hair, flashes of light brown accenting her mane, as dark kohl-lined eyes looked up at him.

"Geez, brothapoo! So you all were going to blow me away, huh? Why are you all so Alpha and sensory-blocked that you can't see? It's just little old me." She flashed a playful smile as Calvin let her in and locked the door.

Kalika was dressed in an orange and red silk sari with gold jewelry that made her creamy rich toffee skin and lush curves stand out against her attire. Calvin often called her Princess, or Kali, and always made sure she got whatever she needed. He picked up her luggage and made it disappear as she moved into the compound.

At twenty-five she was the only female of the House, and she often felt like the matriarch. She had no problem cleaning and cooking for the men. She was the baby sister, needing constant protection, so they felt, but today, thankfully the vibe wasn't directed to her. Peeking around her brother's massive frame, the look in every male's eyes was at a battle-ready-intense level she didn't like.

"Talk to me now!"

Kalika's sari brushed against the wood floor. One glance at Calvin had him whispering a spell that had her dressed in dark denim, skinny jeans, white high-top Nike on her small feet, and a black-and-white graffitied, off-the-shoulder shirt that showed off her belly and plush breasts. Adjusting her gold ankh that had the House crest inlaid on it, she pulled her long hair into a bundle at the top of her hair, using a hairclip as curls fell, framing her face.

Khamun stood to sweep Kalika in a huge embrace as he sat her down then took his usual seat in his big lounge chair. He stretched his legs out, leaning forward to rest a forearm on one thigh and prop up the other on his bended knee. His gun habitually appeared, tapping against his shin. "My Guide may be a Vessel."

Kali's slight inhale eased the tension in the room as she sat lotus-style. Her back rested against a pillow near the fireplace mantel.

"Really? We're talking about the one whose restaurant burned down, right?" Kali casually stated. She raised a questioning eyebrow, studying the man she felt was a big brother to her. His handsome features were stoic as tension rode his shoulders and he nodded.

"Then what's the problem? We need a blood sample to see if it's true."

Khamun shook his head and glanced at his baby sister. Sometimes she could be very blunt, other times she could ride them all hard if they didn't get their shit together. And sometimes she'd turn into the baby sister they loved to dot on. But, as of right now, she was pure Mystic and Slayer, just another valuable team member expressing her experience and tactics. He watched her eyes flicker in processing, "No, we have to get her and her protector ASAP. She's an Oracle."

Kali's mouth dropped at that as she sat forward. "Wait. What?"

"Yeah, Princess," Calvin firmly replied. "Khamun did his interrogation thing and found out that his Guide is not only a Vessel but also an Oracle. We need to get her ASAP. That's our fam."

"Then let's get her."

Kali looked around urgently, every man quietly watching Khamun as he sat back without a word.

"What do you all need to find out?"

"Not sure, Kali, but I trust you will know once you do your thing," Khamun evenly replied.

Kali quickly pulled out her laptop from the air, a trick Calvin had taught her. She quickly began pecking at the keys, her mehndi tattoos glowing with power.

"I know she is family, but I can get an extensive check of her personal background. Go into her medical history, read between the lines, as you know only I can do, and find out the truth before you bring her here scared and screaming."

Nonchalantly watching, Khamun gave a curt nod. "Do that, little sis."

"Okay, so Sanna Steele, born in St. Louis, she's twenty-seven—Wait, are you all just going to sit here and not get her?"

Lenox stood and stretched, running a hand through his dark hair. "I will have to do that tomorrow. I've been keeping tabs on her and the family twenty-four/seven, and I already feel like I'm stalking them. Khamun and Calvin just came back from a fight. We are positive she's safe right now, and we all need to rest, including you. Didn't you just get off a plane from India, little sister?"

Kali rolled her eyes and grumbled.

She promptly shut her mouth as Khamun stood and called his weapons to him. "I will go back and watch her home, and get that blood sample."

"Wait, bro, you need to rest," Marco replied. "I'll watch her, and Lenox can get the blood sample tomorrow. Then we move them to safety as planned." He stood. His hands brushed down his jeans as he held his hand up, a steel gun etched with verses from the Bible on its shiny surface glinting in the fire light.

"We have to look at the whole picture, gentlemen," Lenox interjected.

"Sanna has two siblings. Twins. A brother and sister. Amara is at Spelman College, and the other, Darren, is at the University of Illinois, Chicago."

An apple appeared in Lenox's hand again as he walked with both hands behind his back, the green surface of the apple missing a piece. "This family is about unity. They don't do anything without making sure family is protected first. We have to be smart and logical about this and not go out there in a weak state of mind and body. *We* all need to rest and process this shit. Research." Lenox's voice reflected his own authority and wisdom as he eyed everyone in the room.

Kali decided that was her cue. Clicking on her laptop, she said, "Nox is right. We do need to rest, but look, about that research end of all of this, if San is an Oracle . . . Remember the e-mails you sent me, Calvin? You said you think Kyo's a Gargoyle because of some things you remembered back when we visited them a lot."

Calvin nodded, as everyone focused their attention on Kali. "Well, if everything is true, then she is what will help keep our side strong and survive."

Lenox gave Kali a slight smile, his pearly whites flashing for a moment.

Inwardly laughing, Kali added, "Of course, we need to check out her family too before we start handing out labels. These two women are not the only ones we have to protect. We have to protect both women's families." Not once looking up from the computer, Kali held her laugh as she counted in her mind and waited for the men's reply as she searched for more information.

Every man groaned and stopped everything they were doing, as if lightbulbs flashed over their heads.

Lenox's chuckle filled the room as he sighed, his hand sliding into his dark denim jeans. "We have to report this to Society, mainly your mother, man. See if they can explain why none of them saw this Guide and her family."

Khamun stood again. The tapping of computer keys reassured him.

"You know why, Nox. Mom's been blocked, and this is going to piss her off even further, but I'll do what I can. She's going to want the whole family, shit. What more can you tell us? Break down her lineage. Maybe we can see if an ancestor is registered in Society."

Lenox headed into the kitchen and came back out with a beer. He shook his head in agreement. He knew the team was going to dig up more info and want to do everything they could to protect this family. Hell, he couldn't deny his own desire to rush back out and kick some ass and take names later, but he had to keep a rational head here. Everyone was battle-worn, and all of this info was fresh like baked bread. The team needed to research and sort this crap out.

"Hmmm. First up, Kyo Satou. Age: twenty-six. She is about to be twenty-seven. Mother and father: Takiko and Hideo Satou. Has a younger brother Takeshi Satou, and get this—He's at the University of Illinois, Chicago as well."

Kali glanced up and clicked a button, and images of Sanna, her family, Kyo and her family showed on the TV screen. A picture of Takeshi and Darren in matching frat colors and canes flashed on the screen, as Kali scrolled on.

"Takeshi is enrolled in international business, and Darren is in law. Dang! Why am I acting brand-new about this?" Kali shook her head in frustration, and glanced at the men, who blankly stared at her and shrugged. Playful smirks flashed over their faces as she continued to stare.

"What?" every man said in unison, their playful stances quickly dropping at the seriousness in their little sister's coco-rich eyes.

With a huff, she clicked a button on her laptop, cranking up the volume on the TV of a news article displayed on the screen. The report flashed images of a vandalized and destroyed loft apartment in an old, brick shoe factory. Patio balcony doors hung off their hinges, and shattered glass was strewn everywhere. A close look showed items of fabric, blood, and other debris scattered in the loft. Police, building tenants, and neighbors all vocalized their confusion and fear.

Every team member saw flashes of Stalkers, demons and Dark Seers mixed into the crowd, portraying themselves as ordinary, concerned pedestrians. In that moment alone, everyone knew this was no game.

"We need a team to get Amara from school ASAP because the family is being attacked.

Takeshi and Darren are at the University of Chicago Hospital due to trauma. We need a team up there now!" Kali yelled, her hands suddenly shaking, tiny sparks of Mystic light dancing against her long, painted fingernails.

Calvin shot into motion, almost heading out of the door before Marco stopped him. Calvin spun around, his hands flexing open and closing. He yelled, "Why didn't they call me? Shit!" He reached into his pocket and pulled out his cell. Scanning it, he yelled, "Shit!" He had multiple voice mails from Sanna and Tamar, each one hitting him on the hour. "I need to go to them." He apprehensively glanced around, checking his weapons to see how much ammo he had.

"We'll get them, bro. Just be calm. You'll set off Khamun too, man, if you don't chill," Marco whispered. Both men stopped and glanced at an agitated Lenox.

"You see this?" Lenox said. "The numbers are adding up. These two are important! It's not an accident that you have an Oracle being protected by a Gargoyle, and her brother is being protected by a Gargoyle as well. Check out the sister. Does she have one too?"

Resting be damned, ran through Lenox's mind, urgency fueling his motives and making him process what needed to go on. Units needed to go on alert, and they needed to make sure this family didn't fall through the cracks, not another one.

Khamun casually slid his cell phone open. He began making calls to various loyal Society council members who worked in conjunction with his family House and his own outcast of a House. Having loyal associates was everything within his world. Certain protocols dictated how acknowledged Houses worked, and since his House was unofficial, it made things easy for him to function without technically following the rigid rules of Society.

But because he was also of a royal birth house and a Guardian, he himself had necessary rules and guidelines to follow, although his own House did not. That meant that, as the son of the region's High Elder and of the long-living royal line in the States, he had duties to perform. It also helped having allies within the council. People he could use as liaisons. This kept the eyes of Society members who would like to take his father's place as High Elder off him, his House, and his father. He was no fool to let them use him against his father for their own game. What he established with his own House also provided a means of never-ending protection for those he called family.

The Nephilim world had changed a lot over the generations. A main reason was the fear of being wiped out, the shifting views of the many humans and hidden Nephilims they protected. Also, as generations changed, the many so-called righteous members of Society who thought they were better than everyone were really agents of the Cursed, allowing the Cursed to manipulate them and taint the old ways of the Light's survival, democracy, and history.

This was one of the main reasons he had to be sure to protect his Guide, because if a Cursed spy, or a Phantom as they called them, ever found out his truth and his Guide's truth, then that could adversely affect the balance in this war and lead to a catastrophe.

Shaking off his thoughts, Khamun started pacing. He noticed Kali tilting her head his way to gain his attention, as she continued to punch keys. Multi-tasking, he listened and spoke to the Society members he knew he could trust. It also helped that Marco had gained a seat long ago, due to family rights via his Light royal lineage, so he synced his phone conversation with Marco as they both listened to Kali.

"Doesn't look like she is in danger yet. She's well protected at Spelman, so she doesn't necessarily need one. But looking at her activity via Facebook . . . " Kali laughed and shook her head. "I love my family. I know we are not around them a lot, but they are a very smart family and have smart friends. Looks like the Satous sent a cousin down with Amara to watch her. The cousin was enrolled in Spelman at the same time. Her name is Miya Satou-Katsu."

An image of a smiling doppelgänger of Kyo, just with several distinct differences, flashed in front of Khamun's view as Kali continued on.

"The registry seems to be digging hard for this family. They must be very ancient, which is also key. Your girl Sanna and her family have strong backings. I'll have to check the Asian registry."

Kali held her hand up, ticking each one off as she counted, "One, two, bam! There they are. Satou and Katsu. Now let's see if this is the same family."

Kali was no joke with technology. Khamun had to give her the upmost respect. She was able to crack any code and get beyond any firewall without detection at all, and could find without hassle any old records.

Kali sat with her glowing hazel eyes closed. The laptop flashed pictures on the TV screen as she jerked forward and gasped, her hands resting on her crossed thighs. "Um, they are Imperial! Royal Gargoyles. This is incredible. Calvin, what's up with our cousins? Who in the family was smart enough to have Imperial Gargoyles watch and protect this family?"

With a look around the room, Kali stared astounded, "Did you all hear me? They come from Dragons!"

Calvin shrugged, circling his sister. He kneeled down behind her back, glancing at her laptop screen. "I told you I don't know, li'l sis. I only— wait what!" Calvin cursed in Creole and shook his head. "Ey, man, that's crazy. Dragon Gargoyles are thought to be extinct!"

Kali's eyes reflected the many colors of hazel as they widened with excitement. She searched more.

"Yes, that's why these records were hard to find. I had to dig deep, and they are not on our Internet archives. I'm putting it in my own archives now."

Khamun shifted his thinking. "Whose Vessel is she? Not only is she an Oracle, which is rare, but, shit, who is she? We need to get her now." Urgency filled him, his jaw clenched. "Damn the diplomacy. That family is coming under attack, and the Cursed are not going to stop, especially if they find this out."

"War," was all Marco said as he steepled his fingers in front of his mouth, nodding. "Yeah, they will go to war for them."

Lenox sat back, his ankle resting on his knee as he took a long drink from his chilled beer, his Adam's apple working as he spoke. "As Kali said, this seems to be very strategic. Each Steele child is being protected, yet as I sat in that kitchen with those ladies, neither knew anything. It was the same with the mother. Calvin, give us a family rundown."

Kali and Calvin nodded at the same time, which let everyone know Kali was looking up Calvin's family history of and would fill in with what she found if questions arose.

His fingers laced together as he cracked his knuckles, Calvin rolled his shoulders and leaned against a nearby table. "A'ight. Sanna is my cousin through my G'ma Sera. Bishop, her father, married Sanna's momma, and that's all I know. Bishop's my cousin, but I've always called him Unc. Nothing special about his background, 'cept that his ma and g'ma are Prophetesses. That's where she gets her Nephilim gene then. I assumed it was dormant because he was human too."

Kali frowned as she shook her head and looked up at Calvin. "Bro, that's not true. G'ma Sera sat and told me the truth. She shared her vision with me."

"What? When? Why didn't she tell me?"

The concern in Calvin's eyes made Kali halt her Internet searches. She placed her laptop on the table and stood to move to his side and hug him gently, her hands cupping the sides of his face briefly while he looked up at her with brotherly love.

She loved her brother deeply. Ever since his family had adopted her as a child, her life never felt devoid of love, even with the loss of both her Guardian parents, so to see the distress in her big brother's eyes always upset her. She would go to war for him and her family, which included Sanna.

"Because she knew you carried too much as is, so she talked with me."

Calvin wrapped his sister in a bear hug and simply shook his head, his shoulders slumping in understanding and quiet disappointment. "Tell us."

Kali muttered, "Okay. Unc Bishop was an Immortal and Mystic. His father was a Guardian, and his mother was a human guide, a Prophetess, G'ma's twin sister Sadie."

Calvin frowned, as did everyone in the house. Everyone knew the law—Guardians and Guides never mated for life. It was against Society for Guardians to let their presence be known to their Guides, unless it was to protect them from Cursed attacks. That was it. Any prolonged or intimate acquaintance was against Society bylaws.

Khamun stroked his jaw, his mind churning in thought. That very restriction was the reason why he had never made himself known to Sanna until the attack, and even that was very covert. That restriction was what had him yearning for her at night and waking up in cold sweats, needing to feed and horny as fuck.

He often thought of breaching protocol and risking his status in Society. He wanted to do it just to sit and have lunch with Sanna, but he knew he couldn't, because of his mother and father. It would put them in an already difficult situation, so Khamun used his team to get close to her. Lenox and Marco acted as his mouthpiece when his will broke, and he sent Sanna steamy dreams of being with her.

Kali and Calvin were the anchors, checking to see if she was okay and were not affected by the dreams the very next day or week.

The law of Guardians was difficult, and he had heard tales of many falling and leaving their posts as Guardians to be with their Guides. It was one of the reasons more Halflings were in the human population and had to be watched for an active Nephilim gene.

Calvin's voice broke through his inner thoughts. "Damn! Really? I remember he was killed by a Snatcher. Shit makes sense now."

"No, brotherpoo, it's deeper than that." Exhaling, Kali watched her brother as she continued. "Grammy was ashamed how this happened, but Uncle Bishop's dad ran off and hid with Sera so they could be married. It took a long time before Grammy could even find them to demand that they come home. Bishop's dad had died protecting Sera, and Sera had brought Bishop home to raise him. The summer we spent, when you had just found out about your immortality, that was when we got to meet him, bro. Then a year later he was killed by a Snatcher, dying in the same way his father had died when he was protecting him."

Kali wiped a solitary tear falling down her toffee cheek, with the heel of her hand as she gave a half-hearted smile. "You Freeman-Steeles know family is your life or death."

Calvin shook his head and slouched over in the chair. He had taken the time to sit and cradle his head, the new knowledge swarming his mind. "Why did that shit have to happen, sis? I connected with him. He schooled me in so much. I had no idea he was Immortal. What made a Snatcher come after him?"

"I don't know," Kali replied softly. "She wouldn't tell me that." Tears choked her up, making her draw her knees up to her chest.

"I think we need to find out, because I have a feeling it's connected to his children," Lenox replied hoarsely.

Kali was already combing through her computer again at Lenox's words. She tried to distract herself from the emotional tension of her cousin's background history while she checked out birth records and reports on Bishop Steele's death. Determination caused her to furrow her brow.

"As Kali mentioned, they are not even registered with Society then," Lenox pointed out.

"So how do we handle this, Khamun?" Marco calmly asked, watching his fam. "You're her Guardian."

Everyone sat lost in thought while he paced then stopped then paced again.

"I'm not her Guardian then, since she is a Vessel and Oracle. The law of Guardians doesn't apply here now. I can intervene and get her, but we have to do this intelligently, as Nox said. Everything in me wants to grab her now and usher her in here, you know, but we can't," Khamun said. "We can't drop the ball like the past Guardians did with that lost Oracle. We have to surround her, and we have to gain her and her family's trust. We need to insert ourselves around her." He ran over what he needed to do in his mind.

Marco agreed.

Lenox thought quietly, a Trinity resting between his fingers, while Kali was clicking away at her laptop, and Calvin was pacing with Marco.

"Well, I'm her fam, ya know. I got this. I can go and insert myself." Calvin, a flash of determination and slight humor flickering in his emerald eyes, looked at Lenox then Khamun. "Ey, Lenox, you keep your position as you are doing, you know, acting as their liaison for our company, and Khamun, brah, you'll finally get to met ya Guide."

Khamun flashed a smile.

As Calvin headed to the door, he said, "Kali, I'll let them know you're back from ya trip. I bet they are gonna head up to Chi, so we need to keep a team with them."

Kali suddenly stood, snapping her computer shut, and swiftly moved next to Calvin. "No, I'm coming too. They are my family as well. Plus, everyone here needs to get their asses in bed and rest. You do too, brotherpoo, but I won't fight you, so let's go."

Khamun interjected as Kali hugged her brother. He noticed Calvin's body was tense with emotion.

Khamun's eyes briefly flashed with worry and care. "Cal is right. We need to integrate fast. Early in the morning, I'm gonna transition to Chi and wait for Calvin and his family. Marco, get in touch with the Chi-town team. My Guide and her Gargoyle's brothers need protection now. We'll have to integrate them into this as well. We won't lose any more innocent people to the Cursed. We can't. "

"I'll stay here and keep the ranks with Marco, watch the city and protect our territory while keeping Society council at bay," Lenox calmly replied, his arms crossing his chest.

"Yeah, we gotcha back, fam." Marco nodded, his eyes flashing with care.

Everyone agreed.

Khamun closed his eyes and spoke in the old language of Angels. Both Marco's and Khamun's wings unfurled as power washed over everyone. Calvin's tattoos, Lenox's eyes, and Kali's mehndi and bendi all glowed as they whispered in sync. They needed prayer to guide them through this, to protect a woman who would save a dying race.

Yes, they needed to do all they can, so they would not lose anymore to absolute death and loss. Over the passing generations, many Nephilims had gone missing. Either turned into Cursed, or permanently killed off through attacks by the Cursed. This prayer was a vow to continue to fight until they couldn't fight anymore.

Chapter 6

It was found that the One God's son had a close friend, another who would become a lost disciple and prophet in his plan. She would forever be named The Whore, The Prostitute, The Harlot. But before that, before she became The Lady Magdalene inflicted by demons, she was just a young girl, a young woman on the verge of her eighteenth year. Forever his loyal friend, it is said, she understood him more than anyone, birth just for him by his Holy Father.

In these lost accounts we knew the truth, the truth that this young girl would forever be at his side. Bound to him by his denotation dreams and amicable union, he found her when he was but fourteen and she twelve years. This union forever bonded by the One God in innocence and love.

The three crusaders, the first Guardians, the wise ones, bore witness to miracles of the young messiah. Their accounts are what we carry within us always. The young one sat calm on the cool waters boating, reflecting as only He could. The three crusaders sat at his side, answering all his questions and also learning much from him. The young messiah smiled and pitched his rod as his head bowed, and the waters became silent. It was with this that a multitude of fish rose to jump into the small boat as the young one opened his eyes and smiled.

"She is awakening," was all the young man said as the three wise ones listened to his declaration and asked his parents' permission to find the one from his vision.

They found her in the fishing village of Magdala playing near the water's edge, her long, thick mane of dark hair glowing from the sun's rays being used as a rope to taunt fish toward her. The young protector went to her side that day and they were inseparable, training and educating each other as well as the wise ones.

I smile at the memories of these two. Darkness only was beginning to touch the pair as the young Magdalene became a woman. Eldress Mary was with the young Magdalene when the first prophecies arrived, giving the young girl visions stronger than even Eldress Mary ever had.

Night terrors and head pains plagued the young Magdalene as the first demons were sent her way at eighteen, forever marking her and moving her into what the mortals historically named her. But to us, she was an innocent, a Disciple, the first Oracle to be attacked by the Dark, bitten to be Cursed, until the young messiah healed her and purged the evil from her in later life. For this we know the truth, the truth of this holy anointed pair to be fighters against the Dark, more than disciple and messiah, but united in holy matrimony and spiritual teaching. The young anointed protectors, fighters for humanity and us.

From this we vowed to forever watch over and protect our Oracles. To stop the Dark from taking what they themselves could never sire, vessels of knowledge against our enemies. Vessels of power created to stand at the side of our experienced fighters, varying within them the memories of this present and their pasts. Vessels taken through the generations to be seeded with darkness until our Oracles became rare and almost extinct. We protect them with our very lives, we watch them close. This is our history and no other. The Light will always prevail. This is the end of my entry.

Chapter 7

Sanna and her family had all packed up last night and were just about to head out when Calvin came to the house. Calvin almost crushed Tamar with a bear hug, and Kali was right behind him, running up to Sanna with a tight embrace. Tamar had always treated her cousins Calvin and Kali like a third son and a third daughter, so when they both insisted that Sanna's family travel in his and Kali's Escalade trucks, they could do nothing but accept and head up to Chicago. Calvin had explained to them that he had a townhouse in Lincoln Park, where they could all stay.

The drive was long, so Sanna used the time to talk to her sister Amara on the cell. Amara was panicking and anxious, but Calvin had called and told her that he was sending her plane tickets. He was also sending his frat brother Khamun to wait at O'Hare Airport for them.

Amara was waiting at Atlanta's Hartsfield-Jackson International Airport going stir crazy with her bestie Miya, Kyo's cousin. Sanna could hear Miya trying to keep her calm as she tried to distract her with random questions. Sanna was happy that both of them clicked so well as kids. Miya was good people. It reminded her of herself and Kyo but with a slight difference.

Thinking about Dare and Take, Sanna couldn't help but smile. Their attitudes mirrored each other's—suave, protective, loving, and very supportive of those they called family and friends.

Sanna was scared out of her mind for her brother and godbrother. She had just got done talking to them, and now they were laid up in a hospital probably unconscious or something. This was insane. She calmly tried to breathe, but pain shot into her skull and spread through her like prickly nails as she leaned her head back, sweat soaking her skin. The car suddenly seemed too small. She had to ride this pain out, had to make it to Chicago to make sure her family, her brothers, were okay. She squeezed her eyes shut.

Flashes of light seemed to drown her as she momentarily opened her eyes and saw her cousin Calvin watching her in the rearview mirror. Briefly as if in a blink of an eye, she swore she saw his irises glow with green power. Leaning forward, she quickly rolled down the window and closed her eyes again. That ebbing ache made silent tears roll down her cheek as she bit her lower lip. She could do this. She could make it and check on her brothers then curse them out for being reckless, or for getting hurt in the first place.

***

Five hours later they arrived in noisy, bustling Chicago with the sizzling weather, traffic stalling them. Their Escalade seemed to hit every pothole known to man. One pothole was so bad, Sanna thought it took off a hubcap as the truck lifted in the air then dropped back down.

"Damn!" Sanna yelled. "These streets are a hot-ass mess. And the drivers here seem to be just as bad as the ones in ATL. What the hell!"

Her mother chuckled, and Calvin nodded his head in agreement. "Shawty, you ain't said nothing but the truth."

It was a deja vu moment for Sanna when they finally made it to the hospital and she glanced at a sleeping Kyo.

Kyo opened her eyes and abruptly sat up. She was back. This was part of her dream. She had stood on that exact roof of the hospital. She had floated five levels up peering into the room her brothers rested, and here she was in a reality where her brother may be severely hurt. *How could he get hurt? What was he doing to become so messed up that he was in the hospital? What was going on here?* Nothing had been going right since the attack back in St. Louis, and now this mess with her little brother. No, this couldn't be happening, shouldn't be happening.

Now she was sitting in an Escalade, worried and praying until her hands became cramped from clenching them so hard. The emotion was so high, Sanna had suffered through another migraine but hadn't told anyone about it, playing it off as cramps and keeping her cool as usual. That pissed Kyo off. She couldn't do anything but shake her head as she glanced at her godsister.

Kyo could see the strain it was having on her. Hell, she could feel it. She wanted to scream. Wanted to tell Calvin to stop the car and pull over so she could shake the hell out of Sanna and help her sister with the pain as they both cried.

She remembered the dream, seeing her brothers bloodied and mangled. There was nothing she could do, and it terrified her. Things in the dark were coming after them all, and the only reason she knew this was because Sanna had said it out loud as she dreamed it. The family was under attack from entities neither of them could see, yet no one was saying anything. All she could do was shake her head and pray that this feeling was nothing but nonsense and that her brothers were okay.

Halting the sudden desire to have a nervous breakdown, Kyo was out of the car in a blink as she fleetingly looked around with a strange expression on her face. It had been a long time since she had been to Chicago, but it felt like it was just yesterday, in her dreams.

Sanna furrowed her brows in a grimace, watching her godsister as she glanced with a raised brow, eyes wide, her hands fisting on her lap before spilling out of the car to head into the hospital.

The sterile hospital halls whisked by Sanna as everything felt like a scene from a movie. Everyone around her seemed to move, whereas she seemed to be walking in suspended motion.

Patients coughed. Monitors beeped, rang, and screamed for attention.

Following the color coding strips in the hospital, everyone made it to the ICU, rushing the nurses' station. Hospital staff seemed to not notice the huge number of people standing in the waiting area.

Sanna was two minutes away from grabbing the throat of the next person who had the nerve to ignore them, until her godfather Dr. Hideo Satou walked up to the nurses' station and spoke in a very hushed tone to the curly head of a woman, playing as if she was filling out various forms. His voice became clipped with restrained anger.

Dr. Hideo Satou was a tall, muscularly lean, handsome man. You would have thought he was in his early thirties, but he was in his late forties. His jet-midnight hair curled around his face in a feathery, shaggy haircut, which reflected where Kyo got her style. And his laid-back style of light blue jeans and a white button-down shirt with brown leather oxford sneaker designer shoes made him look like a graduate student.

Dr. Hideo leaned in, smoothly looking over his black-rimmed glasses, and addressed the nurse, "I wish to know which room my sons are located in."

It always amazed Sanna how many confused Dr. Hideo for someone her age. It was only when he opened his mouth, and wisdom and knowledge spilled forth, his age showed. Dr. Hideo was Japanese-American, but was reared in Japan before coming back to America at thirteen. Family tradition had him making trips back and forth, which made him a child of both nations. His world-known pedigree in neurosurgery made him the most bad-ass doctor in the nation, and he now stared down an insensitive woman who looked up at him as if she owned the world.

It took every skilled lesson in meditation and martial arts, as well as the dragon arts, for him to not shift in this unethical practicing hospital. His son, his flesh and blood, was lying in some gurney bed, bleeding out, as his other son, his godson, lay in a comatose state. He could smell their energy and blood. He could also tell that if they had not made it out of wherever they were, they would have been on the brink of dying. Now this unprofessional degenerate of a nurse wanted to stop him from knowing where they were.

He could drop to their uncouth level and bypass all the ignorance and go to his sons by following their scents, but if he did, his already boiling anger would have him shifting in a drop of a dime and that was not acceptable, not right now. No, he would keep his cool and play by the rules and be patient.

Hideo rolled his shoulders as he calmed the dragon within and stared at the nurse, dipping into her mind smoothly, dissecting her brain, to make her pull up files and background information, so that she would get up off her prissy ass and pay attention to what he was saying.

"Sir, I'm not allowed to give you that information. Your son seems to be on blackout, and you are not the father of Mr. Steele, so I am not at liberty to share that with you."

Dr. Hideo bowed his head, his face tightening with frustration as his voice seemed to lower even further. His grey eyes flashed with power as his nails lengthened. He kept himself from leaning into her face and snapping her neck, aware of the people around him. Those blessed people had him checking himself as everyone had to take a double take while they stared at the unusually cool and collected male gripping the edge of the desk, quietly talking to the rude woman.

Sanna swore she saw a haze of cold energy surround Pop Hideo as she took a double take, blinking at what she thought was his nails lengthening before she shook her head. Running a hand down her face, she looked up again, her eyes refocusing. By the grace of the Most High, she saw him as he normally was, resting against the nurse's desk, his facial expression locked in cold, restrained frustration.

The nurse huffed, clicking on her keyboard, one key at a time, her eyes glancing up and locking on Pop Hideo.

Sanna raised an eyebrow. If that chick said one wrong word to her godfather, then it was going to be a fucking problem, ending with her foot in that chick's back. That's how upset she was at this particular moment.

"Of course . . . I am sorry. I understand protocol, but as you see, both young men call me father, so Mr. Steele, as you see, is my son, my godson."

The nurse continued to click. She leaned into the computer screen then abruptly stood up, pushing away from the desk, one hand snapping quickly to her temple. She shuddered then exhaled. "Dr. Hideo Satou?"

Dr. Hideo stood back with a curt nod as the nurse pulled out a clipboard, made notes, and slid it toward him.

"Please sign here and here, and I will page Dr. Toure. He specifically told me to let you and your family pass through. I—I am so sorry. It's hospital policy to keep patient information private when they are placed on blackout."

Hideo Satou shook his head. He wanted to be a smart ass and call her on her disrespect and rudeness, but instead he just glanced at his wife before turning back to the nurse and offered a tired smile. "It is okay. We just want to see our children."

Emi Satou quietly walked near her husband and wrapped her arms around him while he nuzzled his face in her silky ebony hair. She knew her husband and was quietly sending him soothing support to keep him calm. If she hadn't, then that woman would be dragon bait, and that wasn't something they needed right now, not today. Her husband needed comforting, and she was going to give it to him, even though her insides were being eaten up due to the stress and worry for her sons.

Gently cupping her husband's clenched jaw, she gave him a soft kiss on his lips, and both exhaled with emotion. Worry filled them as they glanced toward Kyo and motioned for her as she walked into their open embrace.

Emi was the same height as her daughter. Anyone who didn't know would swear they were twin sisters. Emi just had longer hair with hazel eyes. Her daughter was a beautiful blend of her

Okinawan descent, creamy tan skin, almost pale-almond-hued, with her father's strong Tokyo style, smarts, and sensual mouth.

Emi quietly spoke with her daughter. She smoothed her child's spiky hair, brushing a red strain of bang from her face so she could kiss her forehead. A comforting smile hit her lips, letting her daughter know she was here for her. Tears sparkled in her eyes as she glanced at her other daughter, her dear godchild Sanna and she wrapped her in an invisible blanket of ease.

Sanna sat uncomfortably in the plastic cold chairs in the waiting room and watched the family. Everyone was shaky and scared. Their nerves were on end while sending prayers to the two young men who lay under protective care. Since they were in blackout mode, everyone knew it had to be serious.

Calvin had disappeared. Mr. Hideo spoke to the nurse again, and Kali sat by Sanna, resting a hand over her head. She returned the loving touch back as she rested against her cousin's comforting shoulder. It was something about her cousin, which always calmed her when she was near. It always put her in the mindset of how her mother made her feel. Though Kali was younger, she still seemed to have this inner well of maternal comfort Sanna seemed to appreciate.

A sudden vibration had Sanna's leg shaking. She contorted her face in a frown and pulled out her cell. One glance at the text message had her smiling. She showed Kali the screen. Amara was on her way, having caught the earliest plane she could jump on with Miya. She quickly texted her sister, letting her know that Calvin's frat brother, Khamun Cross, was going to meet them at O'Hare Airport and drive them both to the hospital.

She tiredly laughed as her sister asked her what he looked like. She frankly had no idea at all. Hell, she had no idea who he was, except Calvin seemed to trust him enough to have him pick her little sister up. So she texted that bit of tidbit back. Her cell phone began to fade in and out, the words before her becoming fuzz as her body started to overheat.

Blinking back tears of pain, Sanna stood as she looked around for somewhere private to have her spell. Kali was asking her something, but at that moment all she could hear was mumbling, her hearing fading in and out like a rush.

The migraines were coming back to back now, and she didn't know why. They could be coming back to back due to stress but this wasn't the time for it. She wanted to scream, but she knew she couldn't.

Checking the sign, she walked toward a fancy-looking vending machine. She put a dollar fifty in and hit the bottled water option. Then she reached for it then unscrewed the plastic top and took a deep swig.

Digging into her purse, she grabbed her orange bottle of pills, with shaky hands as she opened the childproof prescription container, white-hot pain ripping through her, making her clutch her hands as she dropped the bottle and pills. Water slowly spread over her feet like a veil, and pills floated like little lifeboats as she held onto the machine. This was horrible, like the last time she was back in St. Louis.

Images flashed across her mind, making her eyes roll in the back of her head, her eyelashes fluttering with each image she saw.

Hands reached for her from the dark, as she heard a clicking sound as two feminine shapes emerged from the shadows, their faces covered yet their eyes glowing red as they suddenly slashed at her.

Sanna wanted to scream while the images repeatedly took her senses over. Each vision dug into her senses like barbwire, branding her brain in fire.

She saw ruby red blood darken as it congealed by her feet in a flowing puddle. She saw Kyo's skin change and harden into stone, her features frozen in fear and pain. Sanna reached out to the statue of Kyo as it turned into dust and rubble as the two shadowed women destroyed it in the sudden moonlight.

Tears flowed down her cheeks as she watched in horror before she heard a worried drawl cut through the thick cloud of images that choked her mind. Muscled arms suddenly wrapped around her, shaking her out of her haze.

Disoriented and exhausted, confusion washed over her face as her cheek rested against Calvin's hard chest. She breathed in his familiar, comforting scent, its fragrance stroking her senses as her hearing returned to normal. She heard her cousin, who she felt was like a big brother for her at times, murmur to her in Creole, singing an old hymn Grammy Sera had taught them as he rocked her.

Calvin had gone back to his car to talk to Khamun as he tried to calm down. He needed the privacy and distraction. The emotion of the family and situation was causing him to spark with magic, and he couldn't afford them to see him in this state. So as he made sure that his young cousin was on her way, he closed his eyes and listened to Khamun's rant.

"Damn, man! I'm tired as hell. The transition took a lot out of me since I hadn't fed to my fullest."

"I hear you, man. When I use Mystic transition, it does the same to me. Seems to unplug me, ya feel me? So will you be able to survive being around us? Because this shit got a brotha running on *E*, brah."

Calvin watched passing female nurses and female doctors eye him while offering a flirting smile. Out of respect he nodded and offered a slight smile as he moved to be by himself. He didn't have the time to return the casual flirting he enjoyed doing. It was his nature to soothe the female personality and make a woman smile, but right now his mind was on his family, especially his cousins.

"Yeah, I'll be able to handle it, brah. Hey. I contacted the Chi-town crew as well. They have a well-placed man in the hospital taking care of Take and Dare. He put them on blackout to keep as many humans out of our business. So y'all should be able to get through without a problem unless some human doesn't know what's up. So is Sanna okay?"

Calvin had to inwardly chuckle. His boy was in love. Now that he could officially cross the line from Guardian to Protector he knew that Khamun was going to turn his cousin's already tilting world even further upside down and right again.

"She's handling the best she can right now. She had another migraine in the car, and my girl sat and rode through it like a warrior—"

Before he could finish Khamun bellowed, "What! She had another migraine, and what did you do, my man?"

"Ey, brah! It's all good. I watched her. Trust. I didn't enjoy watching that. I had to keep myself from pulling over and going into Mystic mode, but I did put a small calming spell on her."

Silence had Calvin thrusting a hand in his pocket and pacing. He heard Khamun clear his throat.

"Okay . . . did it look bad?"

"Yeah, man. We gotta get her through this, but right now we gotta check on Dare and Take. So with that, get my younger cousin here safely and get ya energy right. You know how you do. If you don't feed, you get sick, so it's good you partially got a snack, my man."

"Bro, shut the fuck up. Sometimes I feel like you my damn dad, man." Khamun chuckled.

Calvin studied his cell, smirking while he listened.

"I got the restorative tablets. I'll take some as soon as Amara's plane lands, and I'll get us to the hospital ASAP."

Calvin glanced to the heavens and quietly exhaled. It was true. The two of them often flipped between brother and father role, making sure each was okay in situations such as this. "A'ight. I'll holla, brah. Take care of yaself, and I have to roll out. Something feels wrong."

Khamun's voice hitched as if he was going to ask what was up, but he simply got quiet then said, "Peace."

As Calvin hung up and jetted back upstairs from the outside courtyard, the first thing he saw was his cousin clutching the soda machine and sliding down its slick surface. Her water bottle spilled in slow motion and blended with the scattered pills.

His heart stopped when he saw her like that. It took everything in him not to holler as he grabbed her and held her tight against him. He could feel her body shake with each shattering spasm, her eyes suddenly glowing with quiet power in a way he had never witnessed before.

As he held her, he whispered a healing prayer while her body shuddered in response. An epileptic shock made her body rigid as a board. Tears slid out of the corners of her eyes, and inaudible words slipped from her pink lips. This scared the hell out of him as her power took his body over, her jumbled words wrapping around him.

Instinct had him cloaking them with an invisible spell that made it look as if she had just fainted and he was helping her.

Yeah, she is for damn sure an Oracle, he thought as he saw her Denotation vision. The hair on his body stood strong through the exchange. He had to pull back before he drowned in it, and he gasped.

Reality snapped back around him, and he looked down, gently pressing the back of his hand against her now cooling skin as he gently shook her awake.

"San, I'm here," Calvin gently whispered to her as he held her tight against him while he prayed.

He noticed her eyelashes flutter behind their closed sleep and then slowly open. Her pupils tried to focus on him while her lips parted, and her heaving chest slowly evened.

"I—I just want them to stop. I don't know what to do anymore. Make it stop, cousin . . . please."

She was so tired and exhausted from the pain, from worrying about her brother as well, that all she could do was glance up at her cousin's scared and worried face. Her head then turned from him to stare off in a tear-streaked glaze.

"I will do what I can, shawty. We're going to help you, Dare, and Truth, okay. We're going to keep you all safe, even Kyo and Take. We got you. That's why I'm here. I won't let anything happen to you. You are my blood. I got you always, even if I have to sacrifice myself."

She didn't understand what he was talking about, but his devotion, his love and protection made her just nod in fringed understanding as his touch made the pain subside and she fell asleep.

Calvin kissed the top of her damp forehead while he picked her up and took her back to the waiting room. He watched his aunt's eyes widen as her face froze in an *O* shape. He shook his head in a dazed state. "She'll be okay, Auntie. She is just exhausted. Let her sleep."

Dr. Satou, whom he got to know as Hideo, briskly strode to Sanna's side, his walk full of fatherly concern and stress. He looked at Calvin briefly before taking her from his arms. "Where's her medicine?" he asked, looking her over.

"She dropped it, but I was able to help her sleep," Calvin cautiously said.

Hideo looked up at him briefly.

Calvin swore he saw his eyes flash at him, tendrils of flames, circling over gray lenses, but before he could investigate it, Tamar came up to him and clutched him by his arm, softly tugging with a purpose.

"Come with me, son."

Tamar regarded him with so much determination in her light brown eyes, he felt as if he had no other choice but to let her lead him off to a private area.

"Cousin Tamar, Momma, look, it will be okay. I helped her. Please don't cry." He hated seeing his family like this, hated seeing the women he cared about cry, but it was nothing he could do. He saw Kali come around the corner, her gaze searching.

Tamar turned and briefly smiled at her with love and concern in her eyes. "Both of you come with me now." Tamar commanded her small frame, sashaying with constraint as she walked to an empty room, her heels clicking on the floor. She waited for both of them to enter, and closed the door.

With both arms wrapped around herself, Calvin and Kali watched her back rise up and down as she slowly turned and tilted her head to the side.

A tear slid down her cheek before she fiercely wiped it away. "Tell me right now. Why are you both really here?" she asked in a tight, restrained voice.

"Momma Tamar, you know why we are here. Darren and Take need us. They are our family too. You know why we are here. Ma! Please don't cry," Calvin said, his own voice wavering with emotion.

Kali held herself tightly, the emotion in the room filling her with pain and sadness as she watched the woman she called a third mother fight back from breaking down.

Tamar Steele shook her head, curls vibrating with her emotion as she stared at the two she loved as her own children. "No, let me try this again. Why are you both here? Kali, why? Tell me the truth. My child is laying in a hospital bed, as my other child is laying in the waiting room passed out from pain. Tell me right now—*right now*—why you both are here."

Kali looked confused as she studied her aunt's posture. Something was different, very different about her, especially the way she was speaking to them. She could feel it as she stared.

Tamar looked at Kali and bowed her head. Tears suddenly spilled down her cheeks as Kali gasped.

Calvin looked at Kali, misunderstanding in his face.

Tamar held up a shaking hand, "Protocol, right?" She gave a sarcastic smile as she shook her head. "Protocol is what killed my husband. Protocol is what now has my children in danger! *Danger*! How long will you both just stand by and not protect my children as dictates?"

Calvin's mouth dropped open as he looked at his aunt for the first time in a long time. He could see her aura glowing all the colors of a Disciple and a Prophet. Shaking his head, all he could do was sit down, his hands cradling his face as Kali stood by his side, her hand resting on his shoulder.

"Momma Tamar?" Kali asked, her world now thrown for a loop over it all as she lost the words forming in her mind.

Tamar clenched her fists, dropped her head, and scanned the room, frustration making her furious. "I've been waiting for a long time for you all to realize that my children needed your help. A very long time. Did you really think I didn't know who you were to us? Everything I did to protect my children so that we can survive is because I *know*. You understand me, son? Kali? I know more than you!"

Kali and Calvin became silent with budding understanding, shock rolling through their minds as they digested what was just said to them. All this time they thought they were in the shadows, protecting from afar, when in reality, their aunt, the woman they called Momma, knew everything they were doing, who they were, and what they were about.

Calvin croaked, "I don't understand. How are you a—"

Tamar walked up to him and cradled his face, gently laying a kiss on his forehead. "So you both didn't know? Here I was under the impression that you both knew, since you all started coming around us more often. Ever since I saw my daughter's Guardian outside of our house, or around her in general, I thought you all knew. Oh, my dear babies, I am so sorry."

Tamar gently hugged them both then grabbed a chair and pointed to the other empty chair at its side. "Sit down, baby girl. This is going to be a long story then," Tamar softly said as she watched Kali drop her shoulders and sit. She reached out to hold Kali and Calvin's hands while she sighed and took a seat.

"My babies are coming into their powers. I know, I know. You all are wondering why do I know this." She reached into her purse and wallet and pulled out a folded picture of a younger version of herself with a tall handsome Blair Underwood-looking male.

Calvin and Kali recognized him instantly. It was Bishop Steele, her husband.

"Their father . . . that man made sure that with his last breath he would protect us. I wasn't always an Immortal. I was just a Prophet, a human with the gift of sight. I was just a woman who fell in love with a Disciple with magic abilities. We met in college and knew we were soul mates. My visions of him and his visions of me sealed it. So it made sense to marry and start a life, especially since we loved each other dearly."

"Unc Bishop was more than a Disciple?" Calvin calmly asked as he studied Tamar's butter-brown face as it softened with the memories.

"Yes, my beloved was more than a Disciple. He had your gift, sweetheart, with magic. It passes through your Creole bloodline, stemming from Africa."

Calvin softly smiled, sitting up straight with the knowledge as he glanced at Kali. She also flashed a brief smile as she nodded to listen.

"Very strong magic, gifted from the Ancients. My beloved was going to be your mentor and teach you about the power you have, but the Most High called him back home." She got very quiet as her mind flashed back to her husband's death.

Calvin gently squeezed her hand as she exhaled slowly.

"It's okay. I've grieved. He gave me so many gifts, I have nothing to complain about."

"What happened? Why did he die? How did you become an Immortal? Because that's not possible. Yet here you are." The questions seemed to rush out of Kali as she sat on the edge of her chair.

Tamar chuckled as she gently kissed the back of Kali's hand, which she held with her own. "We had to move the moment I was pregnant with Sanna. The instant we conceived her, everything changed. We both had the dream of Denotation as I carried her. Me, a human Prophet having a Denotation vision. I was incredulous, and I was scared out of my mind from that power. My husband was just as worried for us all. We knew we had to go into hiding and couldn't put our family in jeopardy."

Tamar glanced at Calvin as she said that. She watched him bow his head, emotion tight in his shoulders.

"You know, my husband's father, for the longest of times, didn't want us to meet you all, but when the Elders of the family passed, we knew it was okay go back to where it all began. Home, as my husband's father would say. So we all went, my husband and a pregnant me. We wanted to see if we could hide without putting you all at risk."

Memories of it all flashed in between the triad as they linked in mind and power. Kali and Calvin's eyelids flickered with the movie screen projected images in their mind.

"So your grandmother Prophetess Sera told us to hide in plain sight, but my husband was smarter than that. He knew I needed protection, and he could feel the power our child held. So he contacted his childhood friend in St. Louis, Hideo. Hideo had just married Emi, and so they both suggested we move there, where they could watch and protect over us."

Calvin raised an eyebrow. "So they are Gargoyles, correct?"

Tamar smiled brightly. "More than that. As I said, my husband was intelligent. He had plans of protection set up long before I was pregnant. As soon as I conceived, he set his plans in motions. The Satous are Dragons, the highest level of Gargoyles."

"Yes, next to the mythical Sphinx line, of course," Kali interrupted in quiet glee.

Tamar agreed as she studied her cousins, whom she called niece and nephew. "Yes, my husband knew this. He always said it was the Most High's plan to put Hideo in his life, and at that moment he understood why. So we lived in peace in St. Louis. My husband had to fight, from time to time, to keep us off the Cursed radar, but when Sanna was born it became harder to hide her. My little girl had the gift of sight at birth. Whenever I changed her, she would touch me, and I could see what her little mind held. It frightened me sometimes to know that our child was an Oracle and a Vessel. We had heard from others, through the family, that Oracles were being killed and kidnapped by Cursed, so we had to be careful. That was why we never registered in Society. Society never would have truly accepted us anyway, due to my husband's background, but it was for the best in the end not to register."

Calvin grumbled as Kali interjected.

"Regardless, they should have accepted you all. So, she was an Oracle even at birth? That is powerful. Oracles do not come into their power until they hit maturity! And you do not know who a Vessel is until they awaken!" Kali exclaimed, confused and excited.

"Yes, I know. This is why I think we were able to hide for so long, because they were hunting maturity-aged girls, never once thinking of an infant being born into her or his powers already."

"How is it that she doesn't know what she is then? How is it that she's having migraines, as if she's maturing into her powers now?" Calvin asked, confusion lighting his eyes.

Kali responded, her eyes wide in excitement. "And who is she? She is the Vessel of who?"

Tamar's own eyes lit up with the power of a Prophet as she sighed. "My husband. He did something at his death, and her real identity is locked away from even me."

"That's what's up. It's the way of the Vessels to stay hidden as a means of protection," Calvin explained.

"Tell us how Uncle Bishop died, Momma Tamar. We need to understand because there is so much we just learned before we came here." Kali stood then kneeled near Tamar as she held her hand.

"It was right after we left from visiting New Orleans. Sanna's birth was a trigger that we had to hide, but when the twins were born and Takeshi was born at the same time, we had to be even more careful. It was as if Sanna's powers grew when they were born. My husband told me he had another Denotation dream about them. And I did too, after he died."

"What are they then?" Calvin softly asked as he ran his hands over the back of his neck, trying to ease the tension.

"I'm not sure yet. My husband knew though and died protecting his children. As I said, it happened after we left New Orleans. Sanna was playing with the twins in the back of the car, and she made a power surge happen. She was three. They were giggling and cooing. Sanna was trying to sing to them. They loved her so much, she was always able to connect to them. It was like they all knew what each was thinking, so when the power surge happened, it scared the hell out of us. We knew we had to figure out a way to hide them."

Hesitating, Tamar rubbed her temple and continued on. "It took until Sanna was seven—you were ten, Calvin, right when you were coming into your own gifts."

Calvin bowed his head, nodding in remembrance. He loved his cousin, had started calling him uncle when he was young, because he felt a kinship with him left void by the father he had lost long ago to depression over the loss of his mother. "Yeah, I remembered. He was a cool OG. He taught me a song." Calvin held a hand up then dropped it as he ran his palms over his massive thighs and chuckled. "Ey, I'm a damn chump. That song, a rhyme he taught me, is a spell. I had no idea at the time. I thought it was some rhyme he made up. Man, that shit makes sense."

Calvin observed the woman who sat quiet, her toffee skin glowing with a mother's love. Comfort as well as the wisdom of a Prophetess wrapped around him in comfort.

"Ma Tamar, I think I know what he did."

Tamar gave a ghost smile as she nodded. "Yeah, you do. You just have to remember what he taught you."

Kali sat confused as she listened. Everything was settling in her mind like puzzle pieces, except for the link between the three Steele children. She had never heard of a link that can charge an Oracle, let alone a Vessel.

"My husband was always doing research, creating scrolls of power to protect us. It was like he was a man obsessed. He made sure he spent his time with our children. Teaching them some of his legacy as they played. He even taught Kyo and Takeshi some protection spells as well."

"How?" Calvin and Kali chimed at the same time.

Tamar softly chuckled as she stared at the pair. "He was a very strong Mystic and an even stronger father and husband. That man loved us with all of him. I guess this is why I was a Prophet. There is so much that your Society has documented but kept from you or just lost through the ages. I know what I know because my husband fused his knowledge with me as he passed, and thanks to the later dreams of Knowledge I had as my babies grew up. I also know what I know because of Sanna. It's like she knew what was going to happen before us."

She shook her head and gave a drained laughed as she thought on it. "Of course, she knew. She was only a baby when she gave me that knowledge, and I later was able to unlock it. My little girl is . . . so powerful."

Kali had to bite her lip and let Tamar settle through her emotions before she shouted and asked what happened.

This was a lot of much-needed information, information she knew she would defiantly keep away from Society until she could document it in a way that didn't scare the Elders or rile up the pretentious council members' angelic feathers.

"I'm sorry, babies. I'm just worried for my children, and the doctor is taking too damn long."

She pulled out a bottle of water and took a slow sip, exhaling at the cool feel of the liquid sliding down her throat as she licked her lips. "This is what happened. My husband was at work. He had just dropped off some of his scrolls and then went off to the office, heading down two seventy, toward Chesterfield. The Cursed somehow was able to link him to the power surges occurring, so they started stalking him since the first one when

Sanna was three. Those . . . bastards crossed the boundaries, took the fight in front of human eyes and caused a massive pileup on the highway with him in it. Somehow he was able to escape as they pulled him out of the car. He took the fight away from the confused humans and died fighting Snatchers, Hunters, and . . . a Fallen Elder. A Shroud-Eater."

Kali's mouth dropped open, and she stammered, "A Shroud-Eater! They do not get involved unless what they want is of highest value."

Calvin stood. "Motherfucker! How did they know?" Calvin's roar filled the room and caused the hair on everyone's body to stand with the electrical charge he shot through the place. He slammed a fist on a nearby wall as he thought of his cousin, the man he called uncle. It just didn't make sense at all. He needed to remember the rhyme he had taught him. It was fucking mandatory. He just had to.

He remembered clearly that his uncle had told him that he would need it one day in understanding everything that was going to happen soon. Of course, he didn't understand and pestered his uncle all day to tell him what he meant. But his uncle just laughed, handed him a basketball, and had him go it over and over as he made hoop after hoop. A song, a simple rhyme to him, but what was it?

"I think they traced the surges to him. Somehow my husband manipulated the power to focus on him and, in doing so, deflected the Cursed from us. I do know that. I felt his last word, a rhyme, a poem he wrote, vibrate through me, through our children. I knew then, when I couldn't sense his heartbeat anymore, that he was gone from me."

Tears choked her throat as she remembered the pain and relived it all over again. Her nephew's comforting hand rested on his shoulder.

"My Immortal beloved cut down and killed. The Shroud-Eater took his last breath. But my husband protected his soul from being permanently killed off by his spell. The poem and my children's powers were bound, their memory of their powers locked away, as I was made an Immortal and we were hidden from the Cursed, until now."

Kali abruptly called forth her laptop and went to clicking. "What you just said, I know. I remember it somewhere. When I was visiting my family in India, my great-aunt was talking about something like that. Spirit song? Spirit anchoring . . . something like that."

Everyone in the room got quiet as they watched her click away, staring at the screen as she spoke. "I'm searching. We can learn so much about what he found and help many."

A knock at the door had everyone looking up as a tall, handsome, syrupy cocoa-kissed man with sprinkles of white at his locked fro's temples and goatee walked into the room. His dimpled smile calmed everyone as he quietly closed the door.

"Sweetheart, close that laptop. You can search later," Tamar calmly said, switching into the concerned human mother routine. She stood and smiled at the handsome doctor. He was a tall drink of water. Stood over her in a towering six five, with black, wired glasses that accented his chiseled face and welcoming, dimpled smile.

The speckles of white grey in his low-cropped, spiky fro and goatee added wisdom to his golden eyes. Tamar had to inwardly pray. Something about this man felt familiar to her spirit. Had her blood pressure rising in all the right areas, areas that had been ignored since the death of her beloved husband, and it scared her. She shook her head and offered a warm smile as concern over her sons took over.

"Hello, I'm Dr. Eammon Toure," the doctor stated.

A soft island lilt to his voice filled the room while he held out his hand for Kali to shake. Calvin sized him up and quickly moved to block his view from Tamar.

Dr. Toure chuckled and reached around Calvin fast, gently taking Tamar's soft hand, his eyes briefly flashing, letting Calvin know who he was.

Calvin stepped back to watched Tamar's pupils expand as she held the doctor's large hand. Both Kali and him glanced back and forth as the doctor swallowed and gently let go, blinking as well.

"You must be part of the Chicago team, Doctor?" Calvin gruffly interrupted, slicing the tension in the air as he crossed his arms over his broad chest.

"Ah, yes. As I said, I'm Dr. Toure. I was told by the Satous that you all were in here. Dr. Satou is with your son and his son, Mrs. Steele. Both young men suffered extreme trauma, but they will be okay. They seem to heal fast."

The last statement was said with a hidden undertone that everyone in the room clearly understood. Those with Nephilim blood or who were pure Nephilim typically healed faster than typical humans.

"Due to security issues, I placed the men on blackout. Just as a precaution to keep them hidden from any Cursed spies. I am sorry that you all had to wait so long and had to deal with the inconvenience. I had noted that you all were coming in and should be escorted right away to the room, but as you all saw, sometimes we get mishaps."

Tamar hustled to the door. "Good. Then let me check on my sons then."

Dr. Toure placed a hand on Tamar's shoulder as she stopped and looked behind her. Her head tilted to the side as she gave him a sidelong glance that could cut a man in two. This woman was beautiful. Simply elegant. A queen. And he felt as if he knew her all his life.

Eammon thought as he sharply inhaled her sweet sultry scent and tried to shift back into his professional manner. "There are some things of concern. As you know, your son is past his maturity stage, yet he is going into the 'priming,' as is your daughter. I had one of my trusted nurses check her as well, since she had a seizure in the waiting room."

Calvin inwardly cursed as he moved to head back out of the room but was stopped by the doctor.

"Listen to me, and listen to me quick. If there is a better place for them to transition, then this hospital is the best. I will keep them on blackout, while we help them through the transition. We've had documents telling us of those Nephilims who did mature in later life, so we know what we are up against. They will not die on our watch. But if you keep moving them as you are, they may not make it through it."

Dr. Satou offered a soft smile as he turned to help Tamar relax in understanding. "Mrs. Steele, can you tell me why they may be going through this late transition? I've taken blood samples and saw that they should have gone through this already."

Tamar opened her mouth and then quietly shut it as Calvin took over.

"This late transition happens in our family from time to time. We have the necessary capability back in St. Louis to take care of them. We just need to make sure they are okay. Can you keep them safe from Cursed here and help us move them out?"

"No. Darren and Take will want to stay here. They are in school. I cannot uproot them from their new home. Take Sanna home, but I need someone here to guide them through this here and keep them hidden until they come into their power."

Dr. Toure's soft, slight accent lowered with concern as he agreed. "We can do that. My team can watch over them. It looks like they do not know what they are, so . . . I will leave that to you of course, Mrs. Steele."

Dr. Toure looked at everyone in the room as a need to protect them all suddenly swelled in his chest.

Tamar's head was bowed low as Calvin wrapped her in an embrace, while Kali slid in to hug her as well.

"We have your back, Momma Tamar. You know it's time to tell them."

"Yes, I do, and I will soon. It's for the best," Tamar whispered.

"It's for the best."

Chapter 8

Khamun was shaking his head. It was taking everything in him not to slam his foot on the gas and hoof it down the highway while he listened to Amara and her shadow, Miya, idly ramble. He had picked them up fifteen minutes ago and was now on his way to the hospital.

"So are you single, mister man?"

Khamun had to keep himself from rolling his eyes behind his shades as he drove on, ignoring Amara and Miya's questions.

"Girl, do you see this? Meme, I asked a direct question, and he's ignoring me! Khamun, what's your last name again?"

He almost said V'ance but remembered to give his mortal last name. "It's Cross, and yeah, I'm single. Why are you both so damn talkative?"

Miya was chewing on some gum as she looked at him through the rearview mirror, her yellow-painted, razor-sharp fingernails tapping with nervousness.

"Because we need something to keep our minds off of where we are going. So tell us about yourself, like why you are so fine and single. You gay?"

Amara exploded with laughter as she gave her best friend a high-five. "Meme! I was so going to say it!"

Khamun closed his eyes at a red light that seemed to be taking forever and slowly inhaled. Both were cute and bubbly. If he wasn't under so much stress and worry over protecting Sanna, he would've been able to handle their antics. But as of right now, he wanted to stop the car and walk away.

"Who said I don't have anyone just because I'm single, baby girl?"

Both women glanced at each other then broke out in laughter.

"Whatever!" they said in unison, and they began to ramble to each other, almost sounding like clucking chickens to his ears.

Khamun couldn't help but rub his throbbing temple. He knew he had to protect these women, but damn it, they were slightly annoying. When he'd picked them up from the airport, he had to admire them both. They'd both stopped and gawked at him as he held a sign with their names on it. They looked like they'd stepped right out of a coloring book. Somehow with all that color, they looked very mature. They were very sexy, but were bright as hell. Matching ice cream Nike shoes on their feet. Bubble gum sunglasses that he knew Kali would love. And they sported denim leggings with bright-ass shirts that showed off their ample rear, perky breasts, and deep-set curves, all while they linked arms and gabbed away.

Khamun had to adjust his shades just to keep his eyes on them. He noticed that Amara resembled a younger version of Sanna, with less thickness. Her sandy-brown curly hair framed her soft face like a halo, and the dimple in her right cheek made him want to beat any man's ass who ever tried or wanted to touch or hurt her. The need to protect her was crazy deep as his abs clenched, and he eyeballed every man that stared too long at the young woman. He had to rein that in. Suppress that need to make her his family, his little sister, because he hadn't even really met her older sister yet. The woman he longed for and loved.

Miya was dressed in vivid colors as well. She looked like a living Toykopop model, but with an edgy urban feel that belonged in the next hip-hop video. Her silky ebon hair fell around her face in crinkles, giving her a sassy feel as her curvy body made many men blink twice at her.

He felt them play with the ends of his locks, his jaw clenching at their whispers and giggles. This shit was "cray," as his favorite rapper would say. So he quickly pulled it up into a knot, ready to lay down the law.

"A'ight, look. No, I am not gay. I'm single due to work," Khamun grumbled as he drove through traffic.

"Oooh, really? How old are you, and what do you do?" Amara smiled as she studied Khamun's muscular form.

He was the kind of sexy that one could only dream about. Not too beautiful that you might have to question his orientation, but reality sexy and edgy, with sinful dark-chocolate skin, like burnt caramel or burnt cinnamon. With crinkled locks so well-groomed that you just wanted to grab a few strands and begin playing in them. His body, damn! His body was like, Whoa!

She wanted to see under the shirt just to see if he was really as ripped as his arms displayed. Everything about this man felt like he was the one, the one she had been looking for all her life, for her sister Sanna. She smiled and nodded, twirling her fingers through her hair as she chewed on her gum. It didn't help he had beautiful eyes as well. That seemed to be the icing on his coco cake. He was definitely big brother worthy.

"The hell?" Khamun briefly glanced at Sanna's mini-me in the passenger seat, his eyes searching over her as if he thought she was crazy. He shook his head and deeply exhaled. "Okay, baby girl. I'm twenty-nine and work in a restoration construction firm established by my pops. I have a degree in architecture and art history. I have a purple belt in kenjutsu and a 9th degree belt in jujitsu. In undergrad, I worked as a bouncer, so I have gun training via marine training. My blood type is O-negative, and I'm HIV-negative. And I can't stand spiders. Anything else?"

Khamun gave an annoyed glance in the rearview mirror. Being Nephilim meant he couldn't get the common human's sexually transmitted diseases, so telling her he was HIV negative was just for show. He reached for his all-black, invisible-rimmed sunglasses and slid them on. Though he told her a hell of a lot of information just to soothe her, he left out his Nephilim background and his ninjutsu training.

Amara and Miya glanced at each other as both women giggled and high-fived each other. "Damn!" they said in unison.

"I think my sister would appreciate what you have to offer, except for the spider thing. Might want to do something about that." Amara turned and looked out the car window.

Khamun almost lost control of the car as he watched Amara out the corner of his shades. She said it as if she knew. It was as if all the wisdom of the world had settled into her voice, and that had him processing and reevaluating the younger Steele sister.

Miya nodded in agreement as she quieted down as well. Both women seemed to work in sync and in thought as if they knew everything and nothing at all and as if they knew they were right around the corner of the hospital. That had Khamun appraise them both. They were not fools or immature at all.

"Do you think they will be okay?" Amara quietly asked as he turned the car into the hospital parking lot.

He noticed Miya reaching to squeeze her hand.

"Hey, sis, I think so. Your fine-ass brotha has your blood and all. He always bounces back hella fast. So, yeah, I think so. And Take is of my blood, so I know for damn sure he better be okay, or I will choke him." Miya gave a lopsided smile, trying to lighten the mood.

"I don't know. This feels different . . . like everything is changing. Khamun, what do you think?" Amara's golden-rimmed chocolate eyes focused on him as he turned off the car and slid a hand in his locks.

"I think they'll be okay, because they have a large healing support of family around them, baby girl."

Amara smiled then opened the door, hopping out with ease. She turned to check her makeup, reapplying bubblegum-pink lipgloss and fluffing her curly mane. "Okay, I can dig that."

Miya jumped out and stood next to her, adjusting her wavy hair over her shoulders as she gave Amara a "stank" look, face scrunched up, eyebrows raised. "Oh my gosh! Not dig that. I thought you were going to stop that truth! You know, that's so nineteen seventies!"

"Yeah, yeah, yeah, I know. I like it, though. Got it from Calvin." Amara hooked arms with her bestie, and she and Miya both walked through the sliding doors of the hospital entrance at the same pace.

Khamun just shook his head and checked his cell to see where the Steele and Satou families were in the hospital, as anxiety hit him. He was finally going to see her in person. Be near her. Inhale her sweet perfume and hopefully touch her. He had to close his eyes and inhale slowly just to calm his racing heart as he stood in the slow-moving elevator. Damn hospital had the nerve to have the muzak version of Prince's "Diamonds and Pearls" playing.

Inwardly chuckling, Khamun kept himself in check before he started nodding and singing along.

"You okay, mister man?" Amara asked with a raised eyebrow.

Miya gave a smiling chuckle, her green gold eyes flashing with power.

"Ah, yeah."

How she asked him gave the feeling that she was peering into his soul, and that flash of power in Miya's eyes had him wondering about her as well.

The elevator dinged, letting them know they had reached the tenth floor. As the doors opened, Calvin came into view as he stood waiting for everyone, a big goofy smile plastered across his face.

Khamun reached out, clasped hands with his boy, then pulled him into a shoulder bump as both men nodded, offering a masculine display of support.

Peering over Khamun's shoulder, Calvin grinned hard again. He stepped past his boy and scooped Amara up into his arms as she squealed.

"Big bro! I've missed you! I need some of your cooking, so hook a sista up when we get home."

"You ain't said nothing but a word, peanut. I've missed you much, and Kali is here. She ordered you some fabric from Bombay. Should get to you soon."

Amara's sudden tug at his neck as she hugged him harder had Calvin chuckling while he hugged her back.

Gently sitting her back on the ground, Calvin peered at a beaming Miya with a smirk. "And this must be Miya. Hey, doll." He flashed a smile.

Miya giggled bobbing her head up and down as she turned a pretty shade of red, equally cheesing hard.

"He's cute too. Why didn't you ever tell me you had fineness around you, Truth?" Miya whispered as Calvin gave her a brotherly hug as well.

"Because you'd never go home, and I'd be all alone in the A!"

Amara pouted then laughed as Miya pinched her. "You know that's a lie! I can't do that. I'm stuck to you like glue! For now."

Miya sneered then walked up to Khamun. She stared up at him with her hands on her hips as he looked down at her, shaking his head. Flashing a mischievous grin, she hip-bumped him and hooked her arm through his. "Let's go. I need to know if the fam is okay and Amara has been wanting to see her mom for a minute now."

Calvin became tense and slid his hands in his pocket. "Yeah, follow me. Everyone is in their room. Um, don't trip, Mara, but Sanna had a serious migraine."

Amara stopped in her tracks, her eyes widening with concern. "Is she okay? Is my sis okay?"

"Yes, yes. They gave her a shot and checked her out. She's chilling in a wheelchair—doctor's orders, since she won't go lay down."

Both Amara and Khamun tensed up. Though Calvin saw that his bro also became rigid though he tried to hide it. Everything was still swirling in his mind after Tamar had laid that bombshell of information on him and Kali. Blown away and spiritually moved was an understatement.

Shifting his mental gears, moving on, he knew this was going to be some intel Khamun would definitely trip over.

Time seemed to stand still for Khamun as he rounded the corner and walked into room seven. He could see the back of her thick hair. It was partially pulled back, leaving the back spilling over her shoulders in a thick, wavy, well-kept cloud. He wanted to run his fingers through her hair as he watched her slide her head to the side in weariness. He glanced around as he saw the two males of this tight-knit family hooked up to monitors, resting asleep, their bodies covered in partially bloody bandages.

"Amara! Miya!" Sanna yelled, happiness flowing over her sister and her friend as they both honed in on her.

Tamar and Kyo both chimed in unison, and both women headed across the room.

Dr. Satou smiled, greeting Miya with a fatherly hug as Kyo joined in on the family embrace. Amara broke down in tears, while her mother cradled her in a rocking hug.

Khamun couldn't help notice Sanna's eyes go to her sister in happiness and surprise as she looked over her shoulder. Her stunning eyes hesitated briefly as she glanced over at him and then looked away. As he slowly exhaled the breath of air he was holding onto, he noticed her stare quickly returned as she gaped at him in confusion. Her intoxicating gaze stayed on him as she tried to turn her wheelchair to get a better view.

The blood rushed to his ears as everything seemed to get silent. Nothing but the monitors chiming and beeping as he stared at the woman he'd always watched from afar. His eyes trailed over her sensual face, soaking her image in.

She licked her lush lips, and that made his groin tighten as her pupils dilated. He watched her swallow as her hands clutched the arm of her chair and she began to breathe ever so slightly faster, the swell of her breasts rising like a gentle wave just for him. He watched her skin softly flush ruddy, making her skin glow with a toffee-glazed hue as he stepped closer.

Amara's squeal broke the trance as she rushed her sister and hugged her tight, before looking up and breaking down in tears at the sight of her twin brother's battered sleeping form. Rushing to his side, she held his hand.

Everyone in the room felt a sudden shift of energy as she cried.

Calvin's eyes widened as he noticed the energy shift, and the scene. Now that Amara was near her brother, she stood in the middle of Darren and Takeshi as Sanna made a point at the foot of each man's bed. A triad.

Very interesting, he thought as he noticed his cousin's body go taunt.

Spasms overtook Sanna as she gripped the sides of her head then fell out of her chair. Her eyes rolled in the back of her head as her body shook.

Everything moved in slow motion as Khamun dropped down on his knees. He pulled Sanna into his arms as the wheelchair rolled off.

Dr. Satou, Dr. Toure, and Mrs. Steele all stopped in their tracks as they watched Khamun cradle Sanna, holding her tight against his chest as he brushed her thick hair out of her face.

Calvin quickly and covertly created a magic barrier that maintained the energy in the room, kept it from spreading, as the monitors beeped and both comatose men started to shake in unison.

A thud signaled Amara's sudden loss of her balance as she slumped down over her jerking brother, her body seizing in sync. It was as if the three were hit by an invisible electric current.

Kyo and Miya screamed. Tendrils of energy wrapping around them both and brought them to their feet as they scratched at the floor, sweat sprinkling their brows.

The Priming was fast and unbreakable. The spell that held the Steele children together suddenly dissolved and absorbed into them, waking up the overdue maturation. Everyone in the room stood shell-shocked.

Dr. Toure quickly entered the room and shut the hospital door. His locked 'fro stood up with the charge as his hands shook against the door's surface. He too seemed very affected by the surge.

"My babies, what is happening?" Tamar cried. Her hands cradled her face while power flowed like a breeze over her glowing skin.

"Old magic. Ancient magic. I can't identify the specifics of it, but its ending. They are coming into a large amount of their power right now," Khamun said as he held Sanna's shaking form.

His face was stern and caring as he watched his former Guide's features soften as her eyes slowly flickered opened, pure white light emitting from them like water. He licked his lips. His pulse was dancing within his body at the sudden brush of Sanna's light buttery-sweet scent. His fangs instantly descended as she evolved in front of his eyes.

The "Priming, or Evolution," as Society called it, was when a Nephilim matured into their gifts. Usually if a Nephilim is paired with a "life friend," usually a Gargoyle, they too mature at the same time due to the soul link of the duo.

Kyo had started going through her change fast, while Sanna's Priming was muted or slowed by the spell he was feeling in the air.

Khamun had to rock as he held her in his arms. The strength of the power had him on edge and had him ready to go into mating mode over his charge, and that freaked him out to no end. He had never had that feeling before. Like many men in Society at the age of maturity, picking a mate either happened fast or stalled, so the male could "sew his oats," as they say, and Khamun was in the "sew-his-oats" phase.

The power surge waxed and waned like a wave suddenly stopping as everyone in the room gained their breath. Tamar teetered forward as she tried to stand.

Dr. Toure suddenly appeared at her side, offering his arm as support.

"We . . . we . . . wait on the discussion of this." She unevenly paused to take a breath.

"I will tell them who and what they are soon, but I want to make sure they are okay. I want . . . I want them to have some normalcy before its time." She had to lick her dry lips before she could shakily continue. "My babies will need protection. So you all are their Guardians. Stay that way. But you have the right to now be in their face, be it . . . discreet or otherwise. You do not tell them your true purpose until I talk to them."

Emi Satou placed a loving hand on Tamar's shoulder as she gently stepped forward. Her delicate features flushed with power. "Yes, we as a family need to sit down and tell our children of their history. It will take time, but we will do it, before the Dark ever tries to touch our children again."

Khamun looked up, agreeing as he felt Sanna's erratic breathing stall and stabilize, his fingers finding a way to trace her sleeping face. "Yes, ma'ams. We will do that. Ease them slowly into our world so they do not panic. We can do that. Come around a little at a time . . . as you've both requested."

Tamar nodded. "Good. In the meantime, I guess I will need to be trained in my role as an Immortal and Prophetess."

Calvin walked up to Tamar and held her in his embrace.

She silently held in her tears as he spoke.

"Because of what happened, Auntie, you are a Disciple now and will live a long life with the chance of being reborn if ever something happens to you. I will help you, and so will Lenox. You will be part of our House as we secretly draw up the paperwork."

She dipped her head, and everyone fell silent as the energy finally disappeared.

Mr. Satou, with the help of Calvin, moved Kyo and Miya into chairs. "With these new changes, I believe we are ready for our paperwork to become active, my boy." Mr. Satou smoothed his daughter's matted hair as he stood behind her chair. "It has been our family's long history to protect the royal lineages in Society, and when chaos broke, we went into hiding. With our children and Miya being forever linked to our godchildren, it is time for them to be acknowledged and given their rightful place in Society." Mr. Satou's eyes glowed with power as his wife came to his side.

"Are you sure, honey? We've been in hiding for so long." Emi slid her hand over Hideo's while she kissed his cheek.

"Yes, I am considered an Elder of the family now. Miya's family would be happy at us finally being acknowledged, and you know this has been something they fought with the old Elders for. For her and our children, to regain their history." Hideo exhaled and gave a wary smile.

Tamar smiled at her old friends. "I know this transition is something we've been preparing for, for a while now, and now that it's here, we want nothing more but to turn the clock back and get some stability, but . . . we can do this."

Turning to face Calvin, she rested a hand against his jaw. She continued, "As long as we keep smart and keep this unit close-knit as we have, and trust in these young men and my nephew, my son, we will all be okay."

Calvin was pleased at that. He loved when Tamar called him son because he felt even more connected to her. Tamar filled that void left from never having his birth mother around. She'd died birthing him. So when Tamar called him son, he knew she meant it and knew he'd put his life on the line for his family.

Dr. Toure bowed his head and headed to the door. "We have two Society notaries here. Liz or Ashley can draw up the necessary paperwork and move this along. Also, due to the fact that we are a House Garrison, we have a notary here. They will not need to send for one. I will contact Paulette, and I will also bring in an extra bed for Sanna."

Kali stood from her spot near Darren and quickly followed Dr. Toure. "I am the House's notary and keeper of knowledge. I will work with her on quietly processing the notary, especially since this is a royal HG."

Dr. Toure stopped in his tracks at that and looked closely at the young woman in front of him, a dark eyebrow slowly rising. "Excuse me?"

Kali knowingly smirked as the door slowly closed in front of her. She dropped her voice as she addressed the doctor. "Yes, Ms. Steele's Guardian is the Royal Prince of V'ance y A'lor."

To the human ear, what was said in the old tongue of Society sounded like *vengeance* and *valor*.

Tamar glanced at Calvin as everyone took a seat, eyes focused on the sleeping bodies in front of them. "What does that mean for us, Calvin?

"It means you have the best of the best protecting you, Ma, and the fact that your soon-to-be house of minor value to others in Society is aligned with a Royal Garrison means that you and your children have a contact that many beg to have with the Royal family. It also means that your minor house will be included in top Society functions, and when the snobs of Society find out your family produced a surviving Oracle and Vessel, whose own personal Guardian happens to be the Prince, your minor house will no longer be so unimportant. Ya heard meh?"

Khamun chuckled at the raised eyebrow Tamar gave as he cut in and continued on, carrying Sanna as if she were a feather. "Yes, ma'am. Calvin spoke truth. But this also means right now you are minor, due to us just finding you. But the fact that Calvin is part of this Royal house himself, making him like what your world would call a Duke, provides the means of going into your history and setting you up right."

Studying Sanna's sleeping face, Khamun sat her in a reclining chair that Calvin had dropped into the room. Khmaun held Sanna's soft hand as he spoke. "Kali has already found your husband's Societal will. Once she reads over that and submits it, I can guarantee that your minor house does not stay so minor and that you, Mrs. Tamar, will have higher ranking then the average newling house.

I know you will, because you are the mother of
an Oracle-Vessel, and you have a royal order of
Dragons watching your children."

Pausing, Khamun reined in all of the sensual
and caring emotions he wanted to unleash on
Sanna as he watched her. He knew when the time
was right that she would be more than what they
were currently speaking. He knew she would not
only be Oracle and Vessel, but if she would have
him, she would be Princess and his wife.

"Your house is not so minor, and you will have
funding. I can vouch for that."

Tamar sat astounded, a tear sliding down her
face. "My husband took care of us?"

Khamun agreed in inclination. "Yes, ma'am,
and now I am going to take care of you. You will
have royal Society papers and rights, as well as
additional funding from the royal houses. You
now have familial allowance, thanks to Calvin.
That is my word."

Tamar shook her head in awe. "I mean, sweetheart, that is wonderful, but we don't need all of
this money, ranks, and whatnot. We just need to
be protected and made sure me and my children
can function as normally as possible."

Khamun's head tilted in respect as he offered
a dimpled smile of support. "I can understand
that, but in this world, you need as much protection as you can get. Unfortunately, this means

you need as many networking houses to back you, which provides you with Societal protection and a hell of a lot of money."

"I don't understand the importance," Tamar said, her eyes glowing as she processed the information.

"If anytime your family needs to go back into hiding, with the houses, it is easier to move through and find shelter. Your husband used such backing to have you and your family protected by the House of Satou, a very smart choice as we've found out. But now that you have to be made known to Society, you need more protection. Without this, you will be left without options of future protection and future alliances."

Tamar shook her head, her arms wrapping around her waist.

Khamun moved toward her in concern and quietly squatted down in front of her, resting a hand over her shoulder. A shock of energy went through him as his eyes shut closed. A link was just provided, and he knew she would be his family without a doubt.

"Listen to me, and I mean this with the utmost respect, Momma Steele, but I got this. You do not have to worry about anything. The money and papers you need are due to the fact that it has to make sense with Society protocol. In order to run your life, you need money, you need status. Outside of the fact that I am your daughter's Guardian, why my House and my family's House have aligned with a newling Vessel family has to add up."

"But when they learn of Sanna—"

"No, ma'am. We are keeping that guarded, so that the Dark doesn't find out. There are people in Society who like to live in the gray. No, I live in the gray. These people live more near the Dark. They provide whatever intel they can to our enemies, and we have only just learned of this in the recent years, so . . . we have to keep this quiet. Even though the Dark knows of what they *think* she is, we will downplay this. Make this move fast, but slow as to not draw attention. As I said, your husband and his parents were very smart, as are the Satous."

Khamun glanced up and bobbed at Mr. Satou, who had quietly moved to stand behind Tamar. Hideo crossed his arms over his chest with a curt nod. His stern face was caring as he watched on.

"Momma Tamar, don't even stress. You will all have about two months to three months max of normalcy. We won't even assimilate you all into this right away. Sanna and Kyo need to have this happen slow. I know my fam, and I will make this smooth as ice. Ya heard me?" Calvin lightly chuckled as he gave a slight smile then glanced at Khamun.

Both men gave a silent mental fist-pound.

Khamun replied, "Please trust us, all of you. This will not be easy." He suddenly stood and moved by Sanna, whose head began to loll back and forth. Her fingertips gently touched his forearm. "She's waking up," he murmured.

"So are the others," Hideo said, instantly moving around the room to check everyone's vitals.

Sanna's mind felt like a battlefield. Her body felt as if it had been in a thousand and one accidents as salty tears kissed her cheeks while they escaped from her closed eyelids. She had no words to describe what happened. One moment she was fine. The next, every nerve and fiber in her body felt shredded and stretched. Thousands of tiny needles slashed through her bloodstream and mind. Each slice caused wave after waves of mind-splitting migraines and seizures. All she could do was loll her head back and forth as she tried to open her eyes, the voices in the room soothing her, keeping her pulse from rising due to the concern she could hear in their tone.

She tilted her head in pleasure as she felt her mother's comforting soft lips press against her temple. It was like her mother always knew how to soothe the pain away with just a touch. She could never understand it, but it was what it was, and she was thankful for her mother being nearby.

"Just breathe, sweetie. In and out slowly . . . you remember how I taught you."

Sanna did remember as her mother's peaceful voice put her back into that place of content. She inhaled and exhaled. She visualized every point in her body and relaxed. Each zone in her body lit up in her mind, fluxing and waning with her control to calm down and smooth the tenderness of her pain away.

Yeah, she remembered. She had been doing this since she was twelve, so it was nothing but a thing. So she sank into an abyss. Her body slowly melted against the softness of the sheets she felt against her skin as her breathing calmed, and she was okay again.

She was so thirsty. Her lips hurt. She tried to lick them, but they felt raw.

"Sanna, I have some ice water. Trust me."

She had to flinch and turn toward the sultry deep voice so full of concern. She knew that voice. She tried to open her eyes, but everything stayed blurry, so she opted to keep them closed.

The light brush against her skin made her relax in serenity. She felt his touch against the back of her head and the shock of sweet cold ice water brush against her parched lips. The taste of water felt like a miracle in and of itself as her lips finally unsealed themselves and opened. Her mind suddenly went from being aware of a man's touch to being aware of the cool liquid melting in her mouth.

Her tongue darted out quickly as its pink tip brushed against a fingertip. Her eyes broke open as she tried to focus her eyes, due to the quick spark shooting through her body and nestling between her legs at that brief bit of contact. She knew this touch. This man. And all she could do was frown as was nursed by the hands of a man she couldn't see.

"Ma . . . Ky-Kyo?" she croaked, but her throat closed with dryness again as the man who held her fed her more water.

"Amara?" Her head was pounding as awareness hit her.

"We are all here, sweetheart, and doing fine. Just rest."

Sanna heard her mother's soft voice flow over her in a healing embrace as she spoke.

"That migraine was a doozy."

"Yes. Yes, ma'am." Sanna gulped more water as she shifted then pushed the glass, and arousing hand, away with it. All she wanted to do was not feel like an invalid, but in the end she knew it was a hit-or-miss in trying to move out of the bed she currently lay in.

Inwardly sighing, she heard quiet movements in the room. *Oh, damn. I'm still at the hospital. Gotta push this off. Make sure my brothers are okay*, she thought.

As she tried to move, she didn't hear the additional voices mutter their good-byes or the silent lock of a door.

"I'm going to step back and let you all take care of this while watching the hospital. Calvin and Kali will stay behind, since they are family. They know how to call if problems occur." Khamun glanced at his crew and strolled out of the room, his hands sliding into his jeans.

"Oh, man, he is so fine. Why is he leaving, Momma? And what happened?" Amara groaned as she sat up.

"Mara, he got called away. He'll be back. Now lay down and let the doctor look you over, sweetheart."

Amara shut her eyes with a groan as she complied and lay back with a flash of a sly smile.

"Hey, Sanna." Amara laughed in a singsong voice. "I found you your future husband."

Sanna slapped a hand over her face. *You are too much sometimes*, she thought. She turned on her side in the hospital bed and rolled her eyes with an exasperated whine. "Lord!"

Chapter 9

Waking up in a hospital, doctors combing over her, while her brothers and sister lay in the same condition, was not her cup of tea. Every thought under the sun ran through her mind. She needed to make sure her brother Darren was okay. She needed to make sure Take, Meme, and Kiyo were okay. She needed to reassure her mother that everyone was okay so she could rest, and that she was okay. But, of course, her dear mother was having none of it.

Sanna had to drop the quick pseudo-paternal concern as doctors checked her. Incessant questions hit them all left and right, bombarding not only them but also their waking brothers with questions none of them was able to answer due to the poking and prodding of the hospital staff.

Now that the medical jabbing and blood drawings were over and she was finally discharged, Sanna lay in a truly comfortable bed in her hotel room in downtown Chicago, oblivious to the world around her. Her brother Darren's voice

made her smile as she sat up and watched him
fuss with their mother.

"Ma! I love you, but I'm good now. I don't
need another nurse, unless she's a vixen with
a fly shape. Trust . . . it's not that bad." Darren
ducked from his mother's searching hands then
swiped against his head as he glanced at Sanna
and rolled his eyes and ducked again.

Sanna had to laugh while she watched. "Man,
sitting there with your leg in a cast, you are so
damn lucky that's all you got, Dare."

"Hey, Sanna, shuddup! Okay, damn. But I
love you." Darren half-laughed and groaned
while holding his sore side, his head shaking in
the process. Deep-set gold-rimmed chocolate
eyes flashed.

Tendrils of light flickered and swirled like a
pool of water in sunlight as Sanna blinked. She
swore she saw some power in that innocent
blink.

"All that cussing around your momma now,
huh? Take, sit down and calm that mouth, Dar-
ren-Bishop-Steele! We didn't bring your butts
back here to get hurt again."

Breathing hard with a deep laugh, Takeshi's
grey-green eyes also flashed with a jade-tinted
spark that had Sanna hopping off the bed. She
almost crawled over her sister's sleeping body as
she rushed to the bathroom.

She needed to get herself together. She was clearly seeing things, and she did not need to add hallucinations to her list. Ringing out a wet face towel and dabbing at her face, Sanna stared in the mirror, her chocolate eyes wide with a slight panic. She'd had strange dreams during her conniption, as she liked to call it. People spoke to her, telling her to help protect, to stop a darkness that was spreading.

She saw her family and friends, swallowed up by the approaching darkness. She heard a clicking noise, a sound so nerve-straining that no matter how much she tried to ignore it or run from it, it sliced through her, making her fall to her knees and become swallowed by the darkness. She swore she could still feel herself being surrounded by the darkness, its sticky slick texture running over her body.

Tears sprung in her eyes as she swore she felt thousands of spiders crawling over her while the darkness toyed and tried to reach to places she didn't want it to touch. Each dreamed seemed to intensify, become more fluid, more real. And as soon as the darkness got close enough to snatch her, the familiar touch of a man always pulled her from it. She felt his power replace the darkness, leaving her energized and in sudden need as she watched his blurred form shattered the very darkness with his and her own power.

A power she felt spreading from her spirit to connect with his. That was when she woke up.

Now she was seeing that same power that flowed through her in her dreams now ebbing in her family and in her close friends. She swore could read their souls at times. Soul-reading. That's the only way she could understand it, and she wasn't sure she wanted to name it that either.

"Sis, you okay? I gotta drain the snake!"

Sanna jumped at Takeshi's silky voice filled with unease, and loud knock, as she turned off the running water. "I'm fine, Take. I'm sorry. Here you go," she said. She opened the bathroom door and watched him with worry as he hopped on his crutches into the bathroom.

"Er . . . " Sanna opened her mouth but stopped mid-sentence as Takeshi gave her a sidelong glance.

"Don't. I love you, and you are my sis, but I don't need you touching my johnson. I got it." He flashed a goofy smile and looked her over with his own apprehension before closing the door.

She exhaled and grounded herself. She could never understand how fast they all healed, yet they always did. Shaking it off, she turned to head to the table sitting with her birth brother.

"Ma, get them to talk!" Sanna yelled. She stuck her tongue out at Darren as he shot her daggers of death.

Tamar chuckled as she tried to lighten the mood. "Speak on it, son of mine."

Darren rolled his shoulders and neck. While her little bro ran a hand over his wavy low-cut fade, the swirling tribal tat disappearing into his collarbone seemed to shimmer as Sanna gripped her leg.

"We were on the South Side chillin, doing what we do. Just got accepted to intern with Temple and Company. So we were celebrating with the bros."

"Okay, son, skip to the part where my baby boy ended up falling from a fire escape," Tamar curtly interrupted. Her nails suddenly tapped the table as she watched Takeshi ease into a chair next to her.

Amara and Miya were still soundly asleep as everyone quietly conversed and ate.

"Umm, that was my fault?" Take downed his orange juice and rubbed the back of his neck under his shaggy, jet-black hair.

"We were talking with some sexy—I mean, these women, Selena and Iris. They wanted some air, so we headed outside to talk on the balcony and what not then *boom*!" Takeshi narrowed his eyes, anger suddenly bubbling from beneath the surface. "These big burly guys came out of nowhere and started shit, I mean, began to antagonize us."

Both Sanna and Tamar tilted their heads to the side in a mirrored reaction as they tried to process what was said.

Momma Tamar took the words out of Sanna's mouth as she incredulously asked, "Excuse me. Say what?"

"Long story short, Ma," Darren quickly replied, narrowing his eyes at his godbrother, "they started saying some crazy crap, calling us pure, virgins, fresh meat, and other crazy bull. Talking about how tasty we'd be and how fun it would be to turn us, whatever the fuck that meant. Then they rushed us, them and those chicks. Of course, we couldn't go down like that and had to defend ourselves. We ended up on the fire escape." Darren bit his lower lip in anger as he continued, "I promise you these dudes and the chicks seemed to turn into some crazy-ass shit, and the chicks sat back watching and laughing." His hands suddenly shook at the memory.

"Dare cold-clocked one of the guys. Hit him so hard, the dude's jaw ripped off! Shit was *insane*! And I don't know, but everything moved fast after that, as if on fast-forward. I pretty much don't remember anything else but slamming into Dare as we both fell over the railing."

Darren casually shrugged as he kept his cool and cleared his throat. "I remember Take, your ass moved like something out of a movie, bro. Your eyes were glowing. The chicks tried to stab you in your chest, but the knife or whatever that shit was they had in their hands broke in two.

Then you blocked me, and we fell. I saw some folks from the party surround those punk asses."

Take smiled broadly. "Yeah, I do remember that. Whoever those other people were, they came in and went ape shit on them. It was sick!" He took a swig of his orange juice.

Dare reclined in his chair, one arm resting over the back of it while he glanced to the side, as if his mind was processing a million thoughts. "That's truth right there. That's when I blacked out."

Takeshi bowed his head in a nod, flipping a piece of toast between his fingers as if it were a card. "Yeah, I blacked out too."

"Excuse me, babies, I need a second to process this," Tamar said, slowly standing as she wrung her hands.

Before Sanna could ask her mother if she was okay, she watched her head out into the hotel hallway. Sanna plopped back down. "I know this is going to sound crazy, but I swear I dreamed that happening," she softly muttered.

Darren turned in his chair as he studied his sister before reaching and resting his hand over hers. "Seriously? Another one of those dreams, sis?"

"Yeah, and guess what? I'm pissed at you both for leaving crap out."

Takeshi looked toward the door as he frowned, dropping his voice into a low rumble. "What do you expect? Momma Tamar was on the verge of breaking down, sis. How could we tell her that they tried to rip us from limb to limb?" Leaning forward, Takeshi almost hissed, images from the night hitting his system like a case of PTSD. "And how could we tell her that no matter how hard we fought back, they kept coming and coming? That they spoke some crazy-ass language that Dare could understand, and I couldn't until I touched him?"

Sanna's eyes lit up in amazement as she sharply inhaled. It was like she could see the fight in front of her eyes as Take passionately spoke.

"Or do we tell her that was when we returned the favor to them guys that bled reddish black? Or that somehow as we were in the alley after the fall, that we were okay and that I looked at a nearby wall and prayed it would crumble on the assholes and it did? How can we tell her that? Huh?" Take leaned back in his chair, his hands running down his face as he exhaled. "They were like roaches. They kept popping up, until those cats from the party showed up and handled it."

Sanna studied the swirling thorn-like kanji tattoo that started from the middle of Takeshi's thumb and index finger that crawled up his forearm. She debated in telling them what happened to her and Kyo, but she knew her younger brother would pry it out of her. So as she opened her mouth to spill all, it didn't shock her when Darren interrupted her.

"Tired of you always trying to be Pops, San. You got a kitty, so stop. We already have Momma. Now tell us, big sis. What happened? Something felt wrong that whole day, and I knew it had to do with you, so talk, sis."

Sanna frowned as she squeezed her brother's hand. "Okay, damn! Dare, I'm sorry." She leaned forward and thumped Takeshi on his temple as he chuckled. "We had a similar thing happen to us."

Sanna recounted what happened in her beloved restaurant Aset and how Kyo saved her life. She had to hold her ears as both men stood on their crutches hollering at her.

Amara and Miya woke up to both men's thundering anger as Kyo and her family strolled through the door. Pushing through the forming crowd, Tamar shook her head, her curly mane falling around her face.

Yeah, Sanna knew this was going to be long day.

He ran as if something chased him, instead of him chasing something. More like someone. A lazy smile flashed across his face as he lifted his hand, squeezed and sent his anointed bullets into the legs and arms of the screaming man in front of him. Coolly laughing, he slowed his pace and calmly stalked toward the fallen form. He sheathed his gun and removed his trusty sword from its spinal harness. He was the Reaper, assessing his hunt.

Mrs. Tamar had let him know what had happened with her son and godson. As soon as she let him know that, he then asked for clear-cut directions to the area where it all went down, and his hunting began.

Quickly making his way to the coordinates, he combed the streets of Chi-town, which was nothing for him. The city used to be his training grounds when he was younger. Even with all the changes in his past, his home base was here, and the streets were his.

Finding the trail in the alley and the studio apartment was easy, especially since he saw Slayer runes, letting him know exactly what went down. For his kind, it was like a CSI crime scene, markers flashing everywhere. He could see what protection scriptures were used, what anointed bullets, if any, and what entity went down in the fight, or if Slayers were lost or taken in the fight.

For whatever reason, he was always able to see the scene as if it was happening in current time, something no Slayer could do. As he kicked a random chair in the now empty studio apartment, he watched the phantom bodies of the partygoers appear before him. He could hear the music, feel the environment, as he crossed his arms and watched the scene play out like a movie.

So far from what he'd read, the Chicago team did well. No casualities were taken, but one of the entities slipped way via the uproar during the party.

Khamun strolled around the room, watching the ghost figures of Darren and Takeshi fight for their lives. He was suddenly taken aback by a guy with a dragon tattoo on the side of his neck and some of his friends, all with similar tattoos, who were dancing earlier as if they were on a b-boy dance squad. That squad quickly jumped in to try to help stop the fight. The one who drew his attention seemed to hurdle in the air as if flying, landing a kick to the side of one burly demon's face.

Khamun had to commend the mortal as he watched him and his friends push innocent by-standers out of the studio apartment as the Chicago team, who blended in with the guests, took over. Khamun watched the b-boy who sported a low buzz-cut with sideburns that formed into a goatee stop a demon from feeding on a partygoer.

Assessing the room, he kept an eye on the demon that looked like a wannabe combination of Kanye West in attire and the lead singer of

Maroon 5. The bastard looked like he was savoring every moment of the fight, but something was a little off.

First of all, the b-boy was something different. He could sense it the longer he watched, and a slight smile played at his lips as he watched the tattoo swirl and move as if coming alive while the b-boy fought. Khamun noticed the same thing with the guy's crew, and he knew he definitely would be contacting ol' boy shortly.

Second, the demon the guy kept eyeing seemed to be recording the whole fight while texting like crazy and occasionally glancing out the window.

Pulling out a trinity, Khamun lit it and inhaled. His hands rested in his pocket as he casually walked around the room then headed to the window leaning out and glancing up. "Oh, so you had spectators, huh." He narrowed his eyes and descended to the roof, his cocoa skin glowing with his power.

The quick descent to the roof had him staring directly in to the ghostly face of a woman who he knew all too well. He walked around her, studying her features. He had seen this woman back in St. Louis once, and he remembered her well from back in his past. *I see your ass, Dark Lady*. He quietly chuckled in thought.

Shorty was fine. Body built like a coke bottle. Lips thick and plush, made for kissing, if you wanted to test the waters and end up dead, so he'd heard. He glared. Her hair flowed down her back in dark waterfalls, and she sported Egyptian tattoos all over the side curves of her revealing body with two golden asp-shaped bracelets on each wrist. He knew you never wanted to be on the other end of those things, since they turned into poison-tipped blades that could slice through any type of bone.

Her height, her kohl-lined grey eyes, and dimpled smile marked her resemblance to her twin brother.

Khamun shook his head, letting out a slow trail of smoke as he looked at her well-sharpened nails text away. A key-shaped golden whistle swung, connected to a ring on her middle finger.

"Bad as ever, Cousin Reina."

Scanning the rest of the roofs, nothing seemed to show up as he turned away from the ghost image of his lethal cousin and dropped down into the alley. He landed in a low crouch, his fingertips resting in the phantom pool of blood seeping from Darren and Takeshi's broken bodies. Any other mortal would have died from the ordeal, but he could clearly see they were more than they seemed.

"Yeah, looks like you both are definitely fam."

Observing as the Chicago team handled business with the demons, cursed Gargoyles, and other pets of Reina's, he studied the protection spell being cast, as traces of Darren and Takeshi's blood disappeared, so no traces of them could be taken. He listened as his body shook with the sudden need to feed, sweat beading on his brow. As his enemies screamed around him, he followed the trail he'd originally gone there for.

The demon's trail was easy to find, due to the Locus tracer spreading in its system. Those tracers slowed the demon down until it eventually died from the slow poisonous release in a specific time period. He had to smile at the Slayer who had the skills enough to put the tracer in the demon's system because apparently this was a slow-torture releasing tracer.

Khamun easily followed the blinking Christmas light trail, leading him throughout Chicago's Southside, until he found his target's trail stationed in an old factory building. One text to the Chicago team's network had them on their way to clean up the mess he was surely about to lay down.

Now here came the simple part—breaking into the old factory turned house. It was nothing for him. He landed in and saw the human demon hybrid sitting in front of his TV, surrounded by dead, homeless bodies. The draining of their spirits and blood would give his prey easy cause to shift into its combat form. Yet this bastard sat clueless, one hand on his dick, the other clicking away on his cell, texting, and watching various videos of torture, bloodstains on his fingertips.

The Reaper cracked his knuckles and flexed his fists while he quietly watched in silence, blanketed by shadows. Yeah, handling his business and taking care of the trash was part of protocol, but returning the favor and pushing the screaming demon out of his window into the alley below was for pure sport. As he watched the prick fall, he knew he was going to feed well and enjoy the hunt while he was at it as the sun set.

Khamun rolled his shoulders as his fangs dropped. His silver black wings expanded while his prey lay on grey cement crawling away. With a quick lift in the air, he flew near his target, dropping a little away from him, as he toyed with him and strolled closer.

"Please, don't kill—"

The Reaper slammed his blade down near his prey's head. "Oh, so we are pleading now?"

The bastard crawled, sputtering and spitting blood as he held up his hands to block any attack, his eyes wide with fear. "Yeahhh, I didn't ask for this, man. Please?"

The Reaper's face showed his disapproval as he laughed. "So wait . . . no texting? No YouTubing? You're innocent, right?"

"Right, right. It was all just a joke, you know, staged and . . . and . . . please . . ." He tried to push himself up in a low crouch and held his spot as he watched The Reaper stalk him.

"That's funny, my man. The theatrics was incredible. You get an Oscar for that shit."

"I'll talk! I'll talk! Don't kill me!" The target jumped up then rushed around the open parking lot attached to the building.

"My man, why are you playing yourself right now with all that running? You're going to die anyway, but you know that."

The Reaper shook his head, inwardly laughing as he grabbed his prey by the collar. He slammed his hand around its throat and squeezed until he pulled on the demon's corrupt soul. He could see every death, every sin committed, and it pissed him off to no end. Through it all he knew his objective. He had to get the information he needed, which was nothing but cell phone texts detailing that this demon was to hunt and capture his two potentials, under direct orders.

Khamun shifted deeper within the demon's mental web and shook his head at the crap he saw. So this type of bastard's sins was video documenting. This type of demons was into voyeurism. This breed got a high off the pain they inflicted.

The Reaper winced, digging deep, and turned every evil the demon committed into the purest of unadulterated torture lined in pure Light, as he searched for what he was looking for. There it was, flashed in his mind. He had found it.

The Cursed knew that Darren and Takeshi were powerful. They just didn't know what type of powerful Vessels they were, which was why the whole family was being hunted. The Cursed wanted them all. *Greedy-ass bastards.*

Hissing, the Reaper felt the demon push back, breaking free, and attempt to tear at him.

"Muthafucka, you hit me."

The demon flashed a wicked smile, slowly walking backwards to use the shadows as a cloak.

The entity roared, his fangs dripping with saliva as he leaped to attack. Razor-sharp claws protruded from once human fingers, while torn flesh hanging like peeling wallpaper made The Reaper assess his target in disdain.

He so enjoyed a good fight. Shit made his day as he calmly walked in a slow zigzag motion, pushing an idle hubcap across the cement street. He listened to it scrape while it hit his prey, and he waited for the impending attack.

The entity scrambled on the ground, pushing the hubcap away, spittle running down his face.

Khamun laughed as the entity hissed. It was ready for a kill.

The demon pummeled forward, swinging out to slice, but only ended up face down on the rough concrete, scratching and heaving in disbelief all in one quick move, and with a guttural grunt.

"Look, look, it was reflex. You were hurting me. Okay! I'll talk, my man."

In a swift motion, Khamun lifted and threw his prey like a rag doll, enjoying the fact that he hit the side of a building. He rubbed his hands together slowly, stalking his target with amusement and disgust. "'*My man?*' I'm going to need you to come better than that."

The Reaper watched his kill's crumpled form slowly twist to push up with an eerie power that would have any normal human running scared. But, of course, this was nothing new. Just extreme, boring-ass showboating, in his opinion.

The demon rolled his shoulders and cracked his neck as he turned and stared, putrid green foam forming around his mouth.

Eyes glowing in the darkness of the parking lot, sweat beads rested calmly against the entity's temple. It ruggedly breathed in and out, scanning and looking for a means of escape.

"I get not an ounce of help, Nephilim? Typical. You all preach this love-thou-neighbor BS and hunt us without discern. Don't you think that's some evil shit in itself?"

The Reaper stood steadily, his anger simmering underneath the surface, as his power-glowing eyes. "No." The Reaper whipped his blade smoothly in the air, making contact across the demon's neck. He smiled as he watched the head drop to the concrete in a reverberating thud. "It's called Holy Vengeance."

He reached for the still standing and flailing body and bit down. Liquid elixir almost dripped from the corners of his mouth as he took his fill, and he drew out the sins and trapped souls within. And both the head and the body violently shook and imploded into a red visceral mist of dark blood. The force of it all made him drop to one knee. His eyes rolling in the back of his head as his wings quaked with force.

The ecstasy was supreme. He felt his body purify the spirit and send it to the heavens. This vessel was a pure possession, a film school student who was forced into the darkness that kidnapped him one night while heading home from late-night classes. So it pleased The Reaper that this spirit would get an honorable judgment.

Sound evaded him, but he knew his protection barrier was up. Any threat that came his way was dead and drained within a blink of an eye while he was in bloodlust.

Jolting one last time, The Reaper exhaled and rolled his shoulders. He could hear the Chicago team rummaging through the building, whispering prayers over the fallen bodies as they cleansed the scene.

Slowly running a shaking hand through his
locks, he cleared his essence from the scene
before he rolled out, something he realized he
innately did a majority of the time. No Guardian he knew, Slayer, or Arch could erase their
essence, but he could. He could also manipulate
it so it only showed him using his Guardian gifts,
and not his Attacker gifts, as he called them.
So, he exhaled, his power spreading over the
lot, sizzling and fusing away his essences, while
he manipulated the spiritual molecules and
changed the scene as he walked off.

Descending into the factory building, he was
pleased to see Dr. Toure working protection
runes, while others ran around the building
handling their business.

"That was powerful tracking, young man," Dr.
Toure stated, walking up beside him, his hands
dropping to cross his arms.

A brief smile flashed across Khamun's face.
"Powerful? I wouldn't say that, Doctor Toure.
Felt it was my Guardian duty to clean up some
loose ends. Good thing I knew an Arch who
could help that out, with those ends. Liked how
your team handled everything, by the way," he
added with respect.

"Thank you, son." Dr. Toure reached out to
shake hands and gave a strong squeeze with a
chuckle. "*Doctor* is too formal. Call me Eammon."

Both men walked around the scene assessing what had occurred.

One hand in the air, Eammon motioned to Khamun. "Tamar—I mean, Mrs. Steele is keeping me abreast with everyone, and they all are being watched carefully in their hotel for backup to your team."

Hands behind his back, Khamun stepped to the doctor's side as water spilled over the building floor, acting as an energy-charged conduit for the runes being laid down. This was done to protect any humans that stumbled upon the building.

"Again, I cannot say thank you enough. Hopefully, we will be ready to go soon. We need to keep them guarded and secret for as long as possible."

Khamun muttered and kept his voice low as he shifted out of the way of a unit personnel. He knew he needed a moment with the doctor, so he clasped a hand on Eammon's shoulder. "Step to the roof with me, Mr. Toure."

Both men descended to the roof as Khamun placed a silent barrier around them. His hand still on Dr. Toure's shoulder, he quietly relayed what he found, flashing selective images in the Elder's mind. Each image deepened the furrow forming across the good doctor's forehead.

Eammon stepped back to study the street below. His tone dropped in concern, and his soft accent filled the space between the men. "I believe, or well, I've learned that people are placed in your life to guide you on your personally tiered path, and each way you go, you are forever blessed."

Khamun listened as Eammon quietly crossed his arms over his chest to stand calmly. Eyes cast downward, he watched various cars, ambulances and police vehicles drive by below them. Some vehicles swerved past multiple potholes, others hit each bump in the road as they slightly shook or bounced with the impact.

"Where I grew up, we were limited on Guardians, due to civil unrests. As you know, the protocol dictates that every region must have Guardians. So my family has a history of being just that—Disciples who train as Guardians."

Eammon kept his glaze ahead, studying Chicago's skyline. "When I was twelve, I went back to my father's home in Kingston, where I met my grandfather. He taught me how to be the Guardian Disciple I am today. He explained that you protect the innocent as if they were your family. That is number one always. Then when I went to my mother's home to visit my great-grandparents in Nigeria, they gave me the tools to be strong in my sight. Tamar . . . I dreamed of her. I never understood who she was to me, but I knew if I ever met her that I would protect her with my all. But then I grew up and met my wife. I moved on in my role as a Guardian until my wife passed of cancer, and I got into a car accident that changed my perspective on many things."

"I'm sorry." Khamun glanced at the elder and quietly listened in communal respect. It was embedded in every Nephilim youth that you listen to your elders; otherwise you may miss your blessing or the knowledge needed as a key in life. They had many stories that could help or assist in making you see within yourself. Mainly, it was due to the fact that Elders were chosen not because of how long they physically lived, but by how many soul incarnations they had, as well as diplomatic experience. Nonetheless, he still listened to this man who was his elder in years, because they too were meant to be respected, as dictated by family creeds.

"It is okay. Iyiah was a good woman. She was the one who made me remember my dreams. She told me to protect this woman and her children, and that the car accident will serve a purpose. It wasn't until I met Tamar that it all became clear. It also became clear that, like me, you, my boy, care deeply for her daughter."

"Uh . . ."

Eammon chuckled. "It is okay, son. At your age I didn't understand my heart fully yet either. I just tell you this, so you can know. I will protect them as if they are my own." He pointed to a semi mini-version of himself below and smiled. "My son, Zion. He also has the gift of sight and is a strong Slayer. So do not worry, my boy. We will see each other soon. My role in Tamar's life is not over. I believe it is just beginning."

Silence took over the pair as Khamun took in the rising sun. Colors washed across the sky comforted him as a soft smile played across his handsome face, amusement and respect swelling within at the elder's wisdom.

"Yes, sir, I believe we will meet again, but I wanted you to understand that I know it's against protocol to step over the line. A Guardian never falls for their Guide."

"Well, my boy. You know that everything has changed. She is no longer your Guide, but something tells me that you had crossed that line well before knowing that."

A quiet smirk briefly lit up Khamun's face as he thought on the erotic nights he had spent in Sanna's mind before Eammon's deep chuckle drew him back to reality.

"Ah yeah. Yes, sir, I knew."

Eammon walked near the roof's edge as he spoke to the air. His sturdy and muscled arms rested behind his back. "That role is as old as time, but you do know that it has been broken and will continue to be broken until the old ways adapt?"

Khamun stretched and closed his eyes. His cell vibrated erratically while his mind began to ache with a sudden SOS making him process everything. "Yes, now I do. Sanna comes from such a union, which has changed everything . . . including what I previously knew about her."

"Indeed," Eammon murmured as they glanced over the dark city streets quietly communing.

Chapter 10

"Talk to me." Khamun quietly combed the room, pacing as he headed back to his charge.

"We have an issue."

Khamun stopped in his tracks as he cracked his neck and gripped it, rubbing it to ease the tension. "Speak on it."

"The Nile building has been compromised. We cannot relocate your Vessel there. St. Louis is officially kill zone for her and her family."

"*What*!" Khamun's voice dropped a thousand octaves as he listened on. "Explain to me how that . . . *shit* could happen. I thought you all had the streets on lock! Lenox." He heard the subtle, simmering anger dancing against his best friend.

"When the team secured your Vessel's home, a Shroud-Eater was spotted a couple of days later in the same vicinity. Which you know means that we cannot hide her there anymore. They have her scent. We need to relocate and move the team, including your Vessel."

"*Shit*! I can't believe this. We did everything to the code. Are we sure they are tracking her still?" He could see Lenox racking a hand through his raven hair as he stood near Sanna's now burning home. Shit was an understatement. This had turned for the worse.

"Do we want to risk it? We cleaned what we could. From the intel I've picked up, they are thirsty for her blood, and since other Guides have been hidden as well, they want the freshest pick they can find, and they found yours. Their Dark Witches and Warlocks managed to break through the barriers. We can't keep her in her zone, we need to move to the central outpost. And it's time. You know what that means."

Khamun inwardly cursed and then slammed a fist into a nearby wall. He had been avoiding going home for a decade now. He loved his family, but how could he go home with the changes that were going on with him? His mother would be the first to pick up the transformation in his body. She would see he wasn't just a watcher anymore, he was something more.

"A'ight, okay. You know what went down up here. So as—"

Lenox smoothly cut Khamun off with his sudden appearance next to him and continued the conversation. He was dressed in a clean all-black suit, Italian leather black shoes, and he sported a pair of diamond cuffs in the shape of their House crest. You couldn't see the weapons hidden throughout his athletic, built frame as he moved around. Like his clean-cut suit, you couldn't tell that the man wearing it could kill you without moving from where he stood, or that he could kill you with just a tap of his hand on your shoulder.

Lenox was in his business zone and ready to kill as he flashed a bright smile, "Sorry to cut you off. The rest of the crew is on their way, My Lord."

Khamun was about to respond when Lenox added, "Also, you know I got this. As you settle down and step back into your rank as Lord of the House of Vengeance, the Vessel will be told that her establishment will be moved here. Everything as was planned before is being taken care of as we speak, and we will move her here smoothly."

Standing shoulder to shoulder with Khamun, Lenox crossed his arms and stood wide-legged. "I've already sent the letter of acceptance into my law firm for your Vessel's brother and his protector. Some of the Chi-town crew has moved down to our spot and is already holding down the region. Everything is going to work out fine."

"So you say. But you just don't know how this shit is going to go. You really don't."

"Look, My Lor—"

Khamun shot Lenox an icy look that had him holding up his hands and sighing.

"Okay, Khamun. We've been fighting side by side for generations. What you are, your mother will accept, and you know your dad is going to follow suit because he wants to still have his wife by his side. So. Chill. It is what it is. This is good. Our House has been working on limited resources as is. Hell, we've developed our own resources and made it better. Don't you think the other Houses need our insight? So we can stop losing Guides and Vessels as is?"

Turning to face one another, both men clasped hands and gave a shoulder bump. "I hear you, man. Between you and Calvin, I don't know where I'd be right now. Probably running around killing everything I can touch with Marco. Thanks."

Lenox laughed and nodded. "It's all good. Now let me get to my part of the game. As your conscience, I love inspirationally pissing you off with the cold, hard reality of various situations. Also, as your boy and the legal/financial head of our House, I love consciously toying with the bourgeois' mental every time I present them with new legal documentation and House notaries. No one is as cold as I am with this."

Both men pounded each other's fist.

Lenox reached into his pocket and pulled out a bright green apple. He took a bite before speaking again. "So, okay, I'm heading to my offices in order to get your Vessel's brother in check with a job, and you go do what you do, and I got the linguistics."

Khamun gave a quick nod and threw Lenox his SUV keys. He chuckled as he heard Lenox whistle low.

"Damn. I get to drive the baby, huh? I'll treat her right. Been wanting to see what Marco put under the hood."

That was his cue to head out. Fading through the streets, flying and using the shadows as his energy, Khamun tapped his Bluetooth and rang Marco. Nothing but screaming and varied huffs of annoyance hit his ear as he shook his head laughing.

"Ey, woman! Now I told you, I got it! I know how to work this tech crap, a'ight! *Coño*! 'Sup, cuz. So you know about the move, huh?"

Khamun couldn't help but laugh at his cousin. "Yeah. So you and Kali are going at it again, huh?"

"Of course. Same thing every day since we've been reinforcing the compound and laying down the packing stones. *Every* damn thing has to be tagged and bagged in her 'computer,' so we don't lose anything."

Marco's exaggeration of Kali's voice when he stressed *computer* had Khamun rolling as he let his mind connect to the visual of the compound. Everything was in chaos. Kali was running around with a tagging gun, and Marco clicked away on the main computer.

"She acts like I don't know this shit. Expects me to be the typical *acere* and go play with my cars."

"Hey, hey, Marco, she just don't know, huh?" Laughing, Khamun clutched his stomach as he listened to his cousin's exasperated voice lighten up with humor.

"Naw, cuz, she don't. I like to sit back with my cup of coffee, listen to NPR, and catch up on my sports pages or Washington Post shit!"

Both men started laughing hard as Khamun heard Kali scream at Marco in the background.

"Look, you got me acting extra, *mami*. I'm talking to Khamun, giving him the update!"

"Bet. Let me hang up. I see everything is in line and ready to go."

"Oh, yeah, we'll be up in Chi as soon as you send us the signal. I figured it'll be the old compound."

Khamun quietly exhaled. It had been years since he'd used his old haunt. Nestled in obscurity in the middle of Chicago, he knew Kali would love it for its ultimate security and the fact that it blended in perfectly with the city.

"Yeah, you might want to head up there first, check if the power is on and all that good crap."

"I will, Marco. Just take care of home in STL for me, and I'll handle that," Khamun replied, walking through an opulent garden and punching in an access code.

"Okay, fam, I got you. We'll do that. Know this, though. I'm not ready to return either, cuz, but we gotta do this. I hate to even admit this shit, but Lenox is right. Ey! Bring that ass back here! You play too much, Kali! Let me roll out. We got it on lock here, cuz. Love ya, fam. One."

Khamun chuckled and hung up as he stood outside of his Chicago home nestled in Lincoln Park. He could see the lights on and knew his staff was keeping the place in line. He definitely wasn't ready for this. He wasn't ready to talk on his full role as a head of a Nephilim Society House, especially since it was a royal sector of the Light lines. Within the Nephilim sect, there were no official Kings or Queens. That title was reserved to the Most High, who gave them the original task of protecting the innocent of the world. Even though the title Prince was thrown around, it was more of a de facto title. Those in high rank, and oftentimes with multiple rebirths, were given the title of Elder or Eldress. These privileged elite had central control of all the Nephilim in each part of the world, which was determined by global Houses and a council of dignitaries.

The Elders watched over the community, while the young were allowed to serve within the dignitary council. As a youth in a Royal

House, the first founding House within the Nephilim world, he had a right to being head of the dignitary council. But when Khamun turned twenty-five, which allowed him to join the DC, as he called it, he wasn't ready, and it hit him and his father hard. Especially when his once silver wings began to darken, leaving him with silver feather highlights, and he gained a set of diamond-hard fangs, instead of the normal steel incisors. He also woke up with cravings with an ability to sniff out any demon he could find. Which he later learned allowed him to break bone with his fangs and cloak his area with ease. Yes, he could blend in with his people, but he was vastly different and he was alone.

The day he woke up in a church in Detroit, covered in demon blood and their essence released to the heavens, he knew he had to come up with some reason to start his own house. A house which would later consist of others like himself, people in the middle, people who would be shunned by the Nephilim society.

The memory of it all hit him as if it was yesterday.

"You are serious about this, son? You want to start your own house and not have a dignitary seat in the council?" His father sat at his oak desk, looking at his computer screen. Papers, books, scrolls and other important documents lay in order around him while he clicked his mouse and saved whatever he was working on.

"Yes, sir. I feel that is best for me right now. I-I just am not ready, Pops." Khamun observed his father's incisors crest. His eyes flashed white, and his body tensed. All of this always reminded Khamun that he was standing in front of a full-blooded Arch more powerful than he.

"Ready? You are my seed! You carry the generations of Mi'kahl and Le'la, the founders of our Society, of one of the first houses in your DNA. Hell! You carry the very memories of your past life as a warrior, whoever you may be awakening too soon, and you say you are not ready?"

He wanted to defend himself, but custom dictated listening to one's Elders, and he was double bound to his silence because that Elder was also Head Elder, Region King.

"Boy, you were created ready. Don't give me that rubbish. What is going on with you?"

Khamun could tell his father was fired up because, while he yelled, his Ethiopian-laced British accent thickened. So he did what any scolded child would do. He kept his gaze at his feet, his fists clenched, as he tried to hide his own dropping fangs. He slowly exhaled while his father's booming voice slashed through his mind.

"Nothing. This is just what I want. I'm at the place to pick what I want, and I want what I want. Which is to the start this House."

Khamun watched his father rise from his desk, his hands sliding behind his back as he kept his eyes on him. He sat bone-straight, chin held high, ready to go to battle for his choice in his life. He had been trained and educated since birth under his father's hands, even through college, and here he sat trying not to make his father understand his choice, but to make The Elder understand that he couldn't take his spot. He didn't know what he was yet and did not want to be a threat to his people.

His father leaned against the front of his desk. His arms crossed over his chest before he ran a large hand over the sparse salt-and-pepper hair on his crown. "An unrecognized House, consisting of you and Marco? A House of riffraff, of outcasts, of degenerates, because that is what the Dignitary Council and Region Elders will have you all believe, son. Are you ready for that shit?"

Khamun's nails gripped the arm of his chair. He couldn't believe the shit pouring from his father's mouth. He wasn't degenerate, and neither was Marco. And they both could give a damn what others thought, but his father was speaking truth through it all. What he was doing would bring the Nephilim Society at his feet, ready to go in on what they feared the most.

"Pops, either you give me your blessing, or I do me. Either way, if I don't have it, I have it from Mom. Her House is ready to back me."

His father's body language was next to impossible to read. The man stayed silent. His six eight muscular frame held tight, restrained frustration, as his eyes narrowed and flashed a warm sepia hue.

"Do you?" His father held his hand up quickly to silence Khamun's impending words. "Son, do you understand what you are asking? You are a Prince of this region. My own son, a Guardian more experienced than any at twenty-five years of age. Ready to be groomed by the Eastern, Central, Southern, and even Ambassador to the Mother Region Africa, and you are ready to walk away to form your own House?

"I am ready to hand you the reins, son, and . . . and you do this?" His father's hands spread out in front of him with his rhetorical question, his eyes pleadingd with him.

But Khamun couldn't do it. He wanted his father to understand him in this, but he knew it wouldn't happen. "Pops—"

"No, listen. I love you, son, and I want peace in my marriage, so for your mother I will do this. But understand, you will do all of this on your own. When you are ready to come home and take your place, you take it. I do not have time for this. Any funds you receive from your mother's estate will be limited to an allowance, half of what she already controls."

Khamun didn't want his mother's money and had told her so, but like his father, she was stubborn and insisted, so he kept his game face on and knew he would move that money to another account never to be touched. He was proud that he was going to get to be his own man.

His father continued his rant. "She will be pissed, but this is business. Marco will step in the role as your house's Dignitary council member. Since he is of our Royal House, this will establish some stability in the Society, though not by much. It will amuse me to see the bastard's feathers be ruffled by my nephew taking a seat, and my son working with what they feel is beneath their holy sensibilities."

Khamun was shocked to see a slight smile on his father's stern face. It was common knowledge in the household that his father couldn't stand those on his council, in the DC, and in Nephilim society who twisted everything that was founded and turned it into a bourgeois competition for status. He openly felt that they had lost sight of why their race was created to stay on Earth. Khamun couldn't help but feel the same way, which was why he was doing what he was demanding, to protect his family, himself, and secretly find out what was going on with his DNA.

"But know this, my son. When you hit thirty, if your house is still not established, you will take your place in the Dignitary council and take over as co-regent in the House of Vengeance. Do you understand? Because this is not a choice at this point. This is family law."

It ticked him off that he was being put in his place yet again, with stipulations, but he would take whatever he could. "Yes, sir."

"The paperwork is being drawn. Blessings of the Most High unto you, my son. You leave me as a man taking care of his own. I'll see you again when you are thirty."

How his father just laid the law made him feel as if this was it. That their once fluid relationship was now officially over and strained. It hurt him.

A part of him hated that his father just didn't get him, and he couldn't help himself asking as a means of closure, "Pops, so you are just turning your back on me? Disowning me?"

He studied his father's blank face as a warmth in his eyes shined. Khamun knew they were done with this chapter in his life.

"No. I'm letting you come into your own right . . . although I am not amused."

After that life-changing meeting, he and his father ceased to communicate as father and son. Whenever he had to give a report, he got nothing but The Elder. Which ultimately pissed him off to no end. His father's behavior only resulted in Marco and Lenox being Khamun's middlemen in communicating with the man.

His mother, he could never shake. She stayed on him like glue, insisting she be used as his liaison House oracle since she was already the Region's Oracle, due to the loss of so many. He loved his mother, and the nonjudgmental love she gave had him accepting. He had no other choice. Their House needed an oracle in order to stay in the circuit and function reliably; all Houses did.

The founding of his House had been a challenge. At the start, it only consisted of him and his cousin Marco. Marco was the only one at the time who saw the difference in him and didn't judge him. Hell, Marco saw the difference when they were children and never said a word. He was his right hand, and that would never change.

Calvin, his left-hand man, came into the picture a month later while they were roaming Brooklyn. The brotha was something else with his mishmash Brooklyn swag accent and New Orleans brogue. Dressed in all-black, a military-style jacket with baggy black jeans, black Timbs, shades and a smirk, he made every chick in the spot damp. He took down a crew of demons at a local club he was deejaying and rapping at without breaking a sweat. Every word he spat tore throughout the spot, filling the air in swirling light that only those of Nephilim blood could see. He was down with Khamun the moment the music faded out.

Of course, the tech of the team, Kali, effortlessly became a part of the team without any concern from the men. It hit them all in their DNA to protect her, and protect they did. Even as she equally cut demons into snack food while she crooned background vocals for her big brother, handing him weapons she materialized from her henna tattoos. She was unmatchable with her knives and martial arts skills. Khamun knew without a doubt that he would kill any man or demon who tried to touch his little sister.

Lenox rounded the team out, even naming the growing house. Khamun had been friends with him since high school and college. Nox was the only Immortal he knew who could handle him in basketball, football, and even track. He always was the extra kick to his conscience, and he would later find out that Nox could detect the change in him too.

In college, Lenox and Marco were the lady killers, hunting panties every chance they could, and doing it in a way that was so smooth, they earned the nickname Don Juans of the campus. Many also didn't know that Lenox could kill anyone or demons with his bare hands and swift fighting skills. He was skilled in every hand-to-hand or weapon-on-weapon combat you could ever know.

It later made sense why Nox was so skilled when he went into his immortal evolution and Khamun learned that his best friend was the very first Templar, who happened to be a Moor. They also speculated that he possibly had a past life as a Scottish king during King Arthur's reign and was also a five-star lieutenant in World War I.

Khamun's team was out of the ordinary, and naming his house House of T'em, also known as Templar, made pure sense. His House single-handedly brought back the Templars, and this shocked Society because it was believed that the Templars were the first to become insurgents in Society.

Kali's gifts in searching out knowledge and his own mother's oracle skills helped them prove this was a lie. Since then, Society had been watching them, and every crew member had to tone down who they were within Nephilim Society, or deal with being ridiculed or even shunned. It never amazed Khamun how immature people with money, or with society rights could be, when competition entered the room.

Once his House was globally established, he later learned through Kali that other hidden branches or Houses of Dusk, as it was called underground, were formed around the world to accommodate those who lived in the middle, who were shunned by other Houses of the Light lines, or couldn't find their place within the bourgeois Society, like his own team. These people, like himself, whom he later called the Purgatory Line, helped add to the limited resources of the House and helped save the most humans, Guides, and Vessels throughout the history of Nephilim society. His House had survived and still was going strong.

Inwardly smiling, he knew when he hit thirty that his father's mandate wouldn't hold water and that he now held his own reins.

At this instant, all of that was about to change. With just one step into his old house, Khamun Cross, or according to his Society name, Region Prince Khamun Imen V'ance, would now bring a new element to all the Purgatory Houses around the world and ultimately expose what he didn't even know he was.

Sanna sat lotus-style in her purple drawstring pajama pants and white tank shirt. She was reclining on her plush, cozy, cloud-like bed, staring in disbelief at her clutched cell phone in her hand. "Excuse me. Say what?" She couldn't believe the shit that was being said to her from the other end. Not again!

"Sanna, sweetheart, listen to the man. I think this is for the best, baby girl."

Sanna couldn't help but look up at her mother, who was frowning herself, making her sepia eyes pop with concern.

"This man just told us that our homes burned down, that my business is now moved to Chicago, *permanently*, due to demolition that went awry, and you both expect me to sit here okay with this? Where are we gonna live, Momma? I don't know anything about Chicago. It's cold as hell up here. I do know that!"

Tears rimmed Sanna's eyes as she clutched her cell with heightened stress, anger,

"Ms. Steele, as I said, my company has made arrangements for you and your family. You have nothing to worry about at all."

Sanna just shook her head. "Mr. MacLeod, I mean Lenox, I understand what you are saying, but that was my father's home. We grew up there. The commercial building was my future home for my business. And that was my apartment. This is not acceptable!"

A rustling of papers over the cell phone had Sanna casting a wild look around her hotel room at her mother, who just put a finger up to her lips and tapped a finger to her ear, motioning for her to listen.

"But—"

Tamar shook her head then held a hand up, and she gave a stern look. "Listen, Sanna. I talked to him already, and we have this in order, so listen, baby girl."

Lenox cleared his throat over the cell phone. He was in business mode, true concern in his voice. "Ms. Steele . . . Sanna, your mother had my people look over your father's will, and it states that he has property here in Chicago. Property that I have sent contractors to evaluate and bring up to par. The neighborhood you are in is very well known and safe, so you and your family will be fine. Your father also has a second property downtown which you do, since your brother was planning to move into it." Sanna raised an eyebrow then glanced at her mother, who just nodded.

"I told you, baby, your father made sure we were okay. He has land down South and two places on the East Coast that your cousins are watching over. It's okay. He was a stickler about owning property and renting it out. I also own some property on the West Coast that your aunts are looking over. We will be fine, baby, just fine. Do not dismiss His blessings."

Running a flustered hand through her braid-ed-out 'fro, all she could do was sit in disbelief. "I know I should be grateful, really, but why all of a sudden are we coming into all this property, huh? Where was it before? This is too crazy, Ma, and you know it."

"If I may, Mrs. Steele"—Lenox's voice demanded everyone's attention as he spoke—"from the re-cords I have, your mother has been making profit from each rental property, and as requested by your late father, she placed it in funds for you and your siblings' education, as well as deposit-ing funds for his grandchildren, your children. Monies have been divvied out to charities, and your grandparents in Louisiana, who have now relocated to Savanna, Georgia. Your father was named benefactor over both sets of land in those regions before he passed."

Sanna blinked as her mother motioned for her to continue listening.

"Your mother is very good with money man-agement, very good. So it seems, when the home market busted due to this recession, all monies collected stayed fluid within your accounts. Your mother also was given funds from your father, solely for her survival as well. No, your father wasn't rolling in money, but he was very smart at buying property, property it seems that has been handed down through your family."

Kyo leaned down to whisper to Sanna as she plopped on the bed and listened. "Why is he all in the family business like this? Isn't he just the contracting lawyer for Sanna?" Kyo was chewing on a bagel and dressed in turquoise pajama shorts with a matching tank top while she handed Sanna some grapes.

Sanna bellowed, "Thank you! I was two seconds away from asking that." She reached out to high-five her godsister.

Tamar pursed her lips as she crossed her arms, staring at both women. "If you two do not stop that mess right now! Now listen. His business card says otherwise, and I asked him to help me with some of your father's records after I was going through them. Now listen and stop being rude. This information is not just about you, baby girl."

"Okay, so now what? We are here in Chicago to stay?"

"Yes, your mother has already pushed this forward, and it was only logical to have you set up in a new building. Interesting enough, the building where my law firm is at has a huge opening for a restaurant such as yours, and I can guarantee no issues will arise, if you are interested."

Sanna frowned, quickly biting her lower lip as she glanced at Kyo.

Kyo shrugged as she stretched. "I don't know. This is insane. And I'd have to move up here too, so hell . . . something new! Let's do it." Bouncing up and down on the bed, she flashed a brilliant smile, her asymmetrical cut hair with honey brown highlights flying with her. "Stop being scared, girl. No money is coming out of our pockets, so let's do it. This feels so right, although crazy, but right!"

Sanna signed. "Okay, Mr. MacLeod. You heard my business partner. Let's do this."

"Great. I'll get everything in motion, and it is great doing business with both of you ladies. Oh and, Mrs. Steele, I look forward to our next appointment as well."

"Me too, Mr. MacLeod. Now get some rest. You work too hard, young man." Tamar chuckled as Lenox's warming laughed filled the room via the speakerphone.

"Yes, ma'am, of course. You beautiful women keep me busy, and it is very much appreciated. *Adieu.*"

Sanna placed a manicured nail over the receiver button and hung up with a quick push as she groaned and shook her unruly, crinkled hair. "Mommy, are you serious? Should we do this? We've gone through so much right now. First Dare and Take, and now our homes are gone. My business is gone! Ma!" She eyed her mother cautiously.

Tamar smoothed a hand down her cream-colored pencil shirt, her silver hooped belt accenting her lush hips. She ran a hand over her wavy, curled, ear-length bob raven hair. Her momma was smooth, and wisdom poured from her.

"My love, you hold so much wisdom in you. It is time you truly listen to your spirit, baby girl. You've done so well being led by it, but now it's time you listen. Close your eyes and listen."

"But—"

Rolling her eyes, Tamar lightly pinched her daughter with a smile and held her hand, lifting it to press against her heart. "Sanna, close your eyes and listen."

Sanna complied with an inward sigh, fear suddenly filling her. She didn't know why, but she just knew something was going to happen. And it frightened her to no end. As she sat breathing slowly, she felt Kyo lay a comforting hand on her shoulder, and she let her body relax.

Kyo seemed to always know when Sanna felt unnerved, and all of this that happened to them both didn't change a thing about their friendship. Sanna appreciated that so much.

Fingers digging then flexing against her thighs, her body seemed to hum as she relaxed and listened. Fluid energy flowed around her, and she saw her happiness here and peace. She saw it clearly as she could breathe.

"Yes, I guess it would be good to stay here. Let's break it to Dare. I know he's going to trip over it."

Shaking her head as she listened to her two life supports laugh, Sanna headed into the hotel suite living room smiling. She saw her baby sis fussing over her twin. It seemed that Amara was the elder twin whenever Darren was sick.

Takeshi stared at her baby sis with a quiet hidden hunger and a lighthearted glance as he joked with the pair.

Sanna inwardly beamed while grabbing an apple. One day soon, she was going to play matchmaker and get Take and Amara together ASAP.

"So, um, we are moving to Chicago."

"Like hell," Darren muttered over his cup of coffee, humor lighting his eyes. He flashed a lopsided smile and wiggled an eyebrow.

"Shut up, Dare. You know what crap has happened. Well, Ma said . . ."

"We know, sis. Your ass was hella loud. Kind of happy about it, though. Congrats, big sis. A new city, *baybay*!" Amara grinned as Miya slovenly shuffled out of her room, scratching her messy hair and wiping hand down her face.

"Yeah." Miya yawned and stretched. "New place to visit. *Hiiii*, Dare." She softly smiled. The sleep in her quickly vanished as she accented the hi, getting a wink out of Darren. Hands combing through her messy hair, she smoothed it down, "And bye, Mrs. Steele. Please be safe."

Tamara was halfway out the door as she waved. "Bye, babies. I'll be back. Darren and Takeshi, don't you move from this room. You both need to rest!"

Both men chimed, "Yes, ma'am," as the door shut, and both quickly stood grabbing for their support.

"Where's my sis at?" Take stood and moved around the room, searching for the remote control as he limped on his crutches.

"Talking with your parents about all of this and, um, Take, sit down right now, man. Geez!"

Sanna rushed to Take's side and quickly helped shuffle him to the couch. Helping him was something else, especially when he had the nerve to put his hand on her rear as he fell down on the couch.

"Boy! Here!" she said, throwing the remote.

Take laughed hard, clutching his ribs as he leaned to the side gasping for air. "What? I wanted to compare you and Amara. Dang!"

Narrowing her eyes, Sanna tilted her head to the side and flicked him off with a laugh. "Yeah, whatever, man. You are just being nasty."

"Very! You want to touch my tig-o-bitties, then think of a better way to get at me, Mr. Nasty," Amara teased. She smiled while she bit into a piece of pineapple, and juice ran down her chin.

Take watched that juice slide from her mouth and dip down her neck as his body visibly tensed.

Noticing Take's eyes darken, Sanna ducked as Dare threw an orange at him. He smoothly caught it and turned around and flipped through the TV.

"Watch ya hands, bro. And put it on the game."

Sanna smiled while she hugged her sister. She helped her sister unbraid her thick semi-wet braids, turning to hug Miya at the same time. She would get used to this. She would make it through all this crazy. Her brothers were alive and healing extremely fast. Her mother was doing whatever she does, and Kyo was okay. This change was going to be good. It had to be. Her soul said it was so and said it very loud.

Like her mother had said, she needed to listen to herself. Since being here and coming out of the hospital, she felt different, she felt vibrant, something she hadn't felt since she was a child. Life seemed to go on mute when her father died. She remembered feeling safe when her daddy was around. A feeling she sometimes felt at night. It was as if something was trying to snatch her, and all she had to do was call her father and that fear would disappear.

Sanna felt happiness, joy, and calm, but life was just stunted. The little bit of magic in the world seemed to fade for her and roamed in her dreams after her father had passed. Now, as she stood unbraiding her sister's hair, taking the time to finger-comb each soft, curly strand and looking at the beautiful view that was Chicago, it felt different.

She inhaled and rolled her shoulders. Everything seemed to be vivid and alive with positive change now. She was praying it would stay this way.

Kyo quietly shut the door to her shared hotel room as she stood. She almost slumped against it, studying the group in the room. This was her family, her contentment, now her responsibility. She couldn't believe what was just told to her. Her father, her mother, they had to be out of their mind. She didn't even register telling Miya and her brother Take to go talk with her parents as she stood in bewilderment.

She didn't even register grabbing a bottle of water and standing near her best friend, her sister. Chicago seemed huge, beautiful, rugged, and understanding, yet equally dangerous. With a look at her almost shaking hands, she studied her silver-painted nails, flexing and looking at each sturdy tip sparkle like diamonds. Her father had said it was her duty to watch her best friend.

Yeah, that's nothing new for her, she thought, glancing at Sanna.

Kyo could feel that San was off balance, a little unsure about all of this, and hell, she couldn't blame her. She felt as if they were in the same boat. The dreams, the many times she felt that they shouldn't go to a certain area, or even go kick it some nights. All of it slowly came together to make sense.

Her father had told her that she, her brother, and cousin were something special. Something more. Something anointed. Dragons. It was her birthright to be a Protector over her best friend, whom she called sister, and fight for the innocents of the world. She was told that Sanna and Darren didn't know about them, or that her "god-family" was placed around her at birth as a means to protect them. She was also told that because of her birthright, she would be viewed as a shadow, or an outcast, respected but always suspected.

But that was neither here or there. Her main focus was to help Sanna as she went through her awakening, and it was Kyo's duty to awaken with her.

Duty to awaken? Awaken how? She didn't understand, and her father didn't tell her. He'd just said that she would know in time and that, that time was close. Her father let her know that they had homes for her and that they would move up to Chicago within the coming months, but right now, it was important that she stay with her godsister. As if she would go anywhere else. Her sis needed her, and she needed Sanna, whatever she was. Whatever it meant. She was going to see it through and work it out and make sure no harm came to sister. It was just the way of their world and all she knew, so it made sense.

Before Kyo's mother left, she had told Kyo to trust her instincts and she would know who is safe to be around Sanna and herself. So now she stood not believing what was told, even though she saw it with her own two eyes.

Her father had rolled his shoulders, closed his eyes, and the room seemed to heat up as he spoke. The very air around him seemed to shimmer as he closed his eyes and took out what Kyo had no idea after all these years were contacts. He opened his eyes, and she gasped. They were grey with flecks of beautiful jade green like her own mismatched jade set. The only difference was the fire metallic ring around the irises and the fact that his eyes were solid grey with jade.

His skin seemed to cast occasional specks of sparks, like smooth stone in the sun, as his hair and nails lengthened. His once model smile was now home to a clean, jagged pair of fangs. When her father gave her a reptilian-like blink and exhaled fire plumes from his nostrils, Kyo screamed bloody murder and passed out.

Sighing, she studied her hands, her arms, her skin. She was told that, as her right as a Gargoyle or Dragon, she had certain abilities that would awaken as Sanna woke up. But the thing was, when would that be? She needed to prepare herself.

Am I going to look freakish? She ran a hand through her asymmetrical cut hair. She already got over the hump of being teased for her different-colored eyes, and now she knew why she had them. She could only assume every extra bump in her DNA, in how she functioned in the everyday world, was because her father was a freaking Dragon and married to a human. No, scratch that—her own mother was something special too. She carried the dormant Dragon gene, showed by the same hard nails Kyo had, and was a Disciple with a touch of Dragon mystic abilities. How that worked out all these years, she didn't stick around to learn.

"Well, sis, this is going to work out." Kyo smiled as Sanna nodded. She couldn't help but to think, *What is my godsister? Why does she need protection?*

Shaken out of her thoughts, she felt her brother and cousin at the door as they suddenly swiped the key. She had always known when her little brother was around. Could feel him as she breathed, and now she understood why. Dragons within families could sense each other as a protection mechanism.

She smiled at her family as they both looked at her wide-eyed.

Takeshi strengthened up on his crutches, getting up from the couch, and watched in awareness as Miya bit her lower lip and cast her eyes to the floor, suddenly looking at her nails. It looked as if her bright yellow-painted nails were changing colors like a kaleidoscope, which had Kyo confused.

Take frowned and rested his hand on Miya's shoulder as he calmed her, her nails returning to their bright yellow sheen. Yeah, her family was something special and powerful, something unique altogether.

Chapter 11

Khamun sat with a cold smirk on his face. He sat complacent at the Dignitary Council meeting with Marco and Lenox at his side representing his House. A month had passed, and submitting the documents for Sanna, her family, and the Satous had happened with ease, thanks to Kali's brilliant mind. The council had no idea what Sanna really was and was not interested in learning more about a minor newling house. It was good that the announcement of that house being attached to him was suddenly dismissed. He would thank his mother for that later. Now he sat listening as the council bellowed with covert anger, all while his father sat watching in discernment.

"He placed his seat on bid! He cannot return and take over as head of the Dignitary Council," one young cats almost screamed. His white-as-chalk, fluffy-as-cotton wings shook in annoyance as if he was a PMSing teenage girl.

Khamun slightly chuckled at the image.

"Protocol states that, for him to return and regain his seat, he must have been active in council meetings, which he has not!" This came from an older male, whose mate stood at his side nodding her pretty golden ringlet head, her face red with restrained fury.

"My husband is right. This is an outrage!"

"The only outrage in here is the fact that your grown ass has Shirley Temple curls in your head," Marco muttered under his breath, loud enough for her to hear. He sat back reclining in his chair, an arm resting over the back of the chair next to him.

Another outrage was the fact that no one in the council addressed him by his royal rank, yet another display of disrespect. Khamun deliberately chose to ignore the slight of the council as he laughed under his breath at Marco's comment.

Leaning forward, Khamun stood and slid his arms behind his back as he looked down from his House's private balcony section.

"You . . . you cursed half-breed bastard!" ripped from the golden-haired woman's pursed lips, her eyes focusing on Marco and Khamun as she pointed a delicate finger.

Khamun's amber eyes flashed at the affront, the gold ring around them pulsating as his fangs dropped and his own wings slowly extended.

Marco and Lenox both leaned forward in unison, cold smiles sharply appearing on their faces, their hands ready to draw whatever weapon they so chose, as they represented their house to the fullest.

"Would you mind repeating that again, Madam Council member?" Khamun slowly asked, each syllable dripping with controlled anger as he watched the woman sputter, staring her down like the bitch she was.

His voice radiated with a coldness that blanketed the whole room, and he felt his father's eyes focus on him in quiet amazement. Briefly glancing toward his father, he felt his mother's warming care wrap around him in pure love while she watched from her own House seat.

This was a first. He had never shown his wings in public after he started going through his change. But because a simple bitch had triggered his anger, he now stood in his other form, his Reaper wings spread for all to see. He inwardly chuckled as he closed them, cleared his throat, and slid his hands behind his back.

His head slightly tilted to the side, he stood in his six seven glory, dressed in black pinstriped crisp-cut slacks, black leather shoes, and a sleeve-rolled-up, white tailored shirt accented with a black vest, his locks French-braided down his back.

"Now, we are all familiar with protocol, and the Madam would be correct, but as is *also* stated, I may have representatives from my House to act in my place, since I am often busy with Guardian obligations as was dictated to me at birth. Am I incorrect in my approach, Lord and Lady Elders?" Glancing at the row of Grand Elders, he could see the muscle in his father's jaw ticking.

The Region King focused his attention squarely upon the woman who had the nerve to disrespect his family's way.

Khamun swore he could see warming respect in his old man's eyes, and that kind of support made him stand proud.

"*Region Prince* V'ance would be correct in his assertion. He has a right to his chair. Protocol has not been breached, since he has had a constant representative in his place. Council members who are active constabularies do have a reprieve in allotting a member of his or her house to stand in place of said council chair," an Eldress stated.

Her sea-green eyes turned toward Khamun's as a soft smile sparkled in her eyes before disappearing. She was a beauty. Her red curly tresses framed her cinnamon dark skin, her curvy frame hidden behind the ceremonial robes of an Elderess. He knew she had to be many centuries old though, to the human eye, she appeared to be a young-looking forty-five.

Khamun's father leaned forward to address the room and state his point. "Those who wish to contest this may do so, as is their right, but we can sit here all day or move on with our business for the day or resort to derision and reprehensive conduct."

"I contest!" a voice shouted out, as another rumble moved through the hall and rose like a quiet sea storm.

Khamun, his father, and several council Elders all rolled their eyes. A mental exasperation ripped through the quiet storm. His father, the High Elder, sat back in his chair, arms crossed, as he stared at a young, chestnut, shaggy-haired man dressed in a grey suit. His olive-toned skin slightly glowed, and his dark Armani shades gave away his sunlight aversion, marking him a Dead Wrath Angel.

"State your case."

"I am Gregory Ryan de Mer'ce of House of Mercy. The House of Templar is an unauthorized working Line, regardless of its royal claim! They are nothing but mutts who play Protectors, Guardians, and other so-called titles. They have done nothing but cause havoc where they were stationed. Innocent newling Nephilims' homes burned and made open for attack! City blocks scorched and destroyed because their Mystics were not doing their jobs and hiding the teams. This House is nothing but a jest to appease the spoiled brat Prince and his needs!"

Khamun bit his inner cheek, trying to rein in his anger as coldness filled the hall with each slow breath he took. Dead Wrath Angels were just as ostracized as his own house, due to the fact that they were a Nephilim race that scared the hell out of some in Nephilim society. This fear arose due to their ghostly, temperamental behavior and rumored aims to gain titles and ranks at any cost. After the Great War, many Wrath Angels died out or survived by being broken, due to torture, or, as this bastard in front of him who was trying to start more shit, survived through death.

Through dying, Wrath Angels were able to preserve their souls from being taken to the Most High. This act resulted in their soul forming a sort of barrier that showed over their skin, casting a misty glow, like water droplets on the skin. They say this new race of Wrath Angels was pardoned by the Most High himself, due to their sacrifice in the Great War, and they were allowed to reproduce with hope that pure Wrath Angels would be born. Unfortunately, through the generations, they weren't trustworthy, and no pure Wraths were ever born.

Slowly standing, Marco brushed his arms off. He was dressed in all black. Black slacks, black-and-red pinstriped button-down shirt, sleeves rolled-up at his elbows, and black leather shoes. He had just cut his long hair off, leaving him with a wavy ultra-low fade. The hazel ring around his grey eyes flashed as he licked his lips.

Dimples played in cheeks, accenting the newly grown goatee around his mouth as he smirked, then addressed the bastard below. "It is interesting to me, *coño cara*, that you have the unmitigated gall to disrespect the Region Prince and this House. Let alone the members of both councils with your pathetic groupthink. This House is certified and authorized not only with its *own* Royal Garrison but with its own—"

Khamun watched his cousin through narrowed eyes. He quietly whispered to him *"Marco, this fight is not worth it. Let them think what they want and do not reveal our hand, man."*

"Coño carajo, cousin! Get the fuck outta here. They disrespect our family and you want me to chill? Naw, now it's time to put their slimy asses in their place, especially that fucking Death Wrath! He feels off to me, man. Remember I told you some of these so-called goody-goody Society folk would drop Death Wraths at our door as gifts and we'd return them as spies via the bite?"

Khamun narrowed his eyes, bowing his head, pleased that Marco was in the same mind frame as he. *"He's a Phantom,"* Khamun calmly said, watching the bastard.

"Right. I can taste that shit on my palate, homie." Marco rubbed his hands together.

Lenox brushed his thighs off and stood as well. *"You know the game, fellas. Only way to tell is via the eyes and to check for the bite. So until we can get him cornered and alone, which I doubt will happen, we have to play the game. As you see, his House is thick, and he is well guarded. We have to get him alone and handle what we do. So let me end this meeting and sucker-punch their asses so we can be on our way."*

"*Do you, man,*" Khamun stated with a smirk on his face as he stepped back, making the coldness in the room simmer down.

Marco glanced at Gregory one last time, storing his shifty face to memory before sitting.

Lenox loved this part of his job. All eyes on him, he knew the women of the hall were drinking in his six six frame. His black wavy hair curled at his nape. His icy blue eyes darkened with his mood, which offset his almond milk skin and his black slacks. His white shirt was unbuttoned to show a peek of his chiseled chest, which had many women sending mental lust shots his way as he made way to address the council. The game was on, and he was ready to go into his lawyer mode.

Getting under the skin of these prissy bastards made Lenox's dick hard. He crossed his arms, scanned the whole hall, and nodded at the High Elder, as his arms uncrossed and slid behind his back. "Council members and Elders, let us resolve the discourse, for this is going on too long.

Fellow dignitaries, for those of you who despise us as if you were Cursed yourself, as the House of Templar and Vengeance House Garrison Notary and personal legal representative, as I am for many Houses here, you know my work well, and every document you contest with your *Royal* member is also in order."

Narrowing his eyes, he scanned every face in the hall, even the Elders', just to see if his point was starting to process, and he inwardly smiled as the "Oh shit" face began to appear on many dignitaries' ignorant stares. "To question a Royal and his documents is to question my professionalism, and I will not stand for that, let alone the disrespect to my Houses. In saying so, any more contests will now go through legal court, and any injustice my clients feel will be rewarded as seen fit."

The room became silent in fear as Khamun noticed his father stand. His own fury slapped everyone in their faces as he walked off, promptly signaling the end of this witch hunt on his seed and his House.

Another Elder cleared his throat and eyed the councils. He said, "Your arguments have been recorded, and we have come to our judgment. The House of Templar will retain its seat and merge with the Royal House of Vengeance as was stated. Any more appeals will be met with an Elder judiciary council. So say it, so shall it be. Councils are adjourned, and we send blessings to Region Prince V'ance de T'em. Welcome home, My Lord. Your seat as Dignitary leader is officially processed."

Khamun knew in this moment that he had shown his father he could handle not only his own house but the pricks of Society. He also knew that all of this had only gone on so long as a means of his father making a point to him. Which, of course, ticked him the hell off but made him smile. Society had seen what his House was about and also now knew he was something they had no clue about. He was back with major work to do, and now the gossip would begin.

Sanna couldn't wrap her head around at the ease she now felt being in Chicago. At one point she thought she'd open up a restaurant in Atlanta. She just wanted to get away from the dull Midwest and start fresh. But now, as she stood a month later going over building details for her new home and restaurant, while Kyo spoke on the phone with different food merchants, that want just changed.

Shifting through different documents, Sanna tapped her hand against her thigh as she read and signed various papers. She finally felt some peace of mind.

It had been crazy going over the damage the fire had done to her family home, her second restaurant, and her apartment in St. Louis. Her mother had lost almost everything. Pictures, items from her father, and childhood stuff seemed to strangely survive, and she was grateful for that. As for her home, it seemed that the fire ate everything. All her clothes. Yet her important items, such as her degree diploma, birth certificate, social security card and more made it through the blaze. All the things they needed to transition seemed to endure.

She sighed, rubbing her temples as she looked over the insurance forms for this new place, as well as the one from St. Louis. Her migraines had been flooding her more frequently, and she knew it had to do with stress. Even though she was coming at ease with the new Aset: Chicago restaurant, and the many patrons who used to drive down from Chicago to St. Louis just to eat at Aset were creating a buzz she appreciated, stress was still driving her.

This new restaurant was vastly different, since she had to rebuild twice. She figured that she'd freshen it up, do something new, and combine a small private cooking school with personal chef assistance available, which was something Kyo wanted to always do. She knew already that her unique fusion restaurant would generate something good, and nothing but positivity was going to come from it all.

As she moved around the city and learned her way around, taking the "L," hopping on buses, learning her new neighborhood, she felt like she was being watched and followed. The majority of the time Kyo was always with her, but it didn't stop that nagging feeling that someone was protecting her. It also didn't stop her constant dreams.

Last night she had awaken with the feeling that the man in her dreams—she'd named him Watcher—was surveying and protecting her. He was keeping her from the demons who wanted to hurt her as he found his way into her apartment and held her while she cried. Her face was damp with tears as she woke up and looked around, swearing she smelled faint cologne linger in the air.

She hadn't the foggiest idea why she was crying or why her skin seemed to flush warm with satisfaction, but it just felt like something she needed to do in her dreams. She needed to cry to release the tension, but when the Watcher was in her dreams, she seemed to never really remember them quite well, especially the sensual dreams.

She placed a hand on the back of her neck, massaging herself, then reached for her tea.

"You seem to be low on tea. Let me refill that for you."

The deep, soothing voice grabbed Sanna's attention and had her head snapping up. She quirked an eyebrow as she stared into amber golden eyes, framed by smooth, warm, milk chocolate skin with a light copper tone to it. His smile halted her breath as she studied his braided back locks. Her eyes roamed over his sensually taut running-back-muscled body nestled in a black denim jumpsuit with paint splotched all over. His white A-line tank shirt peeked out from underneath, while his smile seemed to make her body over heat with exotic need while he filled her cup up with more tea.

"Sugar. Cream. Vanilla. Cinnamon and nutmeg. Am I right?"

Sanna blinked as she nodded, confusion hitting her hard, while directing her stare to his brown work boots. She tried to work her mouth to talk, but all she could do was glance up and stare like a mute. He was delicious. She swore she had met him before. Déjà vu hit her hard. It was her dreams all over again, back in STL with the fine-ass painter and mural, but this was clear, solid reality. If she was bold enough, she could reach out and touch his hard, chiseled body and know this was real.

Once again it felt like she knew him. As if she knew him all her life and somehow was meant to be with him. He felt like her dream, the man in her dream. His voice with that silky deep octave had the hair on her body rising as the blood rushed between her thighs. She had heard him before. She was positive about it. And not just at the hospital.

Her eyes locked in on his plush lips, and she felt like she was Loretta Devine in *Waiting to Exhale*. The man had lips meant for kissing, and while he spoke to her, she swore he was playing with her mentally the moment he licked his lips. That simple act had her ready to rip his and her clothes off as she sampled his plush mouth. She wanted to see if that goatee could cause a nice friction against her moist bud. She blushed at her crassness. *Where in the world did that thought come from?* She had to get it together fast.

Exhaling and demanding her body to calm down, sudden frustration made her place a hand to her temple as she reached for her medicine.

"You don't need that. Here, drink some tea. It'll calm the headache, trust me," the man said as he handed her the cup.

His large hand surrounded her own smaller hands, and she jumped. He felt good, and why she knew that by just a brush of his fingers, she had no idea. Yet this man seemed to melt away the pain she was currently feeling from the budding migraine and seizure ready to tear her mind apart.

While he studied her calmly, his eyes sensually held her attention. "I'm glad to meet you finally and not in a hospital. I'm Khamun."

Met her? This gorgeous specimen of Mount Fine-as-wine had met her in the hospital? Oh, no, sir and no, ma'am. Who the hell was mister sexy, and how had he seen her in her worst? She was embarrassed beyond words.

Using her cup as a means of distraction, Sanna slowly sipped her tea and stared at its caramel creamy-colored surface. "That is really, really good. I mean, just right. Mine doesn't come out this good. What did you do?"

Khamun chuckled and grinned, his own eyes taking in Sanna's flush at meeting him while she enjoyed his tea. He couldn't blame her. It was like his world had stopped the moment he landed in her zone. He had been watching her, hidden for hours, as she worked throughout the restaurant.

Dealing with all that crap at the Council meeting had stressed him out, and he knew he had to check on his Oracle-Vessel. When he decided it was time to finally meet the woman he had desired for years in the flesh without any distractions. He meant it and nothing was going to stop him from doing his job and meeting her at the same time.

Smoothing a hand down his work suit, he inwardly laughed while trying to slyly adjust himself from the heat building within. He had to clamp down his need to walk around her in circles, slowly stalking her, seeing how close he could get to seducing her. She had no clue that her mind was open like a book to him, and every time he tried to close it out of respect, it seemed to flip back open.

She wanted to taste his mouth. He wanted her to taste it. She wanted see what his skin felt like, running over his abs. He wanted her to do so, and that had his manhood so hard, he knew if he stood any closer to her, she would feel it jumping just for her attention.

Using the art of discussion to distract himself, he dropped into a meditation breathing ritual, something he always practiced when he was near her. He calmly spoke, his voice rough with the edges of lust. "I didn't do anything. Just added what you like."

Slightly turning in her seat, she had to keep herself from glancing at the bulge in his work suit. The little glimpse had her almost falling out of her chair. The man was dangerous, and that swell seemed to keep growing. She wanted to cry at the assumptions of what his member would feel like within her untouched body, and she shakily exhaled.

"Oh. And how would you know that, Mr. Kha-mun what?" *Who the hell is this man?*

He held out his hand again, bracing himself for that sensual spark with just the touch of her skin. He licked his lips as he took her in, inhaling her sweet, intoxicating scent, and he felt her pulse quicken.

She was dressed is a black pencil skirt with a lilac blouse that gave a hint of her ample crème brulé breasts. He shifted himself again as he realized she had asked him a question.

"Cross. Khamun Cross." He had to quickly think of something smooth where it didn't tip her off that he'd been watching her since she'd made it on the Society grid and he was assigned to her when he was a teen. Basically, he had to remind himself that right now she was just look-ing at a mortal man who knew nothing about her and her special DNA.

"Oh. Wasn't hard to figure out, since I've been here for some time inspecting my crew and making sure they hold up to your designs."

"Oh, really?" Sanna was scrapping her mind, panning back and forth, combing through her memory. How had she missed seeing this deli-cious man? How had she not seen him? She had been slyly admiring many of the men working on her restaurant, yet she had bypassed a man such as him?

She remembered him from the hospital. When she saw him at the hospital, his very presence had her almost falling out her wheelchair. She knew if in that moment that she had a heart monitor on at that time, that bitch would have blown up. Yet today she had bypassed him in the restaurant? No way. Maybe he was here on the days Kyo was supervising the build? Maybe he . . . well, anyway, somehow he'd evaded her, but right now he was standing comfortably in front of her.

She did recall who he was. This was Calvin's frat brother, and now he was working in her restaurant, employed by her? She couldn't help but smile as she looked him over again.

Her mind was poetically beautiful, even throughout the rambles of fear and confusion. It was something he wanted to paint. Something he was painting in the murals for her restaurant. He couldn't help but read her expression as he softly smiled. He liked her style. She wasn't one to be played a fool for, so he decided to ease her mind.

"I had a couple of my staff with me, touring your property, showing the reins. Then I was busy working on a little something for you, Miss Steele."

The way he said her last name made her heart do a shimmy. She felt like a piece of art as he spoke to her and watched her. She felt like the finest of silks in Bombay as she inhaled his delicious cologne. Damn! Is this man married? Does he have a team of women? Children? Is he crazy? Is he a loser? Something had to be off about him, because right now, he felt made just for her. She had to get her mind right. No one man should have her ready to strip naked and get her rocks off in front of a staff of workers.

"Oh, and that's how you knew what I liked in my tea, okay." Softly smiling, she tried to look everywhere but his face, so she focused on his hands. The man had hands designed for holding a woman's waist, paint traces splashed along his long fingers.

She licked her lips as she dared to eye him again. She looked around as he quietly watched her, taking her cup and giving her a new one. "What were you—"

"A mural. Oh, I'm sorry."

She watched him shift as if she was causing discomfort, and she raised an eyebrow. She knew this man could not feel awkward around her. That just didn't compute for her. Maybe she was staring a little too hard, but damn, he shouldn't be so fine and standing so close. She knew it had to be something else because the way he looked at her right now had her wishing she could go hide somewhere and spend a little time practicing self-love.

Khamun's chuckle broke her train of thought as if he was reading her mind, and she blushed a thousand shades of red.

Her sudden butterflies had her taking another big sip of her delicious tea. She sat her cup down then stood. "Um, I'm sorry. Did you need me to sign something or look over something?"

"Actually, no. I wanted to go over what we've been working on throughout the day and show you the mural, the little bit I have done."

Bobbing her head in understanding, she had to run her hands up and down her arms. She almost had asked if he wanted her to run her hands over his body, but of course, that was her aching kitty talking, and she needed Ms. Kitty to cool it right now. But as she watched his rock-solid ass while he walked, she was ready to scream. He was no damn help either! He was so close, smelled so good and how he tilted his head to the side as he spoke to her, assessing her, drinking her in, had her discombobulated.

Anxiety hit her hard as she looked for Kyo. Where in all hell was her partner in crime at? She needed a buffer. Something. Her nipples were so hard right now, they irritated her as they rubbed against her bra. Her breasts felt so tight and heavy, it slightly freaked her out. This wasn't okay.

"Let me get my co-owner, Kyo Satou."

"Hey! Oooh! Who is *that*?" Kyo appeared out of nowhere, startling her and making her jump as she held in her laughter at Kyo's whisper.

Damn! Sometimes it tripped her out the way her bestie could pop up at any given time, as if she heard her SOS. Chuckling, her godsister was literally circling the man, her multi-toned jade eyes scanning his frame.

Sanna quickly mouthed "Sorry," and Khamun flashed a lopsided grin.

On a mission to work her magic as a buffer, Kyo shoved a hand out. "Hello, I'm Kyo Satou. Excuse me as I get nosy. It's not often my best friend has a handsome man pour her tea. Very nice of you."

Khamun chuckled as he assessed Kyo. He made up his mind right there that she was good people and was a great Gargoyle in person, although he had known that already just by watching over the pair previously. He had noticed her approach before Sanna had. Girly was almost stealth-like. If they were in a dark alley somewhere, any demon she stalked would be sorely surprised. Had he been an ordinary human, her movements and approach would not have been detected. The same could be said if he was some ordinary Nephilim, but he wasn't.

So when she popped up, he knew that Kyo heard her Vessel's mental SOS, just as clearly as he had heard it. He wasn't trying to stay in her mind, but he couldn't help it. It was like her mind demanded that he lock with her, especially now as she stood physically in front of him. He knew that, when another Nephilim female found a mate, a mind-lock would alert her of a partner that was suitable.

Khamun had to rock back and forth on his heels and hide his smirk. The lock was strong. This meant that she hadn't gone through her Evolution. Nonetheless, he was amused, horny as hell, and very flattered. Taking Kyo's hand, they both flinched.

At that same moment, Sanna suddenly swayed and caught herself from tipping over.

Power washed over Khamun, and Kyo eyed him instantly as she stepped closer, her eyes flickering that metallic hue her kind is known for. They were awakening, and being near both of the pair had triggered it all.

Kyo let go of Khamun's hand as she slid a chicken salad sandwich with a cucumber salad to her. "Sanna, sit and eat some lunch."

"I'm okay. I'm not hungry anyway. Just felt a little lightheaded."

Both Kyo and Khamun stared with pure concern.

He couldn't stop his protective nature and reached out for her, brushing his fingers under her jaw, tilting her head up slightly to look in her eyes. Which was bad. Her skin seemed to melt into him like shea butter, and he had to grip her as his fangs almost dropped against his will.

They both locked eyes, and Kyo quickly placed a hand on both of them. Her touch instinctively neutralized the sudden energy boost.

Members of Khamun's crew watched in quiet approval as Marco strolled from his spot upstairs, tools in his hands. He stood watching on from a stairway.

The building was hidden from the Curse, so the energy boost that had just occurred would stay cloaked within the building. Even though that was the case, he still twisted the surge, double binding it into the foundation of the land as a means to strengthen the protection sigils from the Curse.

Khamun's mouth slightly opened as his body vibrated in the addictive and sultry feel of her feminine energy. It was so pure, ripe, and light. Drenched in her budding Evolution, he almost came right there as he fought his body's slight shakes.

"My man, you good?" Marco called out, dousing his jones.

Khamun looked up, his eyes reflecting various hues of gold. He slowly nodded up and down, speechless.

Sanna's Protector ripped him from his concentration as she gripped him hard, almost shaking him while pulling him away from his Vessel's touch. Kyo's beautiful mismatched jade eyes flared with confusion and anger as Sanna shook her head.

"Yeah, let me eat something. I'll take that tour in a minute. Kyo, you go with him, please."

Still eyeballing Khamun, Kyo's hand clutched his pulsing bicep, and she never took her eyes away from him as he watched her say, "Okay, sis. Just rest and eat everything on that plate, woman, or else."

Weakly laughing, Sanna raised her shoulders while taking a sip of her still warm tea. She glanced briefly at Khamun, who watched her intensely as she turned away blushing, reaching for her sandwich. She didn't know what the hell just had happened, but whatever that was, it needed to happen again, and soon.

Following the sassy woman who had the nerve to pull him away from his woman, Khamun had to shake his head and sort himself right. He let himself be led by the Gargoyle, making sure she felt as if she was in control of the situation.

She was pretty, very curvy in all the right areas. Her spiky asymmetrical-cut bob with its chestnut highlights accented her almond-shaped eyes as they let him know what she was. Had he been pure human, her nails would have sliced into his arm, but of course, all they did was lightly paper-cut him as he waited for her to dig into him.

"*Who* and *What* are you? What do you want with Sanna?" she hissed, a low clicking sound suddenly coming from low in her throat like that of a reptile, and she blinked in shock. Her hand quickly came up to her throat as she brushed it off and shook her head.

"Calm down, Gargoyle. I'm not here to do harm."

"Excuse me?" Kyo tilted her head to the side. She swore she felt a shift in her body, as if she was fluid. Her mouth suddenly ached, and her skin suddenly felt aflame.

"Seriously, calm down, Kyo, before you stone!"

"Who are you? And what are you talking about? Stone? What!"

She clutched her stomach. Her insides felt wobbly, almost like she had swallowed thousands of butterflies and they wanted to fly around within her, and her breathing sped up. She saw the fine specimen of a man shake his head and reach in his pocket. He pulled out a small cigarillo, lit it, and then blew smoke in her face.

Sweet, spicy cinnamon, coffee and vanilla clouds caressed her face like a lover's hands. She suddenly coughed, flinging out to slap Khamun across his face, but ended up missing him because he'd quickly sidestepped the blow.

The shock of his rude ass blowing smoke in her face had her gasping. Then her erratic breathing slowed, until she suddenly felt giddy and relaxed.

"Hey! The hell is your problem?" she replied. The need to inhale again made her sigh. She smiled, leaning back against the wall.

Khamun chuckled then crossed his arms over his chest. He leaned back while studying her. "Now we can talk? This, my friend," he said, rolling the cigarillo between his fingers before placing it back against his lips, "is a trinity. It helps calm anyone, and your kind especially loves the smoke."

"Oh!" Kyo blinkd. Her hand slovenly ran down her face as she quickly stood alert. "My kind? What do you know about me? And what do you want with Sanna?"

"Chill, woman, chill. You are slowly awakening. You're a babe to the change, so chill. What I want is to protect you both. Who I am is just as I said—Khamun Cross. What I am"—He shrugged and spread his hands out wide, smiling—"you will find out soon. Just keep looking out for your godsister. You are doing good, and I mean her no harm."

Kyo slowly followed as Khamun turned to walk away, taking a long drag and putting his trinity away.

"No harm? Well, I kind of gathered that," she said as she tried to keep up with his stride. "How you were staring my sis down had me thinking I needed to get a room and take a cold shower. But . . . how do you know what I am?"

Running to continue her talk with Mr. Sexy was hard. He seemed to suddenly pick up speed in his pace while he glanced at Sanna. His beautiful eyes darkened then lightened with energy as he smoothly whipped around on her, guaranteeing Kyo would hear him.

"Relax, and we will talk soon. Now I can't check on your sis right now. She got me in a zone. So I'll be back later. Tell her one of my crewmen needed me and I had to go, okay."

His eyes were beautiful like warm honey on biscuits. They seemed to glow and flicker with a gold liquid ring that seemed to pulsate. Why she felt the need to comply, she had no idea, but she knew it would be for the better if she just followed through. She didn't want to jeopardize whatever Mr. Sexy had planned for her and Sanna. As she nodded, she swore the man disappeared right in front of her eyes.

Whatever he blew in her face had her all kinds of loose, and she smiled as she saw Mr. Seduction—a slight Don Omar doppelgänger with a low, wavy and curly fade—hovering over Sanna with a plate full of cucumber salad in his hand.

Sanna seemed to be shaken, yet very pleased by the tall, quarterback-built man standing near her, softly speaking and slightly demanding she eat.

"*Relájese* and breathe, baby—I mean, Ms. Steele. Just quiet that mind of yours and eat this." Marco ran a hand in circles on Sanna's back, watching her closely as she took the plate from his hands. "*Muy bien, mami*. Eat up," he cooed.

A shimmering aura seemed to flow from him and into her sister as Kyo observed, head tilted to the side in awe.

Sanna quietly ate her salad, raising an eyebrow every time Mr. Seduction would nod his head and murmur in approval.

This made Kyo mutter, "Alrighty then," as she slowly walked forward and picked up an icy-cold glass pitcher full of crushed ice and clear water to pour a glass for Sanna.

"You okay, sis?" Kyo looked Sanna over, handing her the glass.

Sanna gripped it with a shaky hand and took deep gulps of water. She nodded and took more bites from her salad.

"Yeah. Same ol', same ol'. Just need to sit for a bit, is all. Thanks."

Glancing up, Kyo watched Sanna smile and hand her plate to Mr. Fine number two. He, in turn, handed her the chicken salad sandwich.

Giving a small thanks, she took dainty bites before briefly frowning and shaking whatever thoughts flickered in her mind away, looking toward the door Khamun had strolled through.

"Thank you. Marco, is it?"

Marco looked Sanna over and bobbed his head with a light smile. "Marco Spear, to be exact." He stepped back with a low chuckle to give Sanna space and to keep from hovering as he assessed both women. "I can see why he's infatuated."

Flabbergasted, Sanna and Kyo said, "Huh?" in unison.

Marco flashed a sensual smile before picking up his tool bag and rolled-up blueprints. "If you both need me, I will be upstairs checking on the crew. I have electric work that needs to be handled. Do not leave without letting me know, ladies." He glanced at Kyo, his pupils undulating briefly with a silver sheen before they shifted back to normal. With a lopsided smile, he gripped his bag. "I would feel horrible if I did not get a chance to check on you two, a'ight."

Both ladies seemed to nod in unison, blushing as Kyo exhaled. Just like with Mr. Sexy number one, she felt that she had to comply. A sensation that didn't feel against her will, but more like a natural trust, an understanding of sorts. And she did not have a problem doing just that.

Chapter 12

Sanna sat in her new home in Lincoln Park, sprawled on her couch in lilac boy shorts and a lilac tank. Kyo was plopped across from her in a nearby La-Z-Boy chair, dressed in a similar outfit, only in all white. She loved her new home. It was a brownstone building restored to its former glory that sat next to Kyo's own similar unit. Though the houses were separate, for some odd reason, there was an underground connecting tunnel that ran to both units that was still safely functional.

According to Mr. Lenox, the only ones who knew about it were the owner of the restoration construction company he worked with, her, and Kyo. Lenox had insisted she stop calling him Mr. Lenox, so she had to remind herself to stop with the formality. He had insisted in decking out their homes with security and other gadgets. Unbeknownst to both women though, the tunnel also ran to a private bunker that led to a part of the CTA subway system no human knew about, and the highway. It would come in handy if ever they needed to escape, or when it came time for them to train in their awakening powers.

The land that the two brownstones lay on sat in a protected blended Nephilim neighborhood, which ensured that the ladies would stay protected and hidden in plain sight.

"Today was too crazy, wasn't it?" Sanna chuckled as she hit play on her DVD. Larenz Tate and Nia Long flashed across her massive HDTV then *Ninja Assassin* as she played with the menu option before settling on *Love Jones*.

Tonight was chick-flick action night. That meant that any movie, be it chick flick or action with cuties in it, Sanna and Kyo would be glued to.

Kyo pushed a massive tin of Garrett caramel and cheddar popcorn toward Sanna. "Crazy is an understatement, girl. Since moving here, we have been surrounded by the holy grail of sexy-ass men." She tilted her head as she raised her eyebrow in a sly smile. "Do you think Lenox or Marco would like a little geisha in their world?"

Sanna shook her head at her girl. She knew Kyo hated clichés and stereotyped references with regard to her race and sexual appetite, but tonight she definitely was playing it up.

Kyo batted her eyes and winked, a hidden flash of danger glinting momentarily before disappearing.

"Girl, do you think they would like a little brown sugar in their world?" Sanna ducked as popcorn suddenly doused her, and she shook her curly 'fro while she laughed. "What!"

"Please. They are off-limits. Plus, you have that ultra-sexy man, Khamun, after you. Please do not act as if you didn't see how he was literally so close that he could be your second skin."

Sanna rolled her eyes, huffing. "Please. Mr. Cross was not into me like that. Did you see how fast he left?"

Kyo gave her a shrug. "Nope. No, I did not, sis."

Quirking an eyebrow, Sanna shook her head. "Man, listen. No one is interested in me. I'm a curvy big girl who just can't seem to draw in them fine, tall glasses of men who aren't looking for stray ass. I keep getting old-ass, dusty, scary, stalking, Flavor Flav-looking men. What is wrong with me, huh?"

Kyo rolled her eyes and studied the movie. Larenz was spitting about how Nia was the blues in his left eye as jazz flowed through the house.

"Sanna, stop. You are in a new city. New world, new everything! Yes, those creepy, elderly, or Flavor Flav men do seem to like you, but guess what? So do those fine men who have their heads on straight. You just have to stop being blind and mean-mugging everyone."

Sanna sighed and quietly shifted on the couch. "I do not mean-mug, and I do pay attention."

"Do you? Okay. So when are you going to give Khamun your card? Hmm? When are you going to let him between those thighs, so the gates of heaven can sing and you can finally know what good tallywhacker is? Huh?"

Sanna flushed a thousand colors as she covered her face with her hands. "Oh my goodness! I hate your jokes sometimes. Damn!"

Kyo laughed. "What? Answer my question pretty please. So when he asks, you're going to give him a chance, huh?"

Sulking, Sanna couldn't help but wonder. She couldn't lie, she had been thinking about him hard since her second brief encounter with him. She couldn't help but be curious about that man. Who was he outside of the workplace? Was he really interested in her?

"Sanna! If he asks, will you give him the time of day?" Kyo watched her sister look away from her eyes, pretending she was looking for something near her seat.

"So Calvin is coming over tomorrow. He's going to work on some stuff in the house that didn't get fixed the first go-'round, and is going to take us shopping."

Shaking her unruly bob, Kyo chuckled. "Scared ass."

"What! Yes, okay. If he asks or hints, I'll give him my card. He's just so . . ."

Clapping her hands in glee as she bounced on her bent legs, Kyo paused then glared at Sanna out the corner of her eye. "He's just so what?"

Sanna couldn't form the words. It was like that man was everything she had been waiting on. As if the Most High slapped her across the face and said, "Here! Tired of you praying for him. Now get on with your life with him as destined." Sanna couldn't help but inwardly laugh.

He felt like the man in her dreams. The man who would creep in at night and glide between the sheets of her bed to smoothly place a gentle hand on her inner thigh, stroking and spreading her open effortlessly. The man who seemed to slide down and leave her body wet with kisses that seemed to send euphoric pleasure through her body. The man whose rod was so hard, his veins seemed to add a ridged ecstasy against her wet bud while he brushed her gently. That man whose locks would spread over her naked body covering her in a sensual protection that made her spirit spread and flux through his solid yet comforting body. It felt as if it was him, and that scared her.

She licked her lips. Her body already felt alive in that memory.

Kyo's voice quickly jolted her back to reality. "Sanna, speak! He's just so what?"

"Oh, he's just the shit! I can't even think of a better word. Did you see his mural? It's like its breathing life. He has poetry painted in it too, girl. That man is something else. Like Larenz Tate wooing Nia on stage, kind of something else, and he is working at my restaurant!"

Kyo chuckled while inwardly sighing. She had stood by that mural all day and not noticed a thing, but after her run-in with Khamun and Marco, she noticed the difference. The words seemed to glow with power, and the people in the scene, the colors all seemed to breathe with a life and light of their own. Everything swirled, letting her know no one would come to harm in the building or near the building, that only good was allowed in. The fact that she was able to read that from the mural freaked her out. She quickly planned on calling her father as soon as she found the time for some privacy.

"Yes. That's what I'm saying. You two would look good together. So when you see him again, just slide him your business card. You know he's constantly working throughout Chicago and St. Louis because he's owner of the restoration construction company. Maybe you can get him to come back here and work on a little some-thing-something." Kyo snickered and tried to block the pillow Sanna sent flying in the air, but it hit her in her face.

"I bet that would make your day, huh!"

"Yes, it would. So now that we have that squared, you think Lenox or Marco would mind sharing a midnight snack with me?"

Sanna laughed. "What? Like, at the same time?"

"Yes! A girl has to dream."

Sanna cracked up laughing. She knew Kyo was as fresh as the driven snow, like herself, but her mind wasn't. "What about that guy in your dreams? The one you said had you clutching at the sheets and grinding all on your pillow?"

Quietly munching on her popcorn, Kyo frowned. "What about him? He's just another wet dream for my mind to torture me with."

Sanna loved how Kyo could be raw with the truth with her, but when it came to her own self, that wisdom always seemed to work backwards. "I don't think so, but that's just me, sis. I think you're going to bump into him one day."

"Where? In St. Louis? Nantucket? I think I have to go to California, because he didn't seem like the dutiful Asian son. No. He seemed like a wildcard like myself, and where do you find that at anywhere? And don't say *ABDC*!"

Sanna just smiled and shrugged as she noticed her cell light up with a text. "Amara and Miya are coming back to see the new house and check on Momma on spring break. Which means my house is going to be flooded. You know Take and

Dare already are annoyed that the whole family is in Chicago as is."

Kyo laughed. "Yes. The whole point of them coming here was to get their own space, but I don't think they really are that upset with it as you think."

"No, they aren't. They love that we are here, especially us."

Chuckling again, Kyo nodded. "Right. Because where else can they go for good food and a HDTV, with all the entertainment they like? Plus all this space."

"Mmm-hmm. So I know Mom is loving her downtown condo? How are your parents? Do they love where they are at?"

"Momma loves being near Loyola, and the fact that they welcomed her with tenure and her own graduate department, she is in heaven."

"Really? I'm so happy for her. She's been so damn busy, she hasn't had the time to tell me whenever I call."

"Don't I know. Daddy has been going crazy. He's been kicking the med students at UIC's ass. Being the top neurosurgeon in the country kind of sets you up with being gawked at by med students."

"I still think it's funny that Take and Dare have to deal with Pops Hideo on their campus now. I heard him saying one day that he was going to get you and Take into that med school even if it kills him."

Kyo exhaled and rubbed her temples. "*Again*, I'm too old to go back. Leaving in my third year was the best choice ever. Juggling both was too hard. I loved that I said, 'Screw it,' and got my pastry degree instead. And, San, Take for damn sure doesn't want to mess with med school."

"I know, I know. That damn photographic memory of yours had you at the top of the class in med school and culinary school. Anyway, I think he's just excited, is all."

Kyo said, "Yeah, I think so too." Then she added, "Don't think I'm playing, Sanna. Next time you see Mr. Sexy, give him your card. Otherwise, I think he's going to snatch you up one day, and I'm just going to have to let him."

"Hmm. I wish he would snatch me up even for a little bit. Did you see his arms and his lips!"

Both women sighed and melted as they laughed and continued to watch the movie, not the least bit aware of the shadow in the window.

Chapter 13

The Reaper smiled. Right now he was just himself, the Watcher. Studying his Guide, it pleased him that she was settling in so well, relaxed and happy with her beautiful self. He knew he wanted her even more now. Her aura seemed to shine brighter as she slowly awakened.

When her mind drifted off into their mental lovemaking, he had to stop himself from kicking the door down and tearing into them lilac boy shorts with his mouth and drinking his fill. Images of his tongue playing tag around her pearl and lapping at her honeyed haven had his fangs cresting in need. Damn, if his dick wasn't still throbbing at the thought.

He had to quietly thank the Most High for the change in status, because all protocol was going to be broken if he couldn't have her—his seat in power, his house, all of it. He wanted Sanna Steele. After today, he for damn sure was going to have her and keep her.

Entering into the house unaware, he stood back and observed. Her father had chosen this house for a reason. Outside of the fact that it was in a well-protected area, this house also had a hidden bunker that connected not only to the main interstate but also to his compound via Chicago Transit Authority and a cavern. He had to do everything in his power to protect what was his and protect the woman who would help revive Society. It had been a long time since a surviving Oracle had been born, so finding one who was also a Vessel, in such a close generation, was a blessing in itself.

Fluctuating like a quick breeze, he misted around Sanna quietly, his fingertips playing with the ends of her hair before he noticed Kyo's sudden stare. For a second he thought she could see him, but he knew better. Gargoyles could sense his kind but not see them. Smiling, he moved away, her eyes following but not processing. *Good*. She was becoming aware.

"Kyo, girl, what are you looking at?"

Khamun inwardly chuckled.

Kyo shook her head in confusion, "Nothing. Just had a moment." She glanced around again and shook her head as she relaxed and watched the movie.

The night was young, and he was starving. Being back in his home city had him on edge. He hated hunting here. The thrill was the best, but he always had to make sure no one from Society ever caught him in the act. Feeding from the enemy was something that no others did. Many had fangs just for decoration. They were useless appendages that would only appear in anger or lust. For that reason, people in his Society couldn't be called vampires. If a Nephilim fed, it was typically done via their mates or relative, donated Nephilim, half-Cursed blood, or not at all. Feeding reminded polite Society of what the First War did to change them from their pure Arch state to that of half-human hybrids that had fangs as weapons to tear the enemy apart, and that was a stain on the Nephilim race, a mark of the First Fall.

Sudden hunger had him in a daze. Since the woman he wanted as his mate was still clueless about her lineage and he clearly couldn't feed from her, hunting seemed the best bet, he thought as he strolled through his compound. His compound was hidden, thanks to protection runes that camouflaged it as nothing but a well-guarded CTA building, surrounded by lethal fencing and cameras that Kali had hooked up.

He drove through retina and bio scanners identifying him, which opened the massive gates. Driving underground, it took only five seconds for him to open his door and meet Kali's angry stare.

"You didn't feed!"

"Hello to you too, little bit," he said, lightly picking Kali up by the shoulders and moving her to the side he walked on. "No, I did not. Don't feel like it." He stepped out of his black Escalade.

"What! You have to feed. Khamun, please go hunt." Kali tried to match his pace as she followed.

"What I want to feed from is not currently available at the time, so it is what it is. I'll grab something in the cellar."

"I'll call Marco." She frowned and rushed forward, her face contorted in annoyance.

"I'm good, Kali." It annoyed him to have to use donor blood from his cousin, mixed with that from a non-relative Nephilim, typically Kali.

Khamun paused in the long corridor and glanced down at the woman he felt was the little sister he never had. Kali stood in tight dark denim jeans that had rips on the thighs, yellow high-top Nike, and a white-and-yellow graffitied shirt that hung off her bare right shoulder. Sometimes he thought she could be Miya's twin sister.

"You know how I feel about it, so leave it."

"No, Khamun, I can't. If you don't feed, you know how sick you get. We can drag a Cursed here for you."

"Munchkin, if it was about the hunt, then I wouldn't be here. This is different. I just don't want that blood." He closed his eyes and ran an idle hand over his locks as he exhaled.

"You want Sanna."

The lilt in Kali's voice and twinkle in her eyes made Khamun inwardly cringe as he walked on. He passed through another set of scanners and flashing lights before standing in the middle of a swank platform that overlooked his second home. If he made a right, he could take the hidden stairway to his estate home. If he walked north, he could end up back in Sanna's and Kyo's homes. Yeah. He liked where he was and the family he had surrounding him.

"Grab me the donor blood and be done with this, Kali, okay. I'm good. Do not mix Marco's blood in there. That's an order."

Kali pouted and walked off before pausing. "You know, you could just ask her in her dreams. Take a small sample. See if it will help you appease your thirst."

"I could, but I'd rather have her be coherent and willing, because when I feed from her . . . " Khamun flashed a seductive smile that had Kali blushing while she shook her head.

"Okay, okay. I'll be back with your food." She rushed off.

He knew she'd mix Marco's half-dark blood with the bag out of love and concern. He hated using Marco in such a way. It often put them both in a bad place due to old memories and shadows of their youth, but he needed that darkness. He needed to have it run through him and cycle out like a dialysis machine, but the older they both got, the less Marco's blood seemed to help. Khamun always felt it was due to his cousin's acceptance of being a creature of the Light, not what he was born in, the Dark.

"Ey, man. How my cousin doing?" Calvin strolled in from the gym that nestled on the first level of the compound. Glowing sweat drenched his white tank as he dabbed at his face with a towel and offered Khamun dap.

"Still adjusting and loving her home."

Damn! Khamun swore everyone was dousing him with fifty questions. He misted and landed on the couch, the remote in one hand and his foot resting on the table in front of him.

Calvin was still on the platform stairway, shaking his head as he hopped the railing and landed with a thud below, before calmly walking to the couch. "That it, man? She a'ight? Nothing dark invading her dreams?"

The concern in Calvin's voice had Khamun sitting up as a warm cup of blood found its way in front of him. "No migraines tonight, my man. All is good."

"A'ight. You know I hate that shit, ya heard me?"

Khamun took the floating mug and downed it fast, out of annoyance for the bitter taste awaiting him. With a lick of his lips, he leaned forward to sit the cup down, but his eyes suddenly widened and rolled into the back of his head. A flash of the woman he craved for all day and all night hit his loins. Pieces of shattered porcelain and red fluid lay across his lap as his fangs crested, his nostrils flared, and he suddenly felt Calvin, Marco, and Lenox rushing to hold him down.

"What the fuck, Kali!" Khamun thundered as his breathing escalated and sweat saturated his shirt, making it cling to him as if ready to choke him. It felt as if his locks were rising on his head, while his body ciphered through the blood that merged into his system, hitting him where it counts.

"*¡Carajo!* What did you do, Kali?" Marco replied in disbelief, narrowing his eyes. Muscles bulged in his arms as he fought to hold his cousin down, ducking from the swings that threatened to connect with his skull. He swore he felt his cousin's muscles constrict then bulk as the man fought his blood lust.

Kali felt like the odd woman out as she thought of ways to divert her actions. Backing away, tears suddenly shining in her eyes, she couldn't help but open and close her mouth like a guppy. "I—I—"

"Speak, Kali, and speak fast, woman! What did you do?" Lenox demanded, his pupils expanding with power as he gripped Khamun's pushing form.

"I gave him what he wanted!" Kali screeched, playing with the ends of her hair, her foot tapping in sudden frustration. "Don't judge me! I hate seeing him go through this. Now that she's awakening and crap, it's like he's losing his damn mind! I had to help anyway I could, and he's been rejecting Marco's blood, so I had to do what he wanted!" she said in a rush, stepping back from the glaring males around her.

"Which was?" every male chimed in unison, while Khamun snarled, swinging, trying to get to the rest of the spilled blood.

Khamun suddenly collapsed against the couch, his body jerking to stop its seizure. The massive swell in his pants descended as he slowly gained his breath.

"I, er, I gave him Sanna's blood. Dr. Toure took a sample when she was seizing, and I happened to snatch the rest to protect her from Cursed spies! Don't judge me."

Every man in the room froze.

Kali backed up slowly again, almost falling over a chair as she thought about running but decided to hold her own. Male pride washing over her made the hair on the back of her neck rise as she fisted her hands and stared them all down.

"What? It helped him, yes. See. He's looking a whole lot better now. Better than when he feeds from those asswipes. So there, I did good."

Lenox shook his head and chuckled, Calvin ran a hand over his face, and Marco pulled out a trinity and lit it, giving Kali major side-eye as he slid his hands in his pockets.

"Kali, love, my man was already going through the effects of the mating lock, and now you just kick-started his damn Craving. He's officially in heat. Damn, woman! Good intentions, but fucked-up results." Lenox laughed and sat back.

Kali processed it all. "Um, oops." She awkwardly smiled as she held up her hands in defense. "I didn't think it was that bad. He can work through it, yes?"

"Hell, no!" every man in the room chimed at once, and they laughed hard.

Khamun slowly came back to reality, his hands flat on his thighs as he leaned forward. Head bowed, locks spilling like a curtain, his back expanded up and down as he inhaled then exhaled slowly. "Lock me up and don't let me leave tonight or tomorrow," he growled as he slowly stood. "Otherwise, your cousin is about to be introduced to a male Nephilim in his prime, and she doesn't know shit about me yet."

Marco walked forward and placed a reassuring hand on Khamun's shoulder while he helped him walk it off and head to his private chambers. "I got you, cousin. Just breathe it out and mediate on that shit."

Hesitating, Khamun kept his back to everyone, his fist clenching as his body shook again, "Kali, I'll talk to you later about this shit right here."

A reverberating punch into a wall made Khamun curse, his body shaking yet again. "Fuck! I need her, cuz," he said through clenched teeth.

Calvin yelled, "Ey, you put your sweaty hands on my cousin, and we got a problem. Ya dig?" He laughed just to calm his boy down as he shook his head and continued his banter. "You know she can't handle your Craving yet, and you fucked up the good couch, my man. Who gonna replace this shit?"

Lenox's brash laughter filled the room as he looked over the shredded and broken couch, wondering what the hell they were going to do with that busted couch.

"Hey! Why don't you all shut the fuck up and suck on a tic tac," Khamun roared, his hands cradling the back of his head. Extremely embarrassed, all he could do was shakily breathe as he slowly headed to his chambers for a long, cold bath and shower.

"I'm sorry," Kali whispered wide-eyed, before she skipped away with a sly smirk on her face. "I wish another female was in this house! Damn!"

Lenox ran a hand over the destroyed couch, using his gift to send it to storage and replace it with a new couch. "She did that on purpose. I hope you know, bro." He calmly plopped down on the couch.

Calvin threw a leg up on a nearby ottoman and took a swig of his beer. "Naw. Not Kali. She was looking out for him, ya know. Naw," he said out loud to himself.

Lenox shook his head. "Really?" He laughed as he reclined, remote in his hand, an apple on his knee. He flipped through the massive HDTV mounted on the graffiti-decorated wall. "She's a romantic, and like you just heard, when Khamun mates with Sanna, that will bring not one but two women. No, four, because you have to count Sanna's sister and Momma Tamar into our world or lives permanently. Kali won't be the only female anymore."

"Don't forget Miya. Damn! Good thing Amara and Miya are in the *A*. The team there definitely will have their hands full. Feel me?"

Rounding the couch, Marco gave Calvin a pound as he smiled. "House full of females? *¡Carajo!* Not gonna work, but damn if it won't be interesting." Taking a beer Lenox offered, he reclined in his chair. "I see why cuz is in love. She is sexy, and her spirit is beautiful. Baby got curves and softness in all the right places. So what we going to do to protect her?"

"Outside of the usual? Kali runs security twenty-four/seven. Calvin and I both drop by the house and Aset as much as possible. What you have in mind?" Lenox casually asked.

"So I was thinking, Khamun combs the neighborhood every night . . . why don't we make sure we watch the surrounding neighborhoods? When she moves, we move. We stay her shadow."

"Marco, man, that's Khamun's thang," Calvin said, "but I like what you saying. We stay in the cut. We move as Khamun's shadow when he can't or as additional backup. Yeah, good thought, because he's chilling now, so one of us can chill and watch her now."

Lenox kept an eye on the TV as he idly replied, "Exactly. We act as Khamun's blind spots. Hit up the enemy before they get at her."

"Drink to that shit!" Marco laughed. The hazel ring around his grey eyes, also known as a soul ring, marking him as something unknown, briefly emitted his Arch power as he roared.

The Bulls flashed across the screen. They'd won another game.

Chapter 14

"So you are telling me that the Initiates are gone?"

Light flickered and danced around, illuminating everything in its touch, leaving nothing but icy white tendrils in a cold, clean chamber. White and black glowing handprints that seemed to move adorned the resonating walls.

"Princess. They were immediately cloaked. Taken as *they* only know how to do. We couldn't risk any losses until we were sure we could obtain them."

"You couldn't risk any losses?"

"Yes . . . we—"

Pain suddenly sliced through the kneeling demon. He only wanted to appease the Princess, but he definitely now knew his choice of words was unfortunate. He looked down in utter shock at the well-manicured, razor-sharp nails, home to immaculate shining rings that now protruded, covered in his shiny black and red blood from his chest.

"I have a low tolerance for stupidity."

The Dark Lady dropped her mouth seamlessly against the demon's neck, tugging at the threads of darkness that sustained their kind. Moaning in ecstasy, she drank deeply, her hand that rested in the middle of the demon's chest slowly turning to clutch his rotting heart. Her fangs sank deep, ripping flesh. She pulled back a piece of flesh nestled between her delicate now ruby shining lips while she chewed then spat out gristle, as the husk of a demon lay at her feet like fallen sheets.

A soft chuckle flowed through the chamber as the Medusa slowly circled the husk of a shell, enjoying its once solid body now becoming dust. She wore her usual attire—thigh-high venom boots, black leather leggings that opened down the sides, held together by barbwire strings, accenting her deep-set curves, and black halter that cut down the middle and gave a peek of supple chocolate breasts and a bare back. Her braids were parted down the middle and fell down her back in two French-braided twists with pearl hair shells and African ornaments neatly braided into each strand. Around her neck was her tag, her black inlaid-diamond choker that marked her part of the Royal House. Along the side of her ribcage and right near her breasts were African tribal motifs beautifully tatted in script that stopped above her hipline.

Flicking her long, snake-like tongue, she walked slowly, each step reminding her of what she was and why she was this lethal hunter. Each step caused razor-sharp pains that steamed from her spine and traveled throughout her body, keeping her alert. She lived with the pain on a constant basis and was used to it. It was her master, and she was its prisoner.

"I assume you are not amused, Princess Reina." She carelessly glanced at her own venom-pumping nails then over at the platinum whistle.

Reina idly played with it as it hung from her delicate wrist. The whistle was not only the Medusa's leash, but it also doubled as a key to her collar.

The Medusa held a slight smile while she assessed her owner and confidant, "*¡Maldita sea!* You know what you have to do."

Reina sat, leg crossed, as she sucked each bloody finger and admired her all-white dress. The dress hugged every curve she owned and adorned her like spilling diamonds, exposing toffee-soft flesh from the dips of the sides of her hips, trailing down to expose ample naked thighs. If she turned, one could see the Egyptian-scripted tattoos that ran down her spinal cord accenting her naked back and hips, as well as the Asp bracelets that adorned each upper arm.

The front cut down her plush breasts, covering her nipples, showing butterscotch mounds that could seduce any man she wanted. If one's eyes traveled further, you could see nothing but exposed flesh leading to her crescent-shaped belly button. Yes, she knew she had a beautiful body, and she used it to her gain in hunting and snatching whatever prey she so chose.

Though her dress revealed all, it still held its own secrets. Weapons were strategically placed on her body and made to look like pieces of her clothes or jewelry, especially the spinal sword she wore, which looked like a back necklace. She could kill anyone with her hands or the many weapons she wore within less than a millisecond.

Dipping her hands in a crystal bowl full of cool water that her pet held in front of her, she cleaned the rest of the blood from her forearms and hands, studying the now pink water. Her reflection cast an image of a beautiful woman with kohl-lined eyes, plump lips, golden eyes, and thick mahogany hair that fell over her shoulder in a braid crowned with an Asp crown around her temple.

"Nydia, this means I want you to play, and I want you to sniff the bitch out and the two bucks who got away."

"Yes, Princess. That will be no problem. I found them once, and I will do it again." Nydia, also known as the Medusa, smiled. She knew how Reina loved good-looking men, and those who got away were just that. They were strong, good-looking, and, unfortunately, tainted by the Light. To break them and turn them would be no small feat, for Reina and Nydia definitely would enjoy watching.

"Once you get me the males, his Protector you can have for yourself. Daddy will be pleased when we take the Oracle, if that is what she is. You know his dreams are jaded."

Nydia nodded and reclined in an adjacent recliner, as they waited for the servants to bring in new toys and food to play with. Nydia didn't want the Protector, though mounting him for a bit wouldn't be a problem, but the one she really wanted plagued her dreams at night. Him and his syrupy chocolate-dipped skin and emerald eyes with the deep sultry Southern drawl, matched with a hard body meant for fucking, had her nipples and bud hard with the nasty dreams. Dreams she didn't want to have, and which were dangerous in this Society.

Being what she was and the fact that she was so close to the Royals, she could not afford to show any weakness. Her desire for the one she toyed with back in St. Louis could be her death and downfall. She wasn't about to let that happen. Even though Reina could be considered her best friend and would let her have anything she wanted, she was also notorious for her flippant predatory behavior. Nydia knew better, unlike the husk of the demon whose particles now floated in the wind.

Nydia knew what it was like to be in the shoes of the Oracle they currently hunted. She knew what it was like not to be protected by those who should have done their job. Should have been on the other side but wasn't. Yes. She knew what it was like to be broken and made to forget. Memories burned through her blood, hardened the protruding spinal disks in her back, which caused her daily pain. Pain and reminders that contorted her, made her cold, and changed her into what she was now. Dreams were dangerous here, and so were old truths.

"Yes. Your father has been a little off track with his dream-probing."

Winter, her close head attendant, walked in gracefully. Her midnight-black hair flowing like calm waves against her sapphire jewel gown showcased creamy, pale café latte skin and curves that represented her African American and Sicilian ancestry. Her sapphire blue eyes flashed as she presented the attendants to the Princess. A glint at her thigh let one know that she was not as she appeared. Winter was a Hunter and a Witch. She was the eyes for this team and was just as deadly as everyone in the room.

"Princess, your tea."

After taking the jade teacup offered, a tall, handsome, shirtless Nephilim in the process of turning Cursed kept his watery, grey-green eyes cast downward as he timidly poured Reina some blood tea.

Observing him from under her lashes, her honey hazel eyes revealed a silver soul ring that quickly disappeared when she blinked. She waited for him to kneel in front of her, as was customary, while she slowly took a sip and let a hand run down his wavy jet-black hair.

She had found this toy one night at a local Nephilim club. In his Prime, he had every woman trailing after him as he flirted through the club. When his eyes had settled on Reina's voluptuous form, he had no idea the tables would quickly turn.

"Amit, is it?" Reina sensuously smiled as he nodded. She hated that his glowing bronze skin was starting to fade due to the change, which was why she typically stalled the shift. She enjoyed turning him little by little, so she could keep him the way she liked it. All of her toys had to have glitter and beauty, and Amit was no exception. His East Indian beauty mixed with his Barbados accent made her eager in riding him hard while she studied him. She picked well. Very well.

Nydia snickered as she rose and looked over her shoulder. Reina was ready for sex, and Amit was expected to perform, as duty dictated. Taking the tea tray away, she watched Reina slid a hand over his collar and force him to look up. His light eyes briefly darkened with anger as his thick brows dropped in a frown and his hands clenched against his thighs.

Bad move, man, Nydia thought as she calmly sat back down to watch the games begin.

A swift backhand landed Amit on his back with Reina hovering over him, her hands clutching his throat as her nails cut into him and poison seeped into his skin.

"Is there a problem?" she hissed near his ears. Her braid draped over him as she inhaled his rich scent. She made sure her pets bathed in her favorite cologne, which made their existence better.

"No, no, Princess," he croaked.

She smiled, her fangs extending, her free hand sliding over his compact abs.

If Reina had been paying attention the way Nydia was, she would've seen how sick he looked. How he cringed at her touch. How he hated her and would attempt to kill her if he didn't still value his life so much. Amused, she tilted her head to the side as she watched.

Reina took a hold of his flaccid member, stroking slowly then roughly then slowly again, while his eyes fluttered closed against his will, and he expanded in her gripping touch.

"Good. For a moment I swear you thought you could be bold enough to challenge me. And we all know what happens if one of my pets takes it upon himself to sign his death warrant. Hmm?" She looked at the wall of pulsing handprints, which seemed to move as if alive. The wall of Purgatory. The home of Nephilim and humans they've chosen to keep as prizes, either for torture or to give the gift of the Bite to. Being on the outside was far better than being trapped within those walls, which expanded throughout the estate.

Amit nodded, anger keeping him in check as his hips suddenly pumped against her strokes. A groan escaped his closed mouth while Reina ran her silky tongue down his chest. Her deliberate search succeeded in finding his engorged head and had her swallowing him with an ease that had Nydia smiling again at her prowess.

Hated or not, she was the spoiled Princess, and what Reina wanted, she always got, especially with such talents as she was showing now.

Welcome to the Cursed chambers of the Dark Lady, Prince Reina A'archy y M'ylce, where leaving wasn't an option. Reina enjoyed the voyeurism. Sometimes it made things exciting for her. Other times she wanted to watch. Watch her favorite pet touch herself in heat from all the sex on display, just for kicks. So just like with all of Reina's toys, leaving wasn't an option for

Nydia. She had to sit and watch, her mind often drifting to the one she battled in St. Louis.

Amit's shiny girth had Nydia raising an eyebrow at his length. Like many Nephilim men, he was not lacking in the least bit.

Reina moaned and slid over him again, her fingers finding her heated core as two fingers dipped within. "Amit, do not ever *think* of challenging me," she hissed. "*¿Comprendes?*" She parted her dress and let him slide inside her dripping cave. Her back arched while she let his length find her spot, and she groaned.

"Behave and you live. Live to serve me and not be lunch for the rest of the Dark Society or the wall." Reina worked her hips in a slow circle, rolling them as she bounced up at the sound of Amit's muffled moans. She could tell he was trying to restrain himself but couldn't. Not with how tight she gripped him. She knew how much he enjoyed her slick walls and couldn't get enough of her addictive grip.

She fed from him through her body. The Light from him hit her core while she shifted the Curse bite and her poison, slowing its nature to change him. She bucked while his hips pounded up into her core. The force made her vibrate with each thrust. She slid her hands in the air then down her body to squeeze her perfect, round breasts. His vibrancy made her ride him harder, while she coated him with her wetness.

This was good. She got to feed, and now she got to fuck. She liked her choice of toy. He filled her nicely but not too much. For some reason she could never find a toy to fill her to that point of blinding ecstasy she needed. This was why she stayed hungry for hours longer.

Reina tilted her head to the side and eyed her best friend. She smiled as she watched her strum her own covered mound, her hips slowly twisting to her own pleasure. It pleased her that her best friend could get pleasure at the same time. That's all that counted. She wanted to share what she gained, and this was one of the gains.

Bowing forward, Reina climbed off her bucking mule and sat in her chair, her legs spread wide, and watched him come to his senses. She knew that he understood what she wanted next. She moaned as his beautiful hands spread her wider. His touch was on that knife's edge of hatred, of the venom she liked, and she bucked as his mouth touched her aching bud, his plush lips drawing it in with an angry suck, making her drip even more.

Yes, this toy was good. She would keep him a little longer, especially with how good and thick his tongue could be. Lost in the pleasure, she felt that tightness, that quick flash of warmth that she hated. The Light in her was coming out, and she hissed, pushing her pet to his back.

She closed her legs and gripped her chair, her body shaking at its cresting release, her wings suddenly ripping from her back.

Beautiful white, almost silver, wings filled the room, and her toy's eyes widened in wonder. She swore she saw a slick smile flash across his face as he crawled up and pushed her back, pinning her to the chair, his shaft surging deep in her, making her wings grow with her orgasm.

She screamed in anger. "*Nydia!*" She didn't want this Light. This was not good. She jerked with her toy's strokes, bringing her to more paralyzing pleasure. She had to stop this before her father saw her other side, the side he'd tried to kill off. The side she hated and which reminded her that she was a danger in this Dark Society. This side was what made her twin disappear because of his treachery, his death reminding her that she was alone in this.

"Winter!" She hated when her mind went there. Her beloved dark twin, now gone from her, killed in his insanity due to this Light in him, and to find out that she too was tainted with the same virus was enough to make her hate everything Light, even more than any Cursed.

Fear rolled through her as the back-to-back crests triggered the good. She formed her mouth to call her Dark Gargoyle again. Her whistle almost to her mouth as her new toy was flung backwards, she saw Winter standing beside her, running expert hands down her back to coax the wings into disappearing.

She closed her legs suddenly to stop the rest of the orgasm, but the sticky wetness between her thighs reminded her how good his touch felt.

Quickly trying to hide her mark of being a part of the Light when she shouldn't have been, she bit her lower lip, drawing blood, and rolled her shoulders in cold fury.

As she panted, she saw Nydia hold Amit by his throat and squeeze, blood trickling over her fingers, her reptile-like tongue flickering in and out in constrained anger. "You overstep your boundaries, servant," she said.

A low, clicking noise sounded from within Nydia as she stepped closer, inhaling the scent of sex and Light in the air. This was not good if the King came into the chambers. Everyone and everything would be killed on sight if the Mad King strolled through. Like father, like daughter.

"Get out now, or she will kill you on the spot— Or I will, regardless of how much she likes you." She whispered so low, she knew he almost didn't hear her. She licked the taint of sex and Light from the side of his neck, and his color seemed to return in a whispery glow.

She narrowed her eyes, something clicking within her briefly to say, "Run. Take the corridors to the grey panels. Then from there, take it to the river of purgatory, then you run. If I catch you, that pretty dick of yours will be on the Princess' mantel by sunrise." She dropped him and looked down at his wheezing frame, and he crawled away, pulling up his pants, then promptly stood.

Winter smoothly walked to the chamber doors and opened them. *"Move fast or die. Remember the help I gave you by influencing the Medusa,"* her soft voice whispered to his confused mind. With a sly smile, she placed a piece of wax paper into his hands without anyone seeing, as he rushed out of the room, eyeing everything around him before disappearing.

"Where is he going?" Reina asked weakly, her wings unhinging and disappearing again within her as she tried to shift forward in her chair with Winter's help.

Smiling, the Medusa slid on her leather gloves and adjusted them, making sure each nail slid in its slot. "Time to play."

Reina chuckled. She inhaled deeply, and her eyes suddenly flipped to a coldness that further chilled the already cold chambers. "Do bring him back whole. I did enjoy him, but I do intend to punish him some more. *¿Comprendes?*"

"As you wish, my Lady." The Medusa nodded slightly.

"If he escapes . . . "

Nydia inwardly flinched. Yes, if he did escape, the punishment would come from her flesh, but right now she didn't care. The rush of the hunt was pumping her blood and made her eyes flash in excitement. She exited the room promptly, noticing the smell of sex and light disappearing instantly.

Slowly moving through the corridors, the pain from her spinal protrusions had her dropping into a lethal predatory mode. Her nails scraped against the brick wall as she clicked her tongue. She could smell him and hear his heart beating a mile a minute as he ran.

He had made it to the woods faster than she thought, so she took a shortcut through an upper tower overlooking the woods from the main estate. The wind hit her face and she jumped. The door to the tower closed behind her.

Wet leaves mixed with dry ones crunched under her weight as she kneeled and touched the ground to pick up his heat signature. Lifting her hips to angle herself, she took off in a sprint faster than the human eye could see.

Behind her, the castle compound shimmered and flickered like dark smoke in the wind, revealing nothing but an old asylum protected by woods and abandoned buildings. While she ran, her breath frosted in the chilly air. She chuckled as she jumped over the creek. He was a determined one and moved faster than she thought.

She narrowed her eyes as she caught a glimpse of him in the moonlight, jumping over a wall and disappearing. Her trek had her following him through the streets of West Side Chicago, winding and panting, combing through cars and buildings. She noticed he wouldn't stop, so she called some of her own demonic Gargoyle brood to make this hunt the more amusing. Tiny beasts spilled on the street, running and hissing, sniffing him out, scraping the concrete asphalt.

"I will find you!" the Medusa yelled as she tracked his scent. It was only a matter of time.

Chapter 15

Sanna lay wide-eyed, tossing and turning, staring into the night air. She couldn't sleep. It was hot. Sweltering. And her lilac tee stuck to her like a second skin as if she had run a marathon. Her body ached, and something in her kept saying she couldn't stop. Her mind ached as usual, but this time it was different.

She hopped out of bed, walked to the kitchen, thinking she was going to grab some cold water. Instead, she ended up with keys in her hand and sitting in her black Toyota Camry. She started the car.

She jumped when the passenger door opened and Kyo climbed in with a yawn. "Where we going, sis?"

Half-awake, Sanna shrugged. "I have no clue. It feels like I need to drive, so let's drive."

"Mmm. Okay. I want a strawberry milkshake and fries from Mickey D's, so let's get some." Kyo reclined back and turned on her side, getting comfortable, and Sanna pulled off.

The streets were quiet as Sanna drove. She was still learning her way around Chicago, but so far she hadn't gotten lost, which tripped her out with tonight's joyride. She was in a part of the city she didn't know anything about, but somehow she was rolling through like she had grown up here.

Kyo lay snoring as Maxwell's "Pretty Wings" softly lulled both women into a sleepy daze. Chicago was strangely beautiful at night. Streets lay empty, outside of the usual wanderers or homeless that walked at night.

"Get up." Sanna shook Kyo as bright lights shined on both women. "I'm pulling into Mickey D's."

Smacking her lips, Kyo stretched and ran an idle hand through her disheveled hair. "Yay. Okay. Let's get White Castle's next."

Sanna stopped paying attention while she slowly drove up. She swore Kyo was sleeping so good that a little drool ran down her face. She huffed. She was doing all this driving in the night because something in her said leave, and now she sat pulling up into Mickey D's because her best friend, her sister, had a hankering for more food. That girl was eating more every day and not gaining one ounce of weight on her thick, curvy frame. She cut her eyes, side-eyeing Kyo with a smirk.

Neither woman noticed a running figure jet in front of them as they joked with each other.

"Damn! Do you have a tapeworm? *SHIT*!" She slammed hard on her brakes.

A young man, bloodied, sweating, and panting landed on the hood of her car, looking at her with pleading eyes. Cuts and gashes marked his body, and his ragged heaving cough seemed to emit a soft glowing mist that wrapped around his glossy dirty skin. Kyo promptly sat straight up as she gaped.

"Uh!" was all both women could say.

The young man waved his arms, screaming for help. He looked to his right then upward. Both women leaned forward to see what he was looking at.

Neither noticed him disappear then run to the back of their car and test the door, before hopping in the back seat. "Please . . . drive!"

Sanna screamed bloody murder as she looked behind her, the fear she saw in the man's eyes promptly made her speed off.

"Who are you? And what happened?" Kyo quickly asked as she looked behind her.

Nothing seemed to be after them, but the need to run was suddenly pumping through everyone's system.

"Slow down please, so you won't draw attention," the young man muttered. He closed his eyes and whispered prayers as they drove.

"Amit. My name is Amit."

Glancing behind her Sanna yelled, "Well, Amit, I'm calling the police! What in all that is good happened to you?"

"You can't. Wait, please."

Both women glanced at each other, and Kyo nudged Sanna.

"He can't come to our house," Sanna fiercely whispered. She shook her head, glancing at him from the corner of her eye, and then studied his disheveled form from her rearview mirror.

He hissed and then groaned in pain while he lay on his side, eyes closed, body shaking, and his arm wrapped around him, gripping his bleeding side. His lips were chapped, and he looked dehydrated, malnourished, and horribly pale.

Without a doubt this felt like the reason why she was up at two o'clock in the morning driving around Chicago.

"Well, you were the one who just *had* to drive in the middle of the night," Kyo whispered.

"What are we going to do?" Sanna gripped the steering wheel harder. "He looks like he needs a doctor, and he's barely breathing as is. This is crazy, Kyo."

Something had Kyo paranoid, looking behind the moving car, biting her lower lip and then glancing back to the bloody, dirty guy. Yeah, he needed help, any kind of help, but Sanna was right, whatever happened to him, taking him to their house would not be safe.

"Yeah, let's take him to the hosp—*Oh, no damn way! Sanna, go faster. Hurry*!" Kyo screamed. Her cookie monster house shoes flew to the window as a means of shielding herself and something landed with a thud that shook the whole car. Everyone looked around in panic.

Sanna hit her brakes, maneuvering her car between other traveling vehicles and gripping the steering wheel as panic ran through her system. "What is the"—She saw something inhuman that blended in the darkness. It scampered its way down the interstate, roaring and swinging a tail so thick, she swore it had to be a cable wire of some sort.

"Please, car, come on, baby. Come on. Move faster," Sanna chanted as she looked behind her again, her hair hitting her momentarily in her face.

"I'm so sorry, so sorry," Amit muttered as he pulled himself forward then ducked. "*Shit!*"

A propelled object of some short flew through the backseat window, blinking as everyone screamed. No bigger than a messaging tube, the object lit up as Amit grabbed it and quickly threw it back out of the window, and the object exploded as it flew behind them, causing the car to propel forward.

Sanna held on for dear life as she maneuvered the car. Tears streamed down her face as a migraine hit her, and her eyes rolled in the back of her head.

Kyo's screams sounded in her mind as her face contorted.

"No! No! Nooooooo, Sanna!" Kyo reached for the steering wheel as the car veered right, sliding down the highway sideways and heading for an approaching semi.

"Wake your friend up! What is going on?" Amit shouted as he tried to shake Sanna. His eyes were wide with fear as his hands wrapped around them, pulling them back. "*Duck!*"

The car hit a median and flew through the air, flipping and falling. Cars blared their horns, and police lights flashed in the night. A light so bright that it blinded everyone imploded through the sky, blanketing everyone and everything.

Sanna woke up, eyes wide as she looked around, her body glowing while she looked at her best friend and the terrified guy. She quickly clutched the steering wheel. Her body suddenly vibrated with power while she halted the Camry's descent in the air. Fear made her look around. She now clearly saw what was hunting them. *Monsters.* That was all her mind could compute about them before it shifted again. *Demons.*

The shape of a lone woman stood off from the light unable to enter the massive bubble as the things that followed turned into nothing but visceral dust and the car safely landed with a skid.

Everyone slowly stepped out of the car, staring in shock.

"Sanna?" Kyo whispered.

Sanna shook her head.

"I got this," Kyo muttered. She inhaled then extended her hands and pushed the bubble forward toward the woman.

Amit jetted to the right and grabbed a piece of steel piping. He smiled. "Time for some mother-fucking payback."

Sanna glanced sideways at him, and their eyes locked. Amit's mouth dropped open. He felt like she was reading his whole soul while his memories of what happened flashed before him, and he saw her eyes narrow as she quickly turned back around, anger flashing in her brown eyes.

Sanna flung her wrist, and the electric bubble seemed to get brighter and hummed.

Kyo jetted forward. Contorted-looking humans exited their cars from the side of the bubble, and she jump-landed a left hook on an approaching demon.

Everyone acted on instinct as Sanna walked forward and spoke behind her. "Rest a hand on my shoulder, Amit."

Briskly nodding, he complied, energy suddenly feeding his depleted body, and he let go, exhaling like he'd just stepped out of a refreshing shower.

"Wow! Thanks. What are you?"

Sanna shrugged and walked forward. "Hell if I know. Watch my back."

Adrenaline pumped through Kyo. She hissed, fangs suddenly dropping, as her mismatched eyes flashed, and her skin lightly shimmered with power. Everything her father had told her suddenly became reality. Memories of her as a toddler learning every style of martial arts she'd seen on TV from her father, mother, and grandparents flashed before her, making her body remember moves she had no idea she knew.

Her hands flung out, and she clawed at the entities that came from her left, right, and even her blind spots. Her body seemed to heat from within with a coolness and fire that collided with her adrenaline. She felt good, felt free. Something she hadn't experienced in a long time, except in her dreams.

As she moved, ducking under flying debris, her vision contorted and shifted, allowing her to see in the night air and adjust to any light that flashed by her. She felt like she was in a movie, and her breathing self-regulated as she ran. She remembered how her lungs used to feel like they were on fire whenever she attempted to run as hard as she was now.

She took a couple of deep breaths and jumped. Wind hit her face as she almost felt as if she was flying, and she instinctively tightened her legs then laughed. Her feet landed right in the middle of a huge barrel of a man. She watched him fly back, taking a door of the truck with him, before promptly standing back up, shaking his body, and spitting onto the ground.

The man seemed to bristle as his face briefly flashed, looking like a rhino and python all rolled up into one. His fangs extended, and poisonous spit dripped from his open mouth.

Something in her had her ready for this fight as she braced herself. If he bit her, she prayed to all that is good that she didn't die.

Eyes flashing, her own hiss sounding in the air, her nails glinted in the moonlight as the big beast of a thing ran toward her. What she was fighting now, she had always thought she'd run from, if ever she was an actress in a movie, but tonight proved to be different. She was protecting not only herself but her family and all these innocent people.

She felt her body lift from the air as the thing hauled her up and threw her down on a nearby car, glass shattering and cutting into her body.

She screamed and sideswiped the demon as she rolled over on her stomach panting. Amazement hit her. She blinked when she realized the glass didn't penetrate one ounce of her skin and shards lay around her. She brushed her hands over her body to dust the crumbled glass away from her then planted her feet on the hood of the car the demon had placed her on and kicked out, landing her foot right into his hissing face.

Another grab by the demon had her soaring over his shoulder as she landed on her feet in a low crouch. She saw the thing turn from her and try to head toward Sanna. She scraped her hard nails across the asphalt surface, sharpening them.

"Hey, asswipe!" she yelled and jetted forward. "We are not done."

She jumped on his huge back, dropping all of her weight on him, to put him in a choke hold, and then flipped him over her body.

Turning in a full circle, she saw an old man watch her, a sinister look on his face as he breathed hard. The way he watched her creeped her out and had her really feeling as if she was in a scary movie.

She jumped on the huge, burly demon she was currently fighting and sliced her hands down his body, ending his life swiftly and severing his head. "Making sure your ass doesn't get the fuck back up!"

Smirking, she ducked at that old man who jumped out on her blind side. Flipping back, she dipped again as he sideswiped her with a quick punch to the face.

Kyo shook her head, her vision blurred. She felt as if the wind was knocked out of her. That little old bastard had a mean right hook.

Stepping back, she fanned herself and took in the sight. This man looked like your average, run-of-the-mill elderly man with grey hair, a newsboy cap, button-down vest, and slacks. *Yeah, looks could be deceiving.*

The old man looked up at her and smirked. Evil filled his face. An animal-like tongue whipped from his mouth before his face disappeared and a contorted, mutated beast of a face revealed itself before going back to its human appearance.

Kyo titled her head back and looked toward the heavens, asking for forgiveness for hitting a crazy elderly man.

Instantly as she motioned toward the crazy old man, she was promptly thrown back by an invisible force cast by that old bastard.

Kyo's form flew in the air and dropped into a rolling thud. She pushed herself up but was held down by invisible hands as the old man stalked her slowly, his movements jerky like that of a zombie but only faster.

She hissed and clawed, but nothing was helping her up, until she felt Sanna's power bubble split and cover her, and the old man let go in sheer pain.

Kyo rolled away, moving fast behind him, and landed a blow that had her amped. "Damn!" She grinned as she landed from a swift roundhouse kick flush to his face. She knocked the old man clean out as he lay on the ground near her feet, like a stretched-out praying mantis on acid. She was done playing. She knew she had to finish him fast.

She dropped down, her hands wrapping around his obtuse neck and twisting it until it snapped. Her stone-hard nails sliced into the thick flesh that seemed to peel away as she ripped the head off.

Jetting up, she moved like the wind. Her eyes scanned the area, finding more prey.

Just then an Escalade pulled up with a team of motorcycles behind it. Something told her they could be trusted, whoever they were. She shrugged and went on with her attacks.

She circled around wherever Sanna moved, and she sped over cars, jumping and soaring in the air, moving like lightning. Nothing was allowed to touch her best friend. Nothing. And she meant it.

Chapter 16

She didn't know what was going on with her, but she knew this guy needed help and after she clearly saw the torture, which she didn't understand he went through, justice needed to be had. She couldn't believe she could do this, let alone fight. She ducked from a jumping monster that snapped at her neck. She screamed then dropped her hand and swung up, snatching the monster woman by the shoulders. She pulled her with a ferocity she didn't know she had and let that beast drop down right against her knee.

The woman grunted and swung out, but Sanna backed up from the slash and sent her Tweety bird covered house shoe right into the she-monster's face. Black-red blood spilled everywhere as she laid her hands on the demon. She felt her power ebb within her then pushed out into the entity's molting form and blasted her into the sky.

"*Duck!*" Amit yelled and he swung the pipe like a bat and knocked off the expanding head of a nearby demon with a bright smile. "*Score!*" he yelled, pointing in the air as the head exploded and disappeared in the night sky. Tendrils of darkness seeped through the air, and Amit began his chanting.

Sanna found herself doing the same, repeating every word he said. As she moved through the congested and destroyed interstate section, she realized he was speaking spiritual hymns and verses from the Bible.

The tendrils of power that ebbed from his body and Sanna's lit up like a thousand Christmas lights as they flew around and misted in the air. "Beautiful," she whispered, looking around at the flowing bursts.

As she moved to run, a tall golden-haired man with chiseled, handsome features that could rival any Hollywood actor's stepped out of a skewed limo. He walked past an unaware human who held up a cellphone recording everything.

While the man locked eyes on Sanna, he smirked, brushed off his shoulders, and punched his hand through the innocent bystander's chest. Blood and flesh rained everywhere as he flung the body, licked his hands, and wiped them off with a handkerchief.

Sanna swallowed deeply as the man-thing continued his descent toward her. She heard him mutter, "I want you."

Ice filled her veins instantly in fear. This man wasn't normal, especially with his eyes glowing pure ruby red, and his body seemed to double in size.

Locking on to him, her mind seemed to connect to his, and she gagged. Tears of anger formed in her eyes as she spat.

This bastard was a well-known social diplomat and PR rep for the Bulls. He had just left his office after working a late night. The thing was, this bastard had assaulted his secretary, a woman he had just hired, raping her and throwing her in a closet to bleed to death. She knew this wasn't his first time doing such a then and she realized this was his M.O. a monster who got off assaulting women.

Fury unlike anything she had ever felt flowed through her, hazing her vision as she ducked from his snatch. She jabbed an elbow into his hard ribcage, searching for whatever she could to hit him hard on his skull with. Her mind ripped open with a synergy unlike anything. She yelled and blocked his punch as she tried to run.

His hand reached out for her and got a fistful of her hair.

Tears spilled down her face. Sanna reached behind her, her nails digging into his forearm as he lifted her in the air with a jerk. The force of it made her mind scream, *Oh, hell naw!*

A static charge jolted through her, and she was ecstatic. Her mind slashed through his body, seeing everything that made this monster evil. She honed in on the very DNA of the thing. She exhaled, pulled then let go as she snapped her fingers.

The monster's eyes bulged out as he dropped her. He reached out and gripped his throat then roared before imploding into nothing but red black visceral mist, each drop glowing with white light as it flowed behind her.

The fast-moving, arching, tunneling droplets of lights made her swiftly turn. She saw a man with locks fly by her, running on the top of cars, his movement graceful yet predatory. She felt her body hum with rapid desire as she watched him. That mist wrapping around him as it shot back from his body into pure light through the sky. It was a symphony of beauty.

"You okay, cousin?"

A hand made her jump and swing as she blinked. Her hands flew up to her face as she saw Calvin duck, a slick smile on his face.

"Damn! Good reflexes. You okay, San?" Calvin looked his cousin up and down. He reached out to turn her around. She looked good. No scratches, just fear and anger swallowing her eyes as his mouth dropped open. She was fully awakening into her power. Her skin glowed softly, and he could feel his body humming with her gift so much, he had to let go because of the strength.

"Yeah, I'm okay. What are you doing here? Wait! Amit!" Sanna turned. She snatched at a bloodied and dirty young man hobbling past her, clutching his sides, something nestled in his hand. He was dressed in nothing but white pants with a black-and-platinum collar.

Glancing down, the guy was holding a steel dented pipe. Calvin knew what was up—an Initiate.

"He needed our help. Well . . . still does. We need to call the police. I don't know what's going on, but those bastards are *crazy*!" Sanna instantly went into rambling, explaining everything that happened.

Calvin just crossed his arms, watching closely. Kyo ran by in his peripheral vision. She flew through the air as she sprinted and jumped off demons' shoulders and back. She screamed and clawed, her skin glittering in the moonlight. Girly was bad, and it was an honor to see both her and his cousin in action.

"Slow down, San," Calvin said. "We have to get you all out of here and contain the mess." He gently tried to lead her and Amit away but only succeeded in being halted in his footsteps.

Sanna grounded her feet and stared ahead. "Wait. Is that Khamun?" A part of her power bubble seemed to follow not only Kyo, but it also trailed a man who looked intimately familiar to her in an instant. It moved with him as he hacked at demons, using a sword she had only seen in movies. Her mouth dropped as she swore she saw fangs gleam in the moonlight. She watched him snatch a running monster and fling it like it was a rag doll.

Calvin quietly bobbed his head, trailing an approaching figure. His emerald eyes glowed as they narrowed. A clicking sound echoing around them made him push Sanna behind.

"What is it, Calvin? Wait. But am I crazy, or was that Khamun?" Sanna tugged his arm, her fear raising the hair on his body as she quietly asked, "What is going on?"

Ignoring his cousin, Calvin shifted on his feet. He watched his team take down demons that seemed to pop up like roaches.

"Kyo!" he yelled. "Come get Sanna and Amit *now*! Take them to the Escalade! Kali is waiting!" His body alerted him of the approaching danger, and he held his arm out to block his cousin.

He sneered as he saw Kyo halt mid-kick to hook a demon behind her knee and flip him to the ground before stomping on its head. She grinned with triumph while nodding to run, and grabbed a fighting Sanna. His confused and battle-amped cousin sent another demon flying with just a flash from her glowing eyes.

She was here. The Medusa. He could sense her, and this was not good. Looking through the power bubble, he could make out her curvy form and he rolled his shoulders, so she couldn't get through. Excellent.

He could tell she couldn't see either, because she kept slashing at the bubble, trying to get in while peering in, but she only ended up burning herself in the process. This was good. The more she tried to get through, the more she hurt herself.

"Sanna! See that woman?" Calvin yelled.

Sanna paused outside of the Escalade and turned to get a good look. "Yes!" she shouted back.

"Knock her ass out with a power burst. Ya feel meh?" Calvin smirked. His eyes glowed with warmth, letting her know she could do this.

Sanna took a deep breath. She bit her lower lip, looked around at the many demons that hopped out of cars and noticed the innocent people who ran, trying to get away. They needed protecting, and if she could do it, she would.

"I'll try!" She flung her hands out with a push, but nothing happened. Closing her eyes, she tried it again, with no results. "Um, see . . . I don't even know how I did what I did, cousin!"

Calvin gave a lighthearted laugh and flung a hand out. His protection sigils glowed on his arms and hair as he glanced at her with glowing eyes. A set of demons flew backwards, knives protruding from their chests.

Sanna screamed, and everything seemed to go silent as demons lifted in the air, hit the bubble barrier, and imploded. She saw who she knew was Khamun on his knees in a shower of black-red blood.

His eyes closed, dark silver wings extended as his head dropped back and white light flowed through him. The tendrils of black mist swirled him and entered him before expelling itself from his body.

"Hey, Sanna! *Mami*, it's me, Marco. Do that again!"

Turning, she saw the one named Marco yell at her as he stood at the bubble's edge, sword ready. She blinked, tears in her eyes while she dropped the bubble, and pushed out, letting her power wrap around Marco as he smiled at the Medusa. She heard him taunt his prey with his laughter.

"*¿Me acuerdas?* Remember me? Tell *mi gemelo*, my twin, that I'm not dead and that we have some unfinished business."

The hazel ring around Marco's grey eyes expanded, and he sent the crazy-looking woman flying with a kick and mental push. Her screech filled the air as she disappeared. His eyes returned to their steel grey color, and he turned to kick a team of demons. He took them down in one move, slicing and shooting them as they crumbled into nothing but visceral matter.

Amit seemed to closely watch. His eyes narrowed as he pointed out demons that were trying to surround Marco.

Sanna screamed again. She saw a tall, dark-haired man running, guns pointed, blasting demons' heads off as if he were doing nothing but shooting at a gun range.

Calvin moved to the side and disappeared before popping back into view, guns blazing. A sizzling pop of power escaped his fisted hands while he flashed a lopsided smile.

"Oooo wee! You see that chump go flying? Lookie here. Nothing like charred demon to make a brotha feel right. After tonight, shit, I'm hunting for some nice, soft booty!" he yelled while laughing. He jumped on a hood of a car, shooting off rounds, kicking entities in the face and occasionally glancing behind him to make sure Sanna was okay.

She saw Marco's smirk as he moved through the crowded streets. Her cousin was something she had no idea about. He moved like an experienced soldier, finding his prey and slicing them down the middle or just blowing them away. Sometimes she swore his body would glow with some inner power.

As she watched, Calvin dropped into a low dip and came up kicking demons on a handstand. The ground underneath where he touched lit up and cooked demons where they stood. This was powerful stuff, and it blew her mind away. She didn't know what was what, or why it was happening to her, but she couldn't help but be impressed by it all.

Looking around again, she saw that Khamun had gotten up and was slicing demons with his wings. They seemed to harden like blades and that tripped her out. He had wings! The man she was just flirting with yesterday, who was doing quality and beautiful work on her restaurant, now stood feet away, moving like an assassin and taking down monsters like it was everyday thing.

"Kali. I need to know what in all *hell* is going on? Who are you people?"

Her cousin Kali sat quietly behind the steering wheel while she watched. Her mouth was silently moving as she clicked on an iPad. Cars seemed to light up and move as if she controlled them.

An old Buick shifted on and drove itself into a tank-size demon, taking it down as a Ford pivoted from the right and ran the thing over, slicing it in two.

"We are Protectors." She activated another car. She sent this one colliding into more entities.

"What does that mean, cousin? Talk to me please. I'm freaked out here."

Kyo stood at her side, her reptilian-looking eyes dilated, and her skin seemed to sparkle with the shifting moon. Her nails seemed to have lengthened, and they sparkled like granite. Fangs protruded from her sister's mouth as she breathed. Confusion danced across her pretty face.

"Kyo?" Sanna gently touched her shoulder, and she shook her head.

"I don't know, sis."

Sanna glanced at Kali, who sat looking at her hands, then resorted to touch her own softly shimmering skin as she tilted her head to the side.

Kali gave Sanna a matter-of-fact look as she spoke. "When I say we are Protectors, I mean you as well."

Everything felt like her mind was compounding on itself. Not like her typical migraines, but as if something was breaking open in her mind. Slowly rubbing her temples, she shifted in her seat. She was ticked. Just a few seconds ago, she stood in the chilly morning air, in her PJ's and slippers, disheveled and sore. She just pulled off the best magic trick in the world, and everyone was clustered around her talking in code? *Yeah, fuck the protector crap!* "I'm going to ask this again, and I want the cryptic dialog to stop. You are my blood! Kali, what is up?" Sanna pleaded again.

Kali frowned. "I can't exactly say just yet, cousin. Trust me. You need time to know what this all is about, and I promise we will talk about it. But, first, your safety is a must. We need to get you to safe land and make sure this area is clear. We have a team coming in to do just that, so it won't take long."

Sanna was about to pry again when Amit chimed in, "She doesn't know she's Nephilim? All this shit that went down and she doesn't know?"

Kali rolled her eyes and eyed the young man. He was fine but dirty and bloody. His skin seemed to flicker and dull whenever he coughed, and she knew that was not a good sign. The attire he wore and the collar around his throat let her know that he was a Cursed chosen, an Initiate.

Frowning she was curious as in how he escaped and why he wasn't turning yet. "Who are you?"

Amit glanced up and wanted to smile, but he wasn't feeling it today. He felt it might be a long time before he felt the rush of flirting again. He just ran a tired hand through his jet-black hair and licked his chapped lips.

"Amit. I was taken two months ago, and I managed to escape because they wanted to hunt me for sport."

Kali raised an eyebrow studying him. He was cute. Very cute. But damn if she didn't feel sorry for him. She noticed Sanna and Kyo looking back and forth as they listened in confusion.

"Two months? And you seemed to not be turning. Hmm. We'll talk shortly," she quietly responded.

"Hey. I had a life before I was taken. I was in school. I know my family is wondering where the hell I'm at. I need to contact them as soon as possible," Amit demanded.

"That will happen soon. You know the protocol. We have to inspect you and clear you for safe return into Society."

The hell with all the questions, Amit inwardly scoffed. He tucked the wax piece of paper his former Initiate trainer Winter had given him in his waistband and waited. Whatever it was, he figured, he'd find out later, but in the meantime his hands felt like they were on fire, and his body like it was hit by a semi-truck. He ran a hand over his hair and exhaled with a quick glance toward Sanna and Kyo.

"Since cousin Kali isn't talking, what is a Nephilim, Amit?" Kyo calmly asked, her eyes narrowing as she crossed her arms over her chest.

Sanna shook her head and glanced at Amit. His tired eyes slowly scanned her again. She felt that tug of concern and exhaled slowly. The screeching and hissing of approaching demons roared around her. People screamed. Cars flew and blew up, yet everything seemed to go into slow mode as she read the answers to the question and couldn't believe it.

Gently touching Sanna's shoulder, Kyo whispered, "You okay, sis? You kind of zoned ou"—As Kyo rested her hand against Sanna, she saw that Sanna's dilated eyes had expanded. That touch let her instantly see what Sanna had gleaned from Amit. That pain and that reality sparked fresh tears in both of their eyes and made Sanna back away in rage.

Kyo couldn't believe it. "No damn way. This is a joke?"

"I'm thinking not so much." Extending a hand, Sanna looked around and shook her head.

Amit dropped his steel pipe and moved to get out of the car. "They have to protect you. It is the way Society works. You are a living legend," he said.

Sanna tilted her head to the side and followed Amit outside of the car. She stepped back as Kyo placed a hand on her shoulder again. "What do you mean?"

"He means that you are something called an Oracle-Vessel. I don't know what it means. I just know daddy told me that I was born and raised to protect you from"—Kyo paused, looking around, ducking before she continued on. "I guess those things out here. He told me that people would come around to help me in protecting you. I guess these are the people."

"Whoa. What do you mean, daddy told you, Kyo? You knew something I didn't know? You've been lying to me?"

Kyo shook her head and she held both hands up. "No, no. I just found out and not by much. I promise."

Sanna locked eyes on her best friend, her eyes dilating again, and she sighed, "Okay. I just need to process this. I'm sorry for accusing you of anything."

Kali slammed a hand on the steering wheel, jerking everyone's attention her way. "Got your ass!" She looked up, smiling as she pointed.

A man built like a wrestler lay smashed under another car.

Sanna rubbed her temples as blood colored the road like finger-painting.

"This is crazy," Kyo muttered.

Amit nodded his head in agreement. "Sure is. But this team seems to know what they are doing. Never seen one in action ever."

Kali scoffed as she adjusted in her seat. "You must be strictly Society bred, huh?"

Amit tilted his head to the side and flashed a smile. "Actually, no. Came here from Barbados. I was in training to be enrolled in the Chicago team while in college, but . . . shit happens, huh?" He tapped his collar and crossed his arms. He shifted on his feet to stand closer to Sanna as a means to protect her.

"Really? What are your talents? Disciple."

Amit shook his head with a chuckle. "I have some sight and a taste of white light power in the form of healing. That's it. I'm good with tech shit and weaponry."

"Interesting. You sure you are just a Disciple?" Kali yelled, "Amit, *block her*!" Daggers flew from her hands and out of the open passenger door, connecting with a flying demon as a gunshot took its head off. It fell to the ground and misted.

"I hate those damn things," a voice said.

Kyo, Amit, and Sanna slowly stood up, eyes locked ahead of them. They saw a figure walk through the mists in all-black, combat boots, and a gun pointed at the sky before shifting to strap to his back.

Blood covered everyone, and Sanna had to keep herself from screaming and crying over it all.

"Damn good work out there, Sanna . . . and about time."

Licking her chapped lips and blinking, she saw Lenox as he smiled. If she had a better sense of mind, she would have commented that he looked damn good in all that black. His curly black hair was pulled back with a grey skullcap to keep it out of his face. He moved through the chaos and nodded. His icy blue eyes almost glowed white. *This is crazy*, ran in Sanna's mind again.

Lenox eyeballed Amit and noticed a small piece of wax paper in the waistband of his pants. "What is this?" he asked as he quickly snatched it and rubbed it between his fingers. As soon as he touched it, the paper turned into a perfumed dust that formed a symbol in the air, and Lenox's eyes slowly closed.

"We have an ally. Whoever she is used old Light magic cloaked by Cursed magic. Very smart and untraceable, it makes me wonder if it is a setup. Let me see your hands, man." Lenox grabbed Amit's hands, flipping them up and down before staring at his palms.

Sanna studied an exhausted Amit who looked as if he was going to speak up, but fatigue made him sway, causing Sanna to step forward. She moved Amit's hands out of Lenox's and dropped them to his side. "Amit will talk with you later about who gave him that. Okay?"

Lenox just smiled and nodded as Sanna looked around in a circle, noticing everyone who had recently come into her life. She opened her mouth to question everyone, but Kyo took the words out of her mouth.

"What the hell is this? Underworld and Blade?"

As Sanna got ready to go into questioning mode again, Lenox moved out of the way and she saw Khamun walk through. Her mind instantly locked up, and her body tensed. She thought she was going to have another seizure. He was the one from her dreams. He stood in the same posture, weapons in his hands, and a look of pure desire in his eyes. The only difference was, he had huge wings that were now folded and a pair of fangs that had her backing up into the Escalade.

"This has to be a joke," she muttered.

Khamun dropped his weapons, walking up to her, and bent down. He snatched the very air from her as his mouth melded with hers.

The world seemed to tilt sideways and then upside down as a moan escaped her mouth. He made her body light up like a beacon. His mouth was sweet and heady. Everything she had experienced in her dreams and his body was exactly what she'd wanted. She couldn't keep herself from fisting her hands in his locks as he lifted her, pressing her against his hard frame. She could feel his length pressing into her, demanding her attention. He drew in her lower lip, suckling, before teasing her lips apart and sliding a silky tongue over her own.

"My damn!" And her world shook as a final seizure overtook her body. Her hands gripped this man as tears spilled down the corners of her eyes and pain sliced through her. She didn't want to go out like this. She wanted this man all over her, through her and in her. *Damn, he smelled so good!* And she blacked out.

In that same moment, she heard his sensually deep voice say, "I'm taking her home."

Chapter 17

Soft music flowed through her senses while she tried to open her eyes. Her body felt like Hell. A smile slid across her face as she turned her head on the softest cloud feeling pillow she had ever felt in her life. Deciding not to fight her body's demand to stay where she was, she tried to access where she was as silky smooth sheets kept her comfortable.

"Just rest and don't fight it," a familiar voice poured out, her making her body hum. She knew she could trust that voice. She knew that voice would set everything right and protect her or give her something more. That something more could happen. Something she so wanted but she was too exhausted for.

"I'll give you everything you need if you let me, but I need you to rest, beauty."

Slovenly nodding, Sanna sighed and let her still shut eyes settle close. She wondered where she was. She remembered being told she was going to be taken home, but where she lay did not in anyway feel like her bed. Actually where she lay felt like . . . Flashes of memories hit her, and everything played in her mind like a movie in reverse. The sights, the sounds, and the crazy. It all hit her hard as she abruptly sat up panting. Her eyes were wide as she hysterically looked around and stopped on the man who sat in front of her.

He was dressed in black drawstring pants, and his white beater loosely hugged his chiseled chest. His locks were braided back in a knot. He held out a glass of water. "Drink for me please."

Sanna frowned and got ready to decline, just to ask where she was but was cut off.

"Have I ever given you reason to not trust me? Look in my eyes and you know the truth."

Something made her comply and she stared, swallowed hard. She quickly felt hot in all the wrong places as she flushed and turned her gaze away, taking the glass and drinking the ice cold water down. Looking around, she saw she was in a nice bedroom. She was in a massive bed, and various works of art hung on the walls.

"You're at my private house. You have nothing to worry about here. You can't be tracked."

Slowly sipping, she dared to look up again as she saw a brief flash of fangs. Something in that had her biting her lower lip. Her kitty was purring too hard right now. She wished it would shut up. She needed to know where exactly she was and how to leave if the need arose, though she didn't feel like it would.

"Where is my godsister at? Where's Amit?"

The man from her dreams and from her restaurant leaned forward on thighs. He took the glass from her, and she swore it disappeared like a magic trick as he reached out and slid a hand through her thick, crinkly afro.

"Kyo is asleep in the room next to you, and she'll be up around five p.m. Amit is at the compound and being examined. He was bitten, but somehow his infection was changed in some way. We are trying to figure out in what way, and if he will be a threat or not."

That had her shaking her head as she stared at the man she knew as Khamun. "He's okay. He won't be a threat. You need him, and he'll be able to help."

A soft smile played at Khamun's mouth as he studied her. "And how do you know that, San?"

How he said that, had her feeling like royalty and she tried to shake it off, clearly affected by his presence and scent. He smelled too damn good. But he did ask a damn good question. She didn't know how she knew Amit would be okay. She just did.

A memory flashed through her of Amit touching her shoulder, and she clutched her temples.

"Drink some water and take it slow, San. You'll ride through it like you always do." Khamun ran a hand down her back, causing her body to react.

She looked up fast then reached for him, her mouth capturing his as she almost fell out of the bed, drinking his sweet mouth like she was starving.

His groan ripped through her body while he adjusted her by gripping her rear, squeezing and pulling her from the bed and unto his lap.

She felt like her body was ready to break into a thousand pieces if she couldn't have him against her. For some reason, she knew he felt the same way.

"Baby, let me talk to you. Let, let me try to— Shit, woman," escaped his mouth as he broke the kiss. He found her neck, sucking, licking and lightly biting, causing her to arch against his hold.

She felt his fingers play at the elastic band of her PJ shorts before shifting and sliding down to cup her pulsating mound. She couldn't keep her hands off of him. She kissed his toffee mahogany skin, licking at his neck and wanting more from his caressing touch. She knew when her hips started pressing and rocking against his eager hand that she was about to lose her sanity. His breathing had her heady, especially as his hand that gripped her ass began massaging.

"Damn! You are real," she half-moaned, as his fingertips pushed the fabric of her PJ shorts and underwear to the side to find her drenched nether lips.

She heard her name break from his searching lips as he stroked then pulled back, eyes closed, fangs getting longer. "Sanna . . . "

She had never been the one to make the first move ever. She had never had a man touch her like this and clearly want her like this. He came to her with no games or lies woven in the mix. She clearly saw this man was in agony. He wanted not just her wet haven but all of her.

That made her cup his face as she curiously kissed his lips lightly then licked a fang. "Talk to me then," she cooed, and she smiled on the inside, proud of herself for being bold in this moment.

Khamun almost couldn't breathe with the pressure of wanting Sanna so intensely. His shaft was at the point of cussing him out from being so engorged, and all he could do was take this woman and lay her on the bed as he attempted to calm his own desire.

He knew if he did what he knew they both wanted, he might scare her in his eagerness, so he had to take this slow. He had to talk in order to pace his overdue desire. He also knew he had an obligation to tell her about her history before taking it to the next level. So he inwardly cursed and pulled back, kissing her fingertips, running his hands over her softness. He kissed her belly, his tongue dipping in her cute belly button before resting his forehead on her stomach to talk.

"I—I've wanted you for a long time. But you don't even understand what I mean by a long time."

He thought he was going to die as he felt her undo his locks. She loosened each strain to comb through them slowly and sensually while she spoke to the top of his head, her fingers occasionally caressing his earlobes. "What do you mean, hmm?"

The lightness and surety in her voice had him clutching the sheets at her side as he heard her smile.

"Shit! Look, Sanna, I need you to pay attention." He almost wanted to kick himself for the whine that came out of his mouth. He was the one in control here. He had to honor her and make this right. It was the right thing to do. Before he got his rocks off and truly showed her how lovemaking between the two of them could be in the reality.

Damn! Her scent was driving him, and the wetness between her legs had him thirsty.

"I am listening. You want to tell me what this means, and you are hoping I won't cuss you out and want to run."

He shut his eyes tight while he swallowed. The spasm of pleasure that ripped through him made him bite his lower lip as her hands slid down his back. It was as if her nails purposely scraped up and down his back, just to torment him. The way she combed through his locks again had his thighs clenching tight. He'd never had experiences with Oracles except for his mother, so the fact that she knew that much slightly tripped him for a moment.

"Yeah, San. See, baby, I've been watching you since I was nineteen. It would have been birth, with my father watching you while he trained me until maturity, but my mother was having blocked Oracles visions, so yeah, slipped through our hands. Now I know why."

Running a hand over his jaw, Sanna cupped his face and tugged for him to slide upward, which he did. Their lips met lightly as both moaned.

Khamun gripped her hip, lifting her so he could position himself to press his already diamond-hard shaft against her waiting yoni. He tugged on her lower lip, drawing it between his own lips, and he nibbled and nipped, being cautious with his fangs. His eyes almost crossed as her leg slid up over his rear and pressed him against her.

"And you've loved me for a long time, I see."

He couldn't talk anymore. He could only let her stroke him as she read him like a book with just a touch. She blew his mind, and she smiled as he felt their minds lock and he fed her all he wanted to verbally say.

Her body tensed, and she let go as he pulled back. "They killed my daddy? Then tried to kill my momma, and my brothers? And me?"

Nodding, Khamun gently cupped her face. He let her read more, and tears slipped down her soft cheeks as she learned her history. He watched her sit up, set her hands on his shoulders to push him back, and he complied, moving to sit back in his chair.

"Talk then," she softly said. She studied his face, her arms suddenly cradling herself.

So he talked and told it all. Talked to her about how brave her father was and how brave her mother still is. Told her about how his cousin had to keep his life a secret in order to protect her normalcy.

He told her how they were all still trying to understand how her father was able to hide her this long. He then told her how the rules of Society dictated that he never cross the boundaries of being with her and how he broke them. Projecting his hard-to-control desires for her through dreams and fantasies, he explained, was his only way he could have her without full-out breaking guidelines.

Exhaling, his hands briefly slid down his face. He told her how Society was broken up by different Nephilim houses, and he explained what exactly a Nephilim was. A breed of chosen angels whom adapted through the generations to be what they were now, Hunters of the Cursed, and Protectors of humans and hidden Nephilims, such as herself. He also explained how she was called a Vessel because she was the reincarnate of a Nephilim warrior in their long past, and that one day that spirit would reveal itself to her.

He watched as she took it all in. Her eyes undulating from time to time, letting know him know she was reading for lies.

He explained that their kind cannot lie but can hold back truths, and that only the players for the Dark can lie.

She reached out and touched his hand, lacing her fingers through them as he spoke on. He knew she was reading him and learning more with just a touch.

Her head dropped as she sighed and wiped tears away. "So my migraines are due to me maturing into this gift, as well as being a Vessel? And Kyo is my life Protector? So what are you then?"

Khamun studied her and leaned forward as he placed hand against her heart. "I'm your lifemate. Kyo would act as a bodyguard of sort of the both of us, since I have no Gargoyle, but I would be your shield because you are my mate and other half of me, baby." He watched her blush, and he quickly added, "If you'd have me, I mean. But we have time for that crap later. What we need to do is get you and Kyo trained and to help you both through the rest of your awakening. I'm guessing that your brother and sister are somewhere sitting confused because they just awoke too. I have Calvin hitting them up. You can call them too if you want."

"Oh. That is good. Thank you. But what *are* you?"

He knew what she was asking, but he couldn't formulate how to explain what he was exactly. "Something different, something dangerous," he wanted to say, but he kept that to himself. He softly smile. "Baby, I'll try to explain that later. We have plenty of time."

Searching her face, he couldn't figure out where her mind was, until she slid off the bed and sat on his lap, holding him, crying.

He exhaled and held her tight, rubbing her back slowly. He knew she needed to process this all, and no matter how much he wanted her, he knew it wasn't the time. Tonight was something else.

***

The afternoon brought with it a warm and soft surprise. Sanna lay melded into his body, her crinkly 'fro wild in his face. Her head nestled over his heart, and he smiled. He had always dreamed about this. Wanted this with all of him, and here it was, with a beautiful woman draped over him. The one he'd been wanting for a very long time.

Smoothing down her hair, he whispered softly, almost humming, while his fingertips traced lightly against her buttery skin. Soft swirling and glowing patterns flowed over her as he wove protection sigils into her flesh, marking her, so he could find her if she was ever taken by the Curse.

His mind jetted to Kyo, lightly kissing Sanna's forehead and tracing her plump lower lip.

Sanna jolted up blinking, half-awake. "Is she okay?" scooting out of the bed, she looked around. "Where is her room?"

Alrighty then. He softly chuckled.

He slid out of the bed, stretching, tying his black drawstring pants and running a hand over his flat abs. "I put her room next to yours. Follow me," he said, holding his hand out.

He waited, and he inwardly smiled as she quickly entwined her hand with his. He slowly walked toward a wooden inlaid wall, pulling back a red-and-gold woven tapestry. He pushed, and a click then a pop sound drew in Sanna's attention.

She watched as the wall opened and he slid it to the side, walking forward. He reached out to gently pull her with him.

Sanna could see Kyo lying in a massive canopy bed, curled in a ball. The room was huge and beautiful, fitting her eclectic style. She wondered how Khamun knew. She quickly recalled everything he'd shared with her last night, and she shook her head. That's why he knew.

"Kyo?" Sanna whispered. She walked forward, flexing her hands at her sides, fear and uncertainty eating at her stomach with each step she took.

"Baby, she's in stasis. She won't wake up until five," Khamun gently replied as he stood back, his arms folded across his barrel of a chest. He knew she had to do this on her own, so he gave her space. He was going to be by her side through her education, even if she had to learn it herself.

Sanna shook her head as she pulled back the curtain, a slight smile playing on her face. She was ready to shake Kyo awake before she gasped. Blinking, she saw Kyo lay curled up, a bundle of sheets wrinkled around her. Her eyes were closed peacefully, but from her legs, her chest, and part of her upper arms was nothing but granite that seemed to fuse with her skin and clothes.

"What is this?" She quickly turned and looked at Khamun.

"Her nature. She's in her awakening too. You both haven't gone through the final stages yet, so right now, she is partially in her Gargoyle stasis."

"What does that mean, Khamun? My sister is half of a statue! What does that mean?" Sanna reached out to touch Kyo, jerking back in shock at the hardness of the granite.

"It means, as the sun rises, her kind goes into hibernation, turning into stone as a means of protection, to rise again as the sun sets. Some rise at midnight, others earlier or later. Kyo is in the early phases of changing, so she will be up early."

"That is not acceptable. Wake her up!" Shaking Kyo's sleeping body, Sanna cried, scared and confused.

"Baby, I can't. It's their way. Not all Gargoyles are the same, though. She may sleep later than others, because of her connection to you, or she may rise early. I don't know. But I can't change it. Sometimes when they are anxious they 'stone,' so just be aware, baby."

Sanna glanced over her shoulder and clasped Kyo's still human hand. "This is crazy."

Heading to the door, Khamun scoffed, "Wait 'til she gets her wings. I'm getting you some lunch. I'll be back."

She watched him disappear, and she dropped her hands in her face. All of this was too much.

Yeah, last night all calculated in her mind, and it made sense. But that didn't mean she understood or accepted it all of the way. It was too out there, too unbelievable.

Her father had sacrificed himself for his family. He didn't die in some obscure war while serving in the Air Force like she had been told. No, he died a different warrior's death. It was strange. A part of her was pissed about all the lies, but after having gone through fighting for her life, not once but three times, due to demons called the Curse, she could understand it. Hell. She could rationalize it all and put herself in her mother's shoes. If it was her and Khamun . . . She had to stop herself and smile. No. If it was her, she would do whatever she could to protect her children.

Exhaling, she studied Kyo's sleeping form. She looked beautiful in her peaceful rest, and exhausted. Sanna knew if she was awake, Kyo would have some colorful commentary for it all. She'd probably joke and ask why Khamun wasn't between her legs right now. Not that she didn't want him in that way, because she did. It just scared her how much she wanted him.

When she touched him, she saw how hard it was for him to watch over her and want her at the same time. She also saw that he was dealing with something more with his personal life.

Something in relation to dealing with what he really was. And she was still curious about it. *Angels with fangs?* That wasn't anything she had ever been taught angels looked like, but here he sat. Hell, she was one of them. Idly touching her lips, she felt him enter the room. She could sense him as he studied her.

"Will I get fangs?" she quietly asked as she ran the pad of her thumb over her straight teeth.

"Yeah. All of our kind have them." Khamun sat opposite Kyo. He held three sandwiches, two Caesar chicken salads and ice cold water on a tray.

Sanna's stomach growled as she licked her lips. "So do you all, like, drink blood and whatnot?" She reached for the salad Khamun offered. She smiled. "Thank you. Did you make this yourself?"

"Yes and no to both questions. I had to fight my personal chef to make your lunch. He forgets that I had to fringe for myself for a while because I chose to and I like to eat, so I learned how to cook like an Iron Chef." He handed Sanna a glass of water. "Some of us feed from other willing Nephilims, some of us don't, so I can't answer if you will have the Thirst or not. Some in Society feel that it's beneath them to feed, but we have these things for a reason, you know."

Throwing down on the salad, Sanna closed her eyes. It was so damn good. It wasn't a traditional Caesar salad. Lightly seasoned grill chicken sat on top of spinach leaves, with red, yellow, and julienned green peppers and onions. The sauce was out of this world, with parmesan cheese on top. She almost cried over how good it was.

She tilted her head in realization. "When you say you learned to cook like an Iron Chef, do you mean I taught you? Or were you there while I was in school?"

Khamun smirked as he slowly chewed his sandwich, pretending he didn't catch what she said. The free crinkly strains of his locks spilled over his shoulder. Like fingers wanting to touch him and get as close to his smooth, dark cinnamon brown skin.

"Khamun!" Sanna's eyes widened as he continued to smile, and he nodded with a slight shrug.

"Yes to both. I told you I've been around you for a long time. Sanna?"

Flushing red, Sanna looked down at her bowl as she quickly glanced up. It was something in the way he said her name that had her feeling cherished and desired. Something she hadn't felt in a long time, or ever, from another man.

"Yeah? I like how you say my name, baby." Biting her lower lip, she almost kicked herself as she blurted out, "I want to go home as soon as Kyo wakes up."

Silence filled the room, and Sanna's heart began to pump a thousand times a minute as she realized how that must've sounded. "I—I mean." She looked up.

Khamun softly smiled. "It's all good. I know you can't stay here forever. I'll take you both home as soon she wakes up and eats."

Staring at her lap, Sanna felt tears well up as she slowly breathed in and out. "I didn't mean to offend you. It's just. You. I want, I want you so bad. But, like you said, I need to know you, and all of this is insane. I need to feel my world. My home."

Khamun just watched her as he nodded and ate.

Silence felt like the best thing for both of them as they waited on Kyo.

Tension made Sanna shift uncomfortably as she ate a chicken salad sandwich that had her shaking her head again at how damn good it was. She kind of felt a little jealous of his skills, but she kept it to herself, or so she thought.

She looked up when he chuckled. "What?" she raised an eyebrow and watched him shake his beautiful locks in a "nothing" motion.

"Khamun!" Her breath hitched in her throat as his eyes flashed, and she saw a glint of fangs cresting.

For whatever reason, she instinctively knew he wanted her, and his fangs showing had nothing to do with a need to feed in the literal sense.

"I imagined myself working with you in the kitchen sometimes. I'm very good with my hands, and I wanted to just be in your world for a while and show you just that. I enjoyed watching the relationship you and Kyo had in the kitchen. You both are very good at what you do. So I watched and I learned, and I went to the compound and impressed my team. Hell. Sometimes they watched you too, and they learned as well. You both are talented."

That tripped her out. They all watched her and learned from her? The very meaning of guardian angels took on a whole new meaning for her. She smiled. Good with his hands? I bet he was.

She jumped when Khamun growled, "Stop."

Blinking, she raised an eyebrow. "Stop what?"

"What you are thinking? I'm having a fucking hard time, as it is, with you in my presence like that, and you want to go home. So if you don't stop, you are not going anywhere."

It was so calmly stated, she had to grab a drink of water and compose herself and glance at the clock. Five o'clock was taking forever. Just sitting was going to drive her crazy, because the need to taste Khamun's mouth hit her every second it could.

"I'm sorry? Are you purposely in my mind?"

Standing and sitting Kyo's food on the night-stand, Sanna watched Khamun pace before he stopped to stand at the bay window, arms crossed over his chest.

"No, not on purpose. It's just habit. We Guardians don't go through your personal thoughts. We just link so we can know all is okay. But, with you, habit has turned that simple act into a mate thing."

Raising an eyebrow she watched his back. Her eyes slowly running over his solid rear, looking at his huge hands. "Explain."

"A'ight, but then I'm leaving you to yourself. There's a TV over there, some books on the right of Kyo's bed, and if you need assistance, the intercom connects you to the attendants. One day I'll give you a tour, but if you need to go to the bathroom or something, use mine. You know the way back to my room."

Sanna nodded. She felt bad for making him feel some type of way as she waited.

"When a Nephilim woman finds her mate, or a partner she wants, biology kicks in, and she sees if his pheromones match hers, and if they do she tries a mind-lock. If the person she mind-locks with syncs just right, then she knows that's who she wants. Ours happened last night. But if you didn't want me, instinct would have you attacking me or calling your Gargoyle or closest Protector to go after me, if I was a threat. If not, it would be a standard rejection or shunning."

"Oh," was all she was able to get out before he walked out. She blinked. "Well, damn!" With a shrug, she sighed. Guess that's why she didn't attract many men. She just ignored them like Kyo said because they weren't the man in her dreams. They weren't Khamun.

That had her thinking things through as she remembered him saying she could call her family anytime. So she did just that.

"Hello? Baby girl?"

Sanna smiled at her mother's comforting voice. Silent tears spilled down her face. Damn, if she wasn't tired of crying. "Yes, ma'am. Are you okay?"

"Oh, Sanna! Yes. I'm on my way to see you. Khamun told me everything. I wanted to sit and talk to you and tell you it all, baby. Baby, I am so sorry I didn't tell you. I didn't know how."

"Momma, it's okay. I know why you didn't get to tell me, and I understand. Did you talk to Darren and Amara?"

"I spoke with Darren. Luckily, he was with me when it all went down. Baby, he collapsed and blacked out. I didn't know what to do, but he quickly woke up and he knew you were in danger. Khamun wouldn't let him come, but he stayed to protect me, so yes, we spoke. And I quickly called Amara. She wants to come home but can't until next weekend. Then she has to go back."

"Oh, man. I know Amara feels confused by this as much as me."

Kyo's sleeping body was so quiet. Every now and then splashes of sunlight would kiss her granite skin, kicking off iridescent sparkles that reminded Sanna of thousands of starlight. It was calming and beautiful in itself.

"Yes, baby. You all are confused, and I hope I can help answer your questions in the flesh, instead of all this mental crap. I'm still learning about this world myself. Your father told me as much as he could, but even he didn't know the true workings of Society. Baby, are you okay truly?"

Sanna played with a strand of her shoulder-length crinkly 'fro and bit her lip. She was choking on her own tears as her mother's love and support hit her full-on. It wrapped around her like a blanket. "Yes, ma'am. Daddy was brave, huh?"

"Yes, baby. Your Daddy was a brave, good man. I miss him so much."

They talked and talked, pulling Darren and Amara in on four-way as they tried to sort out what all of this meant.

Sanna almost choked when Darren told her Take was frozen on their mother's couch. He was partially granite and snoring like a hog.

"Seriously, Dare?"

"Yes, sir. I'm not playing, sis. It's crazy because I saw him go into—What did you call it, Momma? Stasis? Yeah, he did that crap right in front of me. We were watching sports, talking about how to get to you, and he started dozing, head wobbling and shit. Then he freaked out briefly."

"You mean, you both freaked out?" Sanna chuckled. She could sense Dare shaking his head.

Darren scoffed, "Whateva, sis. Shit was crazy. Sorry, Momma. But it was what it is. Take was in a comatose state as soon as the granite hit his bicep. Freaky as hell."

Sanna heard her mother laugh.

Amara chimed in, "Well, Miya fell to the floor of our kitchen. Like dropped like a fly, water going everywhere. I tried to move her, but she was heavy! Now how do you explain to your dorm leader that your roommate is a partial statue and stuck to the floor?"

Amara's soft, bell-like laugh made Sanna smile. "Aw, Mara."

"Sis, I threw a blanket over her ass! She's on the floor with a big quilt over her. We have to learn what the triggers are, so they can be careful," she said.

Sanna couldn't agree more.

While both of her siblings laughed, their mother interrupted, "Well, babies, the big indicator is if the sun is rising, and a second indicator is if they become very cathartic, you know, moving around slow like a drunk. Then get them to a safe spot fast."

"Oh!" everyone sounded.

Sanna heard soft cracking and Kyo's random yawns. "I think they are waking up."

"Okay, babies, let's handle business. Sanna, Darren, and I will be over at your house as soon as you are ready to leave Khamun's, and Amara, baby, handle school and come up when you are able. I'll send you your ticket. Momma loves her babies. Let's hang up."

"I love you too, Momma" was sounded in unison.

Sanna was ready to hang up, but her sister's soft voice stopped her.

"Sis!"

"Huh? What's up, Mara."

"So. How's Mr. Man's house? And how is he? Hmmm?"

Sanna shook her head and smiled, walking around the room, calmly pacing until she sat in the bay window. She was amazed at the massive amount of yard in front of the estate. Well-maintained flowers and foliage protected the estate, and she saw white glowing invisible lines woven together like a grind. She knew nothing would get in here partially due to those lines.

"Everything is fine, Mara."

"Is it? Then why are you leaving? Momma and Dare should be meeting at his house instead of yours, and you *shouldn't* be on this phone with us right now because he *should* have been laying the pipe!"

"Mara! You're as bad as Kyo!" Amara's laughter had Sanna blushing.

"What? I'm just saying. And if Kyo said the same, then you know we are right."

"Ugh! Look, it's not right. We just survived the craziest attack of all time, and Kyo is a statue, and we are Nephilims. I—I don't know him, and you can't tell me you are not scared."

"Oh, I'm scared as shit, big sis. Very. I keep seeing things and feeling your pain or Darren or even momma, so yeah, I'm scared, but guess what? I don't have a Mr. Man to comfort me. You do, and yes, you do know him, sis. You've known him all your life. Ask me how I know?"

Sanna rolled her eyes as she sighed. "Sis."

"No. You are always crying about you wanting someone to love you. But, sis, you know I'm going to tell you the truth. And the truth is, he's

right there and you've known him all your life.
You drew pictures of him as a kid. I remember.
I called him Mr. Man even as a toddler. Ha! It
just took what happened last night to make me
remember. Sis, don't run scared from him, be
with him. It's beyond time. Plus, I'm ready to be
an auntie, and your coota is wasting away."

"Mara!"

Amara chuckled as Sanna heard her rustling
around in her dorm room. "I have to go. Miya is
scratching at the floor, and she sounds scared. I
love you, sis. Go get you some loving."

Sanna looked at the phone as she sighed.
Her sister wasn't nicknamed "Truth" without
reason. She had a lot to process and understand
here. It was something that she wasn't freaking
out more, but when all of this fell on her as it
did, it all made sense. She had dreamed this
before, seen it play over and over like a repeated
old movie, so accepting this as a reality was
surprisingly easy for her.

"San? Sanna, I can't move."

Kyo's panicked voice had Sanna jumping from
where she was and heading to the bed. Kyo lay
frozen. The sparkling granite around her slowly
sloshing off in pumice like pieces as resting
sparkling dust created a ring around her body.

Something in Sanna had her gently holding
Kyo's shaking hand. She knew what she had to

say. "Just breathe and slowly flex where you can. Your body is going to take a quick moment to wake up, since you're going through your Gargoyle change."

"Sanna, I had a dream that we were part of this crazy family. Angels with wings and other abilities. I saw you kissing that fine contractor guy who was killing those monsters last night, Khamun. What's going on?"

Sanna blinked. "Damn! You really are connected to me then, huh?"

Kyo raised an eyebrow, and Sanna explained. Kyo slowly moved her legs, stretching on the bed, then reached for the food and tore into it like it was her last meal.

"Our metabolism boosts when we go into stasis. That much I recall from my dreams. Oh, and why aren't you with Mr. Sexy?" Kyo muttered.

Sanna could only chuckle and roll her eyes.

Chapter 18

The Medusa lay in a puddle of her own blood and pieces of her flesh as she inhaled in pain. She was naked, cold, and shaking. She knew when she came back without the Initiate that the price would be taken from her own flesh, and Reina held true to her word. Yet as she lay there, it wasn't just Reina she stared at but the Dark King himself, Shroud-Eater Caius Primus-M'ylce. The First Fallen of their kind. The one who gifted her to Princess Reina. The Mad King.

See, this punishment was more than losing that young Nephilim. It was about coming across the Oracle and not taking her then and there. Yes. Her payment lay around her in pieces of her flesh and blood. The only reason she was still alive was because of her lineage and because she was the best tracker in their world and due to the fact that she was the Princess's Protector.

So she took the pain. Her braids blanketed her face as each slice into her skin brought her flashes of her old memories, memories that were dangerous because they were lined with hope and more.

"As you know the rules of this Society. What you lose is what we take."

The Medusa clutched the floor, her nails scraping.

The Dark King coolly spoke, circling her with his power. His voice suddenly tore into her brain. She had been going through this torture for two weeks now, and she surely thought she was going to die.

"Father? I think it is time for her to tell us what she has learned from her assumptions and overzealousness. Hmm? Don't you think?" Reina acidly cooed as she watched from her usual iron-and-jewel-inlaid throne. Her legs were crossed while she studied her lethal fingernails.

She wore all-white again. Her long, dark hair was braided in an intricate knot at the top of her head, as curls framed her face, and dazzling diamonds dripped from her earlobes. Her lips seamed to sparkle with diamond dust and glaze as her eyes flashed with a partial madness only her close delegates seemed to notice.

The Dark King eyed his beloved daughter. His eyes skimmed over her revealing form as he smiled and walked her way, but not before he kicked the Medusa, squarely in her ribs. His partially decaying red wings briefly quivered with excitement, his clear arousal evident near his muscular right thigh.

"Yes, my beautiful girl. It's beyond time she spoke. Go play with your Protector." He flicked his hand in mock boredom, and the Medusa swallowed as she prepared herself for more games.

A sharp gasp ripped from her throat as Reina gripped a handful of her braids. She pulled back with a coy smile as she dropped down into a squat, her diamond heels, sparkling in the pool of Nydia's blood.

"So, my darling Protector, what did you learn?"

The Medusa licked her lips. The chamber was full of Initiates, demons, Gargoyles and other Dark Society members, who watched the show with glee. The Medusa knew that the important information had to be given in privacy, so she closed her eyes and relayed what she learned.

"The Oracle has awakened. I could not get to her, but she has a weakness. It seems she knows nothing about what she can do as an Oracle. I witnessed this when I saw her try to project her power but came up empty-handed. This is good. I did not see her face, but I caught her scent!"

The last was said quickly as Reina dug her nails into her scalp.

"Then we know that you will be able to track her. Yes?" Reina slowly stated, her wild eyes flashing clear before clouding up again with a subtle madness.

"Yes, Princess. I can find her. This encounter let us know that she was here in Chicago. This is good. Since she went missing in St. Louis. . . ." a swift punch to the chest had The Medusa flying across the floor. A blood streak indicated where she has slid from.

"Something that should have *never* happened! But I see this is becoming a pattern. Shall I end your life now, so we do not do this for a third time? Hmm?"

The Medusa wanted to reply that the Oracle going missing in St. Louis wasn't her fault. But all she could do was laugh in her own slight madness, grinning as she spat blood and slowly rose up, arms extended.

"Do with me as you will, Your Highness. I am but your Protector and servant, but as I recall, the loss of the Oracle was due to your lower-level Hunters, demons, and Gargoyles, not I."

Reina smiled. Then she laughed. Her pretty hands clapped suddenly as she nodded. "That is true my pet. That is true. Let us move from this and get on with capturing what is rightfully ours, yes, Daddy?"

The Dark King waved a bored hand again, his eyes locked on his daughter's voluptuous form again, seemingly lost in a mad world of his own. "Do what you want."

Reina smiled and balled her hand, pushing forward with her power, sending the Medusa

flying into a thorn wall. The handprints that
adorned the chamber seemed to move, wanting
to help her, but she had to have been imagining that as she felt herself lifted in the air and
slammed the thorn wall again, held in place by
her master's own nailed hands.

Reina's icy lips brushed against her pet's
cheek while she squeezed her throat, her eyes
running up and down her body. "Challenge me
again. You know how I love to play."

The Medusa laughed and gagged as she choked,
blood spilling down her plus mouth. "Almost as
much as I do."

Reina studied her some more and flicked her
tongue out, licking the blood from the corner of
the Medusa's mouth. "That is true."

The room filled with satisfied cheers as Reina
let go and watched her Protector slide to the
floor. Sliding her hands behind her back, she
turned her back on her pet, her ample rear sashaying as she walked. Her long, straight mane
swayed against her back as she looked over her
shoulder at her Witch.

"Winter! Bathe her, heal her, and dress her.
You know how I despise filthy pets."

Winter walked in calmly with a group of Initiate
attendants, all dressed in white with various dark
collars but with Winter's signature sapphire blue.
That blue was also painted in a sash across their

bodies on both their arms, legs, chest, stomach, or back as well, marking them as being trained by the Royal House. Several attendants glanced at the handprint wall, fear emitting from their bodies.

"As you wish, Princess," Winter replied as she turned to curtsy. "My King," she said, her fist against her heart as her dark hair spilled over her shoulder. She inwardly smiled as the king's attention focused on her, scanning her, wanting her. *It was good to divert his curiosity in his daughter*, she thought as she walked to a shaky Nydia.

"Come with me." Winter reached out to grab the Medusa's shoulder but smoothly shifted to her side as the Medusa's nails reached out to scratch her in her face. *Nydia had been tortured too long and was in protection mode*, she thought. Ducking with her hands behind her back, Winter kicked up, blocking each blow with her feet, and turned into a roundhouse kick that connected with the Medusa's face. She sighed. Had the Medusa not been weakened, this fight would have been interesting.

Rushing forward, Winter rammed Nydia with her shoulder and then reached to spin her to hold her tight against her body.

"Be calm, darling," she whispered. "Your healing will not take long, and we have some things to discuss." She injected Nydia with a relaxant via her

Asp ring, marking her a member of Reina's House.
She smiled as the Medusa collapsed against her.

"Initiates, bring her to my quarters," she
commanded, and she watched the attendants
pick up Nydia with ease.

"Your Protector will be healed and back to
standard health within the week, Princess." She
waited for both Royals to wave her off, as a set
of Society Council and general house members
made their way in to proceed with daily delega-
tions.

Her sapphire eyes flashed with power as she
walked through the corridors of the palace. Her
senses were high. She could tell if someone was
following her. It was good that the councils and
Royals were busy, because just that would have
happened, and she would have had to paint the
corridors with Cursed blood.

Nothing here could be done in the dark. That
was why she always banked on the Light. She
never thought she would say such things, but it
took a frightened young boy and his cousin to
trigger memories she never knew she had. Memories that showed her as an eight-year-old child
snatched from her mother's arms and given the
Cursed bite to make her what she was today.

She saw more detail to the previous life she
had, marking her a Witch. A Witch and a Hunter.
She knew her mother had covered her in a pro-

tection spell, a spell that protected her soul and
its memories. A soul that had been dormant
for a long time. Ever since her soul's memories
surfaced, her view with her status in the Dark
Society skewed drastically.

She learned that an abundance of Light in the
Cursed world could draw attention, but if you
worked with it where it cast a greyness, decep-
tion could be had. And Winter was very good
with deceiving those who were here. She had a
lifetime learning what she could or couldn't get
away with.

Resting her palm against a thorn-covered
wall, she pushed, watching black blood spill to
feed the ever-growing roots around it, and a
secret door unhinged to allow her admittance.
Her chambers were covered in blue sapphire
drapings with Louis the XIV furniture, and
various books, scrolls, bottles, bowls, and herbs
lay everywhere.

A sly smile adorned her face as she walked
into her healing chambers and observed a sleeping Nydia. She shared so much in common with
the young woman she sometimes called sister. It
was strange how one attached themselves to the
wrong people, but this was different. She had a
purpose here, and Nydia needed her help.

"You know you almost screwed yourself, Ny?"
Winter grabbed some ointments and peeled

back the white healing sheet that covered her. Sticky red and black blood clung to the sheet, as well as flesh.

She ran a hand down her protruding spinal cord, as she gripped and snapped each vertebrae, lining them up again as they should be.

Nydia screamed and tried to get up.

Healing Cursed worked backwards. You caused harm before healing could begin. Burning ointments sizzled and made wounds fuse and heal. Pulling and snapping massages made sure the circulation and bones in Nydia's body healed in line.

Black smoke filled the room as Winter exhaled and blew sulfuric ash over Nydia's body. This helped cloak the Light magic she often performed in Nydia during her spinal cord sessions.

"So how do you plan upon snagging the Oracle?"

Nydia flinched as she woke up, hissing, her long tongue flicking out. She clutched the healing table, digging into its surface. "Hmm. I plan upon tracking her scent. Winter, it seems Marco is alive."

Winter kept her cool as she inwardly cursed. "Is he now? The rites were performed. There is no way he survived."

"That was my exact thoughts. The King personally took care of his death, seeing that he was tainted. So it doesn't make sense. Ah!"

Winter dug her nails into Nydia's tender flesh and sent grey healing charges through her finger-tips.

"Are you sure it was him? It has been, what, eighteen or nineteen years?"

Nydia shook her head, flinching. "I don't know. I have to do some hunting to be positive about this."

"Of course, you do, darling. We don't need another episode such as this."

"Ah, shit! No, we don't. How bad is it?"

Winter inwardly laughed while she reached into burning ash and grabbed a handle to rub into Nydia's skin. *The work of a Witch*, she thought. "It is what it is. How are your dreams, my dear?"

"They are what they are." Nydia smirked then shouted in pain as Winter snapped a vertebrae in place.

"Hmmm. You still see him in your mind, don't you?"

Nydia tensed and didn't say a word.

Winter smirked as she continued, "You know that I can read that from you. I've taught you how to cloak your thoughts, but you must be more careful."

"I don't need to do a damn thing. I have this in control. I am not one of Reina's weak pets."

Winter stepped back and cleaned her hands. She turned and slapped Nydia so hard that her head turned to the side.

Looking at Nydia's jaw, she saw the flesh nicely healing. "As you say. So how are you going to snatch the Oracle once you have her?"

"That I am not sure about, but it will be done. Searching for her here in our homeland will not be so hard for me. I just have to find if she is doing many of the things she did in St. Louis."

"Ah, of course. Now what if you can't get to her, due to it being white light blessed land?"

Nydia smiled. "We got through to her house in St. Louis before. We'll do it again, or you will, that is."

Winter chuckled and pulled out a jar of leeches, applying each onto Nydia's body, watching as one slipped under her skin to get to her dark blood. "And now we get to it. I figured you'd need my services, which is why I asked. Call me, and I will be there."

"Good. As soon as I heal, I hunt," Nydia said.

A grey salve briefly sparkled on her fingertips as Winter motioned for Nydia to stay on her back. "Then you need to stay off your feet."

Already formulating a counterplan, Winter hoped her gift made it through. Being an Alpha insurgent is not easy when you have no allies, as of yet.

***

Khamun sulked around the compound, watching the Initiate who did the impossible and escaped the Curse. Sanna had been home for two week now, and he missed her. Ever since the night she lay resting safe in his bed under his roof, in his arms, he had been locked into her. Shit freaked him out, he thought as he paced.

He knew he wanted her, but after having drank her blood, triggering his Craving, he knew he was officially hers.

"Amit, explain again how you escaped." Khamun crossed his arms as he studied the still pale male.

His hair was disheveled, but his coloring seemed to be slowly recovering, even though his aura seemed to wane in and out like a flickering light bulb. This kid was something different, but every time he thought he knew what he was, it would go away with a flash. At his neck was a black bite that showed where the poisonous tendrils traveled.

"It was a sport. They wanted to hunt me. The Princess. Look, I told you everything." He held his hands up, the trauma still evident, and he shook his head.

"What else can you tell us, Amit?" Lenox asked, aware that the man was quickly tiring out.

"I know a lot. I don't know why, but shit, I made sure I paid attention to everything. They want Sanna, and they intend to get her."

The room grew silent as they watched him. Every man gripped a hidden weapon as they waited for him to continue on.

"I remember hearing about the Princess's desire to make another pet like the Medusa, and the fact that they took an Oracle once made them hype that they could do it again."

Lenox bit into his apple. Then he spoke up. "Note that there's a connection between Oracles and how the Medusa came to be."

The pretty girl, he remembered her as Kali, nodded as she clicked away. He watched for a moment before eyes burned into him.

Amit looked up to study the one named Marco. Since being here, the man had been watched like a dog, but something about this team made him comfortable, and he felt blessed that he was safe for the time being. He didn't want to fuck anything up being here, but he couldn't help being curious about Marco. He looked and moved like the Princess in some ways, and he remembered hearing her speak about a dead brother.

"I have a question. So, my man, are you her brother?"

Marco eyed him with a cold stare, his eyes flashing.

That alone answered his question. Something in that stare let him know not to fuck with the man and apparently not to ask him questions so personal. He wanted them to trust him, but he liked his life as well, the little of a life he still had, so he decided to play by the rules. He knew he could help them in some way. He just had to prove himself.

When Marco gripped his gun tighter, the machine click of it brought Amit back to reality, and he had to inwardly sigh. Marco stared at him hard, his annoyance hitting him like a bat to the head as he threw his hands in the air. He just wanted some damn help here to understand it all. A new Oracle, one who he felt he'd lay his life down for just for the help she gave him in that moment, made him want to hold his own in this compound, and the one named Kali made the secret spot in the back of his mind that he had to shut off during his torture and turning. Well, it ached to open again.

"Just kill me before I turn all the way," he exasperatedly replied, his accent thickening with annoyance. He looked at everyone in the room. His eyes flashed pale, and his body roughly shook as he coughed, a tendril of glowing mist flowing around his body.

"We can't do that. You seem to be an anomaly," Khamun explained. "After you touched the Oracle you said you felt stronger?" He studied Amit's marked hands.

"Yeah, like she had stopped the venom or something. The Princess liked to infect and bite me while slowing down the progression so that I kept my healthy color. So she said. When I touched Sanna—I mean the Oracle—I felt normal again."

"A'ight. Then we bring the Oracle here, man, and see what she can do," Marco said as he sat, one leg thrown over the arm of the La-Z-Boy chair he resided in, his gun on this thigh.

"I can call her, man, get this going, see if she can get any more info, like finding the Princess' lair," Calvin replied.

"Right. *Mira*, Calvin is talking truth. It's beyond time me and the Princess have some words. *¿Comprendes?*"

Calvin reached over and pounded fists with Marco as he flashed a bright smile. His green eyes flashed against his milk chocolate skin.

"Khamun, what do you think? You are her Guardian. Is it time to bring her here? Because whatever she did for Amit, he needs her help fast." Lenox's eyes stayed on Amit's red palms.

"She wants her normalcy, so I'm giving her that. She'll come when she's ready," Khamun steadily replied, though his mind said otherwise.

"Naw, my man. You don't get it. My cousin is running scared, ya heard meh? Normalcy?" Calvin laughed. "Yeah, right. You know this,

Khamun. Shit. I'll get my cousin. Amit needs her help."

Khamun ran a hand down his face. Calvin was right. He was just acting stupid in doing his job. They had an invalid Nephilim, and the one who can heal him was just around the block. So he nodded at Calvin and said, "I'll go get her."

"Who runs the world? Finally more ladies in the compound," Kali happily joked. She moved to sit next to Amit and give him a sustaining mixture, which consisted of Hemorush, blood donated from Kali herself to replenish the lost blood, water, proteins, and herbs.

The drink tasted like cod liver oil, a hint of blood, and cooked grease. Amit cringed while he drank the mixture, his eyes locked on Kali's rear as she walked off.

Marco chuckled while he noticed and growled under his breath. "You just went through some crazy shit. You want her, you need to make sure you live, and then you need to earn that shit. *¿Comprendes?*"

Amit smiled as he swallowed the rest of the harsh mixture that seemed to connect with his body like thousands of barbwires.

"I'll remember that, my man," he grunted and gripped his stomach, "but in the meantime, get me some damn *help*!"

Khamun exhaled and walked out so smoothly, no one noticed he was gone.

Khamun easily found her at Aset, in the kitchens with Kyo, testing food out and cooking old recipes as crewmen continued to work around them. He smiled and nodded at the men who worked for him and slid his hands in his pockets. He wore dark denim jeans with brown Tims, a white button-down shirt with black pinstripes, his locks pulled back, braided in a knot.

Everything was coming along just right. How she had her restaurant set up in St. Louis was here but more. Pillars accented the main dining area, and his mural, which he was still working on, sat as a focal point for all who entered. He'd added protection sigils into his work as double defense and he watched each glow tendril swirl, letting him know they were firmly activated.

As he walked toward the kitchens, he took in the carefully constructed beauty. Stainless steel was everywhere, to maintain cleanliness. A wood-burning stove was mounted as another focal point for guests to see from the dining rooms. Everything was spaced out just right to ensure plenty of room.

Herbs and wine decorated the walls as art and for cooking. He was proud of the work done as well as the restoration that took place on the building as well.

"Taste this," Kyo said, holding out a small cake, walking his way with a smile on her pretty face.

She was covered in flour with icing on her hands. He felt her natural protection barrier soften to let him through. Anyone that was a threat would have to work to get through, and he was proud that she was learning her abilities.

Grabbing the little cake, he took a bite and kept his eyes on Sanna, who seemed to flush red as he approached. Sweet, buttery toffee crème exploded in his mouth as mellow white chocolate seemed to balance the taste out. He immediately thought about Sanna's caramel taste as he slowly closed his eyes.

"I want a personal cake. Make it up, and drop it off at my estate. My mother is visiting, and I know she'd love this cake."

Kyo beamed, pulling out a notepad. "So it's a success, and one cake coming up. Just, um, give me your address later."

Khamun chuckled as he rounded close to Sanna. "I will, but in the meantime, I'll have Lenox show you how to get to the estate and send him the bill when he gets you and the cake."

Kyo blushed with a pep in her walk as she moved around the kitchen.

"Sanna, how you doing, baby?" He studied her quiet frame.

She opened the oven and pulled out a roasted stuffed lobster, golden with butter and herbs. He got the sense she was ignoring him, but before he could question it, Sanna's arms wrapped around him, and she rose to the tip of her toes to kiss the side of his neck.

"I'm good, and I've missed you," she whispered against his earlobe.

His fangs instantly dropped. His hands found her rear, squeezing, while partially lifting her up. Damn, he missed this woman, and it had only been two weeks. Realizing his stance, he swallowed hard and let go to rest a hand on the small of her back.

He could see Kyo watching them on the sly, a smile on her face as she mouthed to Sanna to hop on his dick. Next time he had the time, he definitely had to gift Kyo with a present for her support.

"Taste this," broke his concentration.

His mind immediately said, *Hell yeah. I'd taste you definitely.* He blinked and realized she was talking about the lobster. He opened his mouth, and she slid a piece of the tender white flesh into his mouth, which he almost spat out due to heat.

"Damn, woman! That's hot!"

Sanna laughed. She held his hand and pulled him toward a fridge. She opened the door. "I'm sorry. Here's some ice water."

Smiling, he just studied her, taking photographic memories of her beauty. She wore jeans that accented her deep-set curves with a red tank shirt. Her curly 'fro was pulled back on one side with a red flower, and her bamboo hooped earrings framed her beautiful face. He wanted to kiss her plump, pink lips and kiss the spot under her ear.

"We need to talk."

Kyo coyly smiled as she mixed batter. "What? Is it time for you both to finally talk about getting some? Because it's beyond time, you know."

"*Kyo!!!*" Sanna screeched as she covered her face. "You play too damn much."

Khamun laughed. The taste of the lobster was *perfecto*. All the flavors balanced just right, garlic, curry, onion, olive oil, and other flavors he was damn sure going to ask her about. He wanted her naked in his kitchen, with food in her hands for him to eat off her body as he cooked dessert for her.

"That's next. But, yeah, I need you both to finish here and come back with me to my compound. Amit needs your help, Sanna. I also want you come meet my mother. It's time for you to get training from her."

He watched Sanna blink, words forming at her mouth but nothing coming out.

"Stop being scared, San. It's time to learn what this is all about and check on Amit."

Khamun was beginning to like Kyo more every day. He reached up and ran the pad of his thumb over Sanna's lower lip, watching her calmly with a slight smile.

"It won't be as bad as you think. Your brothers both came by the compound and left safely. The compound is going to be their second home, and I hope it will be your third home."

Averting her glace, Sanna softly smiled. "Okay. We're just testing some food. We can leave as soon as Kyo is done with your cake and after I visit Darren. I promised to pick up a package for him."

"Okay, baby. Oh, and my mother will love you. She is the only Oracle in this region, so this is business, not"—He dipped his head down and kissed her lightly, softly sucking on her lower lip as he kissed her twice—"personal." He watched Sanna swallow hard as he swore she swayed to the side.

"Okay," she muttered breathlessly.

Khamun inwardly chuckled. Tonight, he was definitely going to have Sanna Steele because waiting was killing him softly. He stepped back, ignoring Kyo's Cheshire cat grin.

"Seriously, do you all have someone for me? Because all of this oxytocin and testosterone is driving me up the wall!" Kyo laughed.

Sanna shook her head, reaching out to entwine her fingers with Khamun's.

Khamun just smirked as he leaned back and brought the back of Sanna's hand to his lips with a kiss. "Check ya dreams, and you may find your answers."

Chapter 19

Darren stood around a mound of U-Haul boxes. He and Takeshi were moving out of the graduate townhouses near campus and moving into an old firehouse close by. With the help of Protection restoration and construction firm, Khamun's business, they were rehabbing it and fitting it to their needs. It also helped that it connected to Khamun's computer and was close to their mother. Even though Darren had moved to get his own independence, he was always checking in on his mother. Now, with learning about the extra bump in their DNA, he had become even more protective over her and his sisters.

Sanna smiled as she studied her brother in too big basketball shorts, red-and-black Jordan, and a white tee that accented his sepia-tattooed biceps. His wavy, low fade was freshly cut, and she saw he was growing a jawline beard.

As she walked through, she had to swerve and pivot as Take rushed beside her with four boxes.

"What up, San!" He smoothly stepped back and walked around Kyo.

Kyo yelled, "Dang! Just run me over!"

Take chuckled and stopped turning around to back up to lower his boxes. He kissed Sanna on the cheek then kissed Kyo on hers before walking about again. "Okay, I'll do that shortly, sis."

Sanna chuckled.

Take was dressed in track pants with a basketball jersey and white Air Force One. A tattooed-looking branding on his shoulder blade made her squint her eyes hard. She glanced at Kyo.

"Yeah, I have the same thing. I asked Khamun about it, and he gave me a book about our kind Kali gave him. You know I hit up Daddy right after and gave him the book."

Sanna smirked. Pop Hideo loved books, so it made sense. "Well, what did the book say? Or Pops?"

"It's our clan marking and where our wings will grow from, once we all go through this final phase. So I need you to hurry up and wake all the way up. I'm tired of the random weirdness."

Kyo hooked her arm with Sanna and pouted. "Well, I love you too, geez."

"Sis, did you go pick up my package yet?" Darren ran a hand down his sweaty face and glanced at Sanna.

Young men appeared out of nowhere in Kappa colors. Sanna shook her head. Looked like the little brothers of Kappa were helping Darren and Take. "Not yet. I just wanted to see how everything was progressing. I'm headed there now." She shifted to the side as some of the little brothers stopped and gawked at her. She blushed red quickly, looking away. She had never been gawked at, except for Khamun, so this was something new for her.

"Move the hell on, newbie!" Darren roared.

Each frat little brother almost tripped over running out as the men laughed.

Everyone blinked when Khamun and Calvin strolled down the stairs with various objects.

"Riii, keep your eyes on those boxes, ya dig?" Calvin said. To reinforce his point, he lowered his voice and glared.

"Um, okay. On that note, I'm going to get your package. You said from the history department?"

Khamun was eyeing her. She remembered how he made her body cream back in his room, and she wanted that again.

"Yeah. Hit up Professor Merril. She should be in her office. She's holding some book for me. Not sure what it is, but I don't have time to get it, since I'm done with her history of law class. Hard-ass wench!"

"Truth!" Take yelled, and he hauled some more items out.

Sanna sighed. "Okay, I'll be back." She turned to leave, and Kyo followed.

"Girl, where you going?" Sanna quipped, smiling. She knew it was no use arguing about it. Kyo was going to go with her, like it or not.

Kyo just hooked her arm with Sanna, and they both strolled out.

The little Kappa brothers followed them both, and some dared to smile when they saw Take and Darren weren't looking.

Frowning, Kyo and Sanna seemed to walk in sync as they both saw women gawking. Sanna kept up the pace, rolling her eyes at the women. Kyo started to laugh as she tried to keep up.

Locating the history department took a while, but maneuvering through the campus was nice, until they felt feet behind them.

"I'm scared to turn and see which one of the damn squad it is," Sanna said. She knew it wasn't Khamun or Calvin. She could sense them. When Kyo tripped over her own feet, Sanna knew who it was instantly.

"Lenox, I take it?" she joked, trying to smother her laugh with a "faux" choke.

"Girl, yes!" Kyo whispered, flushing a bright ruby red before she looked and waved.

"Ladies. Just taking a stroll, making sure everything is good with you both, if you don't mind."

Sanna got ready to say something smart-alecky, but Kyo stopped her.

Kyo grinned hard, and her voice rose an octave. "*Noooo*, you are always welcome, Lenox."

Lenox's soft smile flashed in the corner of Sanna's eye. She spotted Dr. Merril's office.

"I got this," Sanna said. "You and Lenox talk a bit. I'll be a second." She pushed the pair close together and rushed inside, a coy smile on her face.

Inwardly chuckling, she knocked, stepped in, and smiled at the dark-haired woman behind the desk who sat flipping through an old book.

"Hello. I'm here to pick up a package for my brother Darren, Darren Steele." Sanna glanced around the room, her arms protectively crossing against her. Something felt off and was causing the hair on the back of her neck to stand at attention. Her temples began to slightly throb as the room seemed to get hotter.

"Oh, yes, Darren. I'm glad to meet his sister. Please have a seat, and I'll get you that book." Dr. Merril looked up and smiled.

Sapphire blue eyes stared at Sanna, and she suddenly stood. She knew this woman. She had seen her touch Amit. She was the crazy chick's Witch and a Hunter.

Sanna stumbled back, and her eyes widened with paralyzing fear. What was she doing here? She had been close to her brother and to Take. This felt all the way like a trap, and she'd be damned if she'd let this chick catch her.

Dr. Merril smiled with a slight coldness, yet there was something more hidden in that one look. It illuminated her face. She tilted her head to the side and held her hands out.

Books shook on their mantels as Dr. Merril's hair whipped on her head at the magnitude. The power was so strong and concentrated that the hair on her arms stood at attention, and goose bumps rose all over her body. Fear for the first time in a long time hit her hard and heavy, almost suffocating her as tears threatened to spill.

"Please. I am not here to harm you!" Winter almost screamed. Items in her office flew suddenly as the woman she knew to be the Oracle stood in mirrored rigid fear.

Her skin suddenly glowed with intense Light. Her pupils swallowed the whites of her eyes with illuminating power and clarity. That strength, that power, let Winter know that this woman would not be taken, and that in and of itself made her shake with understanding.

The Dark Lady would not have a chance against this magnificent glory. That knowledge made her smile because maybe she could exact the vengeance she now sought for the children like herself who were taken and turned against their will. Maybe this woman was the piece she had found in her studies, a part of a connecting puzzle that would join together and spread holy wrath upon those who sought to harm. That bit of understanding flashed in her eyes and opened the weakened soul she carried. It allowed her to stand and start to mend the broken pieces in her dark form.

Sanna tilted her head to the side and assessed the woman she thought was here to hurt her. She saw something was broken in the woman, something that now seemed to shift and rearrange itself within.

She stepped forward and watched the woman step back. She felt that if this woman was a threat, not to be trusted, that she could kill her as soon as her back was turned. But there was something about that shift in her that made Sanna look closer as the door to the office shook and rattled.

Sanna felt Lenox and Kyo trying to kick the door open. Her body shook and hummed as she felt her brothers and Khamun approach. She knew Khamun would find a way in, so she stepped forward again and wasn't shocked as he stood at her side, her brother Darren with him.

"San . . . " Khamun unsheathed a hidden gun as he assessed her and readdressed her, "Oracle-Vessel."

Sanna saw Darren's eyes light with his own power, and she stood closer to them both.

"Dr. Merril, who are you? And what did you do?" Darren quietly asked. His voice was so low, so deadly, it made Khamun flash a dark smile as he reached to open the door.

"Leave it closed," Sanna heard herself say. "There is not enough room for everyone."

Darren reached toward her and placed a hand on her shoulder. The touch was innocent and filled with concern, but it triggered something else that broke like an overflowing dam. Power seemed to expand and ebb as both Sanna's and Darren's heads dropped back then bowed forward, their eyes locked in on the threatening target as they spoke as one.

"Tell us now what you want with the Oracle-Vessel," they said as one voice, one mind.

Something in the change had Khamun breathing hard, his fangs at lethal length as he stood to block them both.

"Speak, or I will drain you of every ounce of dark sin you carry, bitch." The Reaper was in full mode, and his body shook with a power he never felt before. He had to roll his shoulders to keep his wings from expanding.

Those wings and that thread had Winter scraping at the walls, ready to run. "No, no, don't. Please, please, hear me out. I am not here to play games. I am an ally!" she stuttered, scraping some more.

She couldn't believe her eyes. She was standing in front of bounty hunters for the Most High himself. She felt a trickle between her legs at the realization. This was something none of her kind had ever witnessed for generations.

Yes, her kind was trained to kill the enemy, to kill the pustules who made their love for hunting humans strenuous, and who sat at the feet of the one who shunned them. She was told her kind was an Alpha, but what she was witnessing told her different. She had found information about what she was witnessing, and seeing it in the flesh had her ready to die now for all the wrongs she had committed.

"But you helped some in later life? Your soul opened, and you saw the truths." The disembodied voice of the Oracle-Vessel and Darren filled the room, tearing into her brain as their stare commanded her gaze.

The tall, handsome one with the extended fangs made her soul shake with fear as she felt a coiling tightness in her chest the closer he got.

Tears poured down her lips, and she opened her mouth to speak, stumbling as if she was mentally incapable, "I know the truths. I found the records."

"What records?" the Reaper asked. Suddenly he was in her face. He watched as her eyes rolled in the back of her head, and he inhaled with a malicious smile. His large hands slid over her shaking body and gripped under her jaw to expose her creamy neck. "What truths?" he cooed.

She felt her blood pump colder than anything Reina or her father had ever done to her. Why? Because she knew if she died by *his* hands then there would be no return. It would be nothing but eternal pain and suffering, which had her clawing at his wrists as he squeezed.

"She has found the records of truths. The Nephilim scrolls. Only, it is one. The rest are well hidden, waiting to be found by others," the pair echoed.

And the Reaper squeezed in satisfaction as he lifted her with one arm, his bicep pumping. "Is she to be trusted, Oracle-Vessel? Because I am very hungry, and her sins smell succulent." The Reaper gave a menacing chuckle.

Winter's eyes widened. She instantly prepped her body to kick and flip him over her desk but only ended up with having her leg being blocked.

"Fight me again, and I will suck your knowledge from you," was all the Reaper had to say to make Winter obey, her eyes still locked on the Oracle.

She licked her chapping lips while the door to her office shook and voices bellowed outside. She knew the others would be here and they had to be careful, or the Cursed who watched her would be ready to start a war on UIC's campus. "The book is on my desk. I wanted to give it to you to show my loyalty."

"She speaks truth. Her soul was chained in protection. Those chains have broken over time, as is written in the pages of the Scrolls," the disembodied voice replied.

The door to her office slowly opened as others from their team stepped inside.

The Reaper narrowed his eyes, his head slightly tilting to the side, and he held tight to Winter's throat. "Prophecy? Why hasn't the Eldress seen this?"

"With the loss of potential Oracles, the Cursed knew it would blindside us. This is what has happened. Surviving Oracles have been weakened, and many have been without teachers to know how to reach the Most High, but the awakening has begun. This Vessel will not be taken. Sin-Eater, you are linked with us. It is your duty as is the duty of the linked Gargoyles to carry out the truth. In this, salvation will come."

The Reaper blinked and cast a glance behind him, his attention still on Winter, but also focusing on what the Oracle-Vessel had said. "Sin-Eater?"

"Yes. Your kind goes by many names, but you are a Reaper, as you deduced. But you are also a Sin-Eater. Their sins are your power. Your line has been lost through the generations, hunted, killed, or turned, made to be extinct, just as with the Oracles of anon. The awakening has begun. Seek out your history. These bodies must rest. It has been drained. This joining was unbalanced. Reaper . . . Sin-Eater, protect us now."

The Reaper let go dropping Winter as she slide to the floor. She coughed. Her eyes still locked on the powerful being before her. She wrapped her arms around herself, her knees buried in her chest.

"That one can be trusted. We will keep her cloaked. To the Dark she will appear the same, but we will see the truth. We will also cloak the one named Amit. It is time he came into his birthright as well. He will be a tracker of the Curse. His bite will let him seek those to hunt us. Trust him and use him well. He wishes to be of help, and he is a chosen child of the Truth, just as you all are."

The room filled with power that ebbed and expanded, moving through the streets of Chicago, finding its mark. Amit lay weak and sick, his body so thin, you could make out every bone and vein in his body. The bite had spread fast, and he was slowly dying and turning against his will. It felt like his very life force was being pulled from him, and he fought for breath. His prayers slowly spilled from his cracked lips as Kali fed him water.

Tears spilled down her face, and she prayed with him.

The Oracle light watched the pair. It dispersed an ebb of warmth to fill the compound then wrapped around the two before snapping back and slamming into Kali.

Kali's body arched then bowed forward, her hair spilling over her face, before she sat up and stared at Amit. "Your shell is dying. Changing and activating the dormant Wrath gene within. This too must be healed," she said, her disembodied voice splitting in two, sounding like another's.

Amit sat back in amazement, his body aching and shaking with his jagged cough. Blood spewed from his lips as he looked up.

"Oracle-Vessel? Is Kali okay?"

"We will not hurt this one. This one will anchor us and heal thee. Trust and do not be afraid. Her power will anchor you always."

Bowing his head, he had seen himself. He was nothing but a shell. His eyes had started fading, and he didn't understand why until now. He had no clue that he had the Wrath gene, which meant he was not going into the Death process.

"Do not fear. You will not die, but . . . you will be broken. What you've seen will help you and this team. Trust in Him for we are His mouthpiece."

Before he could say a word, he watched Kali's glowing body bow back then reach forward, clasping unto his chest, and he screamed.

Power rich and ancient flowed through him as it split within him. He felt the silky, energetic, spicy power of Kali mixed with that of the Oracle-Vessel. In that moment, he felt his own dormant power twist and bind with Kali's.

Silent tears streaming down his cheeks, his body lifted in the air.

Moments before Kali had been flipping through a book talking with Amit about new information she had found, and now she was not only a part of her cousin's ancient power, but now she could feel the very DNA of Amit, and he felt good.

The darkness that tried to taint him was purified and changed to help their cause as the Wrath gene pulsed and fought to make him living dead. She didn't want him to die, and it scared him. She already was on edge because she felt the SOS her cousin sent out, but now she was privy to her cousin's true power. She now was acting as an aid in helping the man she helplessly watched contort in shattering pain.

Her hands were controlled by her cousin. They fisted and tugged, pulling the light Amit's soul tried to attach to his skin as if it was a sticky web. She twisted her hand, snapped back, then pushed forward, that sticky web softening and becoming delicate like cotton candy as it misted and flowed back into his body.

His deep screams burst through the compound, hitting Kali in her senses, and she fell to her knees. She slowly connected with an awareness of what was going on. Her eyes adjusted to everything around her, and she caught the vague undercurrent of power in the chambers.

It was a beautiful sight, and she wanted to cry from the magnificent look of it all. She let go, heaving, sweating, and she felt her cousin's power leave her, but not before amplifying her own gifts. Her cousin's power kissed her mind with knowledge unlike anything she had ever pulled through the net, and she was grateful. She stood wavering, slowly looking around, and saw the power spread through the whole hidden bunker and upper-level building.

Tears spilled down her eyes as she cupped her mouth.

"Sanna," she whispered. She knew her cousin was the baddest Oracle-Vessel in history. Her searches through Nephilim records had given her snatches of old first-generation history supposedly lost through translation, oral traditions, wars, and politics. In what she found, throughout Nephilim history, in every Nephilim Society around the world, the Scrolls of Nephilim kept popping up, or the Book of Understanding, as some called it.

As she searched deeper, she learned that others also called it the Book of Truth, and she kept finding words like Mouthpiece, Triad, and something that was the real reason why she kept digging, Sin-Eater. That word rang familiar to her, and it upset her that she couldn't remember why, so she kept digging.

Amit's falling body brought her back to reality. The power that had saturated into his body was now gone as he lay in Kali's arms. His sweat-drenched, shiny, jet-black hair lay plastered to his face, and she couldn't help herself from pushing it out the way.

Once greying and sickly yellow skin was now flushed with health as warm sepia copper skin washed away the grey, and Amit's once erratic breathing regulated. He was okay. He was really okay, and according to Sanna, he was now not only a Disciple but a Broken Wrath Angel.

Outside of the bite where the venom spread like dark fibrous threads from his neck, over his shoulder and down his forearm, the fluid seemed to harden and form an intricate woven design.

She traced it with her fingers, and it hummed with power. Power that felt clean and safe. Something within her made her lean in and place her plush smooth lips against his heated skin where the bite was, and she inhaled. He smelled so good. She knew what had just happened had pulled them together, and though she wanted to deny it, she couldn't.

His arms wrapped around her, and she felt her own power amplify. Strange crap was happening all around, flowing through her mind. She quickly sat up and saw Amit was still asleep.

"Hmmm. Sanna, what did you do, cousin?" Kali muttered as she watched the rest of Amit's color return. She definitely was going to ignore this guy and be about her business, but she was glad that a former Initiate was healed, something no one thought ever possible.

Smirking, she half-heartedly laughed. "Team Light one, Team Dark negative one."

Back at the UIC campus, the same surge of power fluxed through the tiny office as currents lifted Winter from her position against the wall, tears spilling down her cheeks. Everything she was blocked from opened in her mind, and her eyes locked on a tall, handsome man with dark black hair and a jawline clenched in anger and awe. He was hers, and she smiled as warmth filled the coldness and shattered scars through her body while she was dropped to the floor, panting.

"You will be able to be as you are supposed to be, without them being made aware of our enemies. What we gave, only He can gift."

With that, both Darren and his sister crumbled like bricks, both drenched in sweat, their clothes plastered to their bodies.

She weakly watched her other student, Takeshi, drop down and shoulder-lift Darren with a grunt.

The Reaper quickly scooped up Darren's sister to hold her to his chest, sparks of power fusing and flowing between the pair like links, and it was beautiful.

"The one I gave the paper to . . . it is a key. It is sealed on his hands to open that book."

The Reaper hissed, baring his teeth, his gun cocked and pointed her way.

She dutifully dropped her head in acceptance as a prayer she remembered her mother telling her flowed from her lips. She felt a power in her she knew she wasn't ready to connect to just yet, so she patiently waited.

"Talk," was all she heard as she opened her eyes and saw that the gun was no longer pointing her way.

"I found a scroll around nineteen fifty-five, hidden within the healing chambers. It was like it sang to me—"

"Speed it up," a dispassionate voice interrupted.

She looked up and noticed the handsome, dark-haired man staring at her with a slight coldness.

"The scroll took long to decipher, but when I did, I saw it led me to a book. That book. I tried to read it, but it was blank, but it had symbols stamped into the pages like Braille, which let me know the only ones who could read this were those of the Light. I don't know why that book was there and why it went undetected, but there it is. When I helped"—Winter glanced at Marco then the Reaper and saw both men grip their guns tight.

She quickly added, "A boy escaped. That was the day a page opened to me, and I saw what led me to you all. Sin-Eater, Mouthpiece, and Triad."

The Reaper slowly stood, hoisting Darren's sister up like a feather, and he looked down at Winter's slightly flushed skin and saw that she had indeed changed.

He was through with her, as far as he was concerned. Drain her, he wanted to. Snuff her out? Hell, yeah, he was ready too, but the woman in his arms kept him from that task. He didn't feel alone in what he was anymore. He felt more.

The power that rose in him and filled every bit of him scared the hell out of him, but what calmed him was that his power matched Sanna's. He knew that if he touched her, a gauntlet would be thrown and a sensual war would start. But he knew it wasn't time for that, so he stayed away. Plus, something in him said she needed balance, and her balance wasn't all there.

Stepping back, he kept his eyes on Winter.

"That book will tell us what that means?" asked the dark-haired man, dressed in dark grey jeans and a black button-down up at the sleeves. His well-maintained anger occasionally flashed in his icy pupils as he stayed in the back.

"Yes, some of it. The book looks like it connects to another book, so we—you all have to find the next book," Winter whispered. Her head quickly snapped to the side, and she tried to pull herself up. "Some of the Dark are coming. You all must leave quickly. The key is in Amit's skin. The Oracle can retrieve it. That was a spell I also found and hoped it would work."

A tall cocoa-hued man with protection sigils that swirled with his constrained anger walked close to her and dropped down in a squat in front of her. A deep accent made her warm, but the still coldness behind it had her pressing backwards again.

"Just to be clear, shawty, you backslide in anyway"—He quickly grabbed her hand, flipping it, and pressed two fingers into her palm, and a sudden burning sensation hit her. The smell of charred flesh had her sick, as memories flashed across her eyes of her being burned at the stake, and the words *Witch* and *Whore* being thrown at her flooded her mind.

"You will relive every pain of your past lives and what you did unto others while you lived in the Dark. Ya heard meh?"

Winter gulped and shook her head up and down in understanding while the man stared her down, his fingers still pressing deep.

"This mark will remind you, and I will be able to find you wherever you are, Witch. This is magic you can't reverse." He calmly stood and grabbed the book, sweat beading at his forehead, before the Reaper glanced at her one last time, his power emitting that same ominous current the Oracle and Darren had emitted. "You need us, call us."

A heavy, blank, midnight-black card lay at her feet. She smelled the silver in it. Words scripted in silver appeared before her eyes and burned in her mind as she touched it. A phone number and scripture, she had heard, appear just for that cardholder who has the gift of Light in them, lay on its surface and misted to connect with her inner Light.

"Use it smartly, and Calvin will find you. We will be in touch," said the man she used to know as the Attacker but now knew as the Reaper.

Suddenly, the room darkened, and everyone in it was gone, and her office was back in order. She felt at peace, and she took a moment to breathe in that satisfaction before shifting back to "play the dark game."

She quickly cleaned herself up and sent a dark charge through the room to balance out any Light that may be picked up. Just then a member of the Dark society knocked on her door.

Exhaling and folding her hands over her desk where the book once lay, Winter sat rigid, her mind quickly clicking and locking away everything that happened as her dark side came back out to play. She smoothed her hair back, filled up a turned-over coffee mug, and took a sip.

A sly sneer spread across her face while she sat back and crossed her legs. She could feel the daggers she had hidden pressing around her thighs. Her plan had worked, and now her vengeance on the Dark was set in motion. She was going to enjoy every bit of the pain she inflicted on the Dark Houses.

A loud knock and a quick click of her doorknob made her sapphire eyes flash in pent-up anger. If only these bastards had just witnessed what she did, they would now be ash at her feet. As she would kick and dance over with a smile.

She tilted her head to the side, crossed her hands together, and remembered that all things occured in time. She calmly chimed, "You may come in."

A fleeting question hit her mind. She watched the nosy Cursed, who disguised herself as her secretary over the department, walk in. She wondered what the Oracle's name was.

Chapter 20

Sleep felt so good, and so did her body. She woke up in Khamun's bed again and she had to grin. The man just refused to drop her off in her own house, let alone her own bed. Stretching and running her legs over the soft warm sheets, she looked around as Darren came to mind. His touch seemed to amplify her visions, her power, her words, and it freaked her out as they joined minds.

She remembered Darren repeating, "Oh shit, oh shit, oh shit," then "If this isn't some tight-ass shit."

It made her laugh in her mind as words poured from both of their minds. Knowledge flooded them as they processed it all. She knew that her body was going to crash, so she pushed forward and held on as long as she could with Darren's help. What they both learned was that the more they pushed, the faster they crashed and waned in strength. They both knew that the sensory overload needed to be said, but they couldn't and the rest of it, entered them separately even as Darren let her go.

She had to read that book and check on Amit. She had liked what she saw when she healed him completely. Kali matched him very well and vice versa. Talking with her cousin was also on the list.

So she slid out of the bed, ran a hand over her purple romper and headed into the hallway. Khamun must have been busy, because he was nowhere to be seen, and the house seemed ultra-quiet but in a calming way. The scent of food made her stomach growl as she decided to walk through the halls barefoot, hunting down the source. She entered a kitchen that outdid her own restaurant.

"You must be, Sanna. It is a blessing to see you well."

Turning, Sanna's eyes locked on a beautiful older woman who stood cutting various herbs and vegetables. She looked around the same age as her mother. The welcoming woman wore her hair in braided red locs that sat on her head like a crown, and wore an Ankh that nestled squarely against her heart and accented her full, plush breasts in a tan sundress. Her grin was so bright that it seemed as if her skin hummed with a soft cinnamon glow.

Sanna instantly knew who the woman was, and she almost slapped a hand to her forehead, a part of her mind flicking with awareness. This was

Khamun's mother and he had said she wanted to meet her.

"Yes, ma'am. I am. Hello." Sanna timidly smiled and blushed. She couldn't believe he left her here without a warning. She almost felt embarrassed, as if she was displaying some intimate claim that didn't even happen.

Waving a knife holding hand around, Khamun's mother winked and motioned for Sanna to come closer. "You can call me, Neffer. Please help me with this. My son wanted a chicken pot pie, so since this is the first time I've been able to cook for him in a very long time, that is what I am making him."

Cooking Sanna could do, so she reached for an extra knife that lay on the granite marble island in front of her and chopped, nerves hitting her hard. She wondered why Neffer hadn't cooked for her son in a long time. She had to gather it was due to work.

"My son told me everything in how you awakened. You are something powerful, sweetheart. This is good."

She couldn't help but grin at the warmth directed her way and she glanced up while cooking. "I . . . I don't know. I really haven't figured out yet how to do what I've been doing."

"This is true. He told me that as well. Which is why I am here. I wanted to meet the woman I've been dreaming about for centuries. The woman who has helped bring my son back to me."

Silently inhaling, Sanna shook her head. "Oh, no, ma'am. I didn't do anything. And you've been dreaming about me for centuries?"

Neffer chuckled and studied the young woman. She was very beautiful. She was exactly the type her son had occasionally hunted for in Society as teen. She knew this was the woman he was looking for and that she was her son's mate, which put her heart at ease.

"Rule number one, sweetie. All Oracles are made different." She quietly sat her knife down and reached out and lightly rested a hand on Sanna.

Power knocked both women's heads back, and Neffer quickly wheeled it in. She watched slack-jawed at the young woman who sat slumped over, her eyes closed. She dropped her hand quickly and stepped back.

"Of all that is Holy. You are the Legend, a piece to the key of our history."

Sanna panted, a hand resting to her heart. She saw everything this woman had gone through with Khamun: the love of her son; the pain at her son not fitting into Society standards; the fights with her husband in trying to make him understand that their son did not want to step into his shoes as future Elder of all the Houses; the secret she held in protecting her beloved boy; the love and pride she felt as her son took his claim back and proved to Society and her husband that he was a force to be reckoned with.

She saw and saw until the link broke, and she sat trying to keep herself from falling backwards. This woman was a Queen of some sort in Society. No. An Eldress. Her aura exuded regal, and it reminded her of Angela Basset. It only astounded her more that this woman was the only Oracle in the region.

"I guess. Please. Don't treat me differently. I really don't know what I am or what my purpose is." She wheezed, waving a hand in the air, and inhaled deeply.

Neffer slid a hand over her back in a circular motion. "I am sorry. I knew a power link would happen, but now that is over, we will be able to move on, darling. I am here to help you. By the Light you have been hidden well, and by the Light . . . you sound like my son."

Sanna studied the woman. Her eyes undulated and scanned for darkness or lies within Neffer. She blinked.

Neffer did the same.

"Okay, I think Khamun needs to know that you've known what he is, even before his Council welcome him back."

Neffer dropped her hands and gazed at the young woman, a flash of protective warmth flowed from her before she cracked a smile. "You love him. This is good, and yes, child, now that you are here, I believe we have to have a talk."

Sanna agreed and reached out to grip Neffer's hand. "I meant no disrespect. It's just—"

"He's like you. Powerful and has been living alone in not knowing or having anyone to accept him outside of his own House. Except you. That I do know. And you do not dishonor me. It pleases me to hear these words from a fellow sister of the Valor."

"What is that?" Sanna asked, watching Neffer pick her knife back up and resume chopping.

"It is the house you will now belong to, until you and my son hurry up and marry. Then you will be of both Royal Houses, but we will discuss that later. Society has been wondering who this new house is, that is already linked to the Royals. I am going to love seeing those snobs be put in their place yet again, when they learn that you, my dear, are the Key."

Neffer's beaming face made Sanna relax.

"They cannot know that yet. But it will be interesting to see the people that have caused your son, my cousins, and the rest of his family grief. I'm not opposed to a little in-your-face mental smackdown."

Neffer's laugh flowed through Sanna like wonderful chiming bells.

Neffer glanced up and enjoyed the sweet smile on Sanna's face. "I like you a lot, young lady, and not because I saw you and my son together. This is good. It is refreshing to have the old house open again and for me to teach."

Sanna was excited as Neffer spoke to her about current movies, music, shopping, and more. Neffer and her mother would get along great. She would definitely have to set up a luncheon for the pair to meet. Both could relate so much to the feeling of loneliness in the protection of their children.

Khamun strolled in with her luggage. "Smells good in here, Momma."

Sanna quirked an eyebrow as Darren followed, twirling what she knew without a doubt were her house keys.

"Sanna." Khamun hugged and kissed his mother. He seamlessly strolled through and found a way to leave a lingering kiss on her plump lips, before his mother could see.

"Slick," Sanna muttered.

Khamun flashed a coy smile before pausing. "I took it upon myself to hijack you, baby. Momma wants to get this training going. So the sooner the better."

"Yup, and Kali's going to house-sit. She said she'll take care of your home and that she loves you." Darren held a bantering smile on his face.

Sanna rolled her eyes at him. "If I have to train, so do you, Dare."

Darren picked up an apple. Taking a bite and resting an elbow on Sanna's shoulder, he said, "Yup. Lenox, and Khamun got me, oh and his Pops. They want to run some tests at what exactly I can do, due to yesterday."

"Good."

"We're going to leave you ladies to it, since I'm not allowed to cook when the mother is in the house. Some of the staff are on their off-day, baby, but I have one that, if you need anything, you can ring her."

Sanna blushed and shook her head. "No, that's too much. I can figure my way around here and take care of myself."

Khamun stared her down.

Sanna swiveled in her chair and raised an eyebrow. "If I have to have one due to the rules of things, baby, you have to have one too. It's up to you if you utilize her is all. Not changing a thing. Oh, and baby . . . Kyo will be over soon as well. She's visiting her Pops with Take."

With a sigh, she turned back to prepping the food. She knew she needed to check her cell-phone as she watched her brother and Khamun disappear.

Neffer's grumbles interrupted her thoughts. "That boy is stubborn just like his daddy."

"My Light. Really I am not all *that* difficult. Hmm?" A tall, ninety-nine percent cocoa-dark-chocolate man walked in, sheathing a set of guns, his arms crossed over his barrel of a chest.

Sanna almost fell out of her chair.

"You must be Miss Steele. My beautiful wife has been talking nonstop about you."

He held out a giant hand that seemed to swallow her own, and she felt like passing out once again. The visions hit her quick, leaving her breathless while she sat up straight, keeping all knowledge to herself. This man was literally a King.

He was born and bred from the womb of Africa, and though he held a slight lilt in his accented voice, his bone structure said Zulu and Nubian. She could taste his past lives, with a hint of something more to him, something she was not meant to decode yet. Whatever that hidden truth was, it made her quickly look away.

Not only did he look like an older Khamun, but he looked like his own blend of Idris Elba with a walk that could threaten Denzel. Sanna's eye twitched with taking in this man's visage. He was powerful and could snap her in two if she did wrong.

Having a male in her presence like him made her nervous because immediately, with that handshake, she felt his claim on her as daughter. She saw how much knowledge he held about all of Society, many he kept private to protect his people.

His deep, silky voice pulled her out of her zone. She saw where Khamun got his swag from, "Sanna? I stand corrected wife. I apologize for not greeting you via your first name. I am Khamun's father, Omri V'ance or to you of the human world, Omri Cross, High Elder, and Region King of the Eastern, Central, and Southern Nephilim Societies, as well as Ambassador to the Motherland Africa region."

Sanna's mouth dropped. This man controlled half of the US and was a major political power in Chicago. *My damn!* echoed in her mind, and she slowly flashed her pearly whites.

Omri's dark eyes glowed as he slowly presented a beautiful warm smile.

"*I see you crushing my Pops, huh?*" Khamun's sensual low voice with a hint of humor ebbed in her mind.

She jumped then fell backwards onto the kitchen floor.

Khamun was at her side in a flash. He helped her stand as she held his shoulders, and laughter lit his eyes as his shoulders began to shake. He laughed so hard, her body vibrated with him.

"Hey, Pops. I see you scaring women again."

Khamun helped her stand up. His hands naturally fell to her waist. With a smooth embrace they shifted to rest on her hips while holding her from behind.

Sanna flushed a thousand shades of red.

Omri walked up to Khamun to clasp a hand on his son's shoulders, and both men exchanged a silent, strained look.

A moment after, Momma Neffer pushed everyone out of the kitchen to finish prepping as she talked with Sanna more.

Everything seemed to go well at dinner.

Darren dipped out sometime after dessert. After Neffer kept hinting to him about a godniece coming to visit from the West Societies, and how pretty she was.

Sanna was loving it and smiling, thinking karma was a bitch, every time he glanced her way with a pleading look in his eyes. She definitely was going to find that niece and mess with her beloved brother some more.

Looking Khamun's way, she studied his rigid posture at the table. There was a hidden undertone that had her worried for him. When she touched both parents, she saw that tension was the reason why Khamun kept his family at a distance.

She frowned and reached over to slide her hand over his. His glance from the side of his stern face made her heart reach out to him. They definitely needed to talk about it all, and not through some easy mind-lock.

Dinner couldn't have been over fast enough, Khamun thought as he cleaned up the kitchen. His mother had wanted to stay around and tidy up, but his father had other plans and quickly snatched her up and took her home. Part of him knew his father did that on his behalf, to help him spend time with a napping Sanna.

He smiled thinking about her. Through her shyness, she connected well with his parents, and even though he knew she had picked up a lot of hidden dialog between him and his parents, she rode with it like a soldier. It made him sit proud at that table, that he had his own queen to have his back in this all.

He crossed his arms over his chest and watched her. She lay mouth open, eyes closed, and passed out hard. He chuckled as her hand sleepily ran over her belly while she turned on her side. His eyes instantly rested on her plump rear as he smiled. He could watch her sleep for a lifetime. Hell, he did just that over her lifetime, but now it was different. No cloaking, no following protocol. No. Everything was now out in the open, and she was his.

With a quiet ease, he picked her up and carried her to his room. She had her own rooms, but he didn't want to tell her that just yet. He wanted her scent all through his sheets for those nights when he needed to feel her next to him and she wasn't there.

"Khamun?"

He looked down as he held her. Sanna shifted in his arms, making him hold her tighter. "Yeah? I'm sorry I woke you." He paused and pushed open his bedroom door before walking in, kicking lights on with his mind.

"It's okay. Just had a little bit of the *itis*. That potpie was so good." She flashed him a sleepy smile.

As she watched him, she became more alert, and his stomach clenched with sudden anticipation and the need to kiss her. "Yeah, Sanna?" Khamun closed his eyes. He felt her fingers strum through his braided locks, loosening each braid.

She played with the ends of his locks as she muttered, "Hmm?"

Her body seemed to shimmer and he ran his tongue over his fangs. He could feel them threatening to drop, and his body shook with need. He had been neglecting his feedings still. By now he should have been sick, sweating with a fever, but ever since he had that taste of her blood due to Kali, he had been ignoring his huntings to feed.

His last feeding was when fighting against the demons that were chasing Amit. Yet, weeks later, he was functioning fine, but now, with her near to him, that seemed to have changed.

As he gently sat her down, he felt his hands shaking. "I have to go out tonight," slipped cautiously from his lips, and he inwardly cursed. He had other plans, such as seducing her, but now his body seemed to crave something else, and he wasn't about to drink from her without her consent.

So, the idea of hunting shot out of his mouth before asking her, and the look in her eyes had him burning with heat mixed with a need to feed. His Craving was taking over, and he knew he'd fuck her up if she didn't stop looking so damn good.

"Why?" Her pleading voice wafted across his senses.

It made his sight go hazy as he gazed at her pulsing aortic vein and he growled. "I thirst. I need to go, baby." He pulled up and her hand cupped his face.

She pulled him back down, and her lips suddenly brushed against his.

A moan stirred in his belly and worked its way up through his slightly parted lips. As it escaped from it, it spilled out and filled the room as he gripped her.

"Drink from me. I saw you had already before," she calmly coaxed. Her fingertips traced his jawline, and he tilted his head to kiss the palm of her hand.

"I don't want to hurt you, because right now I want to fuck you. No soft, slow lovemaking, but straight take your throat and go so deep into you that I black out." His voice was so low and primal, it rumbled. He was taken aback because that was the last thing he wanted to say. His eyes roamed over her hazy face, and he swore he saw her smile while she shifted under him.

"I know. I saw it in my dreams. I need you to feed, baby, so you don't get sick, so feed."

Khamun felt her cup the back of his head with her hands. She pushed his mouth to her neck, and he hissed, his fangs dropping as he pulled way. "Naw, baby, I want to mark you elsewhere." He pulled his locks back.

He demanded her eyes to follow his movements while he ran his hands down her body and momentarily stopped to pull off his tee. He too had been dreaming about this, and every dream of passion seemed to hit his body as he licked his lips. He dropped down in a sweeping motion to slide her on her hip while he kissed her thick, buttery-soft thigh.

His third eye opened, and he could see her biting her lower lip as power ebbed from her to meld with his own snapping current. The sensation caused his shoulders to roll back as he let his wings open.

"Oh, why are you so sexy and beautiful, Khamun?"

He let his lips draw over the back of her knee to kiss his way to her calf. "Because . . . I'm about to sound corny, but this is divine truth. I was made just for you, baby. No lie."

He kissed the top of her foot and then rubbed her delicate foot between his hands. Her eyes seemed to hum in power as he slid her leg over his shoulder, shifting downward to kiss her intoxicatingly warm inner thigh.

"Damn! Sanna, tell me to stop now because once I kiss your inner thigh again, baby, all stopping is going out the door." He waited for her reply.

He looked up and saw her arching, her hands gripping the sheets, while his third eye roamed over her body like invisible fingers, stroking and caressing her. He smiled as he let one psychic finger tap against her blossoming bud.

She gasped, "No, don't stop."

Tilting his head with a quiet smile, he kissed her. His wings slid under her to lift her up as he slipped down her silky body, sucking her soft flesh at her thigh. Her sweet, honeyed scent took over his air, and he groaned as he briefly brushed the tip of his nose over her covered mound.

"So this is mine?" he quizzically asked, waiting.

From an angle he saw Sanna's head bob up and down with a yes, and he deeply chuckled. The Reaper in him enjoyed this type of hunt.

"I can't hear you, baby. So this is mine? To taste? To kiss? To feed from?"

Sanna's gasp hit him squared in his sacs, almost milking him, and he centered himself, breathing slowly.

She licked her lips, swallowing hard. "Y—yes. I'm yours."

Khamun turned his head to kiss and trace her buttery softness. The tip of his tongue circled in a swirling motion against her inner thigh. He was glad she was wearing the shorts he hadn't changed her out of.

"Mmm! You taste so sweet, Sanna. Can I have you for a lifetime?" He knew if he bit her at this moment, his Craving would turn into a marking, and she would be a part of him as if they were married.

In the Nephilim world, a marking bite was the releasing of pheromones through the fangs that injected into the intended mate. This only happened during the Craving, and when an intended mate had opened their mental barriers for the union. This bite signaled a marriage of sorts.

Khamun could taste the sweet mixture in his mouth as he swallowed and waited for Sanna's mental barriers, body and soul, to say yes. As he glanced up, he saw her body glow from her eyes through her soul.

Sanna softly smiled, her voice humming with power, "Yes, we've waited too long."

Khamun whispered, "Oracle-Vessel? Sanna?"

Sanna's hand slid over her thigh then over his face as she softly replied, "The one and the same."

Khamun's own power locked and synced with her, and he inwardly groaned. His fangs dropped at full length as he bowed his head and took his bite. His fangs sank into her soft silky skin, and he marked her. His lips were so close to her heated mound that, while he drank, he knew he had instantly found her pleasure vein.

Her light, rich taste flooded his senses, and he pressed down more, drinking, as she groaned. Her hands fisted in his locks, and he pulled back some, to let his fingers shift to brush against her covered mound.

As he drank, he listened to her panting, and her hips rocked up against his touch. He hooked a finger to push the fabric of her shorts to the side and expose her shimmering pearl.

The first kiss of air against her hardening bud hit hard.

Khamun smiled at the way she lifted from the bed for him. His hunger seemed to double as he stared at her opening petals. Bowing his head low, he sealed his bite wound with a kiss and the flick of his tongue.

Her ample hips ached to be touched and he slipped his hands under them, then up her back as she looked down at him. Her hands reached up to rest on his shoulders and he found the zipper to her jumper. He slowly pulled down, until it opened for him like a Christmas present.

Sanna turned for him, his wings still cradling her and she allowed him to pull it off of her voluptuous body.

He sat up some to gently lay her back on the bed and his wings slid back as he studied her body. A flash of worry hit her face and he gently took her hand, entwining their fingers. He placed her palm against his heart, and then dragged it over his abs. That spark of worry in her eyes melted away and he kissed her palm again.

"Your blood has me at ease baby. I thought I'd rip through you. Shit. You are so . . . intoxicating. But your blood . . . it's calmed me," he rumbled.

He took her hand and reached for her other, to hook her thumbs on the waist of his jeans. Motioning for her to pull down, he slid up and she pulled down. A sudden burst of nervousness hit him from her scent and he dropped a kiss on her. Kissing a lower lip then a top, he then slid the tip of his tongue in her mouth.

He knew she could taste her blood and the remains of his marking secretion. He let her savor the newest of it all as she shook with need, pushing his jeans down with her feet as her nails dug into his back.

He almost nodded and said, *Take that shit*, as she took the kiss deeper. His rigid member jutted out to hit his stomach, his tip aching as he pushed the rest of his jeans to the floor. His fingers found her bra, and he pulled back to drop his head to kiss the top of her pillow-soft breasts.

Music flooded through his mind, connecting to his surround system as Raheem DeVaughn crooned "Closer (Won't Be Long)."

Sanna sharply inhaled as she cradled his head and he unhinged her lacy black bra, making it drop to the floor behind him with his power. He was lost in her soft skin as he opened his mouth and let a toffee-dipped nipple slip into his mouth.

As he sucked and gently tugged, he felt as if her hands were suddenly caressing him, stroking with the same rhythm he played with at her pebbled nipple. He sucked air between his teeth.

He clearly felt her hands on his back, but this was more. He knew he had opened her third eye. The scent of her desire and his flowed through the room. He slid down to kiss her belly while he slowly pulled at her black boy shorts.

"I dreamed you were this beautiful," he muttered and shifted, pulling the lacy fabric off with one hand while his other hand gently parted her supple flesh. She lay open like a plum, dripping sweet nectar just for him.

He remembered how good she tasted before. He smiled as he glanced up at her. Her beautiful chocolate eyes glowed golden, and it made him kiss the petals of her lips lightly. He tilted his head, bringing her to his mouth and French-kissed her caramel sweet haven. His tongue slipped within her creamy walls, and she arched, shifting and softly gripping the sheets. He held her in place as he widened her luscious thighs and pulled back to dip in and out of her before twisting the tip of his tongue over her swollen bud.

Her panting egged him on as he flattened his tongue and gave her a couple long licks before leaning in to kiss and suck her pearl. His anticipation was heightened as he dipped his tongue within and let her hips ride his mouth before he switched and slowly slipped a finger into her tightness. The tension of it had him pulling back slowly to keep her wet before he attempted again.

After a couple of tries, giving her a rhythm she could take, he felt her milky walls tighten around his fingers, and he smiled, kissing her bud, before making a come-here motion.

"Khamun!" escaped her lips.

He loved that he made her nervousness disappear. Her body was poetry in motion while he dropped his hands and shifted up, kissing until he found her beautiful mouth. He could read her body while he touched her and he felt her tension return.

It wasn't in him to let her hurt or feel this fear, so he took his time and let her body press against his. He let his length let her know how much he wanted her, before he felt her soften.

He shifted to bring her leg up to hook over his hip while he took his tip and dipped into her liquid sweetness. The heat her yoni gave him had him closing his eyes. He let her heat draw him into her slowly.

Her body tensed again, and he kissed her slowly, knowing what he was about to hit. He tilted her neck to the side, nipped, sucked, licked and whispered, "Gimme," and he bit down and took his fill of her sweet blood again.

Sanna whimpered in pleasure, her nails digging as she arched into him.

Khamun pressed his hips down and up to breach her gate, successfully opening her, until he filled her to the hilt. His body almost shut down on him with how tight, wet and hot she was. As he swallowed and slid unto his hunches, he caressed her face and tilted his head to the side in awe. Two small fangs broke through her gumline, and his body shook in recognition and pleasure.

"Mmmm, Sanna," he groaned. He dropped down and kissed her yielding mouth as her arms held him tight. He kissed away her spilling tears.

"Khamun," whispered from her lips.

He felt her tighten around him, making him slowly glide in and out of her tight wetness. He fit her like a key, as if her womb was made just for him, and he slid back arching, holding her hips to teach her how to roll her hips.

He almost came as he watched her plant her feet and slide her hands over his chest. He almost gave up the ghost, as she made her hips wind in a slow grind that had him almost calling on the Most High. He knew she was slightly hurting with trying that move, so he smirked and shook his head at her haughtiness.

"Baby, damn, you bad. Come here. Let me help you out." He picked her up and flipped her, to straddle him. His head dropped back as she took in all of his ten-plus inches.

Sanna curved into him with the new sensation, the intensity making her bite her lip while he moved her hips.

Her tightness had him ready to speak the old language, and he bit his lower lip to keep from doing just that.

As she bucked forward, he cursed due to the pleasure and spat out every language he knew, old and new. "Sanna, work them hips, baby," he pleaded.

The way his voice dripped molasses in that plea had Sanna tentatively move. She worked her hips slowly as she gently grew brave, the rhythm in her soul, her heart and blood, guiding her to rock until she found a tempo that was comfortable for her.

Khamun's wings spread out on the bed as he watched her newling fangs lengthen and her eyes lock with his.

The Craving roared in Sanna's body, making him bare his throat.

"Take that bite, baby. Fi-find the vein, Queen," he muttered, pointing at his jugular.

Uncertainty had Sanna shaking her head. "I want you like you had me," she whispered.

Khamum almost came with just that statement alone. He quietly nodded, tears in his own eyes from the need to nut. He watched Sanna slid him out of her.

Her body shook from the exit and its own anger at the abandonment.

He glanced at his glistening shaft, seeing what marked her as a virgin. He reached for a corner of the bed to pull the sheets and wipe himself clean for her. Her hunger was apparent as she watched him. That need had him motion for her to mark him.

She looked up licking her lips, flushing cinnamon red with not knowing what to do.

Understanding and desire made him smile. "Sit on my stomach."

"Huh?" she asked. Her curly 'fro damp with sweat, she pushed her mane out of her face.

She was so beautiful, he thought. He chuckled, pulling her by the hand. "You heard me. Sit on my stomach, your back to me."

Blushing, she nodded nervously and straddled him as he explained.

He was delighted with the view of nothing but her nice plump rear and sugary-slick openness. "Lean forward and find your mark," he whispered.

His shaft stood erect with anticipation while his hands slid down her back. He fisted one hand into her long, thick, curly 'fro, the other angled her to slide, until her sweet haven hovered right where he wanted it. He knew he was in ecstasy.

As she braced herself on her knees, he let go and gripped her hips, pulling them toward his hungry mouth. He leaned up to drink from her open cup as he heard her breath hitch before she muttered, "Mmmm."

That had him eager and hungrier as she found her mark. She held his shaft and strummed her fangs against his staff.

Her boldness turned him on as she bit down. His body jolted up at the penetration of her fangs. The deep sensual mark of her fangs made contact with his inner thigh near his sacs, making him fist the sheets as his moan vibrated against her swollen pearl. Her tugs of thirst had him finding her hand and showing her how to stroke him as he pumped in her hand.

Pulling back, she looked behind her, and she licked her lips.

That had him seeing red as he flipped her, finding her tightness while he gently slid in again. Her hands found his locks, tugging while her legs wrapped around him tight. Their hands entwined, he made each stroke seal his name in her body.

Protection sigils shimmered through her body as he worked each one in deeper with each thrust of his hips. He bucked while he felt her split the sigils and weave them into his body as well.

With a grunt, he picked her up, so she could ride his lap, while he drowned himself in her sweet, soft mouth, and they came together.

His seed exploded deep, hot and thick within her loving walls, making her body tighten while vibrating into a deep arch, her rear throwing it back against him.

Her beautiful golden eyes flickered like diamonds while her shoulders flexed and silvery white glowing wings broke from her shoulder blades.

The beauty of her wings had him holding her tight while she breathed heavily, her face buried in his neck. Stroking her hair, he slid a thumb over the side of her cheek, catching each tear before it fell. "I love you," he whispered.

Sanna's soft voice flowed over him as she kissed his neck and whispered back, "I love you too." She bit down, drank, and pulled the last bit of seed from him.

He felt her magnificent wings encase him, while his did the same. His fingers dug into her supple rear, and Novel's "We Got It Bad" drowned out their soft breathing and quiet, slow strokes.

Chapter 21

"Ahhhh!"

The Dark Lady, also known as Princess Reina, woke up in a cold sweat, her eyes dilated. Her creamy breasts heaved as she tried to catch her breath. The sheets lay in bunched knots around her as she looked around her dark, fire-lit room. She saw blood—glorious, beautiful, ruby-black blood—drowning everyone and everything.

It made her smile, until she saw the source of that blood. Thousands of her people lay in dusting corpses, their blood washing away the delicious sins and taint they had collected over the centuries.

Her father sat on a mound of bodies under him, his arms held behind his back as he roared. A swift slash of light decapitated him right in front of her eyes. Pure delight filled her as she watched her father die, his sins, his darkness ripped from him by an unseen force.

But anger filled her as she watched light drown out the darkness and her people. Screaming her displeasure as she saw that Oracle bitch in her mind, she fumed. She was the one in her dreams since the beginning of Reina's hunt for her. She watched as she pulled at the bitch's hair when she saw the bloodied body of her twin as a kid, ten years old, staring at her with a smile of hatred in his glance. Confused, a light flashed and made her look away and focus back on the Oracle.

That bitch held an antiquated book in her hands, a large leather-bound book that looked to be connected with other matching volumes. She was flipping through them and speaking the old language of the Light.

A tall, cloaked man, a man she assumed was a Slayer, stood by, arms crossed, ancient weapons in his hands, fangs glistening in the dark, black locks resting over his shoulders.

Something about him made her watch him closely as he lit up with power that frightened her. A power that spread to that Oracle bitch, and it made Reina almost cower in shameful fear. She refused to go out like a bitch, but that current seemed to spread.

She saw a shadowed group touch the Oracle bitch, and the power washed over everything. She screamed, and her vision shifted, and she saw that same book lying hidden by stone-fire beasts.

Beasts, which she thought were mythical, swarmed past her vision. Dragons. She saw it. She saw the marker of a hazy landmark and knew she had to get it before that Oracle bitch got to it. If she could get it, then she could save her people, and she could get the Oracle and kill her. She was a threat to her kind. One that wasn't worth turning, unlike what her father thought, and she intended to kill her. Especially after this vision.

How dare that bitch try to scare her! Her vision tilted again, and she screamed. Her twin stood back in front of her, very much alive, the same age as she. She swung her Asp ring, ready to cut his beautiful face. She watched him laugh, reach out, and kiss her forehead.

"You fear what you'll become," was all he said to her in Spanish.

His touch made her fall to her knees. Light spilled from her hands, her eyes, and then her mouth. She screamed, "No!" and saw that Oracle bitch.

The Oracle dropped down near her and whispered in her ear, "You will not take me, but we will meet."

She too kissed Reina, a kiss full of power against her cheek, and Reina imploded, the light turning her, and she woke up screaming. The bitch was powerful. Too powerful. She had to die. And Reina had to get that book before she accomplished the death of her people and herself.

"Princess?" Winter and Nydia's soft voices blended as one.

Reina gathered herself and threw the covers off her. "Change of plans, ladies," she almost roared as she constrained her anger and pushed the hands away that tried to help her out of her massive bed. "Get off me! I said we have a change of plans. *Nydia!*" she shouted as she stared at her Protector, who stood in a sheer peach camisole nightgown, the fire's glow behind her from the fireplace casting a glimpse of her naked body underneath.

"Have you located my pet?" Reina's hand flew to her disheveled hair while she glared at her Protector, watching her as she waited.

"I have not. His scent has disappeared, but I am backtracking and going to his old hangouts."

Reina glared, walked up to her, and back-handed her hard as her Protector snarled. Nydia clutched her face before reflexively backhanding Reina back with a growl. "I am doing my job, Princess. I am here to protect and honor your will!" She stood panting, her hands clenched.

Reina leered and licked her own bloody mouth as she nodded. "I have another job for you. *Mira.*" She snapped her fingers and walked around the chambers.

Winter reached out to dab at her mouth, and Reina hissed, pushing her back in fringed fury.

"Find this book! I have seen some of the land-marks where it might be, and it is important that we get it before that Oracle bitch and her Protectors get it!" She flashed the image of what she saw in her vision to both Winter and Nydia.

"You find it, and you draw that bitch to you. She wants it. We get that, we get her, and you *end* her!" Reina's eyes flashed with power as she breathed hard. "Do you *both* understand me? Take what you need, and you both get that book."

Winter calmly smoothed a hand down her silk royal blue nightgown and averted her eyes as she spoke in respect. "Princess, your father wills that we keep her alive, and this book you seek . . . we will do all we can to find it."

Moving with a silent swiftness, her gown rus-tled against her stone floor. Fury had control tonight, and she smiled in satisfaction as she held Winter by her throat. She pressed her body against Winter's softness as she spoke. "Do . . . not . . . question . . . me. Get what I said and pre-pare my things. *We* go hunting for this book, and *we* will find it and present the head of that bitch on a platter for my beloved father. *Comprendes*?"

Winter kept her eyes on the Princess and saw Nydia watch with a flash of concern that quickly disappeared. Nodding her head, she realized her nails had dug into Reina's wrist, and the dark aromatic scent of her blood had filled the room. Winter licked her lips and wished this was a moment in time where she was blessed with fangs. She wished she wasn't just an immortal human Mystic bitten by the Cursed and made to be a Witch, so she could defend herself bite for bite.

Reina's bite was swift, and Winter kept herself from struggling with the pain, which felt like a thousand knives cutting into her soul. The dark part of Winter did enjoy this, but the Light in her wanted to poison the bitch and light her ass on fire.

Winter raised her leg and pushed, slamming the Dark Lady to the floor as she held her neck and stepped back. She swiftly kicked the Princess before standing, panting, malicious sneer on her face. The games the Princess liked did make her happy to whup her ass.

Reina sat, face bowed, hair spilling over her face as she breathed hard, licking her glistening dark red lips with a sinister grin. "Bring me a toy. I need to fuck."

Winter nodded, and she watched as Nydia gave her customary bow. "We will follow your wishes. Darkness be."

"Nydia."

The Medusa paused, slightly turning. "Yes, Princess?"

"I still want my other toy. Find him."

Nodding, Nydia's eyes flashed, and she cast a dark smile. "As you wish." Then she quietly walked away

Reina walked back to her bed as her gown fell to the floor, leaving her naked, her creamy caramel, hieroglyph-tattooed skin glowing with the fire. Her plump rear so round and perky, with two dimples that winked, left many Dark Society women envious of their Princess. Her dark brown hair curled on the ends, spilling down her back, covering her plump breasts.

Turning away and opening the door to the suite, Winter had to find a way to warn the others and warn them fast. She also had to find a way to slow down the hunt at all costs. She was known for her knowledge in books, so she knew most of the hunt would fall on her. This sabotage was going to be interesting.

"Will Kwan satisfy you, Princess?" she calmly asked. Winter's hand held her bleeding neck as she tapped her ring and sent healing balm to spread over her neck.

"Kwan and Ethan, send them both."

Curtsying, Winter quickly and quietly exited the chamber and searched out her best well-trained attendants. They were her special little project, and they worked well in her secret game. But in this game of covert affairs, she knew she had to continue to block her mind while going any deeper. She was going to have to adjust her plans to destroy this Royal House. Glancing at her hands, she remembered what she was told and slyly smiled. Warning the others was now a high priority.

Light flashed across her eyes, and she heard a slight tinkling sound, like thousands of tiny bells. She sighed, snuggling into the warmth that claimed her as his. How he made her feel last night was unforgettable. She couldn't believe how bold and comfortable in her skin he'd made her feel. She was hungry for more of him. His taste was addictive, savory, and sweet, like toffee coated in chocolate. He was incredible.

She inhaled and remembered how he awoke her. Everything seemed to slide into place like a puzzle. She felt her body hum and click. Her gumline was slightly sore as her incisors descended. Her back was tense and tender as her wings grew. Her mouth tasted sweet like powder sugar, and everything in her said, "Bite him. Mark him," and she did. Oh, did she.

His touch suddenly made her more aware, as the light and the tinkling sound continued off in the distance.

She stretched, a slow grin forming as his searching mouth brushed her lips. She heard him whisper, "Wake up."

She arched as his large hand found her waking kitty. She thought she was going to lose it, the way he touched her. It was as if he intuitively knew how to make her crave him. Her legs began to rub together, creating additional friction, and she felt him flick his tongue over her hard nipples then suck.

Instantly, her soft mound was in his eager mouth. He lapped at her with a gentle slurp and pulled back, blowing as he whispered, "I know you are awake."

Her head nodded up and down, and she opened her sleepy eyelids with a blink. She looked down at the man who made her body feel like a sleeping volcano. Licking her lips, she groaned and bit her lower lip at the same time.

She felt him slip a finger inside of her and gently slowly stroke her. Her body, especially where he touched, was still tender, but she felt his power blanket her, soothing away the aches she was feeling.

She moaned, "Thank you, Lord, for this man!'

Her head dug into the mattress, and her hips dipped then jutted up to match his strokes, and he claimed her mouth, drinking deeply.

The sound of the bells and the flash of light hit her senses again as distant voices in her mind broke through.

"Ey. Calm that shit down, homie. We know your palms are killing you, but chill. We got this."

"You don't understand, man! It's like I got gonorrhea of the hands. This shit is insane!"

"Ha! Gonorrhea of the hands. Good shit, homie."

Sanna recognized the voices. Amit and Calvin were joking around with each other. She sighed and tried to block them out. They were interrupting her groove while Khamun's kisses lightened, his shaft resting against her swollen clit, and she heard him chuckle.

"My man is a fool, your cousin, that is," Khamun groggily muttered, his nose tracing the side of her neck while he yawned and shifted his weight off her.

She wanted to spread her legs and let him take her to the heavens and high-five every level she passed, but the voices seemed to go on.

"You hear them too?" she asked.

Khamun's sexy chuckle vibrated through her, making her shift against him. Her hand slid down his back to find his rock-solid yet soft, well-rounded rear. He had that rear she could grip or bounce a quarter off, and she wasn't mad about it at all.

"Yeah, baby. We are very much linked right now. I see that light too, by the way and"—He grunted, holding her tight—"I think you're supposed to follow, but I don't want you to just yet."

He wiggled his hips, and she groaned, suddenly kissing his neck with need, her lower lip tracing over the second bite she gave him.

As he had explained it last night, they were unofficially married. A part of her was shocked, but her nature and heart said, "Heck, yes!" So she accepted it. She would have to adjust. And he promised, when she was ready, he would ask her the right way. So he told her to think of it as a permanent engagement, and she was fine with it.

She wondered about those who wanted to break a union made like this, and he told her it was rare, but it involved a lot of protocol and a lot of bodyguards. She just blinked and took it for what it was.

"Tell me, baby, how you learn to work them hips like that?"

She shrugged against him, her legs shifting and her hips rising as he shifted and slid himself within her an inch at a time. Now, see, he was so wrong for that, but oh, so right for it too. She squeezed her eyes tight at his girth, opening wider in tenderness and pleasure.

"I—I was just, I don't know. Saw it somewhere. Thought I'd try."

Khamun chuckled and kissed the side of her neck, licking where he bit her as he shifted up. He dropped his head to kiss the underside of her breast, where he had bit her. "Watched it, huh? So you got a little nasty in you, huh? I mean, I knew that of course, but it's something different in being in the presence of it."

Blushing, she thought back on when he'd told her she couldn't get pregnant unless she was on her cycle, and since he had been around her without her knowledge, he knew her cycle better than she. He'd told her that, since Nephilims were half-human, the Angel side of her had her Nephilim cycle as every other full month. Her human cycle had her typically once a month where she bled, but her Nephilim four-month cycle would consist of her body just cramping until it got to that fourth month, when she'd bleed.

She had to whisper another prayer because if she had to deal with bleeding every full month instead of just one full month every other four months, she'd jump off the highest building she could find. It still sucked that one month she'd bleed for that full month, but she'd deal.

Khamun's length pulled her back to reality as his slow strokes drowned out the voices in both of their minds. She found herself teary-eyed at the pleasure he gave her as he dipped between her legs again and sampled her so deeply. She found herself coming in his mouth.

"Damn! So good, baby. Come here," he cajoled.

Her eyelids fluttered close, and he sheathed himself within her again. This sensual calming of the bodies made her come for the . . . she lost count. But she felt oh so good with the many times he'd made her release.

"A'ight, baby, that light seems to be annoyed, straight interrupting grown folks' business. You think you can walk and we can see where it's at?" Khamun ran his fingers through her hair.

Sanna lay against his chest, twirling her fingers around each strand of his crinkled locks. "Mmmm. I guess."

Picking her up, Khamun took her to the bathroom, where she soaked in a hot tub with him. He scrubbed and massaged her down before lifting her up and drying her down.

She felt pampered like never before while he rubbed her down with nutty sweet oil. She gasped as he cupped her mound with a smirk on his face, rubbing that oil in, dipping into her briefly before dropping his hands.

"Oil of Ruth. It is a special blend used for helping many pains of the mind, spirit, heart, and body. It also used in"—he blushed as he softly chuckled—"in easing the pain of a virgin's first night, so there you go, baby. The house you will belong to with my mother specializes in this oil and others."

Her skin was already glowing like soft gold from their lovemaking, and the oil only enhanced it. Resting a hand over his head and tracing to cup his jaw, she watched Khamun kiss her thigh, hip, stomach, and then rise up to kiss her deeply on the lips.

Khamun moved and headed to this closet and pulled out clothes for himself and her.

She accepted the jersey-soft yoga shorts he gave her and red tank. She watched him dress, his dark cinnamon skin glowing as the muscles in his rear and back tightened while he moved. She had to turn away before he saw how much she wanted him again. The scent of their love-making mixed with the seductive scent of the oils he rubbed on her had her heady again.

"Too late, baby. I want you too, and if you keep on, we not going any damn where." His eyes flashed at her, and a slow, seductive smile spread across his face.

She swallowed, quickly putting her clothes on. She was happy that he gave her shorts that felt like jersey. She knew why, and she was very grateful. She turned back around, and she found him studying her.

His fangs kissed his lips while he closed his eyes and tossed her a pair of black-and-red Nike. "Must your thighs be so damn thick and sexy, all glowing and shit. All right, let's go." He grabbed her hand fast, entwining their fingers, while she hopped on one foot, sliding across the floor quickly to put her sneakers on.

She watched her man pause in the hallway, tilting his head left and right as he listened for the soft chiming. His amber eyes narrowed and seemed to slightly glow with power as he glanced then hitched his head. "That way."

Sanna nodded and followed. The voices in her mind returned, and she shivered. She could feel them as if they were in her face.

"Look, I just want to go back to normal. My damn hands itch and are peeling. I can't even get a decent bite of Wada cake. Shit, I want to see if your sis Kali can cook as good as she can type at that laptop."

"Hey, chump, baby girl can throw down. Let's see if you can do something else but whine, a'ight."

"I can help fix that SIMMS inventory and Logistics section that seems to be acting up . . . I mean, if we cool now."

"Li'l homie? We were good when my cousin signed her sig on the dotted line. So, a'ight, I'll type. You tell me what to do, okay."

"Yeah?"

"You good with finances? We got some backed-up shit in the system too."

"Yeah, man. Double major in accounting."

"Word? Ahh, yeah, welcome to the family, man. Kali will mark your Society papers and make it official. We'll do the tests to see what gifts you got. And stop picking your damn hands, homie. That shit is gross."

"Sorry."

Sanna stumbled against Khamun's back as he laughed and pulled her to him, his arm wrapping around her.

"This shit is hilarious. We got to get to him a 'heal him up good.'" Khamun chuckled.

Sanna blushed, and he kissed her cheeks then pointed to the bobbing light. "It's taking us to the cellars, so I'm thinking it's leading us to the compound, baby."

"Oh, really, this is how you get to it?" Looking around, she saw bottles of wine, dried meat, cheese, and even documents. It looked like something that belonged in Italy or Spain. It was very spacious and cool-feeling.

"Stay close to me to keep warm, baby."

Sanna didn't have a problem with that at all as she hooked her arm with his and matched his long strides. She memorized everything as he placed a hand against a stone wall and watched it move. Darkness took them over, and she felt something brush against her backside, slightly going in circles before pinching, causing her to raise an eyebrow.

Khamun smiled in the dark cellar, reaching around her to turn on a light. He could clearly see in the dark, but he knew she was still learning about her awakening body, so he turned the lights on, out of respect.

Sanna couldn't help herself as she reached out and studied the beauty of the murals that decorated the wall. Before her was the history of the Nephilim race. Well, some of it. Pieces seemed to be missing, and it itched at her mind that parts were lost.

Running a hand over the alternate mosaic then paints, she stopped, deep in the cellar and stared. Chipped tiles mixed with intricate paint and decades of dirt and dust seemed to cover a majority of the scene.

An angel blanketed in light and darkness seemed to hold a blazing sword as the glowing hand of a woman touched him. She frowned because the pair was either covered in muck or missing tiles.

"Khamun, what is this?" she said, tracing the painting, feeling faint power under its covered surface.

She felt him stand behind her, his warmth comforting her as he studied the scene. The glowing light seemed to hover over them as their fingers ran over the smooth ridges.

"This is the older section. Pops use to take me down here and share all he knew."

Reaching over her, his large hand covered hers then moved to trace over the cool surface. "I remember this. I used to play right under this area. The ages deteriorated it. It's so much crap on it that Pop tired of trying to restore it."

Khamun's voice softened with the memories. "Yeah. This spot always drew me to it. I wanted to be him. That soldier with the sword. Pops couldn't tell me the full story, but I know this story extended for a while in the tunnels. I almost got lost trying to read it all as a kid."

Sanna looked up at Khamun as she spoke, "Oh . . . well, maybe you can fix it. I don't know. We can go now." A crease formed between her brows as she studied his face. He seemed to be engrossed in the images that peeked through.

She rested a hand on his bicep, and his power hit her in her gut, making her own sing while she exhaled with a shake and a backward step.

"Something is here," they both said then shook it off.

Glancing over at Sanna, Khamun took her hand, stepping back as he took her back to where they originally stood. "Step here on this floor panel, and it'll take us all the way. As for that mural, I think I'll work on it later."

Sanna nodded in acknowledgment, a soft smile playing at her lips. A whizzing zip made her look past him as the bouncing light landed on his shoulder, making her choke on a quick laugh.

The light seemed to be an extension of the both of them, a part of their consciousness that said they had obligations to handle. So they walked into the corridor.

Sanna gasped as it wrapped around them and turned into an elevator that took them right to the compound, where a door opened, and they both stood in a beautifully decorated bedroom with art-adorned walls.

Sanna blinked. She knew that work, and she blushed as she saw a painting of her sleeping in her bed back in St. Louis, mounted right over a huge super king-size bed. Her face was covered, and she looked like a sleeping living statue, but she knew her shape.

"Your room, I take it?" She pulled his hands to rest on her hips, cupping his hands.

He nodded. "Yes,"

Just then a loud boom shook them out of their embrace, and they jetted out of the bedroom.

Sanna's body still hurt as she ran. She could feel him within, and that had her blushing. She inwardly shook her head at herself. She needed to get her mind focused on what needed to be done here.

"Okay! Marco or Lenox, which one of you mothertruckers is blowing shit up again?" Khamun bellowed, humor lacing his eyes as he took Sanna's hand.

The place was huge! She knew it was two levels, and she currently was on the main level. Light shined in from the second-level windows, brick, steel, iron and other industrial type fixtures housed in the building. A beautiful graffiti-painted mural sprawled across one side of the building as huge military-worthy HDTV screen/computer sat built into another walk. She saw other HDTVs through the compound, but that one was quite impressive.

"Living quarters are down here. Main level is where we train, though sometimes you can find us training down here too, baby. There's a steam room and shower, as well a restaurant-quality kitchen, all Kali's doing. There are multiple garages for multiple cars and air transportation. We all have training in flying planes, except for Kali. Heights are not her thing."

Sanna shook her head as she locked eyes on an engrossed Amit. He sat in front of the huge computer typing away. Kali hovered over his shoulder with an annoyed look on her face, while Calvin watched the pair with a goofy smile.

Calvin's magic flowed over Amit's hands, acting as a protective glove.

"Kali must have found her match." Sanna snickered and Khamun nodded with his arms crossed, chuckling.

Kyo's high-pitched yelling followed behind Darren's fussing and Takeshi's cussing.

Lenox's roaring halted the yelling in the compound as he took control of the situation and put down law. "Look! If you are to be a part of this house, it is your duty to learn *everything*. That means until we know what class you are. You will learn it all. Why? Because not only do *we* have an Oracle-Vessel to protect, but we have *each other* to protect. Got it?" Looking around, he nodded. " Good, now left, left, hook!"

"Sheeit, Sanna's ass needs to be here too, and 'gonorrhea hands' needs to be in here with us. We don't know his class either, my man!" Darren replied in a guttural mutter to Takeshi.

Sanna followed Khamun, who showed her an open room filled with combat dummies and posts.

"I am not a Gargoyle or Dragon, and Khamun has none to teach you, Kyo, and Take, but you will both still benefit from my training, so . . . " Lenox circled and clapped his bandaged hands together. He was dressed in black training pants and a black tank, his hands wrapped in black bandages and his hair pushed back from his face via a thin headband that blended into his hair.

He paused and stood wide-legged, his hands on his waist as sweat ran down his stuck-on tank. His dark maple skin, glistened buttery brown from the sweat, his arms taut with the workout. "Kyo, as they work on their jabs, let's show that roundhouse you pulled off back in that battle."

Kyo smiled in excitement and bounced on the balls of her feet. As she realized what he asked, her mouth suddenly turned up in a frown. "Um, I don't think I remember how I did that."

Scowling, Lenox swung out, his white Nike planted firmly.

Kyo stepped back. Her hands instinctively went out to block her chest as she shifted and dipped in a duck, coming up under the other side of his arm.

Lenox smiled with a nod, switching his stance quickly to double back and swing again.

Kyo stepped back, her black legging clad leg lifting in the air as her eyes narrowed and she saw her opening to hook the back of her knee over his neck, moving swiftly to flip him backwards.

Lenox went down fast but arched his back to kick himself forward into a low crouch, as he slowly clapped using his thighs to balance himself on the balls of his feet. Kyo's leg was still extended out as she watched, shifted her weight and slowly dropped her foot.

"You say you don't remember, huh?" He flashed a lopsided smirk as she flushed a thousand shades of red.

Music suddenly rippled through the complex. Calvin's familiar silky deep voice crooned then flipped into lyrical rapping as the beat mixed, scratched, and made Sanna want to pop her hips and dance.

Khamun bobbed his head as he walked on, motioning for Sanna to follow. She looked around as she continued her tour, finally making it to the main floor.

Walking around, she spotted Amit and headed his way. She passed Calvin as he nodded at her, while working in his studio, blaring and mixing music. He was talking to a handsome Asian guy who sported a swirling, dazzling black, ruby, and gold dragon irezumi with a bar piercing in his right eyebrow, and who had a low-fade Mohawk on his screen.

"Who's he talking to?" Sanna asked, glancing at Khamun.

"RJ. Your brother introduced them. Don't know much about him except that he's into music, teaches a b-boy and hip-hop class and martial arts class at UIC. Oh, he was also at the party your brothers were at."

"Does he know about you all? I mean us?"

Khamun shook his head. "No, everything is kept confidential. Calvin is working on some tracks with him."

Kali glanced as she saw Sanna approach. She grinned hard and turned to embrace Sanna. Kali had rich brown highlights in her loose crinkled hair that accented her rich cinnamon skin with gold hoop chandilier earrings.

She stood at the same height as Sanna, in ripped jeans, an oversized shirt that said DANGER in big black letters, with splashes of colors over the shirt. Her smooth brown shoulder peeked through, and her bangle bracelets accented her wrists. The pink and black Nike she wore emphasized the hot pink in her shirt, and her pink lipstick kicked everything off.

Sanna studied Kali's mehndi-covered hands that were done in a way to state what power level she was at.

"About time you are here, cousin. I have so much to share with you."

Her soft smile warmed Sanna's heart and calmed her nerves. This was definitely a home full of family, and she had nothing to stress about in the least bit. If anything, she had to worry about how much she'd want to protect them all.

Both women chuckled as they quietly spoke and watched Amit move like the wind on the computer.

"Wow, he's really good with computers," Sanna remarked.

She laughed when Kali scoffed. "Not really. I'm better," she muttered.

Amit looked behind him. He shook his head before locking eyes with Sanna, and nervousness hit him. Quickly he saved his work, slowly standing to approach.

He looked healthy and better outside of his hands. His deep cinnamon rich skin seemed to gain its soft ruddy glow back, and he stood a full six seven over her, his thin body filling out into a thicker track runner's shape.

His jet black hair was freshly cut in a shag look that accented his strong jawline and green-grey eyes that now had a grey pale ring around his irises, marking him as a Broken Wrath Angel. His plush lips formed into a smile as he quirked an eyebrow. His V-cut grey shirt showed a slight peek of his hard, cut chest with black veins of his healed and cleaned Cursed bite threading from his neck, disappearing under his shirt and peeking from his pectoral muscle like a swirling tattoo. His dark denim jeans hung well over his white Nike.

Sanna was happy that he seemed to be filling out because she knew once he was at his full peak, her cousin would have to lock herself away from her secret desires for Amit.

"Hey, it's good to see you and not have anything chase you," Sanna joked.

"Yeah. I want to apologize. Everything in me was saying run, and when I saw your car, it felt safe. Now I know why." Amit glanced at Kali, who rolled her eyes, squeezing by him to take over the computer and he laughed. "Damn! She has a righteous attitude."

Sanna bit her lower lip, swallowing her chuckle. "No, that just means she's warming to you. So how does it feel to be a . . . a Broken Wrath Angel, whatever that is? Talk to me and let me see your hands and see what I can do."

"All right." Extending his hands, Amit watched her slowly.

"I'm not sure. It's a huge shock. All this time I thought I was a Disciple, you know, and to learn I have that extra bump in the DNA is kind of crazy to me."

Sanna's hands hovered above his. She was careful not to touch him while she nodded. "I can understand that. Being something you don't understand what it is. I'm glad you didn't die." She flashed a soft smile and shifted her hands. She had enough flashes and jolts from touching folks to last a lifetime, so she just lightly poked a finger at the psychic glove and watched it disappear.

"Me too. I thank you for what you did. Damn! If I hadn't met you, I wouldn't be a tool for the dark, and I'm not down for that."

Sanna chuckled.

Amit leaned in. "I mean it. That world is crazy, and if I was able, I would have tried to end my life, Death Wrath or not. Thank you, Sanna. Oracle-Vessel."

"It is what it is. The Most High has a plan, and it wasn't your time to leave. And you for damn sure were not meant for the Dark."

"Ahh! That hurts. Seriously, what did that bitch to me?" Amit said through gritted teeth, and he watched Sanna do her thing.

Khamun quietly observed her from behind, and Calvin stood by his side watching as well.

"You think you can help him, shawty?" Calvin calmly questioned, concern briefly flashing in his green eyes.

"I think. I don't know but"—Something twinkled, and she looked closer at his blistered hands, shaking her head. His skin was red like it was just dipped in scalding water. How the skin peeled and leaked, she knew he was in pain. Silver strands seemed to be embedded in his hands. She frowned. "Give me some water to clean his hands."

Kali quickly stood and jetted, bringing back a bottle of water.

Pouring it over his palms, power seemed to hum around the room. "Keep your hands cupped." Sanna motioned, her third eye open, guiding her as her hands hovered over his. She felt the tug of the silver slivers in his hands seeking their exit. Power pulsated, causing the pool of water in his cupped hands to undulate as it wrapped around her and kissed her skin. Images flashed across her vision, making her briefly close her eyes.

She saw Kyo running, panting and reaching out to a falling Calvin, blood pouring from his body. Her body jolted as she saw beautiful red and gold wings rip from her sister's back, and she screamed. The woman she saw chasing Amit stood with blood on her hands and mouth. Her eyes shifted like a reptile's. Her cocoa-rich skin glowed with power and she leered. Calvin's blade lay in her side.

Sanna knew this wasn't right, and she almost screamed. She saw a woman dressed in jewels, with Asp bracelets, walk her way, a book in her hand and a gun in the other. The bullet discharged, and she watched as it went past her and hit Khamun, who stood behind her with his own barrel pointing her way, his silver dark wings filling the sky.

She saw more, but it moved so fast that she couldn't retain it all as a piercing pain ripped through her stomach. A blade extended from her body as her neck was suddenly ripped to the side.

A tall, handsome, older man, who mirrored the jewel-clad woman, held her from behind, his hand sliding over her blood-soaked body to cup her between her legs as his wild eyes flashed, and he bit down.

"I will have you," echoed in her mind, and she saw the woman Darren later told her was named Winter attempt to run to help her, when a demon ripped her apart, her Witch power exploding like a bomb. The bodies of the people who vowed to protect her and her own family lay around her in pieces.

Her brother Darren took out a demon with one touch of his hand before nodding at her. His stomach was suddenly torn apart while he fell to his knees dying. That was when she knew her life was being cut short as the bite polluted her body and the man groped her, holding her against her will.

Tears spilled down her face, and a voice within her whispered, followed by a sharp screech that jolted her back to reality.

"Find the keys and find the scrolls to complete the books before they find it," echoed in her mind and she gasped. She pulled, and the silver slivers ripped from Amit's hands as he roared in pain, dropping to his knees, his hands still cupped and up in the air.

The water pulsed, and the slivers floated atop the water, forming a circle, until it became a ticking mechanical disc. The water pulsed, solidified, and wrapped around the silver disk, covering it in a diamond-like case that also shifted and ticked with the disk. Her power kissed the disc, making it glow, and she reached out, holding it in her hand. Gears clicked and ticked as she flipped it between her fingers before watching Amit's hands heal.

"Amit?"

Holding out a hand, Amit shook his head, and his back rose up and down in sharp breaths until they slowed, and he looked up.

"Thank you. It's all gone. All that shit is gone out of me. Thank you, Oracle. Shit." He stood up too quickly, slightly wavering, then reached out to wrap Sanna in a tight hug.

Healing flashes flowed from her, and she smiled. "Call me Sanna, and we are good. I'm happy to have helped."

Amit nodded, backing away. "Okay, Sanna." A slight smile played at his lips as he flexed her hands.

"A'ight, let's talk about what the fuck that is right there, San!" Calvin interjected.

Sanna nodded. "Let's get that book Winter gave us."

Chapter 22

The Reaper stood facing his enemy. They had hunted well and grabbed a target they knew would draw him and his family out. Anger seethed within him as he let his mind relax and process. He couldn't believe how everything had panned out. Just almost a year earlier, he was guarding a woman he had fallen for and knew he wasn't allowed to crave. A woman he knew he couldn't have. He had accepted it, only breaking protocol when he knew he couldn't hold back his desire for her. That slip made him watch her more, made him protect her, even though he had no idea of what she really was. He had to laugh, thinking how blind he was in watching this woman for so many years and not know she was the Oracle and a Vessel.

The one who would help bring Nephilim Society in the US and the world back to where it needed to be. This one who would find more Oracles, women and men who were the backbone to their way of life. He was glad when he learned of her true nature. He felt elated when that truth allowed him to be with her, and now here he stood defending and protecting not only Society itself, but with her by his side. They stood equally yoked, protecting each other and fighting an enemy that was too damned determined.

Rolling his neck, he felt his fangs rip from his gums, slowly extending and flashing in the night air. His hands clutched as the windy night air of Chicago wrapped around him. His fiancée stood at his right, dressed in dark denim leggings, black Nike, and a black tank that showcased her beautiful breasts. He didn't want her here, he needed her protected, but she had insisted.

Prior to the face-off currently going on, everyone was back at the compound glancing at the clear and silver mechanical disk in Sanna's hands.

Khamun stood behind her as she sat in a big chair, looking down at the book. Her fingers traced over the leather cover, not understanding the Ancient Nephilim script. His Shield, Marco, reached out and flipped the book open for her as she looked at the blank pages, with several visible pages.

"*Mira*. Nada here at all. I looked this book over, backward and forward. Outside of five pages that have drawings on them, nothing is here. No braille or other markings. *Coño*. So what do we do?"

"Flip it to the last page. I saw something." Sanna bit her lower lip.

Everyone's nerves seemed to flood over her, and she almost felt sick with the feeling. Marco was gentle with the book, and she was grateful. Khamun had quietly told her that he was a closet bookworm, through all his hard edginess and vulgar language. Marco was into knowledge, cars, and into finding ways to help his people via books, which was why at one point he and Kali were so close and part-time lovers, never mind they were always bickering.

"*¡Coño carajo!* There's something here." He narrowed his eyes, flipped the book to him, and touched the back cover. His fingers ran over the hard leather until they dipped and left an imprint in the inner part of the back cover.

Raising an eyebrow, he pressed and traced until the soft pliable leather revealed raised grooves that formed a circle. Continuing to press the pliable stripping down until it shaped and contorted like clay, his eyes flashed as he looked up at Sanna and flashed a smirk.

Holding the book so everyone could see, Marco slid the book down on the table in front of Sanna. "On my soul, this wasn't there before. The cover and inner covers were hard as typical books should be. *¡Carajo!*"

Khamun watched as Sanna continued to trace the book.

"I know. When I touched the book, my power reacted to it, and something changed." Sanna removed the disc, brought it over the book, and maneuvered it.

Every male in the room except for Marco bellowed out, "Whoa! Whoa!"

Calvin spoke up. "Time out, and hold up, shawty."

Lenox held both of his hands on top of his head, his elbows poking out as he began to pace. "Do we know what that is? Are we sure this shit isn't a trap by Winter? She's good for playing fucking games. Or am I wrong?" He glanced at Marco and Khamun, who both stayed silent, a sudden mask of coldness filling their faces.

Winter was a thorn in both his and his cousin's sides. They had history with the Witch and wasn't keen in rehashing that dark past, so he kept quiet before answering his second hand.

"Baby, what do you feel from the book and disc? Does this feel like a setup or threat?" Khamun's eyes held Lenox's, who glanced off in understanding.

"Everything in me says do this. I feel no threat, but just in case, can we make some protection around us?" Sanna's face lit up with knowledge and concern. She looked around, and Calvin and Kali both nodded, standing to link hands together, fingertip to fingertip. White light flashing turquoise, yellow, then white again ebbed between their palms and fingers.

Both chanted in the old language, and Takeshi and Kyo followed suit. Their eyes flashed and glowed with an inner fire as they stood, walked, and sat on either side of Sanna, their palms flat against the middle of her back.

Khamun kept his stance as Darren moved to sit opposite his sister, and Marco shifted to let him sit.

Power grew, coating the room when Darren linked a hand with his sister. That current grew stronger and attached to Kyo and Take.

Khamun slid his own hands over Sanna's shoulders, and she gasped, her wings breaking free, as did his own, and they both locked as one.

This was what he had wanted to do in the office but knew he couldn't yet, and now he could. His touch fused with her, her brother, and their Gargoyles, as it threatened to spill out. The intensity of it made him let go as his breathing quickened.

His fangs crested, and he ran his hands down his face. Static power sizzled through his locks, making them rise. "Too much, too soon. Amit, sit near Sanna. Marco, Lenox, you both know what to do."

He watched his team gather around his fiancée, and he kept his stance as the power cloaked them all.

Sanna briefly glanced at him as she turned and held the disk, which seemed to glow even brighter and spin even faster as she slid it in place and twisted, a locking sound letting her know it was secure. As she let go, cranking from the book filled the room as everyone leaned back in their circle of protection.

Buzzing and a *Ding*, *Ding*, *Ding* sounded as the book snapped open on its own, shooting blank pages in the air. They rained in the room, freezing mid-air to hover over the book. Nothing but the book cover was left, with many slots and a hinge.

"Okay, so this means what now?" Amit muttered as the pages shifted then locked together. Multiple blank pages linked to five spaced-out illustrations, creating one synched page.

Slowly reaching out, the page settled into Sanna's hand as the whizzing sound stopped.

"Fuck! All of that and we got what, one huge-ass page with nothing on it but spaced-out pictures. Come the hell on," Khamun bellowed, as their protection ring dropped and everyone shook their heads.

Calvin sat back in a slump in his chair, legs spread as he cursed in every language he knew.

Marco pulled out another trinity, tossing one to Khamun. They both lit up and took a similar stance, arms crossed, brooding.

Lenox was the only calm voice who broke up the disappointment in the mix. "Okay, everyone, now look. I know this crap didn't happen without reason so . . . "

"No faith can lead to destruction," Sanna calmly stated as she turned the pages in her hand. She studied each page as if it were a precious fabric before she slid the book cover to Marco, who picked it up and quietly watched her.

Sanna said, "Baby, look at this. What do you recognize?"

Khamun rounded her chair, dropped into a crouch, wisps of smoke escaping his closed mouth before discarding his cigarillo.

Glancing at the ancient pages and random illustrations of patterns that had no sense, he looked closer and saw faint swirls. Each swirl rose then fell like a wave, before moving in circles. Braille-like indentations popped up in the shape of a crest. He frowned, reaching out.

"That's the crest of my family," he muttered. Energy hit him, and the ink from the paper rose up and around his hands, becoming hard and slicing into his hands.

"Shit! Get that crap off of him!" Lenox roared.

While Khamun kept a calm demeanor, ink softened and mixed with his dripping blood onto the crumbling yellow paper. "The fuck is this," Khamun mouthed, his eyes wide as he tilted his head, watching closely.

The paper absorbed his blood and the ink as it glowed. What was once old decomposing paper was now brand-new as if it came straight from the paper mills of old. His blood and ink swirled on the paper, forming words, numbers, and images as a current hit Khamun, making him hold onto the paper before it disappeared with an exhale from him and a flicker of fire illuminated his eyes.

Everyone hovered around him, and he held up his hand. That power felt as if it came from the Ancients. Something so strong, it had his muscles taut, his dick on edge. He glanced at his fiancée. Her eyes glowed in familiar power as she cupped his face. He felt their power pass to each other and settle back into each other.

"Khamun, man, you good?" Marco asked.

Khamun stiffly nodded, trying to work his mouth. Knowledge hit him, and he bowed his head for a second before Calvin sat up, anger blazing in his eyes.

"It's a map. It'll take us to one of the scrolls, and that cover, we use to bind them all together once we collect them. Calvin, man, what's up?"

Hands clenched, his arms almost shaking, Calvin glanced at Sanna before looking back at the team. "We have a situation. We need to roll out and hunt ASAP. A member has been taken."

Khamun knew what was being said within the lines as he quickly stood, the Reaper taking over. "Grab the rides, and we roll out. Do you know where we are going?" he icily asked.

Calvin shook his head. Lenox, Kali, and Marco headed to the second level to grab weapons and a ride, their running feet echoing through the compound.

"Winter's massive was broken up, which means she was rushing, and she couldn't connect all the way. We have to track her."

Sanna stood looking around. "Who was taken? Let me help."

The Reaper looked at what was his, and he growled. Was no damn way he was going to risk her life and have her out there, ass out, not sure of her power. Fuck that shit. "No. You stay here with Kyo, Take, and Darren. I'll hit up Dr. Toure. You all need to stay out of this. Amit—"

"Hell, no. I'm not staying. I passed the class tests and was supposed to be a part of the Chicago team before I got snatched. I may be new, but I know some things. I'm going."

"You're not a Slayer, man, and you still healing. It's best that you—"

Pissed, Amit narrowed his eyes, his fist thumping against his chest. "I can hold my own. I'm a Disciple and a fucking Broken Wrath Angel! I got some white magic in me. Let me help. The Oracle healed me fully."

The Reaper kept his eyes on his fiancée, who kept pacing, throwing angry stares his way. She was who he was worried about. He nodded at Amit. Reaching out to cup Sanna's angry face, he bent down to kiss her, but she stepped back, and he closed his eyes before dropping his hand. "All right. Let's roll out."

"Calvin, I want to"—Sanna reached out to clutched Calvin's arm hard, pain ripping through her as she fell to her knees. Tears spilled down her face, and Calvin cursed as he was locked into the same power.

"Momma!" Sanna screamed and let go, cradling her face.

The Reaper quickly grabbed her, his eyes flashing at Calvin.

"Fuck! Those bitches! They have Momma Tamar? Huh, Calvin?" Khamun roared.

Calvin dropped his head and nodded as he stepped back. "We need to go, my man," he quietly stated.

The Reaper looked down at Sanna's rocking form, and Kyo held her shoulders as he held Sanna against him.

"I'm going. We are going," Sanna croaked.

The Reaper opened his mouth to fight, but Kyo hissed, her mismatched jade eyes blazing at him, and he stared her down. "We go into this, eyes open! You protect her with your life because that's what the fuck I will be doing. Got that?" He glared, speaking between his teeth.

Kyo nodded. "I've had her back all my life. I will lay my life down for her," was all she said, simmering with anger.

The Reaper looked up to get Darren and Takeshi in check, only to notice that they were not there. "Where the hell did they"—The Reaper stopped, homing in on the pair, and he smirked, shaking his head. "My brothas."

"They are strapped and ready to go. Baby, I need you. Be safe out there. You don't understand what will go down if I lose you or anyone here. You got it."

He watched his soulmate stare him in the eyes, the Oracle in her blending as one, and he knew without an answer from her what her choice was. All the Cursed had officially declared war, and his baby was ready to administer her wrath.

Smiling, his spirit clicked with a lethal eagerness, and he stood to walk with her. Kyo and Calvin followed as they strapped up, sworded up, and prepped. He talked them through the many protocols they had, he knew it was a lot for them to try to remember, but he was hoping they remembered some of it.

His crew slid into the Escalade and motorbikes, as he got in his new all-black sports car. He reached over to open the passenger door and looked at Sanna as she smoothly walked with constrained anger and hopped in.

"We communicate in missions with mind-locking, baby. So open that mind and link with me. You can communicate with everyone, until you learn how to link with others who are not me or Kyo."

"Okay, can we just hurry, please." Her eyes stayed on the road.

He whipped out with a nod. "Yeah, baby. We have to track from the half-ass cords Winter was able to get. We know they are somewhere on the Northside. Hiding in plain sight."

He watched her nod. Her nails were digging into her thighs, and he saw her slowly breathe in and out.

Syncing into a mind-link, he felt Sanna's sensual smooth energy meld with his own and in doing so invited the energetic playful flow of Kyo, because she was linked to her brother and Sanna at the same time. Both hit his mind with a rush. Then Darren's protective feel amplified his link with Sanna. He considered this something as important to store away for further investigation.

"T'em House. We all here?" Khamun stated, going into a roll call as every mind linked instantly.

The edgy, gritty, loyal feel of Amit had the Reaper ascertaining him as well while he synced with the newest member and he spoke on. *"All right, tracking in progress, break up in—"*

"Go right," Amit interrupted as his link became antsy.

"Yo, my man, relax with that. ¿Comprendes? We know what we doing. We break up in teams and cover the area, a'ight."

"Right, right. But, really, go right!" Amit demanded again and the link became thick with anxiety as everyone became jittery.

"Listen to him." Sanna's link thickened, spreading a sense of calmness to everyone as the team mentally paused then followed suit.

Lenox restrained voice let everyone know what they couldn't see. *"He seems to sense where they are. His eyes darkened and you know where he got bit? The visible veins are moving."*

"Ahhhh! Yeah, go down that street. It's a lot of them. I can smell them! Shit, I can taste them and feel them."

"A'ight. From this moment on, Amit is our physical tracker in the field. You listen to him and follow suit. The Oracle gave him a new ability that will work in our favor. All right?"

The teamed chimed in unison as Sanna's low voice interrupted, fear and worry making her hide her tears.

The Reaper became pissed. Their blood would be on his hands.

"Yes. His bite will let him know anytime there's Cursed by us," Sanna simply stated.

"Straight ahead! Umm, I'm calling back up," Kali chimed in.

Calvin's chuckle seemed to amp everyone. *"A'ight, homies. Let's get in they asses like a doctor giving a prostate exam. Ya heard meh?"*

"Awww, hell no, Calvin," Lenox griped then laughed.

Marco gloated. *"We got this shit. Nothing we never handled before."*

The team stepped out of their rides, weapons blazing. They were surrounded by mobs of Cursed, demons, and Dark Gargoyles who growled, the occasional flash of lighting hitting their stone-like features. They all stood on the roof of an abandoned building covered in blood, the chill of the night air whipping around them, the thick, sweet smell of demon miasma filling the air.

"Hello, cousin. Took you long enough, don't you think?" The Dark Lady, who the Reaper knew was Reina, Marco's twin, stood dressed in all white, jewels adorning her body. She stood with her hands on her wide hips, her legs spread, her hair up in a braided bun, twin blades in her hand.

The Reaper chuckled. This bitch didn't know him as she thought she did. The wonders of being distant cousins.

"Let us end this as mutually as we can, cousin. Give us the civie and you can walk away."

Reina's bell-like laugh made him narrow his eyes. "Give me my toy."

"That would be who?"

Reina's eyes flowed over the team and stopped on Amit, who stood, fists clenched, his gun hand ready. She flashed a brilliant smile.

A gust of cold anger blasted past the team as gunshots rang.

The Reaper sighed. "Amit," he inwardly cursed, dropping to get into position.

The team spread out, and he watched Sanna duck and move with a fluidity that took his breath away. He acted in unison as his swung his blade and decapitated an approaching Snatcher.

"Get her!" Reina yelled, running after Sanna.

The Reaper followed suit, staying in sync with his lover, shadowing her, connecting, and gutting demons left and right.

Khamun eyed Marco and watched his cousin nod as he jumped and landed in front of a panting Sanna, who threw energy-dripping daggers that hit demons in the throats, blowing their bodies apart like confetti.

Marco slid, the dark miasma from the demons cloaking his appearance, and stood erect as the mist cleared. He had waited a lifetime for this. He knew her madness twisted her love for him into a sick game that resulted in where he stood now. So it pleased him to see the shock on her face as he stared Reina straight in the eyes and she froze in her pursuit of attack.

"*Hola, mi querida hermana* . . . hello my dear sister," he muttered, his hand reaching to his chest and pulling out a gye nyame silver necklace that shone in the midnight sky.

Reina's eyes widened as she shook her head.

The sound of a passing car blasting Kanye's "All of the Lights" remix broke the silence.

"The Gray Prince? No, no, nooooooo. You died! *Tú moriste!*" Her screech filled the air as she stomped and suddenly pulled at her hair. "Nooooo!"

Marco smirked, leaned forward, cupping her face with both hands as he kissed her forehead and sent her flying with a swift kick to her stomach.

As she flew through the air, the Reaper stepped in with a grin, making contact, and dropped his forearm down on her chest, making her drop at his feet. "You ready to give up?"

Reina rolled and blinked, coughing hard, her hand over her chest as her eyes focused, flashed silver then eclipsed with pure darkness. A dark magic emitted from her, and she moved her body in a spin, pushing up and slashing at him. Her movements were controlled yet chaotic.

The Reaper had to step back, blocking each blow that went his way. Blades swung at him as a clicking noise sounded behind him, and he knew what was coming.

"Aw shit," he muttered, ducking under from the blades Reina sliced over his head while the

Medusa's bladed hair and nails swung from behind.

Dropping low, the Reaper pivoted to his left, panting as Calvin covered him and Lenox became his shadow.

Shooting off rounds, Lenox drop back on his knee as he punched up in a clean uppercut, making contact with a Snatcher that quickly covered Reina and the Medusa. Everything was in chaos as the Reaper saw Momma Tamar. She was held by a Snatcher, her eyes closed and unconscious, with another gagged person.

"She was an easy snatch. Unguarded as she shopped downtown. Very sloppy of you all. You think we didn't know who she was? Ha!" Reina flashed a malicious half-smile.

"She is always watched. Do not fucking play me," the Reaper icily stated. He paced back and forth blood accessing the roof. If she was caught, that meant a fucking Phantom had a hand in it, and he had a clue who it was.

Sanna's quick movement caught his attention out the corner of his eye, as she took a demon down in a move so fast, he had to replay it in his mind.

She ran low, twin blades of power in her hands, as she propelled herself up to jab both bladed hands into the approaching demon's chest. Cleanly slicing through, splitting him from within, she turned and grabbed half of the remaining demon torso and bit down, her incisors ripping deep. Blood and sins poured into her, making her body taut as she fed. Glowing tears spilled down her face, and she threw the demon, its flinging body misting.

Darren, shadowing his sister, grabbed a screaming female Snatcher, lighting her up with just a touch. Her body imploded in fire as her dark sins flew in the air and fell like glowing rain.

"Damn right! That was cold." Darren fist-bumped Takeshi as he sped off. Takeshi jumped in the air, reaching for a flying Dark Gargoyle with a swiftness that knocked the entity off guard. His fangs connected to the hard skin of the demon while his nail ripped the monster apart with slight effort.

"Be careful, sis. I'm watching you," Darren muttered in Sanna's mind as she panted and gained her bearings.

The Reaper could sense her worry, shock and pain as he bit down and drank from an overzealous Snatcher who approached him, ripping its throat apart with ease as he flung the molting body. The dark, rich taste of the Snatcher's sins fueled him while he spat then moved like lightning. His body diffused the sins out in electric static that burned demons and Dark Gargoyles into cinders whenever they came in contact with the jolt.

Sanna stood drenched in sweat and covered in blood. Her first taste of demon's sins was intoxicating. She understood finally how her love felt in it all. Glancing around, she made contact with Khamun. His movements were brilliant, and as he ran, the charges that hit the demons and other evils grounded and made the building hum.

Sanna needed to get to her mother, and she needed to move fast. The stress of it was throwing her off her game. Everything she did was awkward. It was as if she couldn't spark her full Oracle potential at times, and it frightened her.

Her wings strained her back, and she tried to release them as her body sparked, but no juice would come. It was like she was one giant knot of tension. She could appreciate one thing though. Her knowledge had helped her shoot off rounds from a gun she had no idea how to use.

Seeing an opening, she ran, ducking under flying pieces of monsters' carnage. Marco suddenly shadowed her.

Kyo ripped demons apart with her bare hands as she also trailed her and her beloved brothers.

Dare and Take worked like a unit of their own, tagging each other, and killed the beasts that tried to take her.

Tears stung her eyes as she ran head on into the burly, molting monster that held her incapacitated mother and another gagged figure. "Give her to me!" she yelled.

The demon laughed and reached back, and pieces of spikes from his skin suddenly shot her way.

She screamed and ducked. Everything moved in slow motion as a body ran into the monster, knocking Sanna's mother to the ground.

Sanna slid forward, catching her in a low crouch. She glanced over quickly then looked up and saw the good doctor.

Dr. Toure stood, anger contorting his handsome face while he swung a bat-like axe in his hand. The Chicago team flooded the roof while he shouted his commands.

A clicking sound surrounded Sanna as a rough flick brushed against her cheek made her gaze up. In front of her was what the team called the Medusa. Sanna swallowed, clutched her hands, and pushed her mother back quickly, standing to shield her. "Back the fuck up!" she yelled.

The Medusa stalked her with a deathly smile, her tail whipping around in pleasure. "And what are you going to do? Hmm? I've been watching you this whole time, and you are nothing but a weak shell of a thing. Oracle? Yeah, right." The Medusa chuckled, her laugh sounding like a reptile's cackle.

This bitch is crazy, Sanna thought.

The Medusa reached out, and her long nail traced Sanna's cheek with a slow smile. "Bye," she said, reaching back and slicing forward.

Sanna's eyes flashed as energy pulsed from her like a shield.

Where the Medusa slashed was where those lethal nails of hers broke into a thousand pieces, and Sanna effortlessly ripped the arm off the screaming Medusa.

Sanna's wings ripped free from her back as they hardened like knives and wrapped forward to slice at the retreating bitch.

"You bitch!" the Medusa screamed. Poison shot from her fangs as she whipped her blade-in-laid braids and razor tail Sanna's way.

Sanna sideswiped her and landed a kick that lifted her in the air and had her foot dropping down square against the Medusa's head. That move helped knock her attacker unconscious, as Sanna fell into a crouch near her mother.

Hooking her arm under her mother's waist, Sanna slowly stood and turned, and ran right into the Dark Lady. Quick annoyance had her stepping back as she tilted her head to the side, flashing a coy smile while she narrowed her eyes. "You will not take me."

The Dark Lady flinched, madness pooling in her eyes. She smiled back with a mutter, "I know."

Jerking her arm back, Reina ran a blade into Sanna's stomach, bringing her forward with a flicker of satisfaction in her dark eyes, and Sanna's blood spilled everywhere while her mother fell back to her feet battered and bruised.

The Dark Lady's fangs ripped out in contentment as she moved in one swift motion.

Sanna felt her life rip from her, tears spilling down her face. A quick blur ran in front of her, shielding her, before the Dark Lady could finish cutting her in two. Fire surrounded her, a loud roar rent the air, and she heard Kyo's and Khamun's voice yell out, "*Sanna!*"

Sanna swore she saw fear flicker in the Dark Lady's eyes as she noticed Khamun appear at her side, grabbing and pulling her back.

In his fury and worry, his power folded over them both. Wings and a gold tail shadowed his movements and flooded the sky as they knocked Reina back.

In that quick moment Reina swore she saw a dragon stand before her. The blade that was meant for the Oracle bitch actually rested in the prize she had worked so hard to get. Glancing at the Oracle bitch, she glared at her stomach and smiled. Yes. She was hurt too, but the brunt of her blade was through the dragon, whose bindings fell around it in ash.

Khamun looked up and felt his mind sync with the dragon in front of him. *His Gargoyle*, ran in his mind, making him blink as the dragon crumbled and turned back into its human form.

Lying in front of him was the b-boy who'd helped Darren and Takeshi. The man he had just made contact with to learn more about, via Calvin. His Gargoyle, something he'd never had in all his twenty-nine years of life.

Next to him was his love, his Sanna, bleeding to death. Vengeance was about to be a mother-fucker. "RJ?" was all he got out as Kyo's scream filled the sky.

Kyo moved like the wind as she ran to the falling body. Lenox was behind her, trying to keep her calm as he shook his head and let her go.

Power flowed between Khamun and Sanna while he looked her over, blood flowing from her. He moved fast, grabbing the Dark Lady, who stood distracted at the man who was once a massive dragon but now lay in a crumpled heap, her blade idle in her hand.

"You fucked with the wrong ones," Khamun coolly said. He twisted her blade from her hand and finished what she had intended to do to Sanna.

"*Kill that bitch!*" Kyo screamed as she held RJ in her hands. She wiped his dirty face and pulled off the rest of his molting ropes as she sat near Sanna, protecting them both.

Khamun's bite was swift. He watched as the paling Dark Lady screamed, sucking her and ripping the darkness from her. She clawed at him and kicked, but he held her tight.

Marco's laughter filled the air while the Medusa fought her way through, only to end up being halted by Calvin.

Vengeance echoed in the air as the Medusa slashed at the man she desired for so long, concern in her eyes. Dropping into a backflip, her braids slashed at him as she got close enough to the Dark Lady to pull at her.

Marco rushed forward, guns blazing. His muscled body slammed into them both like a ton of bricks and sent them flying over the edge of the building.

Khamun also cocked his Glock and sent rounds of bullets flying, blood dripping from his lips while he backed his cousin.

"Aw, fuck, no! We not done, *hermana*!" Dark wings ripped from Marco as his yell formed an energy jolt.

A mystic light from Calvin ripped through the air and covered the screaming women. A web of white holy light absorbed into their skin, fusing and twisting, causing burning pain through their bodies, making Calvin and Marco smile in satisfaction. Calvin looked down from the edge of the building as the women landed with a thud and disappeared. "Try to take from me and I leave ya ass burning. Ya heard me?" His emerald eyes flashed in the night mist as he yelled. The protection sigils on his arms and hair swirled and glowed, and sweat dripped from his brow as fatigue hit.

Winter's quiet voice hit everyone's mind as she disappeared in the cloaking mist, ducking past a fighting Darren, Take, Kali, and Amit. *"I'll see where they went and report to you."*

Kyo's choked cries hit every member hard. Take stopped his final beat-down on a misting demon and ran to his sister's side, Dare, Kali, and Amit right behind him.

"Sis?" Takeshi questioned.

Kyo looked at her sister lying unconscious, and her beaten godmother leaning against Dr. Toure. The man in her arms was the one from in her dreams and lay dying against her. "What did they want?" she muttered, tears thickening her speech while she rocked.

"More like, who did they want?" Takeshi whispered. He watched the partially breathing man named RJ brush his hand across Kyo's dirty face, and swirling sigils on his arms that matched the markings in the Nephilim book lit up.

"Me and the Oracle," was all he said as silence fell over the team.

Time seemed to stop as rain spilled over the roof, drenching and washing everyone and everything, as the Oracle lay in pain. The world ebbed in and out for her as knowledge waned with each slow beat of her heart.

Her mind ticked and struggled to stay whole as her breath stalled in a quiet whisper, "He's the Key to the second book."

Epilogue

(Lost Scrolls of Nephilim: Text two)

I believed this would be the end of my entry, but I am wrong. It has happened. Betrayal in our Houses once again. They have taken a Disciple and polluted him with Darkness. His noble House sits in ruins and pain. The Templars mourn his betrayal, yet The One God's son has known this betrayal would come. He tells us that Betrayal will form our Houses and guide us in protecting the innocent. I do not understand how, but I will never question my faith in His word.

He also prophesied that the one who betrayed us will return to correct the wrong. It is hard to believe, but believe, we must. They have taken much from us and have desecrated our line, stole our children and planted seeds of malice and pain within us, but we stay strong. We will not be taken.

This loss of the Judas shows that we must do all we can to protect those innocent in the world. The Humans. Who are now the carriers of half our seed, our children, Nephilim. The One God has put in his books warnings of the enemies' dark Nephilim seeds and how it is our turn to protect what we love. The Children of this World.

Our vows to the One God's son has expanded, and we will eradicate that which tarnished the Light. Betrayal is what founded our Houses, and Betrayal is what will end their Curse. Ashes to ashes, dust to dust. She will be our mortar, the Triad, her strength, the Dragons, her armor, the Reaper, our and her weapon. The Sin-Eaters will fill the skies, reap what was sown and wash away the sins of the Fallen. The Cursed.

We the Founding Archangels of the Houses of Light will prevail through our seeds and our memories. As was Ordained, so shall it be.

~Elders Gab'reel and Chii de V'ance/Neffi and Anjii de V'ance

Sin Eaters 2:

Retribution Devotion Book Two

by

Kai Leakes

Prelude

The past . . .

"Where are you going to go *boy*? You're sur-rounded!"

"Like hell, woulda ever let ya take me down boss . . ." thumbed in his mind as he ran. More like sprinted through the thick grasping trees that surrounded him. Rigged branches reached out to him as if they had a mind of their own. Their thick almost-black rooted stems twisted in their uprooting from the bowels of the earth to make him trip, but he was smarter than the trees. He leaped and veered out of their men-acing way and his arms jolted outward to part through bushes.

With all of the trees that surrounded him, he would not have believed that he was back in Yon-kers had he known any better but for those who don't know it by that name, New York was where he was. The bustling city lights covered the skies like fireflies splashed across the skies black can-vas. The noisy zipping of various buckets and hacks driving past careless tourist and city folk gave him a sense of how close he exactly was to civilization. It also gave him a sense of purpose.

Twigs snapped suddenly and the rustling of leaves tussling against each other let him know they were still hot on his trail. His mind was racing as he looked for an out. All of this was too familiar to him. Beady red eyes flickered at him in the darkness of the wilderness, *no*, of the park. He was in Central Park. He should have realized that. Those piercing eyes stared at him in delight, ready to seize the opportunity to hog-tie him so that he could be their little plaything but he would not give them that satisfaction. Not yet.

Beads of midnight dew kissed his face the moment he stepped through the thicket. His wing-tip shoes abruptly skidded as they made contact with wet slick grass. He jumped. Then he lifted in the air, almost floating for a mere second. Both of his large feet clacked against pebbled stone, the moment they met the ground.

He could hear the enemy. He could feel them breathing against the back of his neck. Each hair on his body stood in salute, coming alive in electric awareness. In this life at lease he knew he could die on his terms and die giving them a fight. In seven minutes, his time would be up soon anyway, so what could he really do about not being bumped off?

7 . . .

A whizzing sound sizzled past his ear and he felt the hot trickle of blood mixing with his sweat and the quick pop of the gun after the fact. They wanted to play dirty. They wanted to make him appear to be a patsy and a hood. He had to laugh, he was better than a hood. Sure, at one time, he had to fill that slot but now he was his own man, a bruno to a well-known trouble boy who protected the meek of Harlem. They worked together with his gang to find those who were kidnapped or were bumping gums to the wrong people. They worked to regain money lost in predatory loans and schemes and wrongful repositions. They worked to build up their people and to protect all who walked the streets of Harlem from the highbinders that made it their mission to tear down the community. But these men who were after him, the very scum and thugs themselves, were no normal men. *Corrupted monsters in the flesh of coppers more like it. Oh, what he wouldn't give to go out between the gams of a looker for a change.*

6 . . .

The menacing snarl of dogs in the distance made him grimly chuckle before closing his eyes with the feel of his body vibrating with his gift.

His gift allowed him to use the sound waves around him to channel it into music. With a slight part of his lips he let out a low hum. Whistling he changed the pitched and dropped into a low crouch. Both hands extended outward and he observed his skin lighting up in swirling patterns against its burnished surface. That was his clue to project that vibrating power out in waves toward the hunting dogs. A change in his vision allowed him to suddenly see through their glittering eyes and he knew where to run next. With a quick shift of the pitch of his song, he caused the dogs to halt their barks, whimper, and then stopped in their tracks to turn. *Attack*, was his simple mental command and watched the dogs attack their owners before sprinting away in retreat.

His sweat dripped down his face like rain on the ground before him. His ragged breath came out in sharp bursts and he pushed up to start his run again. They wouldn't get what he had been given a vision to find. That he was sure he had hidden well, he had taken something priceless, something rare and something they wanted destroyed but couldn't. Something they had to hide from his people because he had learned, it could kill the leader of their kind.

5 . . .

This was a once in a lifetime win for their side and he had to make sure they would never get their hands on it. He knew the enemy had Warlocks and Witches who could work into his mind, luckily for him, his Mystic gifts were too strong for them to break through, so he inwardly laughed and stopped once he met the end of a pond. *Shit*. He could hear them and he knew he was at his ropes end. The gig was up. He felt himself snagged by the ankles and thrown to the ground. The heckling and putrid nostril burning plumes of a Dark Gargoyle let him know he was caught by the enemy. Yep, it was nothing for him to do but practice constraint, settled in his mind.

4 . . .

"Boy gave us a good show but tonight, we will feast on your filthy Light filled body," a voice sounded around him, causing him to glare towards the thicket then narrow his glowing jade eyes.

Two Anarchy Snatchers stood before him, something that was very rare for him to meet. A blonde with a finger wave bob and curves that clearly whispered she was lethal, stepped forward. She wore a form fitting ruby gown that fit the current times and her movie star looks, with a tiny dot near the corner of her blood red plump lips that dripped that 'It' factor. Sure, he was familiar with her from where he worked. She was new at the Phoenix club. Her ambiguous race made her the bees-knees with the patrons at the club, but her ass and those lips and sultry voice always told those she so wanted to join, her true birth. He had to laugh because as he watched her, black currents dripped from her fingertips like squid ink and snaked its way towards him while forming a slick black rope. Yup, this broad's true birth was nothing her meat bag of a shell perpetrated.

"What a shame, what a shame. I would have loved to keep you around a little longer my dear sap," the woman cooed; he listened to her give off a chilling light laugh then sashayed forward.

At that same moment, her companion, who was what the women would call a 'beef cake', strolled near her side. He flipped his lighter and lit a white cigarette with an impassionate sneer across his chiseled face. The tall, jet-black haired Rudolph Valentino doppelganger whistled and more coppers appeared from behind the trees to surround them on all sides.

"You took from us boy. Do you have anything you want to say before I make you my bitch and give you to our master?" His captor snapped his fingers and flashed his pearly whites, staring down at him, his leather shoe pressed against his windpipe cutting off his air, "Nothing to say? Stand him up darling, I can't hear him."

3 · · ·

It felt good to get off the wet grass. He felt his body being snatched up by his feet to stand upright. The pair had moxie which amused him. But they were as stupid as rocks for not frisking him. Working his wrist, his blade snaked from his hands and gave a raspy reply, "Hey . . . *C'est si bon* mista' right?"

It was simple for him to drop the blade around his ankles and use his power to cut his ankles free. His fists landed into the first copper that jumped him. An elbow connected into the ribs of another. A quick neck grab then lunge over his broad shoulder had him light a third minion aflame in holy Mystic power.

"My name ain't boy and screw your torpedo scum squad. You may have caught me this time but it is only because I let ya . . . by the way, spiffy shoes cat, but mine are much better," his jubilant brawl with the enemy had him blindsided and shackled by black ropes from the female Anarchy Snatcher.

Sparking trusses of power snaked around him. She pulled which had him falling backwards hard on the ground. The hussy's demonic strength allowed her to hoist him into the air; another thick rope tightening around his throat. He knew what was about to occur before it even happened and that familiar sound of rope snapping against a tree limb made him close his eyes in acceptance.

2 . . .

"What a pitiful shame," he heard the blonde coaxed; the cords she controlled, tightened around his throat, cutting into his flesh at the same time.

"He has nothing to snitch about so end this because this is nothing but a vacation for him," his captor yawned exasperatedly. He turned on his heel to light up another ciggy then coolly walked away, "until we meet again boy."

It was time. He bore his teeth in a triumphed grin and his eyes blazed their familiar jade iridescence. *Never break your cool*, he told himself. He connected to his birthright and power blazed around his body making the mob around him back up in fear of being touched by the light. They were going to burn tonight, like all those innocents, they snatched from their homes or cars and as they blazed, he was going to have his moment of peace.

Yes, he'll get to see that glimpse of his family at the gates before coming back to exact his vengeance but he hoped that maybe this time he'll get to see her. He fought for her, his true love, the one they kidnapped and every return entry back into the divine plane let him know she could still be out there, reborn somewhere, whenever he didn't see her. This gave him hope to save her as he should have before, but now he had something that would give his side the advantage over this never ending war and soon he'll start this cycle all over again.

So with a happy birthday to him, he focused on his spirit, willing it to remember all and he spit at his enemies feet, "My name is Calvin . . . never boy."

The taunt snap of a rope and crack of a tree's limb sounded in the night. The image of a man in a long sweeping black coat with a bobby in his hand, a blade in the other with icy blue eyes and long black curling hair, cutting at his enemies before his eyes made him smile one last time. A whoosh with a flash of dimming light and the sound of a gong signaled . . . he was gone.

. . . 1

ORDER FORM
URBAN BOOKS, LLC
97 N18th Street
Wyandanch, NY 11798

Name (please print):_____

Address:_____

City/State:_____

Zip:_____

QTY	TITLES	PRICE
	16 On The Block	$14.95
	A Girl From Flint	$14.95
	A Pimp's Life	$14.95
	Baltimore Chronicles	$14.95
	Baltimore Chronicles 2	$14.95
	Betrayal	$14.95
	Black Diamond	$14.95

Shipping and handling-add $3.50 for 1st book, then $1.75 for each additional book.
Please send a check payable to:
Urban Books, LLC
Please allow 4-6 weeks for delivery

ORDER FORM
URBAN BOOKS, LLC
97 N18th Street
Wyandanch, NY 11798

Name (please print):_____

Address:_____

City/State:_____

Zip:_____

QTY	TITLES	PRICE
	Black Diamond 2	$14.95
	Black Friday	$14.95
	Both Sides Of The Fence	$14.95
	Both Sides Of The Fence 2	$14.95
	California Connection	$14.95
	California Connection 2	$14.95

Shipping and handling-add $3.50 for 1st book, then $1.75 for each additional book.
Please send a check payable to:
Urban Books, LLC
Please allow 4-6 weeks for delivery

ORDER FORM
URBAN BOOKS, LLC
97 N18th Street
Wyandanch, NY 11798

Name (please print):_____

Address:_____

City/State:_____

Zip:_____

QTY	TITLES	PRICE
	Cheesecake And Teardrops	$14.95
	Congratulations	$14.95
	Crazy In Love	$14.95
	Cyber Case	$14.95
	Denim Diaries	$14.95
	Diary Of A Mad First Lady	$14.95
	Diary Of A Stalker	$14.95

Shipping and handling-add $3.50 for 1st book, then $1.75 for each additional book.
Please send a check payable to:
Urban Books, LLC
Please allow 4-6 weeks for delivery